BROOKE MONTGOMERY

Copyright © 2024 Brooke Montgomery
www.brookewritesromance.com

Only With Me
Sugarland Creek, #4

Cover designer: Wildheart Graphics
Cover photographer: Regina Wamba
Editor: Lawrence Editing

All rights reserved. Edition I. No parts of the book may be used or reproduced in any matter without written permission from the author, except for inclusion of brief quotations in a review. This book is a work of fiction. Names, characters, establishments, organizations, and incidents are either products of the author's imagination or are used fictitiously to give a sense of authenticity. Any resemblance to actual persons, living or dead, events, or locales is entirely coincidental. Ed. I.

Sugarland Creek series
Reading Order

Come With Me (Prequel)
Here With Me (#1)
Stay With Me (#2)
Fall With Me (#3)
Only With Me (#4)
Sin With Me (#5)

Each book can be read as a stand-alone and ends in a happily ever after. However, for the best reading experience, read in order.

Take my heart, don't break it
   Love me to my bones
   All this time I wasted
   You were right there all along
   You and I stargazing
   Intertwining souls
   We were never strangers
   You were right there all along

                    -*Stargazing*, **Myles Smith**

Playlist

Listen to the full *Only With Me* playlist on Spotify

Slow It Down | Benson Boone
Stargazing | Myles Smith
us | Gracie Abrams, Taylor Swift
Carry You Home | Alex Warren
Everywhere, Everything | Noah Kahan, Gracie Abrams
Disconnected | Anna Clendening
Close To You | Gracie Abrams
I Like It | Alesso, Nate Smith
Die With A Smile | Lady Gaga, Bruno Mars
Intrusive Thoughts | Natalie Jane
Next Thing You Know | Jordan Davis
The One That You Call | Mackenzy Mackay
Creek Will Rise | Conner Smith
My Home | Myles Smith
Cowboys Cry Too | Kelsea Ballerini, Noah Kahan
Untouchable | Taylor Swift

Welcome to

SUGARLAND CREEK
RANCH AND EQUINE RETREAT

SUGARLAND CREEK, TN

~Welcome to Sugarland Creek Ranch and Equine Retreat~

The town of Sugarland Creek is home to over two thousand residents and is surrounded by the beautiful Appalachian Mountains. We're only fifteen minutes from the downtown area, where you can shop at local boutiques, grab a latte, catch a movie, or simply enjoy the views.

We're an all-inclusive ranch. While we provide rustic lodging, each cabin is handicapped-accessible with ramps and smooth walking trails. If you need assistance with traveling between activities, we'll provide you with a staff member to pick you up in one of our handicapped-accessible vehicles at any time. Please request at the front desk or dial '0' on your room phone. We're here to help in any way we can.

To make your stay here the best experience, meet the family and learn about everything we have to offer at the retreat to ensure you have the vacation of a lifetime!

Meet the Hollis family:

Garrett & Dena Hollis

Mr. and Mrs. Hollis have been married for over thirty years and have five children. The Sugarland Creek Ranch has been home to over three Hollis generations. When the family officially took over twenty years ago, they added on the retreat to share their love of horses and the outdoors with the public.

Wilder and Waylon
Twin boys, the oldest

Landen
The middle child

Tripp
Youngest of the boys

Noah
The only girl and baby of the family

Whether you're here to relax and enjoy the views or you're ready to get your hands dirty, we have a variety of activities on the ranch for you to enjoy:

Horseback trail riding & tours
(10:00 a.m. and 4:00 p.m.)

Hiking, mountain biking, & fishing
(Maps available at The Lodge)

Family Game Nights
(Sundays and Wednesdays)

Karaoke & Square Dancing
(Friday and Saturday nights)

Kids Game Room
(Open 24/7)

Swimming
(Pool open 9:00 a.m. to 9:00 p.m. each day)

Bonfires with s'mores
(Fridays)

…and much more depending on the season!

The Lodge building is staffed 24 hours a day. It's home to our reception & guest services, The Sugarland Restaurant & Saloon, and activities sign-up.

Find all of our current information at sugarlandcreekranch.com.

We pride ourselves on serving authentic Southern food, so please let us know if you have any dietary restrictions or needs to better serve you. We offer brunch from 8:00 a.m. to 1:00 p.m. The restaurant is open for dinner from 5:00 p.m. to 9:00 p.m. If you wish to dine or find other activities off the ranch, we're less than an hour from Gatlinburg and are happy to provide you with suggestions.

*Thank you so much for visiting us.
We hope you have the best time!*

-The Hollis Family & Team Sugarland

See map on the next page!

G	Hollis Fishing Pond & Hut
H	Bonfire Area
I	Family Game Nights Area
J	Gift Shop

SUGARLAND CREEK
RANCH AND EQUINE RETREAT

SUGARLAND CREEK, TN

Trigger & Content Warnings

Dear Reader,

This story features deeply personal content that will be triggering to some people. There are many aspects of Harlow's and Waylon's family life that are intertwined with mine, and I wanted to highlight them in a way to bring awareness and understanding of what it's like living life with someone who's disabled, suffers with chronic pain, struggles with mental health, and lives with depression. This book showcases only two people's lives and is not meant to speak on everyone's experiences, but rather, how their lives are one of the many ways families struggle and deal with trauma.

I want to make sure everyone is aware of the possible triggering content that's weaved through this story, but also, highlight that the prologue consists of the following: witness of non-suicidal self-injury (cutting), blood, and discussions of depression. If any of these make you uncomfortable, please skip (or skim) to chapter one. You don't need to read the prologue in full to understand the rest of the story as it'll be talked about briefly in other chapters.

Other mentions throughout the book on page are conversations and topics surrounding mental health, suicide attempts, chronic pain, non-fatal and fatal overdose, aggravated assault (flashback and present day), and death of a parent.

I want to acknowledge that these themes of struggle and resilience can resonate deeply with many people. If you or someone you know is experiencing feelings of hopelessness or distress, please know that you are not alone.

I encourage you to reach out for help. The National Suicide Prevention Lifeline is available 24/7 at 1-800-273-TALK (1-800-273-8255), and you can also text "HELLO" to 741741 for the Crisis Text Line. These resources are here to support you. Your well-being matters and seeking help is a sign of strength.

If you need more details on any of these content warnings or which chapters to avoid, you may email me at brookewritesromance@gmail.com or DM me @brookewritesromance. Please take care of your mental health and don't push yourself to read anything you're not comfortable with.

With care and love,
Brooke xo

Prologue
Waylon

THIRTEEN YEARS AGO

A crashing sound in the distance wakes me up from a dead-ass sleep and the throbbing between my temples makes me wonder if it wasn't my head that woke me. I squint across the room, trying to make out if my twin brother is in his bed or not.

Yep, even at nineteen years old, we still share a room in our parents' house.

Luckily, it's spacious, so we still have our areas, but that's what happens when you have a larger family. At least when we outgrew the bunk beds at age nine, our parents got us full-sized ones.

Leaning over toward my nightstand, I turn on my lamp and notice his covers are pulled back. We went out last night and came home together, so he's got to be around here somewhere. There's no way he'd drive after how much he drank, but it wouldn't be unlike Wilder to wander downstairs or even outside if he couldn't sleep.

Our family's ranch sits on a couple hundred acres fifteen minutes outside of Sugarland Creek. It's a Southern small town of only two thousand people. Most of them have been here all their lives—like me and my four siblings.

Brooke Montgomery

Half of the ranch is used for our equine retreat business. Five cabins sit along the bottom of the mountain for guests to rent out, and then we offer horseback riding, swimming, fishing, hiking, and a handful of other activities. Wilder and I spend a lot of time together since we manage the trail horses and guide the guests on horseback rides.

The other half consists of the family's personal and boarded horses as well as the stud farm. My younger siblings work there mostly between their school schedules, weekends, and over the summer. It's all we've ever known, but we love it nonetheless. Growing up in East Tennessee provides great weather and amazing views. I can't imagine living anywhere else.

Since the clock reads four o'clock in the morning, I contemplate going back to bed, but the nagging feeling in my gut has me walking out of our room in search of my brother. We've had this twin intuition for as long as I can remember and mine is currently on high alert. A feeling of…dread, almost, and waves of sadness consume me. Whether it's from being half asleep or something to do with Wilder, I need to find out.

The rest of the house is eerily quiet. My dad's alarm goes off at five. Ranch chores don't stop on the weekends, so we'll be expected to be up and ready for work by six. My mom loves to cook and makes everyone breakfast before we head out, so the house will be brightly lit and loud within the next hour. It's the worst after going out all night, but that's the price we pay for having a social life.

I could do without the partying, but I don't like leaving Wilder. He loves to have a good time and can be a handful, so I prefer to be with him to make sure he's safe and gets back home. Even though we're not *legally* allowed to drink, that's never stopped anyone in this small town—barn, field, or house parties. We've been to them all. Sometimes in one night.

As I walk down the hallway, I notice the bathroom door is ajar and the motion night light is on, so someone must be inside.

Only With Me

Not wanting to walk in on Wilder doing his business, I knock softly.

"Hey, you okay?"

I'm not sure how long he's been in there, but when he doesn't respond, I push open the door to peek inside.

I chuckle under my breath at his drunk ass passed out on the bathroom floor in only his boxers. Couldn't even make it back to bed after he took a piss. Typical.

Kicking his arm with my foot, I say, "Dude, get up. Dad and Mom will kill you if they find you like this."

He doesn't so much as grunt when I kick him a second time, even harder.

After several seconds of no movement, my heartbeat ticks faster in my neck. Something feels wrong.

"Wilder? Get up, man."

Moving around him, my bare foot steps in something wet.

I lift it and try to shake it off. "Jesus Christ, did you pee on the floor?"

Again, no reaction from him.

"Okay, time to wakey-wakey, bro."

This time I flick on the light and the room bathes in brightness. This should get his attention.

"I swear to God, I ain't carryin' your drunk ass—"

When my eyes adjust to the light, I realize it's not piss on the floor.

It's *blood*.

"Holy shit..." Kneeling next to him, I quickly glance around his body, checking for a wound before I notice his black boxer shorts are soaked.

The blood is coming from his thigh.

"No, no, no..." I murmur, grabbing the hand towel nearby and adding pressure to the thigh with horizontal razor cuts. "I think you nicked an artery. Fuck."

There's no telling how long he's been unconscious or bleeding out, but the fetal position he's in probably helped him not to bleed out faster.

I check for a pulse. It's faint, but it's there.

Then I listen to his shallow breathing.

Since I don't have my phone on me and I'm too scared to leave him or remove my hands, I shout for help instead. Even though everyone sleeps like the dead around here, one of them should hear me.

"Help! Someone wake up! We need help in here!"

By the third time, my mother rushes in and her face pales the moment she realizes what's happened.

"Oh my—"

"Call 911, now!" I cut off her words and she scrambles back to her bedroom.

"How long has he been bleedin' out?" Dad asks, rushing next to me.

"I dunno. I found him a few minutes ago. He's still breathin', but he won't wake up."

Dad props Wilder's head in his lap to clear his airway, then feels his pulse. "He probably passed out right before you got here."

"What's goin' on?"

My younger brothers, Landen and Tripp, stand in the doorway. I give a quick recap so we don't waste any more time.

"He doesn't need CPR?" Landen asks.

Dad leans down above his mouth and shakes his head. "Still breathin'."

"Barely," I add.

Landen took a lifeguard course and first aid classes last summer when he was sixteen and then taught us what to do in case of an emergency.

Mom returns with the phone to her ear, speaking to an operator, and then kneels next to me to grab Wilder's hand.

"They're on their way," Mom chokes out.

Dad orders Landen and Tripp to get dressed and unlock the

Only With Me

front door for the EMTs. My little sister, Noah, wakes up shortly after and panics.

"Wilder!" she shouts, shaking his arm.

"He's gonna be okay," I tell her but also because I need to hear it myself.

"He's lost too much blood. He'll probably need a blood transfusion," Dad explains.

Sadly, it wouldn't be his first one. Or his second.

When we were fifteen, he accidentally sliced his leg open from a sharp metal piece on a fence. He didn't realize how bad it was and continued working. The blood gushed down his leg and pooled in his boot. I found him unconscious in the barn and Dad rushed him to the hospital.

By the time we got him there, they were throwing around words like sepsis, infection, and blood transfusions. He was fucking lucky I found him when I did.

The second time was self-inflicted a year later.

We were sixteen, and I found him in the bathtub.

There was so much blood in the water, I couldn't see where the injury was at first. The opposite thigh from the fence accident was covered in little cuts. But it was the vertical one that did the most damage.

It was the first time I saw my father cry—from anger and fear.

It felt like a part of me was dying, and I couldn't understand why he'd done it. And now again. I wish I could take away his pain.

My brother—the class clown since the day we started kindergarten, the loud and obnoxious one always up for a party, the most rambunctious person I knew—was hurting himself.

It didn't make any sense.

Wilder has no danger-o-meter. He's a risk-taker to his core. The adrenaline rush he gets fuels years of antics that have led to him getting injured numerous times. The time he invented Barn Roof Trampoline tournaments and did a cannonball off the roof.

Instead of landing on his feet, he bounced and flew right into a tree. He got a concussion and a broken rib.

You'd think that would've slowed him down, but a month later, we went to Blackhole Granite to swim in the quarry. He had a little bit too much to drink and when he jumped in from the twenty-foot cliff, he didn't swim back up. Landen and Tripp rushed in and pulled him out. I gave him CPR until he finally coughed up water.

It's almost like he doesn't care about the risks and there's a small part of me that wonders if he does it on purpose.

After the first time he cut his inner thigh, our parents made him see a therapist and psychiatrist to properly diagnose him. He promised he wasn't doing it because he wanted to die. Rather, he just wanted to numb the pain. Dull the sadness that overtook his mind sometimes. Feel relief from the overwhelming emotions he didn't know how to handle.

I suspect that's why he drinks until he blacks out, too.

Still, they took him twice a month until he turned eighteen and then Wilder was old enough to make the decision not to go anymore.

I wish he had continued.

The depression he was trying so desperately to cover up suffocated me more than he'd ever realized. I felt those feelings too, but I never put a label on it. I thought it was my own sadness consuming me, and maybe part of it is or maybe it's something we share as twins, but I couldn't comprehend how he felt it so deeply that he had to find ways to numb it. Ways to live around it.

Perhaps he felt mine too and the weight of each other's feelings was too heavy for one person.

I wish I could turn them off, take them away from him, and be the one who suffered for both of us. I hate that I can't.

As far as I knew, he'd gone three years without cutting. This would be the second time he's cut deep enough to lose consciousness.

Wilder rarely talked about his feelings, even when I tried to

Only With Me

get him to tell me how he was doing, he'd swear he was doing great. As if he didn't want to burden anyone with the knowledge that maybe he wasn't. Or perhaps admit them to himself. Either way, keeping it in was causing more damage.

My throat tightens as I stare at him, keeping as much pressure on his thigh as possible. I love him more than anything. Even when he's a real pain in my fucking ass, I've worried more about his well-being than my own. I don't want him to feel sad and would prefer he'd talk to me when he did, but knowing he never does is why I go everywhere with him. It's the reason I don't make a fuss out of him acting up or doing dumb shit because then at least for a moment he's laughing and happy. Whether or not it's an act, I can't always tell.

He's good at putting on a facade.

"They're here," Dad tells me when I zone out. I haven't stopped staring at Wilder.

As soon as the EMTs walk in, I quickly explain what happened when I found him and then move out of their way. They do a quick clean and wrap job before getting him on the stretcher and taking him out to the ambulance.

"Waylon..." My dad's booming voice shakes me out of my trance.

His hand's on my shoulder, squeezing me. "Your hands and legs are covered in blood. Wash up, and then I'll drive us to the hospital. Your mother's ridin' in the back with him."

All I can do is nod.

After rinsing my hands in the sink, I step into the shower, grab the shower head, and then spray my bare legs until they're clean. My mind's blank and my heart races nonstop as I go through the motions of getting dressed and meeting the rest of my siblings downstairs. It stays empty as Dad drives us into town.

It's not until hours later that a nurse approaches us in the waiting room and says he's awake and asking for me. The doctor gives us a quick rundown of what they did and what to expect.

Wilder's hooked up to an IV and blood pressure cuff. His

thigh is bandaged and covered with a blanket, so I can't see it, but the doctor said it took them a while to properly suture. He's going to have one hell of a scar.

The psychiatrist on call has already met with Wilder and our parents. Now that Wilder's an adult, he can speak on his own behalf. Since he claimed it wasn't a suicide attempt and was under a lot of stress when he did it, the doctor chose not to admit him as an inpatient. But they're setting him up with appointments to speak to a psychologist to determine the root of his depression.

If I knew he wouldn't laugh in my face, I'd tell him he needed to go to regular therapy appointments. Hell, I'd go with him.

But I know my brother and he'll never commit to anything like that. Doesn't mean I can't try, though, when he's not drugged up and can listen to my concerns.

"Hey, 'sup, Way-Way?" Wilder says as I approach the side of his hospital bed, and I want to smack the lopsided grin off his face.

When we were toddlers, he couldn't say my full name and ended up calling me Way-Way for years, even when he could finally say it. Now he just does it to antagonize me.

"Oh, not much," I deadpan. "Just a typical night hangin' out in the ER."

He nods once. "Fun times."

"Yeah, real fun." I stare at him with intense narrowed eyes. His reflect back, except they're filled with shame and guilt. I remember the previous times he felt awful for putting us through this and then trying to simmer down my frustration. "Are you in pain right now?"

"Nah." He jerks his thumb. "Mr. IV over here is pumpin' the good shit in me."

"Good. Then you won't feel anythin' when I punch you in the face."

His eyes beam with amusement. "I'd probably feel that."

I roll my eyes. "I dunno whether to hug you or beat your ass. I'm so angry. And sad. But mostly, scared. You lost a lot of blood."

Only With Me

"I know. They've been givin' me that too." He nods toward the other IV.

Grabbing a chair, I sit closer. "Talk to me. What happened yesterday that made you do this?"

I'm not sure how else to ask, so I blurt it out. He knows I want answers.

His gaze looks past me as he lifts a shoulder. "I dunno how to explain it. There's this overwhelming doom feeling when it comes to depression. Like the stress of havin' to be an adult and make grown-up decisions. The expectations of being the oldest sibling. The pressure to impress Dad and do a good job on the ranch. There's this underlying sadness that consumes me in weird ways and it's uncontrollable. Even when there isn't anything particularly making me sad, it's just there—haunting and taunting me. I want to curl up in a ball and sleep through the pain, but I can't. I have responsibilities, so I try to ignore it and do everything in my power to distract myself, but eventually, it becomes unbearable. I needed to release the pain, even if it was momentarily. Eventually, it becomes an impulse I can't fight anymore. That moment right before I pass out is when I'm finally numb, and then it becomes somethin' I'm desperate to feel again and again. *Relief.*"

Every word of his confession stabs me in the gut. The weird sadness? I feel that, too. The pressure and stress—check and check. That level of pain, searching for relief, I also feel waves of it. Whether it's mine or his I'm experiencing, I don't always know.

"Unfortunately, I do get it," I say softly, reaching for his hand. "Though I've never thought to do…" I nod toward his thigh, unable to say the words aloud. "I understand the feelin' of it becomin' too much."

"I get the urges and find ways to cope without doing it, but this time, I just…needed to. It was almost like an out-of-body experience. Something I couldn't control but at the same time like I couldn't stop once I started. As soon as I saw the blood, my mind went blank. The depressive thoughts vanished. I only had to focus on one thing at that moment and that was cuttin'."

I noticeably shiver as he talks about it. It's not that blood makes me squeamish, but just the thought of seeing my own makes me nauseous.

"Doesn't it hurt when you...do it?"

"Fuck yeah, it does, but it's like a high. As soon as the edge of the razor pierces through my skin, my focus is on the physical pain. My brain stops repeatin' negative thoughts and my mind goes blank for the first time in weeks, months, or even years. That's when the flood of endorphins hits because I'm no longer being told how worthless and unlovable I am. It's freeing."

I sink my teeth into the inside of my cheek to prevent my emotions from taking over.

"I went too far tonight," he admits.

"So you ain't tryin' to end your life?" I finally choke out because I need to hear him confirm it.

"No. Just cope with it."

"So why didn't you stop before it got as bad as it did?"

He shrugs. "I guess I wanted to see how much I could take so that relief lasted longer."

My head and heart ache hearing him talk about this, but I'm glad he is. Better to be honest with me so I can hopefully notice the signs before he cuts again. I want him to open up to me before things get worse.

"Trust me, I don't feel good about it," he continues. "The guilt of puttin' y'all through this again. The shame that I relapsed. It ain't worth it when the consequences are worse. But I didn't think about 'em at the time."

Makes sense. *All he could think about was relief.*

"What about seein' a therapist? Or psychiatrist? Get somethin' to help with the depression so it's at least a bit more bearable when you feel it takin' over your mind."

"I did all that before, remember? The meds made me feel numb as shit—and not in a good way—and gave me the worst neurological side effects. Talkin' about my teenage problems to an adult just made me feel like an idiot."

"You're not, and there are other variations of meds you can try. It ain't a one-size-fits-all drug. Everyone's brain chemistry responds differently to medication. You gotta keep tryin' till you find the right ones."

"That sounds like a pain in the ass," he mutters.

"*You* are a pain in the ass," I retort.

He chuckles. "Yeah, yeah. What else is new?"

"Nothin' apparently." I snort, though he knows I'm only giving him shit. "I better let the others in so you can finally get some rest."

Standing, I lean over the bed and wrap my arms around him. He's stiff at first, not sure if he should reciprocate, but eventually, he does.

"I love you, ya know?" I tell him, leaning back.

He rests his head back on the pillow and nods. "Yeah, I love ya too."

I step around the chair to walk toward the door, but then he grabs my attention. "Waylon."

Facing him, I lift a brow. "Yeah?"

His tortured expression makes my heart sink. "I'm sorry for puttin' you through this again."

One side of my mouth lifts at how genuine he sounds. Although my emotions are threatening to spill over at seeing him like this, I force a small smile to give him some reassurance. "I know. Don't worry about it, okay?"

He nods firmly with pursed lips, fighting back his own emotions.

When I go toward the exit, there's a stabbing pain in my chest that has me blowing out a sharp breath. I swear, he's going to give me a heart attack one day. These anxiety attacks come and go, mostly during high-stress situations, but nevertheless, they're annoying and inconvenient.

Before I get to the hallway, one of Wilder's machines beeps at an ungodly high-pitched volume. A nurse barrels in before I even have time to turn around and see what's going on.

His eyes are rolled back as his body convulses.

"What's happening?" I blurt to the nurse, but she ignores me as she holds his head in place.

More nurses enter, pulling me out of the way, and soon, I'm standing at the end of his bed, watching helplessly.

"What's goin' on?" Dad asks as he and Mom walk in. My siblings are close behind.

"I-I dunno. We were talkin' and he was fine, but then suddenly, he—"

"He's seizing," one of the nurses responds. "I need everyone out, please. I'll come get you when he's stabilized."

Another nurse pushes us out into the hallway. My chest feels like it's going to explode and there's nothing I can do about it because my twin brother—my other half who shares similar feelings and physical pain with me—is in there, fighting for his life.

And mine.

Because my life will be over if he doesn't survive this.

Chapter One
Waylon

PRESENT DAY

"Goddamn!" Wilder whistles. "It's a full house tonight."

The blaring country music invades my ears as soon as we walk into the Twisted Bull. It's the most popular bar in town with a decent-sized dance floor that brings in plenty of women looking to shake their asses and drink the night away. It doesn't matter what time of year it is—like now in mid-November when it's freeze-your-nuts-off weather—the place is always packed on the weekends.

Wilder's the only reason I'm here on a Saturday night instead of enjoying a quiet evening at home alone.

Sure, I like to drink, but I know when to stop. Wilder doesn't. Making sure he gets home is my main priority, but so is making sure he doesn't make an ass of himself.

The latter isn't always possible.

"Hey, darlin'."

Wilder's drawl grabs my attention as we make it to the bar.

"I gotta ask ya somethin'," he continues speaking to someone.

Looking around him, I notice he's talking to some chick I've never seen before. Considering how small our town is and that everyone knows everyone, she must be visiting or just moved here.

"Hey," she replies. "What's your question, cowboy?"

Wilder lifts his cowboy hat, threads his fingers through his messy hair, and then places the hat back on his head. "Do you believe in love at first sight or should I walk by again?"

Pinching the bridge of my nose, I shake my head at his pathetic pickup line.

"Does that actually work?" the girl asks. "I heard that one five years ago."

I chuckle at her not immediately dropping to her knees for him like most chicks do. Although Wilder and I look identical, it's his outgoing personality that differentiates us the most. I'd rather be in a small crowd around a handful of people I know versus going out with loud music and obnoxious drunks.

"I got you talkin' to me, didn't I?" he muses, and I know he just flashed her his infamous wink. "I'm Wilder. Lemme buy your next drink."

"Fine." She rolls her eyes, but she's grinning as if being offered a free drink is a hardship.

I grab the bartender's attention, order my beer, and then Wilder orders for him and...

Nope, he hasn't even asked her yet.

Classic Wilder.

He starts a tab and then I follow them to a table. As soon as she turns toward him, he buries his face in her neck, murmuring something. She blushes and giggles.

I love being the awkward third wheel.

"This is my twin, Waylon," he finally introduces us.

This is my cue to ask for her name.

"Hey, nice to meet you..."

"Bethany," she supplies. "Nice to meet y'all too."

"You from 'round here?" Wilder asks.

"Nashville. I'm here visitin' a few friends." She waves her hand in the air. "They're 'round here somewhere."

Only With Me

"Cool. Should we dance?" Wilder holds out his hand.

"Yeah, sure!" Her eyes beam, and as usual, I stay and watch their drinks.

We're supposed to meet the rest of our siblings here, too. But Wilder wanted to come early. Tripp used to be our DD, but now he's married with two kids, so he only hangs out for a couple hours since Magnolia stays home with them.

After they dance through three songs, they return to retrieve their drinks.

"You don't dance?" Bethany asks me.

I lift one shoulder. "Sometimes, yeah."

"I'll get some of my friends over and—"

"Oh, that ain't necessary. I'm waitin' on my other brothers to show up."

She ignores my words and waves them over.

As soon as I see one of the girls in the group, I bring my glass to my lips, shielding my amused expression as I gulp down my beer.

This is going to be entertaining.

"I found me a cowboy! His twin needs a dance partner!" Bethany shouts over the music.

The blonde turns and her wide smile shifts into a scowl. "You piece of shit. You're hittin' on my friend after I was in your bed last weekend?"

"Whoa, what?" Wilder jerks back, holding up a hand. Whether to feign innocence or to avoid getting slapped, I'm not sure.

"You know him?" Bethany asks Jen—my brother's on-again, off-again *fling*. They'll go from hooking up every weekend to ghosting each other for months until one of them reaches out again and repeats the whole annoying process.

They're exhausting.

"I didn't know she was your friend," Wilder explains.

"Oh, bite me," Jen snarls.

Wilder waggles his brows. "In the same spot you like?"

Brooke Montgomery

Jesus Christ.

I chuckle, shaking my head at how he constantly finds himself in these messes.

"You wish. Never again. We're done," Jen snaps, grabbing Bethany's hand, and then storms off into the crowd.

"She always says that," Wilder muses, then straightens his spine and stands taller as he shouts louder, "You'll be back! You always are!"

"You're a real piece of work, ya know that?"

He shrugs. "We've never been monogamous."

"Did she know that?"

"Yes! She was in for a good time, not a long time," he reassures me.

I snort under my breath. "Wow…it's a wonder why you've never had anything serious."

"Oh, and you have within the last decade?" he taunts, then takes a swig of his beer.

"I've had one," I remind him.

"Shit, that's right," he muses. "Delilah Fanning from what… nine years ago?"

"Seven," I correct.

We were together for two years, but even so, in that timeframe, we barely had a chance to make it work. Between her dad's work accident and her sister's incident, she had too much going on to make time for us. I understood that family needed to come first, but when she suggested taking a break instead of letting me be there for her, I assumed it was over for good. I hooked up with someone a couple weeks later and she claimed I'd cheated on her.

Never gave me a second chance even when I begged for one.

I was only twenty-five at the time and mostly immature.

But she broke my heart when she told me we shouldn't be together "right now" because I'd trusted her and confided in a way I never have before with previous girlfriends. She knew more about what I'd been through with Wilder than anyone else.

Only With Me

The next time I open up to someone will be when I'm on the autopsy table.

"My bad," he deadpans. "So I guess that makes you the expert."

Rolling my eyes at his dick comment, I scan the area for anyone I might recognize. Most are younger than me, kids who weren't even in high school yet by the time I graduated. To be fair, at thirty-two, I'm too old to be here. It's why I rarely meet anyone because most of these women are in their early twenties.

But me not having a relationship or never getting serious with someone has nothing to do with having commitment issues like him. But I've never told him the real reason, and I hope he never finds out.

"Hey, Hollis!"

I turn to my last name being called and grin when I find one of my close friends I've known since elementary school.

"Jake, hey. How's it goin'?"

He walks up with a beer in his hand and nudges my shoulder.

"Shit, I'm good. You?" His goofy smirk tells me he's been drinking for a while.

"Same."

Shortly after, my brothers arrive and we continue hanging out. We move around from the dance floor to the back room and play a round of pool and then a game of darts. I stick to water after my two beers, but Wilder's had at least six and a few shots.

Jake's texting on his phone every few minutes, but he doesn't have a girlfriend that I'm aware of, so I give him shit about how he must be secretly dating someone.

"Nah, I'm flyin' solo right now. I'm mentoring this club and we started this group chat, so it goes off all day long with random convos."

"What kinda club?" I ask, taking a seat at the nearest table. We just finished the last round of darts, where I smoked him.

"It's gonna sound lame, but I swear it's not. It's a horse club."

My brow lifts. "A *horse* club?"

"Yeah, for people who like horses."

I snort. "Yeah, I figured that. But what's it all about?"

"Most of 'em are in the rodeo industry—barrel racers, bronc riders, various types of show horse competitors. Some are trainers or just experienced riders. We just shit talk about random stuff, but it started as a means of support. Anyone who wanted help with a specific skill, share knowledge and experiences…stuff like that."

"That's cool," I say.

Jake Murphy's family owns a horse ranch, and even after he moved into an apartment in town, he continues to work there as his full-time job. He's been around horses as long as I have—since birth.

"I'll add you to it! You know tons about horses and could probably answer questions or offer suggestions. Most are younger than us, so they'll appreciate the extra expertise."

"No, that's—"

He pulls out his phone before I can finish and adds my number to the text thread.

"There, you're in. I'll do introductions tomorrow when I'm sober." He chuckles. "But everyone's nice."

"Are they all local?"

"Most of 'em, but there's some an hour or two away."

I don't think much about it while I search for Wilder. After Jen stormed off with Bethany, he found a few other girls to occupy him. They've been dancing and drinking for hours.

"Oh shit. Your brother's gettin' up on the bull." Jake points to the other side of the bar. "He ain't lastin' eight seconds on that thing."

I sigh at him waving his cowboy hat in the air. "Fuckin' hell. I swear he thinks he has nine lives or some shit."

Landen and Tripp left an hour ago, leaving me to deal with his drunk ass.

Jake follows as I walk closer and by the time I get to Wilder, he's face down on the mat.

Only With Me

All the girls he was hanging out with scream his name. Meanwhile, I walk into the makeshift arena and try to pull him up by the back of his shirt.

"Can you stand?" I ask. "Or do I need to carry your ass outta here?"

"Nah, I'm t-totally fine," he stutters, crawling until he gets to his feet. "Did I make it?"

"Almost." I snort, glancing at the clock showing five seconds on it.

"Dammit. Next time." He smirks.

The next rider is already pushing through to take his turn, so I drag Wilder out of the way.

"Time to pay the tab and call it a night," I tell him, moving toward the bar.

"What? But they're open for another hour."

Jake wraps his arm around Wilder's waist, helping me keep him up. "'Sup, man?"

"Who're you?"

I shake my head. He's known Jake as long as I have.

"Teddy," Jake responds instead of his actual name, and I suppress a laugh. It's an ongoing joke that every time Wilder's too drunk to remember him, he gives him a different fake name each time.

"Teddy? Okay, cool. Wanna take a shot before we go?"

God, he's relentless.

"Maybe next time, okay? I gotta go home soon," Jake responds.

I glance at him, silently thanking him for his help.

Once the bartender tells me how much is on the tab, I hold out my hand for Wilder's card. Lord knows how many chicks he bought for tonight, and I'm not paying his three-hundred-and-forty-dollar bill.

I add a hefty tip on his behalf, sign it, and thank her again — mostly for putting up with his shenanigans. He relentlessly flirts with her even though she turns him down each time he tries asking her out.

"Sure you don't wanna meet at my house after your shift?" He leans against the bar, wagging his brows at her.

"Hmm…as temptin' as that sounds, *truly*…not sure my girlfriend would appreciate that."

"Why not? She can join. The more the merrier…" He flashes his tongue piercing. "I've got a wicked tongue trick."

"Alright…" I drawl, cuffing the back of his shirt again. "Time to go, Casanova."

I give Rainy an apologetic look before the three of us make our way toward the exit.

"Is Teddy comin' over so I can kick both of your asses in Fortnite?" Wilder asks, climbing into the passenger side of my truck.

"Can I take a rain check? I gotta work in the mornin'…or rather"—Jake checks the time on his phone—"in a few hours."

"As do we," I remind Wilder.

"Pussies," Wilder slurs, falling back in the seat.

"Yeah, yeah. Buckle up," I tell him before closing the door on him.

Jake smirks, and I shake my head. "Thanks for your help."

"Anytime, man."

"You need a ride?" I ask before getting into the driver's side.

"Nah, I can walk."

Jake lives two blocks away, so I don't push it. "Alright, well, I'll talk to you later."

"Yeah, in the group chat! They'll love havin' ya."

"Sure." I release a humorless laugh. He knows I'm not that social. Especially to people I don't know. Unlike Wilder, who could make friends with a brick wall.

Fifteen minutes later, I'm helping Wilder into his apartment above mine. It's technically a duplex in the ranch hand quarters. Mom kicked us out at twenty-one because she was sick of us

Only With Me

coming home at three in the morning. Not that I blame her. We partied a lot on the weekends.

"C'mon, one round?" he prompts, tripping over the shoe he just flung off his foot.

"Go to bed. You're gonna be hungover for chores."

He waves me off. "You're no fun."

I walk backward toward the door. "See ya in four hours."

"How about…six?" He grins. "Cover for me."

Turning around, I give him a middle-finger goodbye wave and go down the steps to my place. It'll inevitably take me an hour to fall asleep and then my alarm will go off far too early.

Chapter Two
Waylon

Just as expected, I get three hours of sleep before my phone screams at me.

I go through my routine—put on my work clothes, scarf down a half-toasted bagel, fill up my massive jug with ice water, then head out to the retreat barn. We keep our boarded and guest horses separate, and since Wilder and I are the tour guides, it's our job to muck the stalls, feed them, and fill their water buckets.

Then I take them out to the pasture so they can graze for a bit before we do our first tour of the day at ten. Our second one isn't until four, so we take our lunch and do random chores in between.

In the evening, we'll feed them and refresh their water once more, and then call it a night by six or seven.

Twelve-hour days, six days a week.

The weekend shifts are usually shorter, and we get a full day off each week, but it's never consistent which one we get.

The days are long and sometimes hot, but I get to ride horses and work with my family. There's nothing else I'd rather be doing.

Currently, the weather is bearable. It's a couple weeks until Thanksgiving and has been in the mid-sixties. The mornings and late evenings are cooler, but it beats sweating my ass off in peak

Only With Me

summer when it reaches the nineties. Especially while riding in jeans and work boots.

"Howdy."

My head pops up from where I'm shoveling one of the stalls, amazed that Wilder's strutting in an hour earlier than expected. And he sounds awake and energized.

"Surprised you made it," I say, returning to my task. "I figured I'd be knocking down your bedroom door to get your ass up."

"I'm wounded at your accusation, Way-Way," he drawls, pressing a hand to his chest.

"Stop callin' me that. And you could barely walk a few hours ago, so forgive me for assumin' you'd be bitchin' and moanin' over a headache."

"Oh, don't worry. My head's killin' me. I'm just choosin' to ignore it."

I chuckle under my breath. "Alright. You can start over there, then. I'm almost done with this row."

"Aye aye, captain." With a cocky smirk, he gives me a salute and walks toward the tack room.

I shake my head at his ability to wake up and act normal.

My phone's been vibrating on and off for the last thirty minutes, so when I finish this stall, I finally check it.

Forty-seven text messages.

What the fuck? I don't even like forty-seven people.

When I click on my messages, it's Jake's horse club group chat that's blowing up my phone.

Damn, they start early.

I scroll through them talking about someone's injured horse and asking for updates on how it's doing. There's a bunch of *thinking of y'all* and *keep me updated* messages. The problem is I have no idea who anyone is except Jake. All I see are random phone numbers, and I don't recognize any of them.

Since I don't want to intrude during a vulnerable moment, I'll wait until Jake introduces me.

At nine-thirty, Wilder and I wrangle up the horses needed for the first trail riding session. When the guests check in at The Lodge, Tripp helps at the registration desk and decides which horse is best for each person based on their experience or knowledge. Then they ride that horse during their entire stay.

"You were at the Twisted Bull last night, weren't ya?" Gabby asks, smiling at Wilder after my safety and guidelines speech.

"Sure was. But I woulda noticed a beautiful woman like you." Wilder's thick drawl makes me roll my eyes.

"My friends and I saw you on the mechanical bull," she explains, waving to the other three riders. "I was gonna offer you a shot, but you left shortly after."

Wilder shoots me a death glare as if I'm the reason he didn't get lucky last night. If he'd pace himself, he could make it to the end of the night without having to be carried out.

"We'll just haveta plan a do-over, huh? Whaddya doin' tonight?" Wilder drawls, and I clear my throat to grab his attention.

Wilder holds up his hand, then leans in closer toward Gabby and whispers, "Gimme your number later and we can hook up tonight."

Gabby grins.

"As I was sayin'..." I drawl, glaring at Wilder. We have a group of four and it's important I get through everything before we leave. "These are experienced trail horses and know the routes, but in the event yours goes rogue or you get lost, do not panic. Screaming will spook or confuse your horse and squeezing your legs will cue them to run. So it's crucial you relax and stay calm. There are safety checks every quarter mile, so one of us will reroute to come find you if you're not with the rest of us. Any questions?"

Everyone shakes their heads and then I begin my demonstration and instruction for getting into the saddle. Most have some experience, so I'm not too worried. It's Wilder acting like a moron that I have to watch out for.

Exhibit A: Wilder turns completely around in the saddle and

faces the guests behind him instead of holding on to the reins and facing forward.

"So Gabby, where ya from?"

"Livin' in Knoxville right now. I'm a junior at UT."

My eyes widen, and I chuckle under my breath at how young she is. Probably twenty-one.

"Oh, nice. What're you studyin'?" Wilder asks—as if he cares.

"Engineering," she replies.

"Oh shit." I bark out a laugh, glancing over my shoulder at her and then meeting Wilder's eyes next to me. "She's too smart for you."

"I like me an intelligent lady," he retorts.

"Yeah, I bet she could teach ya a thing or two."

Gabby's three friends giggle.

Wilder finally turns back around and we finish the hour-long tour. We go through the mountains and show them through the retreat before heading back to the barn.

As expected, Wilder gets Gabby's number, and I take the horses to the grooming stalls to remove their saddles and brush them. Wilder finally joins me fifteen minutes later.

"She's too young for you," I tell him.

"You're just jealous."

"Of a barely legal chick? Nah, don't think so."

"She's way legal, so fuck off." Wilder grabs one of the brushes and works on one of the other horses.

"What would y'all even have in common?"

Someone that much younger would be at a different stage in their life. She doesn't even live around here and is still in college. Though it worked out for my sister with a guy twice her age, I just don't see how it'd work long-term for most people.

"Exchangin' orgasms. Or as you said, maybe she could teach me a thing or two. Smart chicks who always have a book in their faces are the freakiest." He smirks like he's so clever.

Shaking my head, I drop it because there's no sense in trying to reason with Wilder.

Brooke Montgomery

There never is.

After the six horses are back in their stalls, fed and water buckets refilled, we head to The Lodge for lunch. It's where the guests and staff can help themselves to a full Southern buffet for brunch and dinner. Since Wilder and I don't cook, we eat here at least once a day.

"Are you gonna call her?" I ask him when we walk through the reception doors.

"Yep, we're makin' plans now," he says, texting while he walks and nearly runs into a table.

"It's Sunday family supper night," I remind him.

Mom and Gramma Grace cook a feast for all the children and grandchildren once a week and we're *required* to be there—no exceptions, except maybe death. After we eat dinner and dessert, they get out family albums and spend another couple hours gossiping and scrapbooking. We usually get out of staying so we can finish the evening chores, but I try to stick around at least once a month to make Mom happy.

"So I'll leave early." Wilder shrugs.

I scoff. "Good luck with that."

Once I've filled up a plate and grabbed two slices of pie, I find a seat at our usual table. My phone's been vibrating on and off for ten minutes, so I finally check it.

UNKNOWN #1

> I think there's a nail in Gretchen's hoof. She's been limping and not wanting to lunge.

JAKE

> Get your farrier out there to check. Probably infected.

UNKNOWN #1

> I already called. He's backed up until Wednesday. Everything I look up says to soak the hoof but she won't let me near it to even look or put it in a bucket of warm water.

Only With Me

> **JAKE**
> Maybe try with someone else there to keep her calm so you can lift it and check. If it's bleeding, you need to get it out asap.
>
> **UNKNOWN #3**
> I can come out and help! I'm heading out soon and can swing by.
>
> **UNKNOWN #1**
> Are you sure? I don't want to burden you.
>
> **UNKNOWN #3**
> Of course! I'll be there in 20!
>
> **UNKNOWN #1**
> Thank you! You're a lifesaver.

Although I haven't a clue who two of these people are, it's clear they're a tight-knit group. Since Jake hasn't introduced me and I don't have anything to contribute to the conversation, I pocket my phone and finish eating.

"Hey," Noah enters, grabbing our attention. "Can one of you swing by the stables after lunch? I need an extra hand."

"I thought that's why you have ranch hands," Wilder says between chewing.

Noah ignores him, looking directly at me. "I need help sweeping the training center. Ellie's coming this afternoon for training, and I wanna make sure it's in perfect condition."

Landen's wife is a pro barrel racer and she's headed to Vegas after Thanksgiving to compete in the National Finals Rodeo. The whole family's going to support her and it should be a fun time.

"Yeah, no problem," I tell her. "I'll be there in twenty."

"That's why you're my *favorite* brother," she drawls, shifting her gaze to Wilder.

"Kiss-ass," he murmurs.

I chuckle as Noah walks away.

"She just knows which brother to go to that'll get the job done right."

"I could sweep that arena in my sleep," he mocks.

"Probably because you've done it hungover more times than not."

"And it still got done, yeah?"

Shaking my head, I go back to eating and ignoring my messages.

The training center is Noah's bread and butter. Hell, it brings in a lot of revenue for the ranch in general. It's where all her professional training takes place. Noah's well-known in the state and surrounding areas for being a horse whisperer and usually has a two-year waitlist. Mostly because she's skilled in various pro rodeo events. I don't think there's anything she's not knowledgeable about when it comes to horses. She's been this way since she was a teenager.

If you didn't know who she was before meeting her, you'd never guess she was only twenty-six. She's already married, with a two-year-old daughter.

Fisher, her husband, is the ranch's farrier and ironically, her ex-boyfriend's dad.

Landen and Tripp might've threatened him a time or two before they confessed to having a secret relationship.

Wilder and I part ways after lunch, him to the retreat barn and me to the ranch. I'm not on this side much, only if there's a big job that involves extra hands or someone's out sick.

"Hey, Ruby," I greet. She's one of Noah's ranch hands.

"Hey, whatcha doing?"

I explain where I'm headed and before I can get to where the sweeper is stored, two trucks drive up the gravel road toward the stables. It's a long driveway, but I think one of them is Ellie. Although she and Landen live on the other side of the ranch, toward the mountains by the lake, she was probably running errands in town.

"Busy afternoon, huh?" I ask.

Only With Me

"Per usual," she says.

"How's that boyfriend of yours?" I ask, keeping up a conversation while she follows me to the four-wheelers. The sweeper attaches to the back and then I'll ride in circles around the arena inside the training center until it's clean and flat.

"He's amazing. Great. *Perfect*." The stars in her eyes make me laugh.

She finally dumped her loser ex-boyfriend months ago when he refused to propose after six years together and started dating his best friend, Levi. Her ex, Nash, ended up kidnapping her and would've killed her had Levi and Tripp not found her in time. Nash shot Levi at the same time Tripp shot Nash in the chest, and then Tripp jumped into the lake to save Ruby before she could drown.

It was a whole scandal.

The town called Tripp a hero and Levi spent months recovering from a gunshot wound.

Considering how crazy in love they are, I wouldn't be shocked if they get engaged soon.

"And what about you? Thoughts on settling down yet?" Ruby asks when I hop on the four-wheeler.

I get it started and then point to my ear. "Can't hear ya, sorry!"

"Nice try!" she shouts over the engine, and I back out before she can interrogate me some more.

I dodge the question anytime someone asks me about getting a girlfriend or starting a family.

As if it were that easy.

Chuckling at Ruby's annoyed expression, I drive over to the sweeper, get it hooked up, then drive across the gravel driveway toward the training center.

Or at least I try to.

One of the trucks that was driving toward the stables nearly runs me over.

Brooke Montgomery

"Jesus!" I brake as fast as I can, inches from hitting the hood or flying over it.

Fuck, I was so lost in my head, I didn't even notice she was driving toward me.

And *she* is Harlow Fanning—beautiful, young, outgoing.

Her long, golden brown hair is pulled back and her green eyes catch mine.

One of my sister's clients.

Over a decade younger than me.

And my ex-girlfriend's little sister.

Chapter Three
Harlow

"Oh my gosh, I'm so sorry!" I blurt the moment I jump out of the truck. "I stopped to help a friend on the way and was running behind."

Waylon's wide blue eyes meet mine before he turns off the four-wheeler.

A sexy, six-foot-something, muscular cowboy who I've known for years.

Not that we've talked much. He hardly notices me.

Waylon's the quiet Hollis twin and hardly looks in my direction. He's my older sister, Delilah's, ex-boyfriend and probably still sees me as a little kid.

"It's okay, Harlow. I shoulda been payin' better attention, too."

His intense eye contact and deep voice send a chill down my spine. Waylon might be reserved and keep to himself, but he's all man. Tall, brooding, and too attractive for his own good. He's a hard worker like the rest of his siblings, but Waylon makes it look effortless. I've been on the ranch enough over the past four years to notice how dedicated he is.

"Damn, almost had a collision." Ruby joins us. "Y'all okay?"

"Yeah, fine." I brush a hand over my forehead, glancing nervously between Waylon and Ruby.

"I'll get outta your way," Waylon starts the four-wheeler, then shifts around my truck.

Ruby smiles briefly at me before walking back toward the stables. I hop back into my truck and make my way to the parking area. Once I reach the stalls, I find Noah and Ellie.

"Hey, how's it goin'?" Noah asks.

"Good. I was hopin' to lunge Piper and take her for a ride before our session."

Piper's my six-year-old Appaloosa show horse. Noah and I have been working together with her since I was sixteen—four years ago. She gave me riding lessons and taught me the skills for show jumping. I started competing a year ago, so I still have a lot to learn and experience, but I enjoy it.

The season ended last month, but I'm trying to get in as much practice as possible before the next one begins in spring.

"Yeah, of course. Ellie will be done in an hour and then we can start," Noah replies.

Noah stays busy enough that she needs to work on the weekends, too. She takes off when she can, but for as long as I've known her, she always has a full plate. Since I'm not competing right now, Piper and I train with Noah whenever she's available or when I'm not at my part-time job.

Since I didn't want to put all the expenses of Piper's boarding fees on my parents, I work at a Western clothing boutique called Rodeo Belle. It's a cute place downtown that's popular with tourists and college-aged girls.

"Hey, sweet girl." I rub my palm up and down Piper's white-spotted nose. "Ready to get outta here?"

She bobs her head underneath my hand, and I laugh.

Getting fresh air and trail riding with Piper is the core of keeping my mental health stable. After fighting for my life and being unable to walk when I was a teenager, I've learned not to take it for granted.

I brush her for a bit before attaching her lunging tack.

"Alright, let's go." I click my tongue and lead her out to the

Only With Me

corral. I lunge her for twenty minutes since I got caught up at home and haven't ridden her in a couple days.

"Thatta girl," I praise when she walks up to me. "Let's get ready to ride."

After I bring her back into the stables, I cross-tie her in the aisle and put on her saddle tack.

"Where're you ridin'?" Ruby asks before I head out.

"Up to the retreat trails. There shouldn't be any guest tours right now, so figured it'd be a good place to go."

"Okay, be careful. It gets icy up there this time of year," she warns.

"Don't worry. Piper's a baddie, ain't ya?" I pat her neck.

Ruby snorts. "Text if you need anything."

"Will do."

At the mention of texting, I remember to check my phone that was vibrating while I was outside.

Annie's horse had a hoof issue, so I swung by her ranch before coming here so I could lend an extra hand in helping her check if there was a nail in it. Unfortunately, there was, so I distracted Gretchen by brushing her and speaking softly while Annie managed to soak her hoof in a bucket of warm water.

Since Annie's farrier couldn't get out there until Wednesday, I texted Noah and Fisher to see if he could help since he normally has Sundays off.

> **FISHER**
> I'm heading out there now if you want to let your friend know I'll be there shortly.
>
> **HARLOW**
> Thanks so much, will do!

I quickly change over to my text convo with Annie to let her know.

Brooke Montgomery

ANNIE
You're a lifesaver! Thank you!!!

HARLOW
No problem - give me an update on Gretchen when you can 😊

One of the many reasons I've loved growing up in Sugarland Creek is how tight-knit the community is. I've met so many amazing people through their love of horses and the rodeo. Although Delilah's been a professional trick rider for years, I didn't get interested in riding until after I'd spent three years in and out of hospitals.

When I finally recovered from the assault that altered my life — "the incident" as we call it — my mom and her thought equine therapy would help keep my mind occupied so I wouldn't fall into a deeper depression.

I was reluctant at first since I didn't know much about horses, only what I'd witnessed from my sister riding over the years, but I'm glad they encouraged me. Delilah's ten years older than me and spends most of the summers traveling across the state for her job, but she's always been protective of me.

Whether it's because she's my big sister or she felt guilty for not being home that day, she's always been my biggest supporter. She helped me get lessons with Noah so I could learn from the best. I'm no expert in show jumping, but I'm having fun with it and getting to do something for me.

Only With Me

After taking Piper for a trail ride and doing an hour of training with Noah, I'm home before dinner. Delilah moved out a couple years ago into an apartment with her best friend, so it's only my parents and me with our three dogs.

"Hi, Daddy." I lean down to his power wheelchair level and kiss his cheek. He doesn't look like he's in a great mood today. "How was your day?"

He grunts. "Fine. Yours?"

Fine means bearable but not great.

"Good. I stopped at Annie's before going to the ranch. Took Piper up to the mountain trail before her training session. She made all her jumps except one, so not too bad."

I leave out the part where Piper and I got lost on our ride. I ended up walking her through some brush to get back on the trail. Though it made me nervous to be out there alone with only God knows what, I managed to keep it together long enough to find our way back.

"That's great, sweetie," Mom chimes in, entering the living room with an apron across her waist. "Dinner will be ready in a half hour if you wanna shower beforehand."

"Sounds good." I take the hint that I smell like a barn and walk down the hallway. Mom's never been a lover of ranch animals, even though we have pets, and is obsessed with keeping everything clean at all times—including me.

Moose, my childhood boxer, follows me to my room. He's ten years old and loves sleeping under my covers. When I was bedridden, he never left my side. He became my little therapy dog and still is.

Once I've washed off the smell, I meet my parents in the kitchen. Dad sits on the end, and Mom and I are across from each other. Her two Pomeranians, Shelby and Sasha, lie by our feet.

Moose tends to stay in my room and wait for me to return. He knows I'll bring him treats or leftovers later.

The table's already set, so after we say grace, we dive in.

"Is there parmesan cheese?" Dad asks Mom.

"I sprinkled some on top of the sauce," Mom replies without glancing up from her plate.

"More like half a sprinkle..." Dad grumbles.

"Do you want some more, Daddy?" I ask, smirking around my words.

This is a regular occurrence. Mom wants Dad to eat healthy and he wants to eat whatever he wants without being told otherwise.

Pushing back against my chair, I stand and go to the fridge. Dad sits in a regular dining chair at the table, so he's not mobile until he goes back into his power chair or uses his walker.

"Here, Daddy. Not too much." I set the cheese next to his plate.

"Thanks, sweetie." He grabs a handful and smothers his pasta.

When I sit, Mom's narrowed eyes meet mine, and I shove food into my mouth to hide the grin forming across my face.

It's bad enough that he has minimal control over his life, so if a little extra cheese makes him happy, then so be it.

After dinner, Mom serves fruit and Greek yogurt parfaits. A few minutes later, Dad groans in agony, his eyes pinch closed, and he releases a whimpered groan.

"You okay?" I ask, already knowing the answer.

"I'm gonna take some meds and go to bed," he responds, not bothering to finish his dessert.

Mom brings over his chair and helps him get settled before he takes off through the living room toward their bedroom.

It's not uncommon for Dad to go to bed early. Or take a few naps throughout the day. He suffers from chronic phantom limb pain—ever since his work accident eight years ago when he lost his leg.

The amputation cut is above his knee, close to his hip, so wearing a prosthetic is next to impossible.

But his brain still sends signals, thinking it's there, and because the nerves are damaged and oversensitive, he experiences

Only With Me

pain from the part of the leg that no longer exists. His body and brain are at a constant war with each other.

There's no cure for phantom limb pain because it's neurological, but there are temporary treatments. There's mirror therapy, nerve pain medication or opioids, but nothing that can numb it completely. Dad's almost always suffering, and even though he's developed a high pain tolerance, it's not always tolerable.

It puts him in a bad mood more often than a good one.

If that wasn't traumatic enough, the following summer was when my incident occurred. He witnessed it, unable to intervene because he couldn't walk, and that fucked him up mentally even more.

When he's having a bad mental episode, he takes more medication than he should. When he wants to knock himself out, he takes extra sleeping pills and mixes them with pain pills.

Almost every morning I wonder if that'll be the day I find him no longer breathing.

He attempted to overdose once, five years ago. And then once again, two years ago.

Since then, I've tried to stay strong and remind him how much we love and need him. I ignore my grief about how our lives should've been, so instead of adding extra guilt to his plate, I pretend everything's fine.

Our family had it rough for a few years—hell, Daddy still does. I recovered from my incident.

He never will.

"I can clear the table, Mom," I quickly say when she starts fussing over the dishes.

She sighs, frustrated that there's nothing we can do to help Dad. "Thanks, sweetie."

She opens the dishwasher and starts rinsing the plates I hand over. We work in silence, sticking to our routine afterward where she tidies up the house, and I hang out in my room with Moose. When Daddy's in bed, we try our best not to wake him since he only sleeps a few hours at a time before the pain inevitably hits him again.

I wake up sometime after nine in the morning to a video of rain noises still playing. Reaching over, I close my laptop and that's when I feel a weird burning sensation.

"What the hell?" Sitting up in bed, I stretch out my arms and see they're covered in red bumps.

And they're itchy as fuck.

Moose's head pops up and nudges me.

"Oh my God...what the hell is this?" Flying out of bed, I rush to the full-length mirror in the corner of my room. So far, the rash only reaches to my elbows, but I can't help scratching it.

Grabbing my phone, I snap a few photos and send one to my horse club group chat. Someone in there might know what it is and hopefully how to treat it.

I'm too scared to leave my room in case it's contagious. The last thing Dad needs on top of his pain is to get covered in whatever the hell this is. We typically go for a walk in the morning since it's when he feels his best. Well, he rides in his power chair, and I walk next to him with Moose. But it's a good way to get him out of the house and for us to talk.

After a few people guess random possibilities, Jake asks for a closer pic.

UNKNOWN
That's poison ivy, sweetheart. Don't scratch it.

Only With Me

Sweetheart? Who the hell is that?

> **HARLOW**
> Don't scratch?! I'm about to peel off my skin.

> **JAKE**
> You must've rubbed up against it within the last 12 to 24 hours.

> **HARLOW**
> Shit...I went riding yesterday and got lost so I walked through some brush to get us back on the path.

The sun was beating down on me, so I rolled up my sleeves. *Shit.*

> **JAKE**
> That'll do it.

> **UNKNOWN**
> Apply cool compresses and get some itch-relief cream.

I don't bother asking who the random number belongs to since I'm in the middle of a crisis, but I thank him anyway. Jake's the one who added him a couple days ago, so it must be one of his guy friends.

Exiting the chat, I Google how to treat poison ivy and if it's contagious.

Luckily, it's not, but it can appear on other parts of my body since it develops in stages. I was wearing jeans yesterday, but that doesn't mean it won't show up on my neck or face. If I touch any part of my body after being exposed, it's only a matter of time before it shows up.

And of course, it says to avoid scratching so it doesn't get infected.

I'm in hell.

Chapter Four
Waylon

Mondays are always hectic, but they're specifically exhausting when I have to drag myself out of bed in the middle of the night to pick up Wilder's drunken ass and then go to work a couple hours later.

As planned, he left family supper right after dessert and met up with Gabby.

Turns out a twenty-one-year-old college student can hold her liquor as well as he can and they went toe-to-toe. They partied for hours at The Twisted Bull, and when it was near closing time, Rainy called me to get him. She has my number on speed dial at this point and knows not to let him drive.

Wilder has a lot of inner demons he's still battling—ones I wish he'd seek help for—but I vowed to always be there for him no matter what. Loving him unconditionally means I bear the stormy seasons with him. Even though he can be a royal pain, especially when it's during the most inconvenient times, I'll never abandon him when he's spiraling.

After all these years of masking and compartmentalizing, he's good at it. You'd never guess he's drowning in depression based on how he acts around everyone. Charismatic and funny, acting like he's fine, but in reality, he's using alcohol and sex to ignore the demons choking him from the inside out.

I feel them, too.

As his twin, I sense when things are bad and it's why I don't scold him the way I should. I worry if I do, it'll make things worse by triggering him to not only cut but do it too deep again.

Thirteen years ago was the last time he was hospitalized, but since then, I've noticed fresh cuts on his thighs from time to time. Not deep enough to pass out but enough to see he was able to stop himself. Finding him bleeding out on the bathroom floor and then witnessing him seizing in the hospital was traumatic enough, and I never want either of us to experience it again.

I'd never felt my heart drop the way it did when I heard that machine beep like crazy and saw his lifeless eyes staring at me.

And that's why I continue watching him like a hawk and being there the only way I know how—showing up and reminding him he's loved. Even when he doesn't want me to or want to hear it.

I can only hope it's enough to get him through the hard days when he's tempted to harm himself and then chooses not to.

Although we've found different ways of coping with our mental health, I understand him in a way no one else can, which is why I don't get angry when he stumbles in two hours late for work.

Frustrated? Definitely.

"How's your head?" I ask, grabbing the rake.

"Feels like I slept in vise-grip pliers, but other than that, wonderful."

"Great, then you won't mind ridin' out to the pasture and checkin' the troughs."

"Yeah, sure..." His eye twitches as if he can't stand the idea of getting on a horse right now.

"*After* you finish muckin' your half of the stalls," I add.

I may not scold him in so many words, but I'll put his hungover ass to work.

Brooke Montgomery

Once my half is finished, I take a quick break to check my phone that's been vibrating nonstop. A couple are from Landen, one from Noah, and several from the horse group chat.

I do a quick scroll through their conversation until my eyes land on a photo. It looks to be a girl's arm showing off a nasty rash and freaking out because she doesn't know what it is or where it came from.

UNKNOWN #1

Guys, it itches so bad! Oh my God.

UNKNOWN #2

Maybe you have an infection.

UNKNOWN #3

Could be ringworm. Or a bad case of Eczema.

UNKNOWN #1

OMG what is that? Am I gonna die?

UNKNOWN #4

Kind of looks like Psoriasis. Though it could be a heat rash, too.

UNKNOWN #3

You're not gonna die. But you might wanna get it checked out. Ringworm's contagious.

UNKNOWN #1

CONTAGIOUS? This can't be happening.

JAKE

Can you send a close-up pic?

Only With Me

The girl does, a better one that reveals what it is.
Wilder and I had it when we were teenagers.

> **WAYLON**
> That's poison ivy, sweetheart. Don't scratch it.

UNKNOWN #1
Don't scratch?! I'm about to peel off my skin.

JAKE
He's right. You must've rubbed up against it within the last twelve to twenty-four hours.

UNKNOWN #1
Shit...I went riding yesterday and got lost so I walked through some brush to get us back on the path.

With it getting colder, it's less common to be exposed to the plant but not impossible.

JAKE
That'll do it.

> **WAYLON**
> Apply cool compresses and get some itch-relief cream.

UNKNOWN #1
Thanks.

I feel bad because I know how awful it can be.
Wilder had this grand idea that we should play hide-and-seek in the dark and then the following day, we were covered nearly from head to toe.
Wilder and I take the first group of riders on their tour, and he, of course, chats up the cute girls and even grabs one of their numbers before we get back.
"How you haven't knocked up someone by now, I'll never understand," I taunt when we bring the horses back to the barn.

"Pfft. I'm not going bareback. Ain't that stupid."

I chuckle at the irony. "Stupid enough to sleep around."

"I don't sleep with all of 'em! Just because we hang out or party doesn't mean they're all gettin' a piece of me. Sometimes we just make out or fool around."

"You mean, you get whiskey dick."

"Fuck off, I do not!" He shoves me against one of the stalls and makes me lose my balance.

I bark out a laugh at how offended he sounds. "Chill, dude."

After the saddles have been removed and put away, we brush the horses and then put them into the pasture to graze. Since we'll use different horses for the afternoon riders, they're done for the day.

"Lunch?" Wilder asks.

"I'll go later. Noah asked me to swing by, so I'm gonna head over to the stables," I tell him.

"Okay, see ya."

Wilder and I go our separate ways, and I meet up with Noah at the training center.

"Hey." I grab her attention and walk up to her with one of the boarders.

"Sorry to bother you, but I'm short-staffed with Ruby off, Landen's off with Dad to get feed, and a client who was supposed to come and exercise her horse is out sick today, so I need a little help catchin' up."

Noah's good at what she does, but she often runs on fumes trying to do it all, so I don't mind helping her out when I can.

"Sure, just tell me whatcha need."

"You're the best." She grins appreciatively. "Piper needs to be lunged and then you can keep her in the pasture for a half hour. Miss Swift and Lacie-Mae need to be moved to the west pasture, and then if you can tack Mac up for me so I can train her next, I'd appreciate it."

"Sure, but ya owe me one!" I taunt, walking toward the stables.

Only With Me

"Yeah, yeah!" she calls.

Piper's a brown and white spotted Appaloosa who's been here for the past four years. Noah's been training her and Harlow, and from what I've seen, she's a decent show horse.

It takes less than an hour to finish and once I get Piper back into her stall, Landen and Dad are back with the trailer of feed.

"Y'all wanna hand?" I ask, not bothering to remove my work gloves because I already know his answer.

"Yeah, it'll help us get done faster," Landen responds.

There's only half of the bags left, which means they've already stopped at the retreat barn, and I doubt Wilder returned from lunch to help.

"Ellie gettin' nervous yet?" I ask Landen while we haul bags inside the stables.

"More like an excited anxiousness..." he confirms. "She's workin' out like crazy to stay in shape and practicin' as much as Ranger can handle it."

"I can't wait to watch her."

Considering I've never been to the NFR or any rodeo event that big, I'm excited about the trip, especially since the whole family is going. Ayden, the stables manager, will stay behind with Ruby and they'll make sure the other ranch hands stay on top of mucking stalls, feeding, and exercising the horses.

Since the event is ten days long and Ellie has to be there earlier for press, she and Landen are leaving the day after Thanksgiving with their trailer to drive Ranger across the country. The rest of us will fly out there to watch the final few days and hopefully see her win the championship.

Brooke Montgomery

When I get home later that evening, I scroll through more texts in the group chat and find an update from the girl with poison ivy.

She sends a photo of her upper chest and neck area that's starting to turn red and form bumps. Then another photo of her arm looking worse than it did this morning.

> **UNKNOWN #1**
> My mom got me some anti-itch cream but it's not helping. I want to claw off my skin.
>
> **UNKNOWN #2**
> Did you try soaking in a warm bath?
>
> **UNKNOWN #1**
> Yes, with some oatmeal. It feels better when I'm in there but as soon as I get out, the unbearable itchiness returns.

Deciding to pitch in, I offer another solution.

> **WAYLON**
> Do you have any baking soda?
>
> **Unknown #1**
> I THINK SO. PROBABLY. WHY?
>
> **WAYLON**
> Mix it with water to create a thick paste and apply it over the rash. It'll absorb the excess moisture and help relieve the itching. Then once it dries, you can rinse it off.
>
> **UNKNOWN #1**
> That sounds messy, but I'm willing to try anything at this point.
>
> **WAYLON**
> You can do it a few times a day as long as it's not making things worse.
>
> **UNKNOWN #1**
> Thanks, I appreciate the tip!

Only With Me

WAYLON

> No problem. Good luck.

I should've asked her earlier what her name is, but now it feels almost too late. Or maybe it'd be awkward to ask only her in a group chat of several others I don't know.

Once I've showered and had a bigger dinner than usual since I worked through lunch, I video call Bentley—my fifteen-year-old "little brother." I joined the Big Brothers Big Sisters program last year after Landen got into training some 4-H Club kids. He said it gave him a purpose outside of being a rancher and that hit home for me. Outside of my family and work, I don't have much that feels meaningful.

Getting to mentor someone, a kid I can be there for in any way he needs me and be an extra ear, has helped give me something to look forward to.

"Hey, man. How's it goin'?" I ask when he picks up.

His hair's wet like he just got out of the shower and he lifts one shoulder. "Fine, I guess."

Bentley lives in the next town over, but we hang out a couple times a month on the weekends and sometimes video chat during the week. He loves coming to the ranch and getting on the horses. He didn't know how to ride until I taught him and now he's as comfortable as ever. I plan to teach him how to rope soon.

"Just fine?" I lean against the table that my laptop is on. "What's the matter?"

Bentley had a rough childhood after his dad died, so I try to encourage him to talk it out instead of holding in his feelings. I have firsthand experience of what happens when you don't and how it affects you into adulthood. However, he doesn't always want to talk. I understand why because I can be the same way. But I always try to encourage him on his own terms.

Instead of answering, he looks down and shrugs. I know he has a hard time in school. He suffers from ADHD, so he struggles with comprehension and staying focused. He doesn't like asking for help, though, so I always have to pry it out of him, question by question.

"You have homework tonight?" I ask, noticing he's leaning over an open notebook.

"Yeah."

"What's the subject? Maybe I can help."

I wasn't an A student, but I did well for someone not interested in anything besides ranch life and girls.

"Geometry," he replies, already sounding defeated.

"Alright, well, that doesn't sound so bad. Tell me what you're workin' on and let's figure it out."

"It doesn't even make sense," he groans, rubbing his palm over his eye.

"It's a good thing you have me and this handy thing called the internet," I tease. "What's the lesson you're on?"

Bentley shrugs, leans back, and flips through his notebook. When he holds it up for me to look at his notes, I see what he's currently studying.

"Pythagorean theorem, nice. First, let's make sure you understand the formula and then we can figure out how to solve it. What's your first question?"

Bentley shows me the problem and I write it down on a notepad so we can both work on it at the same time. It takes me a minute to remember since it's been over fifteen years, but once we get going, it all clicks.

We go through about fifteen problems and by the end of them, his confidence is up.

"You know, there are websites that can help walk you through math problems like this, too. In case I'm not around or something. That way you ain't strugglin' on your own."

"Yeah, but it's easier when you explain it," he says.

"It's all about comprehension and practice. The more you do it, the better you're gonna understand. But you know you can text or call me anytime. I'm always here to help with homework or listen."

Only With Me

He nods. "Yeah, thanks."

"Anytime." I smile back at him. "Anything else goin' on? You find a date for the holiday dance?"

When his cheeks turn red, I laugh and shove my notepad out of my way. "Alright, who did you ask?"

He rolls his eyes, clearly embarrassed. "I haven't yet. I'm scared she'll say no."

"Who'd say no to you? You're the best-lookin' kid in your grade."

"Pfft. You don't even know what anyone else looks like."

"Maybe not, but still, you're a cool kid. I bet I could give you some advice on askin' her out."

"You?"

My mouth falls open at his hesitant tone. "What's that mean?"

"You haven't mentioned a girlfriend since I've known you."

"Okay, so? I've been single for a bit, but that doesn't mean I can't help. In fact, it means I know exactly what not to do to get a girl's attention."

"Uh-huh." He crosses his arms. "So tell me, then. How do I get Hannah to go to the dance with me?"

"Hannah? Okay, we've got a name. What're Hannah's interests or hobbies?"

He scratches the back of his head. "Um, well...I think she likes horses because she has a couple notebooks covered with 'em."

"Perfect, considerin' you're into that now too. Okay, what else?"

"Music. She plays in the band."

"Nice. Do you know what instrument?"

"Saxophone."

"Very cool. Sounds like you know enough about her to start up a conversation about stuff she's interested in and you can mention how you learned to ride horses recently, too."

"And how does that get her to go to the dance with me?"

"Well, you gotta be patient. You're playin' the long game if you wanna see her again after the dance. Have a few convos and make her laugh. Girls love guys who are funny and nice."

"*Funny and nice*? Oh my God, you sound like my grandpa."

Furrowing my brows, I scowl. "Dude, I'm only thirty-two."

"And single," he reminds me.

"You act like I have one foot in the grave. I'm single by choice."

"That sounds like somethin' a single old man would say."

"*Allllright...*" I drawl. "Well, since I'm *so old*, I better get my old ass to bed."

He snickers at my irritation, and I shake my head.

"Good job on your homework tonight. I'm proud of you."

He lowers his gaze as if he's not used to being told that, but I am. Even when frustrated, he didn't give up.

"Thanks. I'll talk to you later," he says.

"Yep. Night, Bentley."

"See ya."

We end the call, and I stretch my legs, then walk to my bathroom to brush my teeth and get ready for bed.

Once I'm under the covers, I set my alarm and then check the group chat to see if that girl sent an update.

I'm curious if she tried the baking soda paste and if it worked.

But there's nothing, just random messages from other people talking about other topics.

I don't even know who this girl is.

But I can't help being curious.

Chapter Five
Harlow

After three more days of being housebound, I'm going stir-crazy because I'm not about to go out in public looking like I tried to hug a porcupine after rolling in a field of fire ants.

It feels like when I was bedridden all over again, but at least I can move around the house. I'm still fighting the urge to scratch the shit out of my skin every two seconds.

I hate how red and splotchy my arms look.

It's not exactly a pretty view for someone who works at a clothing boutique.

My manager, Ashley, has been understanding, but I hate missing shifts.

I've been soaking in the tub, doing the baking soda paste, and lathering on the anti-itch cream.

I think it's working, but not as fast as I need it to.

I miss my horse and taking her riding.

In between Dad's naps, we watch TV together, play cards or a board game, and have finished a thousand-piece puzzle.

At this point, all I'm missing is a Bingo addiction.

When the dogs start barking, I know Delilah's here.

Thank God.

We've been texting, and I begged her to come hang out with me after work.

When she's not traveling and trick-riding, she manages Lacey's, the luxury lingerie shop downtown. It's a couple blocks from Rodeo Belle, so we'd meet up for lunch or swing by each other's stores when we're both working.

"Hey!" I swing my arms around her. "Thanks for comin' by."

"No problem." When we pull apart, she looks at my arms and chest. "Yikes. Are you positive that it ain't contagious?"

"Ha-ha," I mock dryly. "If that were the case, Mama and Daddy would have it, too."

She chuckles. "Just messin' with ya. Looks a smidge better, though, than your pictures a few days ago."

"Could take up to three weeks to clear up," I groan.

"I stopped by the drugstore and got you some antihistamines and calamine lotion. I read up on it and those were the most recommended for dealin' with the itch."

"Ooh, thank you. I'll bathe in this lotion if it promises to do the trick."

I take the plastic bag from her hand and then we walk into the living room where Dad's watching *The Price is Right*.

"Hi, Daddy." Delilah hugs and kisses him. "How ya feelin' today?"

"Not too bad."

Today's been a good day. We never know how many of those we'll get with him, so we take what we can get.

"I crushed him in Monopoly earlier," I say.

"And then I wiped you off the floor in poker," he retorts.

Delilah barks out a laugh, her blond hair bouncing across her shoulders. "I see nothing's changed 'round here."

The three of us sit and chat in between guessing the answers on the gameshow. Eventually, Mom comes home from work. She's a nurse at the hospital in the next town and works ten-hour shifts four times a week. The other days, she cares for Dad, cleans the house, or runs errands.

Only With Me

Although we have cameras in and outside of the house, I adjust my work schedule based on when my mom will be away so someone's home with Dad and the dogs. Sometimes I'll work the evening shifts for a few hours if I'm needed, but after everything we've been through, Mom doesn't like him home alone too long.

"Delilah, stay for dinner. I'm makin' chili and cornbread," Mom says once she's showered and changed out of her scrubs.

"That sounds delicious. Let me help you in the kitchen," Delilah offers.

"I'm gonna take Moose for a short walk before we eat," I tell them. "I need some fresh air."

I put on a sweatshirt and boots, then grab his leash.

As we walk around the block, I pull out my phone to turn on some music and find a text message from an unknown number.

The same number who's in the group chat and told me the rash was poison ivy.

> UNKNOWN
>
> Hey, hope you don't mind me privately messaging you, but I wasn't sure if you'd want to talk about it with everyone else in the group. I just wondered how you were doing with the rash and if the baking soda paste worked for you.

I don't know why, but my heart races as I reread his message for the third time. Him reaching out to check on me is incredibly sweet.

Truth is, I've been wondering who he is and have been tempted to text him before but wasn't sure what to say. When it comes to talking to guys, I'm...not experienced. Like, *at all*.

But him being concerned for me makes me smile like a giddy teenager.

Brooke Montgomery

> **HARLOW**
> Hi, not at all. Thanks for checking on me. It's working well. My sister brought me some meds and lotion to soothe the itch in between being a paste mummy.

> **UNKNOWN**
> Ha, that's good. My brother and I got poison ivy in high school and our mom made us wear oven mitts on our hands so we'd stop scratching.

I snort at the imagery.

> **HARLOW**
> That's hilarious. Luckily, I've been hanging out with my dad and staying busy so I don't think about it, but it's the worst at night when I'm trying to sleep. I have nothing to distract myself so all I can think about is how itchy I am.

When Moose and I return to the house, my nose fills with the aroma of meat and beans, and my stomach growls.

"Dinner's almost ready, so make sure to wash up," Mom announces, setting the table.

I check my phone and find myself smiling again.

> **UNKNOWN**
> If you ever need someone to help distract you, hit me up. I can't always sleep either.

This is where I should ask for his name. Or at least how old he is.

If he's Jake's age, he's probably in his early thirties.

But he could be fifty for all I know.

Still, he hasn't asked for mine, and I suck when it comes to talking to guys, so I don't ask either.

> **HARLOW**
> Thank you, I appreciate that!

Only With Me

Mom calls everyone to the table and once we're all seated, we say grace and then dive in.

Chili is one of my favorites, especially topped with extra shredded cheese and sour cream.

"How's work goin', Delilah?" Mom asks.

"Great...we're enterin' the holiday shopping season. All the husbands buyin' lingerie for their wives and mistresses will keep us busy through New Year's."

Dad nearly chokes on his food, and I chuckle at Mom's shocked face.

"What? I caught a guy today!" Delilah exclaims, flinging her spoon around as she continues. "He bought two identical pieces, except one was red and one was black. However, they were noticeably different sizes—one was an extra small and the other an extra large—so I mentioned that to him. I even offered to grab the right one because I figured he didn't realize they were different. Instead, he threw his credit card at me and said, 'No, those are the sizes I need,' so I rang him up, looked him up on social media, and then sent his wife a little *hey girl* message."

"Oh my God!" My jaw drops, and I quickly cover my mouth when my mom glares at me for dropping the Lord's name in vain. "I'll never understand why men don't just get divorced if they're unhappy."

Truthfully, I don't understand a lot about men, but that especially.

"Because they're cowards," Delilah explains. "They'd rather sleep around than go to therapy."

"Some like the thrill of sneakin' around and the possibility of gettin' caught," Mom adds.

Delilah shakes her head. "Men are dirtbags."

"This a bad time to ask if you're datin' anyone?" Dad smirks before eating a spoonful of his chili.

Delilah snorts. "There are zero decent or single men in this town. Heck, maybe the state."

"You ain't gettin' any younger," Mom reminds her. "Especially if you wanna have children."

Delilah's deadpan expression causes me to laugh because the last thing on her mind is getting married or pregnant.

"If you're holdin' your breath for grandchildren, you're better off waitin' on Harlow."

"Me?" I gasp. "I've never had a boyfriend, remember? I'm the last person to depend on givin' y'all grandchildren."

"Yeah, but you're not even twenty-one. You have plenty of time," Delilah says. "I'm basically an old maid."

I scoff. "You're thirty, so I don't think so."

"There's no rush," Dad interrupts. "When you find *the one*, then you'll know it's time. Until then, focus on your own dreams and goals. Marriage and babies can wait."

I appreciate his words because at this rate, I'll be single for a long time. Not that I'm overly eager to find a boyfriend, but it'd be nice to have someone special to spend time with. However, I'm not a go-out-and-party type of person, and even when I'm legal to go to bars, I'm not sure how often I'll want to. I can't imagine meeting a guy at a bar and it working out.

But maybe the universe will prove me wrong and my Mr. Right will walk into my life when I least expect him to.

"Oh, hello, McDreamy..." Natalie singsongs as soon as Dr. Shepherd appears on the screen.

I chuckle around a handful of popcorn, nearly choking at her words.

"He ain't that good-lookin'," I say.

"*What*? You better get your eyes checked."

Only With Me

I roll them instead.

Natalie's crushed on him since we saw the very first episode of *Grey's Anatomy*.

We started watching the series together when we were only thirteen years old and roommates in the hospital. It's been seven years and we're still trying to catch up.

Our parents met first since we were brought into the emergency room a day apart. There had been a huge pileup on the highway with several traumas and to make space for them, they put us in the same room.

Natalie had been hit while riding her bike and needed several surgeries on her abdomen, pelvis, and legs. It took her two years of physical therapy to walk again.

I'd been put on life support while they waited for the swelling in my brain to go down and then had to prioritize which part of my body needed surgery first.

When we were both lucid and could finally talk, we became recovery buddies. I spent weeks at a time there with her and when one of us had to go back as an inpatient, we'd often visit each other and start up the show where we ended it.

Since we live two hours apart, we video chat at least once a week to watch a few episodes together.

"I'm still bitter about McSteamy." I frown.

We're only on season ten, and I've cried more times than I can count, especially when he died. I'm attached to most of the main characters and that's why I can only watch a few episodes at a time.

"Maybe you should find your own instead," Natalie says. "McNasty."

I huff out a laugh. "Funny enough, we were havin' a similar conversation at dinner tonight." I continue explaining Delilah's lingerie story.

"You should try a datin' app. I'm sure there are plenty of eligible bachelors you'd like."

"Uh…I dunno. That seems like a million percent out of my comfort zone."

"Says the extrovert. You can make conversation with anyone."

"Not with cute guys," I retort. "I always assume they're way out of my league and wouldn't be interested." Considering my lack of experience, I'm not sure guys would find that attractive when I tell them I want to wait before getting into the physical stuff.

"Harlow, I ain't sayin' this as your bestie or because I've known you a long time, but I'm sayin' this as someone who has eyeballs. You're *stunning*. Like, drop-dead beautiful. And I should hate you for it because you don't even haveta try. If I was even a smidge bisexual, you'd be my gay awakening."

I burst out cackling so hard that it causes my side to cramp.

"You"—I wipe my cheeks from the tears she made fall—"are ridiculous."

"But you know it's true. I bet you a hundred bucks you'd get ten messages from guys within the first hour of your profile being active."

"I don't even know what that means. I've never been on a datin' app."

"You swipe on the profiles you like and if they swipe on yours, you're a match. Then you can either message 'em or they'll message you. There are variations of how it works dependin' on the app. Some have it where the woman has to message first."

I curl my lips, hating the sound of that.

"And what if they ask to meet up but look nothin' like their photos?"

"That's why you always assume they won't and deduct half the points for his looks. So if his photo is a ten, he's now a five. But if his personality is a seven, his overall average is a six. Truthfully, though, I'd probably fold for that."

I snort because that's the dumbest thing I've ever heard.

"And what if I'd like to find an average-lookin' nice guy who won't pressure me to get drunk or have sex with him on the first date?"

Only With Me

"Oh...well, then you're gonna need to download a different type of app for that."

"Which one?"

"Virgins 'R Us."

She says it so seriously that it's not until her face cracks with a smile that I know she's fucking with me.

"I hate you."

"Ha! No, you don't. You *love* me."

"Mm-hmm."

I firmly believe Natalie's so boy-crazy because she spent her early teen years in the hospital, like me, except she also went to an all-girls high school. So as soon as she went off to college, she found the first hot guy to pop her cherry.

We continue shit-talking and watching our show together until midnight. After she pressures me to show her my arms and chest rash mural, we say good night.

Before I go to bed, I take two of the antihistamines and dab on some calamine lotion. Since I don't want to get it all over my blankets, I'm stuck lying on my back like a statue, which is as uncomfortable as it sounds.

Thirty minutes of staring at my ceiling has me grabbing my phone and pulling up the text thread with the unknown guy.

HARLOW

> Hey, sorry it's so late. Any chance you're awake?

When the text shows delivered, I second-guess sending it.

What would I even say if he is awake? Or what if he only said I could text him to be nice and didn't mean it?

Ugh.

This is why I'd suck on a dating app.

But maybe Natalie's right. I'll never get comfortable with the idea of dating if I don't put myself out there and try.

Chapter Six
Waylon

My heart sinks at missing her text last night. Though to be fair, it was way past my bedtime.

WAYLON
> Morning. I'm so sorry for not seeing your text until now. I was already asleep. But if you wanna chat tonight, I'll be up late.

I mentally slap my forehead at what a douche I must sound like, but surprisingly, she responds right away.

POISON IVY GIRL
> Hey, don't worry about it! I didn't realize how late it was and figured you were sleeping.

Poison Ivy Girl—the not so creative name I gave her so I can keep track of her in the group thread.

WAYLON
> How's the itch doing today?

POISON IVY GIRL
> It's turned into blisters…I'm in hell.

Only With Me

> **WAYLON**
> Oh shit. I know that's painful.

> **POISON IVY GIRL**
> I woke up feeling the burning and immediately took a cold shower. Now I'm covered in calamine lotion and trying not to cry about how much this sucks.

Fuck. I feel so bad for her.

> **WAYLON**
> I'm so sorry you're going through this. I'm off to work, but I'll check in during my breaks.

I should ask what her name is and how old she is, but the last thing I want to sound like is a creepy old guy who's trying to hit on her.

But it's more than that.

My family's well-known in Sugarland Creek and as soon as I tell her my name, she'll have all these preconceived notions about who I am—most of them linked to Wilder. Based on what she's heard or seen about me online, it could override everything I've shared with her.

Which honestly, hasn't been too much, but more than I'd typically share with a stranger.

I'd rather let her get to know me outside of what everyone thinks they know before we exchange names.

She could also decide once she finds out who I am that she wants nothing to do with me. Even as friends.

And that'd suck.

It's not easy making friends outside of being Wilder's babysitter and working ten-to-twelve-hour days.

Instead of dwelling on it, I make some coffee and get my ass to work. Wilder's on time for once, so I don't have to rush through mucking my half of the stalls and we get done early.

"Wanna grab some breakfast before the first tour?" he asks.

"Sure."

The downtime will give me the chance to catch up on the group chat. The last time I checked my notifications, there were another dozen or so.

We take my truck to The Lodge and find Tripp and Magnolia sitting at a table with my two-year-old niece, Willow.

"Hey, kiddo. Whatcha eatin'?" I rest my palms on the table next to her.

She does her best to say scrambled eggs and sausage.

"Can I have some?" I tease, but she sticks out her fork with a piece of meat, so I playfully bite it. "Mmm. That's good."

"Get your own food and quit stealin' my kid's," Tripp scolds.

I snicker at how grumpy he is. Considering their son's only a few months old, he's probably not getting a full night's sleep.

"Where's Laken?" He's usually attached to Magnolia's chest.

"Mom and Gramma Grace are watchin' him this mornin' since Willow has a doctor's appointment," Magnolia explains.

"Doctor? Is she okay?" I ask.

"She's fine. It's just a wellness check, but I thought it'd be easier only bringin' one. This way we're not jugglin' 'em both while answerin' questions."

"Gramma Grace was more than happy to babysit anyway," Tripp adds. "She nearly pushed us out the door before we could even say goodbye."

I laugh because I'm not surprised.

She's our mom's mother and has lived with our parents in the main house since our grandfather passed away eight years ago. She loves to bake and scrapbook with us.

She's also known for her witchcraft of always knowing everyone's secrets.

Wilder and I head to the buffet and fill up our plates. Now I won't have to eat lunch and can maybe get ahead on my to-do list.

Once we're at the table, I pull out my phone and read through some of the conversations the group chat is having.

Only With Me

Someone asked about a trick-riding saddle. Apparently, they want to learn and make sure they get the best kind.

Before I can type out a reply, *she* responds with a specific brand that I would've recommended too based on what I know Noah uses.

> **POISON IVY GIRL**
> Just make sure you know what you're doing on it or your ass will look like mine.

> **UNKNOWN #4**
> What do you mean?

Instead of a text response, she sends a photo.

Of her ass in a pair of lace see-through panties.

And her skin is covered in bruises. Not only her ass cheeks but her upper thighs, too.

My eyes expand at how revealing the photo is, and I nearly choke on the piece of bacon I just stuffed in my mouth.

What the hell is she doing?

> **POISON IVY GIRL**
> Safe to say, I fell...a lot. And it was painful.

For how dark the bruises are, I wonder if she fell on cement or even stayed on the horse at all.

> **JAKE**
> DAT ASS THO. Never missed a glutes day, have ya?

Oh my God, I want to kill him.

> **POISON IVY GIRL**
> You act like you've never seen an ass in a bikini before.

She has a point but still...this is a close-up shot I don't think any of us were expecting.

UNKNOWN #5

Bruised or not, that's a fine-looking ass!

Whoever that dipshit is added a peach emoji with a tongue.
Fucker.

GRETCHEN'S OWNER

Damn. I didn't know it looked that bad. But everyone's right, you have a nice booty!

That's the girl who had the horse with the nail in its hoof. I changed her contact too so I could start keeping track of which number belongs to who.

POISON IVY GIRL

Yeah, they take forever to heal too. I couldn't sit on my horse comfortably for two weeks.

GRETCHEN'S OWNER

Two weeks? You need to do some at-home remedies to help them heal faster. Like cold and hot compresses or even Arnica gel.

UNKNOWN #4

Spend one night with me and you wouldn't sit for a month, baby...but for a whole different reason.

When the dipshit sends a winking emoji, I want to reach through the phone and strangle him.
His new contact name is *Perverted Asshole*.

GRETCHEN'S OWNER

Shut up, dumbass.

PERVERTED ASSHOLE

Or what?

Only With Me

GRETCHEN'S OWNER

> She could snap you like a twig and you know it.

Oh, he's scrawny. *Good to know*. He just got a name upgrade.

SCRAWNY PERVERTED ASSHOLE

> Ooh, keep talking naughty. You know I like that.

I roll my eyes at his gross attempt at flirting and decide it's better if I ignore him —*for now*. My concern is how bad her bruises look and if that's normal for her.

WAYLON

> Do you always bruise like a peach?

I've had my fair share of falls, Noah too, and I don't think either of us has had bruises look that bad.

POISON IVY GIRL

> Yeah, ever since I was a teenager. It doesn't take much. Just bumping into something will cause a bruise to form.

WAYLON

> That's not normal. This might sound weird, but you might have a vitamin K deficiency, which is why your blood isn't clotting the way it should be.

POISON IVY GIRL

> Actually, that makes sense. I was put on blood thinners for a couple years when I was thirteen. I'll call my doctor to do some lab work when this damn rash goes away.

Great, now I have more questions than answers about why she was on blood thinners at such a young age, but I'm glad she's willing to get it checked out.

"Waylon!" Magnolia's loud voice startles the shit out of me, and I drop my phone.

"What?"

Looking up, Tripp and Wilder are laughing at me.

"I've been tryin' to get your attention for five minutes. Who the hell are you talkin' to?" Magnolia lifts a brow. "A girl?"

"None of your damn business."

I lock my phone and shove it into my pocket.

"That confirms it." Tripp smirks. "Who is it?"

"It's a group chat my friend Jake added me into. They just talk about random horse or ranch stuff, mostly," I explain.

"So Jake's makin' you all flustered like that?" Wilder taunts, kicking my boots underneath the table, and I kick him back.

"Fuck off. There's a handful of people in there, and I don't even know any of 'em besides him."

"So why're you in there then?" Magnolia asks.

"I read through it from time to time and sometimes reply to messages." I shrug, hoping they don't push for more.

"Hm…I dunno. You're actin' weird, which means it's way more than that." Magnolia narrows her eyes skeptically, and I grab my fork to continue eating.

"Anyway, what did you want?" I ask, hopefully changing the subject.

"Just that we were leavin' and your niece wanted a hug goodbye."

I look over at Willow and then pick her up so she can wrap her little arms around me. "Be good for your mommy and daddy, okay? Make sure to get a sticker and a sucker from the doctor."

"A sucker!" Her eyes light up like the Fourth of July.

"Thanks, man…" Tripp deadpans.

I grin. "Anytime."

Once the three of them leave, Wilder and I finish eating, then head to the retreat barn to get the horses ready for the first tour of the day.

Only With Me

It takes everything in me not to text *her* as soon as I get home and clean up. I like talking to her even though I can't explain why. There's this…*energy.* This pull has me checking my phone way more than I ever have before.

Not wanting to come off weird or creepy is what stops me from randomly messaging her, but then she's the one who texts me first the following day.

> **POISON IVY GIRL**
> So I mentioned the vitamin K thing to my mom and she says she bets you're correct based on my previous health issues. If that's the case, you're basically my hero.

> **WAYLON**
> I like the sound of that. What do I win if I'm right?

> **POISON IVY GIRL**
> Win? Is saving my life not enough of a prize?

> **WAYLON**
> Of course, assuming you're not some seventy-year-old grandma who's knitting a voodoo doll of me.

> **POISON IVY GIRL**
> Dammit, you caught me.

> **WAYLON**
> Nice ass for your age, then.

I smack my forehead as soon as my brain catches up to what I've typed out. But it's too late because I already hit send. *Real smooth.*

Brooke Montgomery

POISON IVY GIRL
Why thank you. Lots of anti-aging and firm cream. But now you gotta show me yours.

WAYLON
My ass?

POISON IVY GIRL
Fair is fair.

WAYLON
I didn't ask to see yours in the first place.

POISON IVY GIRL
But you still looked.

WAYLON
Not on purpose.

POISON IVY GIRL
The bruising looks much better now, in case you wondered.

Dammit, I was.

WAYLON
Is that so?

POISON IVY GIRL
I'll prove it.

Just as I'm about to send another message stating I'll take her word for it, she sends me a photo.

Of her ass in a bikini.

I nearly choke on my saliva.

Jesus Christ.

What am I supposed to say to that?

WAYLON
I think you're lying about your age.

Only With Me

POISON IVY GIRL

What makes you say that?

WAYLON

That's too perfect of an ass for anyone over forty.

Oh God, why did I type that?
Better yet, why did I send it?
Now I'm no better than Scrawny Perverted Asshole.

POISON IVY GIRL

And now you've seen it twice. So your turn.

WAYLON

Against my will!

POISON IVY GIRL

HAHAHA you poor baby.

WAYLON

Okay, fine. I'm all about equality, so here ya go…

And then I send her a photo of a donkey.

POISON IVY GIRL

Wow… hairier than I expected but cute nonetheless.

WAYLON

Cute and hairy, I'll take that.

POISON IVY GIRL

Gonna be disappointed if you're ugly and hairless.

The fact that she has the same humor as me makes me even more curious about her.

"Who the hell has you blushin' like a teenage girl who just met her pop idol?"

Wilder's voice grabs my attention, and my gaze follows him from my kitchen to help himself to a beer and then to the living room where he promptly plops his ass in my recliner.

"Do you ever knock?"

"What for?" He pops the tab of the can. "Even if I did, you wouldn't have heard me with how lost in your phone you were."

"I was not." I lock and pocket it to prove a point. "What're you doin' here anyway?"

"Let's go out tonight."

"No, thanks."

He frowns. "Why not?"

"I worked all day and am tired."

I'm also hanging out with Bentley tomorrow afternoon and don't want to be dragging ass after work.

"That's never stopped you before. Plus, Ashley's gonna be there and she wants to hook up."

That sounds more painful than having poison ivy.

"And how did you hear that?"

"She told me."

"Then *you* hook up with her. I'm not interested."

"Been there, done that."

"Dude." My upper lip curls in disdain. "Then why would I wanna be with her?"

He shrugs like the carefree asshole he is. "Why not? She was a decent lay. She has a Daddy kink, though, just FYI."

"And we're done talkin' about this." Nothing against her preferences, but I wasn't interested before I knew and still not after.

I stand and walk to the kitchen for a beer since the freeloader didn't even bother to get me one.

"I'm stayin' in, so you're gonna haveta go without me," I tell him when I return to my spot on the couch.

"You're no fun."

Only With Me

"Why don't ya stay in and...oh, I dunno...get more than four hours of sleep?"

"Sounds lame."

Defeated, I roll my eyes and grab the TV remote. "Well, call me when you need a ride."

Chapter Seven
Harlow

TWO WEEKS LATER

I curl my body into itself on the pavement of our driveway and my hands cover my head as a metal bat slams into my ribs. Screaming out in pain, the tears flood down my cheeks.

"You fucking bitch!" the guy shouts above me for the second time.

The first was after I kneed him in the balls.

"Please stop," I cry out.

"Get away from her!" Dad yells from inside the doorway of the garage, but he can't help me. He's in his wheelchair and no one else is home. "I'm gonna kill you, ya bastard!"

Dad's roaring voice lands on deaf ears because the guy continues kicking me. When his heel digs into my chest, he forces my body to unfold and then the toe of his boot slams into the side of my head.

Unfortunately, or maybe fortunately, I can't feel much anymore.

My legs are probably broken. I know a few ribs cracked.

I taste blood from my nose.

"S-stop," I whimper, the air constricting in my lungs.

My eyes can hardly stay open, but when I hear a shotgun blast, they struggle to see where it came from.

And then a second blast.

Only With Me

A harsh ringing in my ears and the sound of sirens are the last things I remember, and then I lose consciousness.

"Harlow! Sweetheart, wake up." Mom's panicked voice echoes as she palms my cheek.

The bed shakes when she taps my arm a few times and I finally come to enough to open my eyes.

"What is it?" I ask, looking around and finding Moose resting his head on my thigh.

"You...were screamin'. I assumed you were havin' a nightmare."

Oh shit, she's right.

Blinking away the fog, I swallow hard and clear my throat. "Sorry, I didn't mean to scare you."

She helps me sit up and then sits on the bed next to me.

"Was it about—"

"Yeah," I say quickly. "I haven't had a nightmare about it in a while."

"Could be stressed induced," she offers. "Or maybe side effects of some of the new vitamins you're takin'."

"That's possible," I agree.

After being aware I could be vitamin K deficient, I made an appointment to get my blood checked and found out Mystery Guy was right. I only started taking supplements this past week.

But I don't think that's what's causing the nightmares.

She probably doesn't realize it—and I'm too nervous to remind her and Dad—but the man who broke both my legs and put me in a coma is up for parole soon.

I look up his case at least once a month. Mostly to ensure he's still behind bars. Logically, I know he is, but I need to see the confirmation in order to sleep soundly at night.

After he was caught and I was able to confirm he was the one who did this to me, he made a plea deal instead of going to trial.

The police had video evidence from our neighbor's security cameras, so there was no denying what he'd done. After that,

Brooke Montgomery

Mom hired someone to put up cameras in and out of the house. It traumatized all of us.

I was in no condition to testify anyway, so him pleading guilty was the best outcome. Since Dad shot him in the shoulder, he had to undergo surgery before he could be arraigned.

Ten years for aggravated assault with the possibility of parole after eight. And he'll be eligible in a couple months. He can apply for it, but he's not guaranteed to get approved if he's had any behavior issues while behind bars.

"Want some pancakes for breakfast?" Mom asks, breaking up my thoughts.

"Sure, that'd be great." I smile.

Mom kisses the top of my head, then walks out toward the kitchen.

She's off work today, which means I have a shift at Rodeo Belle this morning. Yesterday was my first day back since getting poison ivy. The rash is ninety-five percent gone and there's very little itchiness, just some scabbing. I could've probably taken another few days off work, but I was bored out of my mind. Ever since Black Friday, the stores have been packed with early Christmas shoppers, so I wanted to get back and help out.

After my shift, I'll come home and change before driving out to the ranch to see Piper. I missed her too and am so relieved I'll get to ride her this afternoon.

Checking my phone, my cheeks heat at seeing a new message from *him*.

> **MYSTERY GUY**
> Good morning. How did you sleep?

We still haven't bothered asking each other our names. We talk in the group chat sometimes but mostly separately now about anything and everything—mostly small talk.

We dived a little bit into mental health. He asked what got me into horses after I mentioned I'd only been riding for four years and that it was a form of therapy to help with my anxiety and

Only With Me

depression. I didn't get into where they stemmed from and he didn't push me to explain further. But then he admitted it's something he and one of his brothers also suffer with and understood the challenges it brought from day to day. His brother has been hospitalized for it and he worries about him every day.

Something I sadly relate to as well.

The more he talked about it, the more it validated my own experience because he understood that depression isn't black and white, and it doesn't look the same for everyone. Some days are good, but then some are bad and they can seemingly come out of nowhere.

Although I'd love to put a name to his messages and maybe even a face, I'm enjoying the simpleness of having a friend who doesn't know anything about me outside of what I tell him.

Someone who doesn't know about my past or what I've been through. Someone who won't look at me with pity and see a weak, scared little girl who was traumatized years ago.

Every time I meet someone new and tell them my name, they already know who I am based on what they heard. It was big news in Sugarland Creek, and since Dad's accident was the year prior, our family name had been in the local and state news *a lot*.

And even though the conversation turns flirty sometimes, it's been harmless fun so far and I'm okay keeping it that way for now.

HARLOW

Fine, until I had a nightmare. How about you?

MYSTERY GUY

Aww, sorry to hear that. I've had my fair share of nightmares, too. Luckily, I slept good until my alarm went off at 5:30. But I was sad we didn't get to chat before I went to bed.

Yesterday was Thursday, which means it was *Grey's Anatomy* night with Natalie. Besides last night, we've texted every night for the past week. Usually until one of us falls asleep and then we start up again in the morning during his break. We don't talk about anything specific, mostly random stuff. Nothing too personal but enough to keep the conversation flowing.

So far, I know he works on a ranch—which isn't uncommon around here—and has a few brothers and a sister.

HARLOW

> Sorry 🙁 I'm with a friend on Thursday nights and keep my phone on silent so there aren't any interruptions.

The jumping dots appear on the screen and then disappear, *twice*, before he leaves me on read.

Well, damn. Now he probably thinks I meant a boyfriend.

"Harlow, breakfast is ready!" Mom calls from the kitchen.

I set my phone down on my nightstand and make my way to the table with Moose trailing behind me. Then I greet Dad with a kiss before I take my seat.

"Morning, Daddy."

"Hi, sweetie. I heard you had a bad dream?"

I sigh, my shoulders drooping as I nod. "I'm fine."

Smiling in his direction, I try to give him reassurance so he doesn't worry, but he already knows what it was about.

Delilah slept in my room with me most nights before she moved out because I'd have them so frequently after the incident. But it's been at least two years since my last one.

Halfway through breakfast, Dad's fork clunks loudly against the plate as he groans in pain. He squeezes his eyes and his hands ball into fists.

"Deep breaths, Dad," I softly remind him.

He tenses when another wave of pain shoots through his body.

Mom and I stop eating while we wait for his pain to decrease. Sometimes it's subtle and tolerable, but other times, it can be extreme and come out of nowhere.

When a piece of farm equipment fell on his legs, it cut his upper thigh so deep, it was irreparable. They had to amputate to

Only With Me

avoid infection, so sometimes when the phantom pain is at its worst, it feels like his leg is being crushed. Almost like his brain is having a flashback of the accident and since it doesn't know that part of his limb is gone, it sends nerve signals to alert another part of his brain that there's pain.

But since the physical part of the body doesn't exist, narcotics and other pain medications don't work.

"Daddy, you okay?"

He shakes his head, purses his lips, and smacks his stump a few times. Sometimes that works to startle the nerves, but oftentimes, he has to suffer through it until it goes away.

"Finish eatin'. I'll be fine in a few minutes," he grumbles.

I hate seeing him suffer. *Hate* it with a passion.

Mom and I continue eating so he doesn't feel awkward having us wait for him. But instead, the room stays silent.

When his accident happened, we dropped everything to help him through his "new normal." I was only twelve and took it hard because I had never seen him so helpless. Mom was a wreck but was trying to remain strong for the rest of us. Delilah and I were left alone a lot so Mom could stay at the hospital with him. Besides my own incident, it was the scariest moment of my life being told my dad had a bad accident and they weren't sure if he'd survive.

Once he was home to recover, he quickly fell into a depressive state because he was bed-bound and physically limited. For someone who'd worked every day for the past thirty-five years, he didn't adjust well to it. He helped support the household and felt pride in his hard work, but then had to sit and do nothing while the rest of us did everything for him.

Years later, and he still hates every second of it. The accident took away his independence. His ability to drive—although there are ways to alter a car, him being on so many types of medication makes it unsafe for him to operate heavy machinery. It took away his ability to take care of us in the way he was used to.

Brooke Montgomery

"How long do you work today?" Mom asks, breaking the tension.

"Until three, but I'm gonna visit Piper after," I respond. "I'll be back in time for dinner."

Dad's only watched me compete a few times. Usually if Delilah's performing in a trick-riding show, he'll come out to watch us both. Mom puts his power chair on a rack on the back of the truck and then Dad can ride it around the event. The biggest obstacle is his agoraphobia, which he developed a few years after his accident.

When the depression worsened, so did his anxiety and his fear of being out in public.

Dad finishes his food in silence before asking Mom to grab his chair. I give Moose my leftovers and then help clean up the kitchen before getting ready for work.

Checking my phone before leaving, I frown when there's still no response from Mystery Guy. I know he stays busy at work and usually checks in when he can, but I can't help feeling like maybe I said something wrong.

I also know there's something wrong with me for even caring that much when I have no clue who this person is besides a few details.

One night, we got talking about our favorite movies and then another time about our top artists. There were a couple moments I was so close to asking him to video chat for a "face reveal," but then I chickened out.

I don't want to ruin this little safe space we've created where we can chat freely without any expectations. At least until I feel more comfortable about the idea of "meeting" him.

But there's also this part of me that gets stupid excited to hear from him.

Still, I know it won't last.

Because like most things in life, good things have to come to an end.

Only With Me

"Harlow, darlin'. So nice to see you." Mrs. Harper smiles warmly when she walks up to the register with a few shirts and a pair of boots. "How's your mom and dad?"

"Just fine, thank you for askin'," I say, although most people know his situation and that he's anything but fine. "How have you been?"

"My younger sister's comin' to visit this weekend and she was supposed to bring her new boyfriend, who looks like a serial killer, and when I told her so, she got all defensive like how could I say that without even meeting him, but I said no offense, and I guess she took offense because now he ain't comin'."

My eyes grow bigger the longer she rambles, but I quietly ring up her items, and once she finally stops to take a breath, I tell her the total.

She continues talking about her sister's serial-killer-looking boyfriend while she pays with her card and then even after I hand her the receipt.

"Well...good luck. Hope you have a great weekend," I say, realizing she never even answered my original question and apparently needed to vent to someone who couldn't run away mid-conversation.

"Thanks, you too."

She takes her bag and then swiftly exits the store.

Funny enough, I don't even know who her sister is, but now I'm still curious about what makes her boyfriend look like a murderer.

Once things slow down, I walk around the store to organize the racks. When the bell above the door rings, I glance over to find Magnolia and Noah walking in with their girls.

"Hey!" I greet, then notice Tripp and Waylon walking in behind them.

"Hey, girl," Magnolia singsongs. "We're here for the friends and family discount."

I chuckle. "I gotchu."

"Nah, I'm here against my will," Tripp says, standing like a statue next to his brother.

"Me too." Waylon looks as comfortable as he was when we nearly collided a few weeks ago.

"Why's that?" I ask.

"We were promised BBQ for lunch," Tripp replies.

"Yeah, well, we're makin' a detour. Deal with it." Magnolia hands Willow off to him so she can browse.

"We need some cute outfits for the NFR," Noah adds, moving Poppy to her other hip.

"I'm so jealous! I wish I could go." I point to the other wall. "We have some cute tops and skirts. Oh, and new boots that'd pair well with 'em."

"Here, take your niece." Noah lifts Poppy into Waylon's arms.

Poppy reaches for his cowboy hat.

"That ain't gonna fit ya," Waylon tells her.

She giggles when it covers her eyes.

"She's playin' peek-a-boo with you," I tell him.

"Yeah, she loves stealin' my stuff. Don't ya?" He puts the hat back on his head, which looks damn good on him.

"Are you lookin' for a cute outfit, too?" I tease, leaning against one of the tables.

"Oh yeah, definitely. Though I'm not sure pastels go with my skin tone." He lifts a shoulder.

I grin at his teasing voice.

"No? I think you'd look stellar in baby pink."

"Especially with ruffles..." Magnolia returns, holding up a blouse she found.

"I love that. I have it in white!" I exclaim.

Only With Me

"Well, now we can be twinsies." She smirks, then shows me a jean skirt she found. "I only hope I can squeeze my ass into this."

Magnolia had Laken only a few months ago, but she's gorgeous no matter what her body size is.

"I'll get you a dressin' room." I grab the keys and she follows me to the back of the store.

Noah follows with a few items, and I set her up in one, too.

"Just let me know if you need a different size or wanna try on anything else."

My manager, Ashley, comes over and clocks Waylon.

"You look like a natural with her." Her over-the-top flirty voice has me cringing. She gets closer to him and playfully tickles Poppy's tummy. I roll my eyes when Waylon smiles and comments how he's the favorite uncle. Magnolia and Noah show off their outfits before trying on a few more. In the meantime, Ashley's plastered to Waylon and asks if he's going out this weekend.

I can't fault her for being interested in him. The Hollis boys are all good-looking and charming. They're close in age, which means she's legal to get into a bar. Unlike me.

Oh, and he didn't date her sister, so I'm sure that makes her ten times more attractive.

"Most likely if Wilder is," he tells her.

"It's cute you two hang out together so much," Ashley coos.

"Mm-hmm, sure, you could call it that." Waylon's tone makes me think he's not excited about tagging along with his brother.

"Sunny, we gotta get going. Willow's gettin' antsy," Tripp tells Magnolia. His nickname for her is adorable.

"She is or you are?" she counters.

"Both," he deadpans.

"And we're hungry," Waylon adds.

It's past noon, so I don't blame them. I wasn't hungry on my break an hour ago, but I am now since BBQ was mentioned.

"Fine..." Magnolia groans. "But you're buyin'."

Noah snorts, carrying her items toward the counter. "Mine, too."

"I don't think so," he tells her. "You got a husband for that."

I chuckle at their sibling antics and at how serious Noah's brothers can be. Well, besides Landen and Wilder. Those two love goofing around.

As I ring up their items and bag them, I watch Ashley and Waylon out of the corner of my eye. At one point, she takes his phone and adds her number to his contacts.

"Text me when you guys are out this weekend."

She's not even trying to hold back her flirty tone.

"Sure, will do."

Bringing my attention back to Noah and Magnolia, I hand them their bags with a smile. "You better take photos when y'all are in Vegas."

"We will," Magnolia says. "And don't be surprised if you can hear Noah screamin' for Ellie all the way from the arena."

I laugh, only slightly sad I can't go. Maybe one day.

"Have fun at your lunch," I call out when they head for the exit.

"Hope to see ya later, Waylon!" Ashley waves.

When they're out the door, she looks at me with her jaw to the floor. "He is so dang hot."

"Who?" I play dumb. "Waylon?"

"Uh, yeah! He's a few years older than me, but I've seen him out at The Twisted Bull and was always too nervous to ask him to dance."

"Oh."

I walk to the dressing rooms to clean up and she follows, not getting the hint that I don't want to talk about her crush on him.

"I'm gonna need to find a new outfit myself."

"I'm surprised your closet ain't packed with how many clothes from here you must have…"

"I need something hot. Sexy. Jaw-dropping. Something to stand out from all the other girls."

Perhaps a muzzle.

Only With Me

"Mm-hmm," I mutter, putting the clothes Noah and Magnolia didn't want back on the hangers.

"Maybe I'll stop by Lacey's for a new push-up bra."

Oh God. Maybe I should give Delilah a heads-up. Imagine if I told her my manager was coming in to find something to impress her ex-boyfriend.

I chuckle to myself.

"I wonder if they're into threesomes…"

"Wait, what?" I ask, realizing I stopped listening to her but caught the tail end.

"I know it's cliché, but twins sharin' one girl is so hot. I would fold so fast for either one of 'em, but together? I would die a happy woman."

Please do so this conversation ends.

"Shit, sorry. I shouldn't be talkin' about this around you. You're too sweet and innocent."

"*Innocent?* Why do you say that?"

And how would she know? I don't tell her about my personal life.

"Because you're young and look too sweet for your own good to be anythin' but innocent."

Great. Is that why I can never get out of the friend zone when I do talk to a guy? I must have the word VIRGIN on my forehead.

"Anyway, I'm gonna take my break." She walks to the backroom, leaving me with four new customers who just walked in.

Instead of getting frustrated, I put all my energy into helping the girls who are looking for cute bachelorette outfits and make a good chunk of commission. When my shift ends, I check my phone and smile stupidly at the text waiting for me.

MYSTERY GUY
So maybe Friday nights can be ours?

HARLOW
I couldn't love that idea more.

Chapter Eight
Waylon

TWO WEEKS LATER

> **WAYLON**
> What's next on your romance wish list?

> **POISON IVY GIRL**
> Hmm...you'll make fun of me for it.

> **WAYLON**
> I'd never. I told you one of mine even though it was embarrassing.

We've been going back and forth on random things we'd like to do or have in a relationship before we're forty. Considering that's only eight years away for me, my list has me in a bit of a mental tailspin.

I don't know how old she is, but after some of her answers and getting to know her little by little, I'd guess in the twenty-five to thirty range.

> **POISON IVY GIRL**
> Yours wasn't embarrassing! But fine 🫠

I laugh at her melting-face emoji.

Only With Me

POISON IVY GIRL

Dancing at sunset in front of headlights. I saw it in a movie once and it looked so sweet and romantic.

WAYLON

I love that! And then your favorite music plays on the radio, and if you're lucky, it starts to rain in the middle of the song.

POISON IVY GIRL

Wait a minute…are you a closet romantic? 😊

I snort.

WAYLON

Maybe. But truthfully, it's been a while since my last girlfriend, so who knows if I even have it in me anymore.

"Dude, pay attention." Wilder snaps his fingers between my phone screen and my face.

I snap my gaze to his.

Furrowing my brows, I lock my phone. "What?"

"Why're you so glued to your phone lately?" Landen asks, nudging me before I walk into something. The airport is packed with hundreds of people leaving after the NFR. "Especially at seven in the morning."

"None of your business."

He rolls his eyes. "C'mon, I tell you everything, so share with the class."

"Yeah," Wilder agrees, though he's still drunk from the night before, so I doubt he cares.

Wilder and I flew into Vegas three days ago to watch Ellie crush the barrel racing competition. Landen's been here for nearly two weeks since the event is ten days long, but he's flying home with us since Ellie's driving the horse trailer back with Noah and Fisher.

Brooke Montgomery

Even being away from the ranch for a few days feels foreign. Once we're back, we'll be working even longer days to catch up. But it was worth it to see her win the championship and get away from the ranch for a bit.

When the three of us make it to our gate, there's already a line for boarding.

"It's a chick, ain't it?" Wilder continues.

"Technically, it's a group chat. But there's one in here who always flirts with me," I admit, except I leave out the part where we've been texting each other separately for weeks. On Friday nights, we stay up and text until one of us passes out. But I'm not adding more fuel to their nosiness by giving them any extra information.

"What kind of group chat?" Landen asks.

"My friend Jake added me to this horse club he's in. They mostly talk about random shit, horses, and some rodeo stuff."

"A horse *club*? Are you sure that ain't code for something else…" Wilder taunts, waggling his brows.

I punch his arm and he snickers.

"Sounds suspicious to me…" Landen adds.

I scoff. "Fuck off, it's not."

"Do y'all have a code word?" Wilder asks. "Big Donkey Schlong or Monster Horse Dick."

Landen elbows Wilder, fighting back laughter. He knows he's purposely annoying me.

"What would you know about big dicks anyway?" I muse, and Landen cracks up.

Wilder puffs out his chest. "I dunno…why don't you ask your ex-girlfriend? She's seen it…"

Landen's eyes grow wider as he looks between us, probably wondering if I'm going to kick his ass in the middle of the airport walkway.

"Stay away from Delilah, you fucker," I demand as we make our way to our seats.

"What? She wanted an upgrade…"

Only With Me

I'm almost tempted to shove him on his ass. Not because I want Delilah but because he's being a dick.

"Ooookay…" Landen drawls. "If I have to sit next to y'all on the plane for the next four hours, save the ass kickin' for when we get home."

Landen sits in the middle seat while I take the aisle and Wilder hogs the window.

I didn't get the chance to reply to Poison Ivy Girl's last text, so I take out my phone to respond before takeoff.

"So tell me about the girl who flirts with you," Landen asks, leaning closer and interrupting me. "What's her name?"

"I dunno. I only see her phone number."

"Y'all didn't do introductions or anything?"

"No, Jake didn't do that. I was added in after they already formed it and they were mid-conversation. When someone said something I could help with, then I chimed in. And it just went from there…"

He doesn't need the details about when she showed off her ass bruises and me asking about them.

"Well, you've got her number, don't ya? Just text her and say, Hey, I'm Waylon from the group chat. What's your name?"

A little too late for that.

"That sounds so high school."

He arches a brow. "Asking a girl for her name?"

Nah, just asking her a month after we've been talking. The moment I admit we've been having full-on private conversations, he'll never let it go and tell our siblings so they can give me a hard time, too.

"I'll think about it." I shrug.

"Is she local?"

"I think so." Based on her knowing parts of the area, I assume she is anyway.

"Well, lemme see her number. Maybe I'll recognize it."

"How? From your manwhore ways five years ago?" I chuckle but then hand over the phone with the group chat open.

"That one…" I click on her contact and point out her number that ends in 666, which is kind of hilarious.

He furrows his brows when he reads the name I gave her but doesn't say anything. Just studies it.

"Well…do you know it?" I finally ask when he's been silent too long.

He hands me back the phone, shaking his head. "Nope. Sorry, man."

A part of me hoped he'd recognize it so I could put my curiosity to bed, but another part is glad he doesn't because it means he probably hasn't slept with her.

"Good luck figuring it out, though," he adds.

I lift a shoulder. "Yeah, thanks."

After we land and drive to the ranch, it's nearly six hours later. I'm exhausted, hungry, and need a hot shower.

Not a good combo.

With Christmas in less than two weeks away, the airport was already chaotic with travelers.

But my mood immediately lifts when I get a text from Bentley of a photo of him and Hannah going to the holiday dance.

WAYLON

Y'all look so good! Have the best time. No drinking!

BENTLEY

Okay, DAD.

Only With Me

WAYLON
You know you can always call me, right? No questions asked. If you need a ride or whatever. Day or night.

BENTLEY
I know. Thanks.

WAYLON
Good. Now be a gentleman and stay off your phone.

He replies with a middle-finger emoji, and I snicker.

Once I've cleaned up and thrown my dirty clothes in the washer, I head to my parents' house for Sunday dinner. Even traveling all day doesn't give us a pass. But since Ellie, Noah, and Fisher are on the road, the table is less crowded.

"I've watched the video of Ellie winning like ten times," Mallory says when we're all eating. "Totally jealous I couldn't go. So unfair!"

My sixteen-year-old cousin pouts dramatically, which makes the rest of us laugh. She's lived with my parents since she was nine after her parents died in a tragic car accident. Watching her grow up from a little kid to a full-blown teenager has been an interesting experience.

When Wilder and I caught her making out with a boy in the barn last year, we nearly lost it. Wilder swears the boy was getting handsy and pinned him up against a wall.

Now she has her driver's license and goes to all of our secret hiding spots with her boyfriend, Antonio.

To just talk, is what I tell myself.

"Yeah, it was cool to witness," I say. "A moment I'll never forget."

"Me neither." Landen nods. "The whole competition was surreal. I still can't believe how incredible she did. I was a nervous wreck for her, but she was calm and focused. A real badass."

I smile at Landen because he's been hyped about Ellie making it to the NFR more than anyone and has been the biggest supporter of her career long before they were together. Even through the years she hated him.

You can see how proud he is of her hard work and how much he loves her. Sometimes I wonder if I'll ever have that type of relationship—someone I can encourage and support to be whatever they want to be.

"Pretty sure I lost my voice screamin' so loud," Magnolia chokes out, then clears her throat. Willow's on her lap and Laken's on Tripp's. They left the kids here for a few days and you can tell how much they missed them.

"Sure, rub it in, jerk-holes." Mallory scowls, and Mom warns her with *the look* for her choice of words.

"What? That ain't a cuss word." Mallory rolls her eyes.

Lord have mercy, she's full of attitude.

"You're too young to enjoy Vegas for what it's meant for," Tripp tells her.

Truthfully, she would've been bored. When we weren't at the arena watching Ellie, we were drinking at the hotel bar or checking out the casinos.

"That's so ageist!" Mallory scowls, flipping her dark hair behind her shoulder.

"No, that's the law." I snort. "You gotta be twenty-one to get into the fun places."

"How about we take you for your twenty-first birthday?" Tripp offers.

Mallory perks up. "Really? You will?"

"I'll be an old maid by then, but I'll go, too," Magnolia teases, but in reality, that's only five years away.

"We'll be goin' every year that Ellie is racin'," Landen says. "Probably the next few at least."

"And how're y'all gonna give me more great-grandchildren in between all that?" Gramma Grace blurts.

"You literally have three right here." Landen points to Willow

Only With Me

and Laken, then over to Poppy, who's sitting between Mom and Dad. All three kids stayed here while we were gone.

I heard it was organized chaos the entire time.

"Okay, and?" Gramma Grace scowls. "I ain't gonna live forever."

Gasps circulate around the room, and she waves us off with a laugh.

"I'll make sure to tell Ellie we're on a deadline," Landen taunts.

Dad chuckles. "That'll go well."

We all know Ellie's independent and stubborn. She hardly takes orders from her husband, who was once her trainer.

Once we finish eating, I walk around the table and collect empty plates, then bring them to the sink.

"Waylon, darlin'," Gramma Grace coos, standing next to me while I rinse the dishes.

"Hope you're not about to ask me for more great-grandchildren because I hate to break it to ya, but there's no Mrs. Waylon, which means no Waylon babies."

The corner of her mouth lifts in a confident smirk. "Maybe not yet, but I can tell there's someone special in your life."

I furrow my brows, confused. "Why do you say that?"

"You've been happier these past few weeks. Lighter. Not so tense and moody."

"I'm not moody," I defend, opening the dishwasher to load it. This is something Noah usually does since Wilder and I tend to leave after dessert, but I'd rather be helpful than make my mom do everything.

She snickers, removing her apron, then sets it on the counter. "Well, whenever you decide to share her with us, I can't wait to meet her."

Meet her? *Me too.*

Or hell, I'd like to figure out who she is first.

After the kitchen is cleaned, Mom brings out the scrapbooking supplies and demands we all stay. I grab one of the unfinished books and look for photos and stickers to decorate the page.

Noah and Fisher have made one for each other already. Same with Tripp, who made a cute baby book for Magnolia when she was pregnant with Willow.

Landen made one for Ellie last year so they could document her year leading up to the NFR. Now he gets to add in a final page of her winning it all.

I hope one day I can make a special one for my partner — whoever she ends up being.

"Look how cute you two were as kids…" Dad holds up a photo from Wilder's and my first day of kindergarten.

He mostly sits next to Mom and watches her flip through photos, but he's made a couple anniversary ones for them that are kept in the living room for everyone to enjoy.

"I can't even tell who is who." Mallory squints.

"Really? You can't tell by the goofy grin on Wilder's face?" I nudge him next to me and grab his attention. "You got caught liftin' Bridget Mueller's skirt on the playground."

"Oh damn, I forgot about that! She wouldn't tell me what color her underwear was and told me to figure it out myself. So I did."

"That sounds like assault," Mallory deadpans.

"She was my first kiss too." He waggles his brows.

"Was she a willing participant" — Magnolia giggles — "or did ya have her pinned against the slide?"

"She chased me and forced her mouth on mine, I'll have ya know." Wilder pulls out a few photos from our elementary years and holds one up. "Can you blame her, though? We were good-lookin' kids."

"That's because you take after me," Dad gloats.

Mallory scoffs. "Don't encourage 'em."

We laugh, and I look at my father, who's a spitting image of us. Wilder, Landen, Tripp, and I look more like him than our mom, but Noah takes after her. From the photos I've seen, Noah's her

Only With Me

mini-me. Golden blond hair, blue eyes, and an I'm-always-right attitude.

"You know, he was the most eligible bachelor in town," Mom praises. "I was lucky to steal those genes for my children. Y'all are welcome."

"You mean, he corrupted an innocent church girl," Gramma Grace quips.

Magnolia gasps with a holler. "Ooh, boy. Are we about to get some hot tea? Tell us more."

"Corrupted?" Dad huffs, folding his arms and leaning back in his chair. "It was love at first sight. If anything, she corrupted *me*."

Mom raises her brow, shooting him a look that can only be interpreted as *Don't test me right now*.

He shoots her a smug one right back.

"Mrs. Hollis would *never* chase a man." Magnolia beams. "She was probably the prettiest girl Mr. Hollis has ever seen and he did the chasin'."

It's sweet how much she loves our mom and how well they get along. No surprise, though, since Noah and her have been best friends since they were in elementary school. Magnolia practically lived here throughout their high school years, but then she married Tripp and now lives on the ranch permanently.

"You got that right," Dad agrees. "That's why I couldn't wait to make her mine. There were basta—uh—losers tryin' to take her from me even after we got married."

I chuckle at his quick catch of almost letting out a swear word. Even though Mallory's older now, she still makes us put money in the swear jar.

"They were not!" Mom argues. "They got one look at the *rock* you made me wear and left me alone."

Dad's head falls back, bellowing out a cackle. "You think your ring scared 'em away? Darlin', I threatened to make 'em horse feed if they even *looked* at you."

Mom's jaw drops and the room erupts in laughter.

"That explains some things…" Magnolia's gaze shifts toward

Tripp, who shrugs unapologetically. He's overly protective of Magnolia and their kids, but I don't blame him after everything she went through.

"Like father like son," Dad gloats.

"You mean, crazy and crazier..." Mom mocks.

Dad winks at her. "You love it."

It's funny watching my parents after all these years. You can tell they're deeply in love and have mutual respect. They were engaged and married within three months of meeting and then went on to expand the ranch and have five kids. Honestly, them moving so fast in their relationship explains why my younger siblings shacked up with their partners so damn quickly.

In the past few years, I've been to three weddings and became an uncle to two nieces and a nephew.

I shouldn't be surprised at our family tradition considering Gramma Grace married a former teacher turned pastor—who was quite a bit older than her—and they went on to have a couple daughters.

Then we learned her great-aunt Polly married her second blood-cousin and then they had seven kids.

And now that I'm thinking about it, maybe I should blame my relatives for fucking up my ability to get a relationship. Between the cousin incest and the expectations to get married and have kids, it's no wonder I have issues.

I'm ready to pass out by the time I get home, but I still haven't replied to Poison Ivy Girl's last text after I told her it's been a while since my last girlfriend.

Only With Me

> **POISON IVY GIRL**
> Oh. How long?

Staring at her message, I contemplate how to reply.

It's been hours since we've talked, but I told her yesterday I was traveling today.

My reply will either make me look like a loser for not being able to get a girlfriend or a failure for not being able to keep one. Either way, saying seven years is going to make me sound like I suck at relationships.

Which I do.

But I can't keep stalling, so I eventually type out my response.

> **WAYLON**
> Long enough to know what I'm looking for in a partner so neither of us is wasting our time.

I anxiously chew my lip and wonder if I should've said something less personal.

When I see her typing and stopping, then typing and stopping again, I groan.

Yep, now I made it weird.

After what feels like forever, my phone vibrates with a message.

> **POISON IVY GIRL**
> Maybe we should finally meet?

Chapter Nine
Harlow

Oh God, maybe I shouldn't have said that? We don't even know each other's names and now I'm offering to meet him?

This sounds like the start of every true crime episode.

Cue the: *"She lit up every room she walked into like a bright shining star. Too bad she was dumb as fuck and didn't learn the never meet up with strangers rule."*

MYSTERY GUY
> I'd love to.

My eyes widen that he agreed, and I internally scream.
True crime episodes be damned.
I do a little happy dance in my room before responding.

HARLOW
> Awesome! I'm off work on Friday.

MYSTERY GUY
> I can make Friday work. Where do you wanna meet?

Only With Me

> **HARLOW**
> Assuming you're in Sugarland Creek too, there's a newer cute cafe downtown named The Grindhouse.

> **MYSTERY GUY**
> Yeah, I've been there a couple times. How's noon?

> **HARLOW**
> Noon is perfect.

> **MYSTERY GUY**
> Great. How will I know it's you?

Ooh, good question.

> **HARLOW**
> I'll wear a pink bow in my hair with it halfway up.

> **MYSTERY GUY**
> Pink bow. Got it.

> **HARLOW**
> See you then.

Now I just have to figure out what to wear.
And how to be way cooler in person than I am over text.

"How could you not tell me about this sooner?" Natalie scolds during our weekly Thursday video chat.

It's been four days since Mystery Guy and I made plans to meet. We've texted each day since then, but I'm still nervous to see who I've been talking to.

Brooke Montgomery

Especially since I'm starting to like him.

Her jaw dropped to the floor after I told her everything starting from the poison ivy group discussion, me showing off my ass bruises and the vitamin K deficiency discovery, which then led to Mystery Guy and me texting separately, and now how we're meeting in person tomorrow.

"And you still don't know his name? How's that even possible?" I don't blame the skeptical look on her face because I'd ask the same thing if the roles were reversed.

"Neither of us brought it up," I explain. "I kinda liked him not knowing. The moment anyone searches my name online, they'll see all the news articles from seven years ago."

The ones that talk about a home invasion gone wrong and how I was nearly beaten to death with a metal baseball bat.

Natalie gives me *the* look. The one of pity and sadness.

"Stop it," I scold, pointing at her through my laptop screen. "That's exactly why right there."

"Sue me for feelin' bad about what happened to you."

Frowning, I continue, "I wanted him to get to know me *now* in the present before he learned of my past. The scarring on my body from the attack, surgeries, and tubes aren't easily explainable in a quick sentence or two. I wouldn't wanna share those details with someone I just met without them knowin' who I am now."

It's too personal for a stranger.

Nodding, she sighs. "Yeah, I get it."

And I know she does, considering she has her own body scars and trauma from her accident.

"It sounds weird, but it's also…*exciting*. Like some mystery guy is talkin' to *me*. Givin' me attention and lettin' me get to know him. It's been thrillin'. As cliché as it sounds, I wake up every day with a smile because I know there'll be a message waitin' for me."

Perks of him starting work so early.

"Well, ain't that sickly sweet." She gags. "Meanwhile, I'll be in the middle of the road waitin' to get run over."

Only With Me

"Oh my God, you're so dramatic!" I holler at how extreme she is.

She acts like she has no dating experience, but she's already lost her virginity at least. I haven't even kissed a man.

Basically, I'm going into all this naive and blind.

We continue watching a second episode before calling it quits for the night after we both excessively yawn through the last half.

"So if you call him Mystery Guy, I wonder what he calls you."

"Oh, I never thought about it. Now I'm curious, too."

"Let's hope he ain't some weirdo who labeled you as Nice Ass Girl."

"He doesn't give weirdo vibes, but I'm not exactly experienced in the area of men, so he could be a sixty-year-old priest for all I know."

"Hmm...forbidden love and he'll die soon so you'll get his life insurance? Jackpot."

"Natalie Jo!" I burst out giggling. "You read too much smut."

"Smut? Girl, that's a thriller plot. The heroine finds out the priest has been inappropriate with her little sister but no one believes her, so she comes up with a plan for revenge. She seduces him and makes him fall in love with her, but the kicker is she takes out an insurance plan on him without his knowledge. Then she murders him in the worst way—like it was so graphic and disgusting—by cutting off his dick and shoving his balls down his throat. But also, like...respect, girl. Making him suffer and doing the Lord's work gettin' rid of that piece of shit."

I grimace at the image she just put in my head. "Jesus...that's gruesome."

"Oh, and then she sets up someone else to take the blame."

"No way...who?"

"Her own mother! Since she didn't believe her about what he was doin' to the sister, she planted evidence to make her the only suspect. She came up with this whole crazy plot and the crazier part is how it worked because the mom went to prison."

"That's madness. Is that how it ends?"

"The epilogue is the best part...not only does she get the money, she moves with her sister to another state and changes their names. Then they start going to another Catholic church and she basically repeats the whole thing—seduces a priest, takes out life insurance on him, cuts off his dick and kills him, then plants evidence to pin it on someone else."

I gasp. "So now it's a whole murder for life insurance scheme?"

"Pretty much, but she's also a little...psychotic. An unreliable narrator, if you will. I haven't read the sequel, but I heard it's even better than the first. She goes from priests to other types of predatory men and it's supposed to be even more disturbin'."

"I haven't even read it, and I'm disturbed."

"Well, I can give you a ton of smut recommendations. Especially if you wanna learn a thing or two..." She smirks, arching her brow.

I chuckle at her clear implication. "Maybe. I'll get back to you once I find out who he is. Might need to read that thriller one instead, after all."

"Speakin' of murder, you should share your location with me—just to be safe."

"We're meetin' at The Grindhouse. There'll be employees and other people there."

"But what if he wants to take you for a drive...ya know—a *drive*," she emphasizes the last word with a drawl.

I pinch my brows. "What's wrong with that? Drives out in the country are my favorites."

"I swear to God." She pinches the bridge of her nose. "There's only two reasons a guy asks to go on a drive with a girl." She holds up one finger. "To get you naked in the back seat for some horizontal gymnastics." Then she puts up another finger. "Or to murder you in the woods and bury you there."

"Damn, okay. No goin' on drives."

"At least not until you know him better," she clarifies. "So until then, share your location with me right now."

Only With Me

"Fine, geez." I grab my phone and add her to my Life 360 app. "Happy, *Mother*?"

"Yes, thank you. Now I can stalk you without being a creep."

I snort. "Well, I'm glad one person will know where to look for my body."

"I'd bring out my shovel and find you myself before even calling 911. Then I'd find the bastard who did it, smash his head in with said shovel, and leave him out for the coyotes to eat."

"Ooookay, this just got morbid like your thriller book. I'm gonna have nightmares tonight."

Her laughter causes me to laugh and soon we're both wiping away tears at her reaction to murdering the person who killed me.

"I better get to bed," I say.

"Yeah, you gotta take an everything shower and shave before your *date*, don't ya?" She waggles her brows, and I shake my head at how obnoxious she is.

"Only because I'm wearin' a cute dress, but that doesn't mean there'll be any touchin' underneath it."

"Mm-hmm. *Right*."

"Good night," I singsong.

"Nighty-night."

Once I close my laptop, I roll off the bed and go to brush my teeth. Then I check my phone and unknowingly smile when I see a text from him he sent earlier.

> **MYSTERY GUY**
> We're still on for tomorrow at noon, right? Pink bow in hair?

> **HARLOW**
> Yep. I'll be there.
>
> Wait. Pink bow in my hair or yours?

I'm obviously teasing, but I know he'll go along with it.

MYSTERY GUY
I was hoping you because I just ran out of pink ribbon the other day.

HARLOW
Ha! So how will I know who you are?

MYSTERY GUY
I'll be in a cowboy hat.

HARLOW
You and every other man.

MYSTERY GUY
Ha! Don't worry, I'll find ya.

HARLOW
Okay, can't wait.

MYSTERY GUY
See ya soon.

HARLOW
Night!

Butterflies invade my stomach at the thought of finally meeting him.

As long as Natalie's warning doesn't become a reality.

I don't know what it is about him, but chatting each day and talking about normal stuff has me excited to finally put a face and name to the mystery guy behind the screen.

We've made enough small talk where it makes sense to add in more details about my past and not worry he'll treat me differently once he knows.

I'm anxious, but I've never been giddier about meeting someone either.

Only With Me

My nerves are on fire as I sit at one of the tables in The Grindhouse.

By how hard my heart's beating and how fast my leg's bouncing, I don't think I've ever been this nervous in my life.

Not even for my first show horse jumping competition. I didn't have this overwhelming urge to throw up. That seems like a breeze compared to this.

But I focus on the beautiful holiday decorations around the café and try to settle my nerves. With Christmas only a few days away, downtown is covered in holiday spirit.

As planned, I put my hair up in a half ponytail and wrapped a pink ribbon around it, then tied it into a bow. I put on a matching color maxi dress that flows to my ankles and a white cardigan over my shoulders since it's chilly outside. When I worked on Tuesday, I bought a new pair of tan boots that go halfway up my calves.

I look cute as hell if I say so myself.

When I sent Natalie a full-mirror selfie, she replied that I looked hot enough to put any man into cardiac arrest.

Let's hope that doesn't happen, but I do hope he's not disappointed in who I am.

Truthfully, I'm not sure what I expect, but I'm ready to find out.

At a quarter after twelve, I check my texts in case he messaged about being late.

Nothing.

When I look around behind me, my eyes meet Waylon's.

He's not dressed in his usual work clothes. Rather he's in dark denim Wranglers, a button-up shirt, and a cowboy hat. He looks *good*.

But he always does.

"Hey!" I turn completely until we're face to face.

"Harlow." He clears his throat. "Hi."

"I wouldn't have thought you were the type to come all the way into town for some coffee."

"Uh, right." He scratches over his scruffy cheek. "Just felt like gettin' out today."

He looks slightly uncomfortable—which isn't unusual for him—but I give him a small, comforting smile anyway.

"Yeah, it's a beautiful sunny day."

I face toward my table to continue waiting with my nerves in overdrive.

Looking down at my phone again, I frown that he's not here nor given me a heads-up he'd be late. I'm tempted to text him and ask where he is, but I don't. At least, not yet.

Instead, I watch Waylon at the register. He orders a drink and then points at a muffin in the display case. When he looks over his shoulder, our eyes meet, and I smile at him again.

This time, he returns it.

When he dated my sister, there was so much going on in our family that I rarely saw him. The most was after I started training with Noah and even then it was sparingly since he works on the opposite side of the ranch.

After Waylon receives his order, he goes to walk past my table but then stops.

"Are you here alone?" he asks.

"I'm waitin' on someone. He's a little late," I say, the words nearly choking me because deep down I know he's not coming, but I'm too embarrassed to admit it.

Waylon gives me a look, one I can't quite place, and then his face morphs into a sympathetic grin.

Great. As if I couldn't look any more pathetic sitting at a table by myself, he must think I'm a loser now for getting stood up.

Only With Me

"Okay. Have a good rest of your day."

I swallow hard. "Thanks, you too."

He nods and then walks away.

If I had more confidence in myself and wasn't afraid of his rejection, I would've invited him to join me instead.

Chapter Ten
Waylon

I sit in my parked truck that's half a block from the café and watch as Harlow walks to her car across the street ten minutes later. There's a coffee cup in her hand, so she at least grabbed something before she left.

But her expression is a combination of sad and mad as hell.

I would've texted her that I was running late, but my phone slipped out of my hand while I was driving and got caught underneath the passenger seat. Since I didn't want to waste more time by pulling over to look for it, I waited until I parked and then spent another few minutes trying to dig it out from where it got caught.

The moment I recognized her long, golden brown hair and noticed the pink bow, I panicked. I almost left the café before she saw me.

All this damn time.

It's been her this whole fucking time, and I had no idea.

Probably didn't help that I didn't know many specific details about her in the first place. If we had exchanged names, there's no way we wouldn't have realized, and then it would've stopped before it ever started.

Only With Me

And clearly, she has no idea either by her reaction to seeing me and assuming I was there on a quick coffee run.

The only reason I asked if she was sitting alone was to confirm—rather, *triple-check*—that she was, in fact, waiting for someone. *Me.*

I need to text her and put her out of her misery. Though I hate lying, especially to someone who doesn't deserve it, the truth would hurt her more.

I can't be *friends* with my ex-girlfriend's little sister.

And if that turned into more? There's no way Delilah would be cool with that.

Harlow's too young, too sweet, too forbidden.

Though I'm surprised we had some things in common, we're at two different paths in our lives, and there's no point in leading her on to think we could ever be something more.

Fuck. Now I have to pretend to be this other person from the group chat and act like I still have no idea who she is while knowing who she is in real life.

WAYLON

> Hey, I'm so sorry I didn't text sooner. A work thing happened, and I wasn't able to get away.

I can't suggest we reschedule because I have no intentions of revealing myself after some of the personal things I've told her. Not that I don't trust her, but I wouldn't have said them if I knew it was her.

Like a creep, I crouch in my seat and wait for her to check her phone.

She gets in her seat, buckles, and then I see her hold it up. It hides more of her face from this angle but enough is shown to see she's not happy with me. Instead of responding, she sets her phone down and starts the car. *I deserve that.*

At this point, I'd be surprised if she responds.

Brooke Montgomery

By the time I get home, I feel like utter shit. The guilt is eating at me, and no matter what I do or say, it won't fix what's already happened.

I was so wrong about her age and never once considered I knew her in real life or that we'd be connected somehow because nothing seemed familiar.

But still, I can't be too disappointed it ended up being her because Harlow's gorgeous, sweet, and honest. I know she'd never tell anyone what was said in our conversations.

I think back to some of them and can now piece together what she told me and what I already know about her.

She admitted there was a time she struggled with her mental health and turned to equine therapy. But now that I'm aware it's her, I know where those struggles stemmed from.

Her dad's work accident when she was twelve.

The incident when she was thirteen.

Spending years in and out of the hospital until she was sixteen.

Delilah was a wreck during that time frame and as much as I tried to support her, I was young and selfish in wanting her to spend more time with me. I was also still reeling from what happened with Wilder two years prior. It became obvious neither of us was in a position to be in a relationship.

I hardly saw Harlow while she was recovering, and even after, she only came to the ranch to train and we rarely spoke.

It seemed like I shouldn't, considering her sister's and my history, and only God knew what Delilah had told her about me.

Now I wish I could take it all back and not get involved with the group chat because she's going to feel rejected by me standing her up when there's nothing wrong with her.

Only With Me

If the situation was different, I would've happily introduced myself and had coffee with her.

But there's no circumstance where it'll be okay for us to continue texting.

And that sucks because I enjoyed her company and talking to someone I wasn't related to.

"Wilder? You in here?" I call out, walking deeper into the retreat barn.

He told me he was going to eat at The Lodge, but his truck is still parked outside. It's possible he walked, though.

Grabbing one of the rakes, I peek into the stalls to see where he left off so I can continue. After I check into the fifth one that's been completed, I head to the next and am startled to find him passed out on the ground.

"Wilder!" I shout, tossing the rake and opening the door. "Hey, wake up." I kick his leg, but he doesn't move.

"What the hell, man? You're sleepin' in horse shit. That's a new low, even for you."

I move around him, getting a better view of his face, and realize something's wrong. There's something around his mouth.

Kneeling, I listen to see if he's breathing and feel for a pulse. It's there, but his breathing is shallow.

"Wilder, wake up..." I shake him and then look for any bleeding around his legs, but there isn't any.

When I look on the other side next to him, I find a pile of vomit.

"Oh fuck. What'd you take?" I murmur even though he can't hear me. "We gotta get you to the ER."

Waiting for an ambulance will take too long, so I haul him over my shoulder and carry him to my truck. His body is limp as I put him in the passenger seat and buckle him in.

"Wilder, if you can hear me, I need you to hang on, okay? I'm takin' you to the hospital."

My heart hammers against my ribs as I speed down the country roads. I call my dad and tell him to meet me there, then send a voice memo to our sibling group chat to tell them.

When Wilder got to work this morning, he was in a good mood, which he usually is anyway, so nothing seemed off to me. As far as I know, he wasn't hungover or drinking for breakfast, so my mind is spiraling with what caused him to lose consciousness.

I called the emergency room to give them a heads-up that we were on the way, so once I arrive, they have a stretcher waiting for him.

"He's been out cold since I found him twenty-five minutes ago," I explain.

"His pulse is weak," one of the nurses states. "Stay here and we'll get you when he's stabilized."

The three of them take him away before I even have a chance to say anything to him.

Not that I had any idea of what I'd tell him.

Please don't die.

I love you.

I pace in the waiting room, reading through the sibling group chat and their responses. Though I don't have much of an update, I tell them we made it and he's in their care now.

> **TRIPP**
> What do you think happened?
>
> **LANDEN**
> Was he still breathing?
>
> **NOAH**
> Did you check his thighs?
>
> **LANDEN**
> Any idea how long he was passed out before you found him?

They're worried sick about him just like I am. It's been years since his last emergency hospital visit, but we're still traumatized from the last time.

Only With Me

WAYLON

> When I left for lunch, he was fine. Yes, he's breathing but irregularly. And I did check. No blood from what I could see. No idea how long or what happened. Hoping to find out.

And then a thought crosses my mind. *If only I'd stayed and gone to lunch with him, I would've been here for whatever happened.*

But then I remind myself that if I had stayed to have coffee with Harlow, who knows how much longer it would've taken for me to find him. We're lucky I was only gone for thirty minutes as it is.

NOAH

> As soon as Fisher gets back from a job to watch Poppy, I'm heading up there.

LANDEN

> Tripp and I are on the way now. Be there in 10.

Before I have a chance to respond, Dad and Mom rush in. They must've sped here.

"Any word?" Mom asks, wrapping her arms around me.

"Not yet. They just took him back five minutes ago."

Dad squeezes my shoulder. "I'm gonna let them know we're here."

An hour passes and the rest of my siblings arrive, all asking for updates and information, but we still don't know.

When the emergency room back doors open, the last thing I expect to see is Harlow with her mom. Mrs. Fanning is in her scrubs and works here, so it's possible Harlow came to visit after I stood her up. It's obvious she's upset and has been crying.

But then I notice there's a bandage around her hand.

"Harlow?" Noah calls out, standing and rushing over.

Instinctively, I get to my feet, wanting to console her, too.

"What's wrong?" Noah asks.

"It's my dad."

Chapter Eleven
Harlow

I'm tempted to chuck my phone out the window as I drive home.

I repeat his message in my head over and over, getting angrier each time.

> *Hey, I'm so sorry I didn't text sooner. A work thing happened, and I wasn't able to get away.*

Normally, I wouldn't get upset about someone having to cancel at the last minute because shit happens, but he didn't text me until he was already twenty minutes late nor did he offer to reschedule.

When it comes to dating and guys, I seriously have no *asshole* radar because he fooled me big time.

Another part of me wonders if he's lying and was here, saw me, and then left.

But his loss. I look damn good today and he missed out.

Yep, that's what I'm telling myself.

Since Mom's working at the hospital today, I'm home with Dad, but he went to take a nap shortly before I left. Even though I want to storm into the house, I don't want to wake him.

Only With Me

Moose greets me at the door, acting like he has to go potty. "Hold on, sweetie."

Figuring the other two dogs need to go outside, too, I go to my parents' bedroom and quietly open the door. The backyard is fenced in, so they can roam freely.

"Sasha, Shelby...outside," I whisper the magic word just loud enough for them to hear me.

They usually sleep on the bed with my parents, but they're sitting in front of the master en suite, whimpering.

"Dad?" I step in and flick on the light, noticing he's not in here.

I call out his name again, this time louder, and knock on the bathroom door. "Dad, are you okay?"

No answer.

Looking around, I notice his power chair is in the corner, but his walker is missing. He typically uses it to hop from the bed to the bathroom since the power chair is too big for the space.

I knock harder and then try the knob. It turns, but it won't open. Something's blocking it.

"Dad! Can you hear me?" I scream, trying to push through whatever is against it.

After a few more attempts, it opens just enough for me to peek inside and look at the floor.

My dad's face-down and there's blood around his head.

"Oh my God, Dad! Wake up!" I try shoving the door again, but the walker or his leg is blocking it, I can't quite see, but I know I need to get in there. Who knows how long he's been there and bleeding out.

I rush out of the house and run toward the bathroom window. The screen pops out, but it's locked.

"Goddammit."

Sprinting to the garage, I grab my metal bat and smash it through the glass. Then I reach through and unlock it, accidentally drawing blood across my palm when I slice it against an exposed piece.

Ignoring it, I push up the window and climb through—which is harder than I anticipated, but I manage to stabilize myself on the toilet seat and then step down so I can reach him.

"Dad, can you hear me?" Kneeling beside him, I press my fingers to his neck and blow out a relieved breath when I feel his pulse.

"Harlow?" he barely gets out.

"Oh, thank God." I grab the hand towel and press it against the cut on the side of his face. "Don't try to move. You must've fallen into the counter and smacked your head."

"I tried to catch myself with my right foot," he mutters, his eyes barely fluttering open. "Forgot it wasn't there anymore."

"I know, Dad. It's okay. Gonna call for an ambulance."

Even after all this time, he instinctively tries to use his foot, but then goes down because there's no support to hold him up.

"No, no, I'm fine."

I snort. "You need to get your head checked out. Also, I think the bottom of your stump is bleedin'."

He groans. "It hurts like a son of a bitch."

When they did the emergency amputation, they eventually had to do skin grafts, so there's no fatty tissue to pad the bottom. It's mostly bone with a thin layer of skin on top.

Once my call is connected, I explain the situation and that I'm too afraid to move his body, but it's blocking the door for anyone to come in. The operator walks me through how to carefully shift him without further damaging anything or adding to his pain, but when I do, Dad groans.

"Shit, I'm sorry."

"I can crawl," he says, lifting on his elbows just enough to get the door open.

"He's conscious?" the operator asks.

"Yeah, but I'm worried he could have swellin' in his brain or broken a rib from how he fell," I explain. "I dunno how long he was out before I found him. He has a head wound, too."

Only With Me

She continues asking questions while we wait for the EMTs to arrive and then I notice Dad's breathing sounds off.

"You okay?" I ask, studying his face.

"I dunno," he replies. "I think...it might be a panic attack."

"Oh shit. What's their ETA?" I ask the operator.

This isn't my first rodeo with calling for help. Dad's had a few big falls over the years, but this is the first time he's ever smacked his head hard enough to lose consciousness.

"Three minutes. Keep him talkin'."

"Dad, tell me about the day you met Mama."

I've heard this story a dozen times, but it's one he should without a doubt have memorized.

Although his speech is slow and he breaks to catch his breath, he tells me about how he spotted her at a party and the noise around him just stopped when their eyes locked. She was the most beautiful woman he'd ever met and was determined to talk to her before the end of the night. But then he learned she had a boyfriend, the quarterback of all people, and he was a—

"Dad?" I shake his arm when he stops talking and his eyes close.

"I think he blacked out again," I tell the operator.

"The ambulance should be there," she tells me, and then a second later, I hear the dogs losing their shit.

"They are now," I tell her.

"Okay. They'll take good care of you."

"Thank you." I hang up and get to my feet so I can direct them where we are.

Multiple EMTs and firemen enter with their gear and a stretcher. The house suddenly feels too small with this many people, but I quickly show them where he's lying.

"He was speakin' a moment ago and then stopped," I explain. "Did they tell you he's an amputee? His stump got banged up too."

"We'll check him out. Don't worry, miss." A woman who

doesn't look much older than me says, patting my arm before walking past me.

A few of them squeeze through the bathroom door that's still halfway blocked, and I quickly wrangle the dogs into their crates so they don't get loose.

I still need to text my mom and Delilah, but I'm anxious for an update. I can't see since they're still in the bathroom, but after ten minutes, one of the bulkier firemen carries him out of the bathroom and gently places him onto the stretcher.

My dad's not a massive guy, but he's not small either. He's six-foot and his upper body is muscular from years working on the farm with livestock. The lower half of him is weaker due to muscle atrophy, which is why it's so easy for him to fall when he loses his balance.

"Is he gonna be okay?" I ask nervously.

"His blood pressure is low and the cut on his head needs sutures. I'm guessin' a CT scan and fluids, too."

"Can I ride with him?" I ask.

"Absolutely. You should get your hand looked at while we're there, too," she says, nodding down toward the blood flowing down my wrist and arm.

I forgot about it until she mentioned it.

"I'll worry about it once I get an update on him," I tell her.

While they get him situated in the ambulance, I quickly text Mom and Delilah, giving them as much information as I can. Mom's already there, so she'll meet us in the ER. Delilah's trying to get someone to cover her shift so she can leave work early.

I hold Dad's hand during the ride, the sirens blaring as we drive to the next town. He's still unconscious, but they're checking his vitals and giving him oxygen and fluids.

Twenty minutes later, everyone rushes out of the back, and they put him into a trauma room.

Nurses swarm his side, and I stay back frozen, feeling helpless.

"Harlow!"

Only With Me

My eyes snap to the side when I hear my mom's voice rushing toward me.

"Are you okay?" She smothers me in her arms, holding my head to her chest.

"I'm worried about him."

"I know, sweetie. They're gonna take good care of him."

They won't allow her to treat him, so all we can do is wait for now.

"Lemme check out your hand," she says, grabbing it.

"It's fine. But we're gonna need a new window." I tense, hoping she's not upset about that.

"I can't believe you did that," she says softly, leading me to a triage room. "Your fight-or-flight response is always one step ahead of your brain."

She's referring to the home invasion.

Had I not reacted the way I did—in fight mode—the guy would've never gotten the bat out of my hand and then used it against me.

But maybe he shouldn't have tried to rob us in the first place.

"At least there's a lot less blood this time," I say to lighten the mood.

"Thank God," she murmurs. "But you're still at risk of infection if we don't get the glass out and clean it."

It's not until after my hand is bandaged and we're sitting outside Dad's room, waiting for him to return from a CT scan, that the severity of the situation slams into my chest. Tears well in my eyes as the emotions overwhelm my senses and my heart races to catch up with my rapid breathing.

I count to twenty, waiting for the anxiety attack to pass, and squeeze Mom's hand.

"I know the situation is different, but is this how it felt waitin' to hear if I was alive or not?"

Mom wraps an arm around my shoulders, bringing me closer. "Think about the worst moment of your life and then times that by infinity when it's your child."

I choke up, wiping my face because I can't even imagine how bad it must've been. "I hate that you guys went through that."

"I've never prayed harder for God to spare your life because if he hadn't, I threatened to go into that boy's hospital room and make sure he didn't live. After your dad shot him, he needed surgery to stop the bleeding, but at that moment, I didn't care. If you didn't make it, he didn't deserve to either."

I've never heard her speak this way before. She was always so gentle and caring, but knowing what I must've looked like and how many injuries I had, I can't say I blame her for being so angry.

"But after I prayed and prayed, I knew there was another Mama nearby beggin' for her child's life too, and I just couldn't do that to another parent. We were both sufferin' and beggin' for a miracle, and I knew prayin' for his death wouldn't affect your ability to survive. So I asked God to save both of you because your families need y'all no matter what."

By this point, I'm full-on snot-crying and shaking.

She holds me tighter, her tears mixing with mine. "Your daddy is strong and he's gonna get through this. It's where you got it from. All your strength and resilience."

"You're strong too, Mama. Look how much you've been through. You're the strongest person I know."

And she is.

Taking care of Daddy and me, having no time to take care of herself, and still working in between so we could keep a roof over our heads. She never gets a day off. Even years later, she's always taking care of us at home or her patients at the hospital.

"Mrs. Fanning?"

Our heads pop up and a nurse and doctor stand in front of us. We both stand. "Yeah? Is he okay?"

"He has a concussion and a head wound, but there's no cerebral edema, so that's positive. He didn't break any ribs or any other bones, which is impressive considering how fast he went down," the doctor explains.

Only With Me

My palm clenches my chest at the relief I feel.

"Oh, thank goodness," my mom says, squeezing my hand. "Can we see him?"

"We have him on some meds to keep him comfortable and he'll stay overnight for observation, but if all goes well, y'all can take him home tomorrow afternoon."

Mom nods at the doctor. "Thank you. I appreciate you takin' good care of him."

"Of course. As soon as he's transported to a patient room, you can go up there."

"Might take an hour or so to get the paperwork through and find a room, but I'll page you or find you in the waitin' room," the nurse adds. By the looks of it, they know each other.

"Thanks, Paige. We'll sit out there and wait for my other daughter, too."

I can't help the tears of relief that fall down my cheeks. I hate that he's alone right now, but hopefully pain free and comfortable for once.

"C'mon, sweetie. We should call Delilah and give her the news."

She texted earlier and said it'd be a couple more hours before she could leave since there wasn't another manager available to cover her shift.

Wiping my face, we walk out the ER doors, and I'm startled when I hear Noah calling my name. But then I see her parents and all of her siblings, except Wilder.

Noah rushes toward me and Waylon gets to his feet, which is weird because he was just at the café a couple hours ago. So whatever they're doing here had to have just happened.

"What's wrong?" Noah asks.

Her gaze moves over my face in concern and then down to my bandaged hand.

"It's my dad," I tell her. "He fell."

"Oh my goodness, is he okay?"

"He has a concussion and is banged up a bit, but overall, he'll be okay. They're keepin' him overnight, so we're just waitin' for 'em to move him to a room."

"That's a relief. I'm glad it ain't too bad."

"Wait, what're y'all doin' here?" I ask.

"Waylon found Wilder unconscious in the barn. We're still waitin' on answers." Her voice is strained like she's trying to hold back tears.

"Oh no. I'm so sorry."

She smiles weakly. "Thanks."

"Harlow, I'm gonna call Delilah outside. I'll be right back."

"Okay, Mama. I'll wait here."

"Come sit by us." Noah leads me over to the rest of the family, and it feels awkward with Wilder's condition up in the air.

"What happened to your dad?" Waylon asks, taking me by surprise. I can count on two hands the number of times I've heard his voice in the past four years.

I explain everything, from the bathroom door being blocked to why my hand is bandaged and how he fell and smacked his head on the countertop.

"Thank goodness he's okay," Waylon says.

"Yeah, I'm lucky I got home when I did. If my date hadn't stood me up, who knows if it would've made things worse finding him later."

Waylon flinches slightly, and I don't know if it's because of the word *date* or that I got stood up. But either way, he reveals a kind and sympathetic expression.

"You found Wilder in the barn unconscious?" I prompt. "Did he wake up at all?"

"No, I carried him into my truck and sped to the hospital. I usually stay for lunch, but today I didn't, and now I feel guilty as hell. If I'd been there, I woulda found him sooner." He shrugs, and I can tell he's fighting with his emotions.

"You can't think about the what-ifs. It'll choke you to death, trust me."

The guilt I feel for trying to go up against a guy twice my size

Only With Me

instead of letting him steal our belongings weighs heavy in my chest because of what it put my parents and sister through. The constant worrying, staying with me in the hospital for weeks at a time, and driving me to physical therapy for a year. That type of guilt doesn't go away after recovery.

"I know, but I can't help it," he admits.

I've heard about Wilder's past, all secondhand from Delilah, but I have a feeling it's much deeper than what I've been told.

"Hollis?" The same doctor who spoke to my mom and me enters the waiting room and calls out for the family.

Garrett and Dena stand, as do the rest of the family, but I continue sitting to respect their privacy.

Realizing I should respond to Mystery Guy's text now that I'm not so heated about him blowing me off, I grab my phone and click on his message.

HARLOW

> Sorry for not replying right away. I ended up having a family emergency and had to call an ambulance for my dad. He's gonna be okay, thankfully. Hope your work thing got handled. If you want to reschedule, it might be a while before I can, but I'd still like to meet up whenever you're free.

I'm probably being too nice and forgiving, but after what happened with my dad, I know I'd miss talking to him after spending the past month getting to know each other.

As the doctor speaks to the family, Waylon grabs his phone from his back pocket, looks at it, and then glances at me over his shoulder before putting it back.

"Is everything okay?" Mom grabs my attention with her whispered words, and I turn toward her, keeping my voice down.

"I dunno. He just started talkin' to 'em."

"Delilah checked on the dogs and now she's on her way."

"Okay, good."

"She's very upset."

Brooke Montgomery

"I know," I say, frowning.

Her texts were frantic with tons of questions I didn't have answers to.

After Dad's accident, she took on a lot of the responsibility as the oldest child. It was months before Dad got a power chair, so his only form of mobility was his walker or wheelchair. He was weak and spent months in agony, so it was hard for him to hop.

Everything got worse after my incident because Mom was torn between being at home for Dad—who was still recovering from multiple surgeries—and being at the hospital for me—who broke multiple bones. Delilah took on a lot of the burden, making sure someone was always with Dad or me.

When Mom told her it was okay for her to finally move out two years ago, she felt guilty for leaving us. But she didn't get to live a normal life for so long or focus on her own needs, so our parents nearly pushed her out. It was time she took care of herself.

Trick-riding was all she had to look forward to, and honestly, I think it saved her.

When a text message pops up, I smile at seeing his contact name.

But then it quickly fades.

> **MYSTERY GUY**
>
> I'm not sure rescheduling is a good idea. I'm sorry.

Chapter Twelve
Waylon

"He took *ketamine*?" I blurt after the doctor says they discovered the pills in Wilder's pocket.

"Yes, and it's a good thing we were able to figure out what he took because we could treat him properly right away. He's stable now, but it's possible he could suffer from withdrawal symptoms."

"That's illegal without a doctor's prescription, right?" Noah confirms.

"Correct. These were not legal," the doctor hesitantly states.

Great. Where the fuck did he get those?

"What's that used for?" Dad looks around at us suspiciously as if one of us gave him the pills. I wouldn't even know where to find them.

"Pain management, PTSD, anxiety, depression…but when it's used recreationally in higher doses, it's usually to get high," the doctor explains. "It's hard to tell exactly how much he took or how long he's been usin', but it'd help if he told us. It'd also help if he were open about anything else he might be takin', so we can make sure we're treatin' him properly."

Oh, he's gonna fucking tell me.

It's one thing for him to drink as much as he does, but I never suspected he was taking pills. Even if he was taking it to help with his mental health, he knows there are legal options.

Wilder will do everything besides go to therapy and get the right medication.

"But he's gonna live? He's okay?" Mom asks.

"Yes, ma'am. We're distributing fluids and meds as well as watchin' his blood pressure carefully. He'll need to stay a night or two, but if no other issues arise, he'll be discharged."

Christmas is in three days, so it'd suck if he had to stay longer.

"Oh, thank God," Landen blurts.

Mom's shaking with fear and anger, but I don't blame her.

I know his depression takes over his mindset sometimes, but it's frustrating to watch him not help himself when I've offered time and time again to go with him. I'm willing to do whatever it takes to get him help, but he has to want it—I can't force him.

"The nurses are gettin' him ready to be transported to a room and then y'all can visit him."

"Thank you." Dad holds out his hand and shakes the doctor's.

"You're welcome."

Everyone releases a collective sigh before we go back to our seats. Harlow and her mom are talking, but her back is to me. I hate that I have to do this, but if I don't do it now, it'll just be harder on her later.

WAYLON

I'm not sure rescheduling is a good idea. I'm sorry.

Keeping my distance, I sit on the other side of the waiting room, but I glance over when she lifts her phone.

Her gorgeous face shifts into a frown, and I feel like absolute shit about it.

Guilty is an understatement.

But the moment Delilah walks into the ER and sits next to her sister, I'm reminded again why I have to stay away.

Only With Me

The sun has long set by the time I'm able to get Wilder alone. I stayed out in the hallway while our parents spent time fussing over him and my siblings went to visit, but once they left, I was ready to go in and strangle him.

"Well, lemme have it..." is all he says when it's finally the two of us. I have no idea what he's told everyone else, but I'm not leaving until I hear everything.

I lean back in the chair next to his bed with my arms crossed. "You weigh a fuckton when you're limp."

He huffs a laugh, shrugging. "Muscle weighs more than fat."

"Where'd you get the ketamine?" I blurt, not wanting to waste any more time getting to the bottom of this.

He scrubs a hand over his scruffy jawline. "Jake."

"Our friend *Jake*?"

He nods.

"You're shittin' me. I'm gonna beat his ass."

"It ain't his fault," he defends. "I asked him for some."

"Not his fault? Why the hell is he sellin' illegal drugs?"

"He ain't sellin' 'em, but he said they're helpin' for some of his issues, and I thought they could help for mine."

"What issues does he have?"

"I'm not gonna air out his personal shit. You're gonna haveta ask him and see if he tells ya."

He won't get the chance to after I knock him out. Jake knows I'm constantly worrying about Wilder and for him to do this feels like a betrayal.

"So you thought you'd try some street ketamine instead of gettin' medication legally from a doctor?"

"They'll only prescribe it if you talk to a therapist."

"Uh, yeah...that's kinda the point."

"I ain't doin' that."

"Christ. You're so goddamn stubborn. You coulda died!"

"I didn't even take that much! It musta been mixed with something else or I had a bad reaction to it because it bottomed out my blood pressure, which is why I lost consciousness. When I finally woke up, I was dizzy as shit, too."

"And if I hadn't found ya when I did, you coulda gone into organ failure, shock, sepsis, or *died*..." When I overheard the doctor explaining it to our parents, I saw red at just the possibilities of what could've happened to him.

"But ya did find me, so we don't need to worry about it."

"Yeah, this time. What about the next? And the next after that? God forbid I make a life outside of babysittin' your ass and find a wife and have some kids. But I can't do that, can I?"

His brows pinch and he jerks back as if I've slapped him. "Why not?"

"You seriously don't know?"

His hands rise and fall, smacking against his thighs. "I guess not. Spell it out for me like I'm five."

Fitting considering his maturity level.

My shoulders lift, deciding to no longer sugarcoat it. "You refuse to get help, and I've tried to be understanding and sympathetic to you not wantin' to go that route, but in the meantime, you use alcohol and sex as a copin' mechanism. I pick you up from the bar at least three times a week, sometimes more, so you don't get behind the wheel and wrap your truck around a tree. Or worse, kill someone else."

"You know I never drive when I've been drinkin'."

"Because I'm always there to pick you up! And you know that. So while you're out actin' a fool, I'm draggin' my ass out of bed to get yours. I can't even fully blame you because I've enabled it for so long."

It's hard not to when the alternative is risking him making drunk decisions that could hurt him or others.

Only With Me

"Okay, fine...I'll call an Uber from now on. Will that help your sex life?"

I pinch the bridge of my nose, trying my hardest not to lose my cool. "You don't get it, and I don't think you want to."

Standing, I step around the chair to leave, but his panicked voice stops me. "Okay, wait. Don't go."

Arching a brow, I keep my feet planted. "What?"

"Stay and talk to me. I don't want you to leave being upset like this."

Frustration streams through me, but I reluctantly return to the chair.

"Are you sayin' I'm the reason you ain't in a relationship?" he asks.

"Not entirely, but it's why I don't pursue 'em. How can I when I'm always worryin' about you? I live in that duplex so I'm close in case I need to check on you. We work together all day so I can keep an eye on you. I track your location so I always know where you are."

"Geez, stalker much? I feel like I need to get a restrainin' order."

"Fuck off," I spit out, and he has the audacity to laugh.

"You don't need to babysit me, Waylon. I'm a grown-ass man, and I know there have been times where I've not been reliable in terms of takin' care of myself, but I don't wanna be the reason you die old and alone."

"Thanks," I deadpan, rolling my eyes. "However, witnessin' my twin brother almost bleed to death—more than once—has given me enough PTSD for a lifetime. Our siblings are married and busy with their own lives now. I can't help but think if I do the same, you'll get left behind, sink deeper into your depression, or harm yourself again, and I won't be close enough to find you in time."

"I'm sorry it weighs on you this much. I ain't purposely tryin' to scare y'all."

"Well, you do—more than you probably realize. You can't

continue livin' like this forever. It's gonna catch up to you, and eventually, the drinkin' won't be enough to numb the pain you're tryin' so hard to ignore instead of managing it. It'll lead to you tryin' other ways to cope, and most likely, they won't be good ones."

He stares at me, sadness covering his features, and I know he understands where I'm coming from. He just isn't ready to admit it.

"You're not alone in this because I feel it, too. The sadness and anxiety," I remind him.

"I know," he says. "And I'm glad you're stronger at not lettin' it get to you than I am."

I don't know that I'd say *stronger* versus focusing my attention on other things, such as him and keeping his stubborn ass alive.

"If the roles were reversed, what would you do? If you had to witness me spiralin' out of control, how would you help me?"

"Probably beat your ass." He smirks.

"Trust me, I want to, but I have a feelin' the staff would frown upon that here."

"Pfft. Don't let that stop ya. You even have the upper hand. I'm connected to an IV, so I have limited range of motion, but no rib shots." He points at me. "That shit hurts."

"Do you know how to take anything seriously?"

He grins, lifting his other shoulder. "Life's too short to be."

"Wilder," I say his name firmly. "What's it gonna take for you to see that you can't continue livin' like this? Tryin' street drugs is one step away from rock bottom. Next you'll be addicted."

"Probably knockin' up some chick or wakin' up hitched. Because at that point, just give me a shovel so I can dig my own grave."

"Jesus Christ," I groan, scrubbing a hand down my face. "I can't tell if you're just being an asshole for fun or if it's the meds they gave ya makin' you extra annoyin'."

"A little of both."

Only With Me

"Medication prescribed legally can help you if ya just gave it a chance."

"Do I look like the lie down on a couch and talk about my feelings type of person? I can't do that."

"How do you know if you don't put in the effort? There's no harm in tryin'."

He shrugs. "I'm already exhausted from tryin' to block it out of my head all damn day. There's no energy left at the end of the day to talk about it."

"Wilder, you and I talk all day long about random shit. Sometimes you talk too much, so why not use those skills and talk to a professional once a month?"

"About what? I doubt they'd wanna hear about my recent hookups," he mocks.

"Do you wanna continue putting Mom and Dad through this?" I ask seriously. "It's not just me it's affecting, but our parents, too. Dad might not say it in so many words, but losin' you is his biggest fear."

His gaze lowers to his lap, and even though I hate guilt-tripping him, sometimes it's all that works on him to take shit seriously.

"He cried the night you nearly bled out in the bathroom. And you know him. He never cries."

He blows out a breath, staring at the beige wall in front of him before he meets my eyes. "If I tell you I'll think about it, will you leave me alone for a bit?"

"Depends how long you take to think about it."

He contemplates for a moment, chewing his bottom lip. "Three months."

"One," I counter.

He scowls. "Two."

"Fine," I agree firmly. "You have two months to decide on your own or I drag your ass to a therapist's office myself come the sixty-first day. Got it?"

Reluctantly, he holds out his hand. "Deal."

I shake it. "We'll go together."

"Oh goody, couple's counseling."

I'd never force him, even though I act like I would, but I want him to think about it. At least take time to get used to the idea instead of shutting it down each time I bring it up.

"If I do this, you haveta get a woman so you stop focusin' so much on me."

"Prove to me that I can."

"I will. Promise."

Chapter Thirteen
Harlow

"So are you ready to get on a datin' app now?" Natalie taunts after we finish three episodes of *Grey's Anatomy*. Now we're just video chatting on my laptop. "I found one called CowboyMatch."

"You're jokin'," I say skeptically.

"I swear it! It's an app for ranchers and farmers to find wives. You could set your location to Montana and move to Big Sky Country." She waggles her brows.

I snort. "I'd freeze up there."

"Not with a beefy lumberjack-sized cowboy. He'd keep ya nice and sweaty."

Laughing, I shake my head at her. "Sounds more like your thing."

"Oh, I'm on there. I wanted to test out the waters for ya and now I have a date this weekend."

"No way. With who?"

"His name is Jackson and he's six-foot-six! That's all I needed to know. He's a whole foot taller than me," she says with stars in her eyes.

"That'll make things…interestin'," I tease.

"I'll be climbin' him like a tree no matter what position he puts me in."

"At least make him take ya out for dinner first."

"Don't worry, he is. And then we're gonna go back to his apartment for…*dessert*."

"Uh-huh, I bet."

"And then hopefully crack me like a glow stick," she adds unapologetically.

"Natalie Jo!" I crack up at how open she is about sex. "I don't even know what that means."

"It's time you find out, Harlow. You're young and hot. Those perky tits and your tight ass ain't gonna last forever, so use 'em now while ya got 'em."

"And now I feel violated."

"Says the girl who sent an ass pic to a group chat," she mocks, arching a brow.

As if I needed the reminder.

"Look where that got me…" I sigh. "Mystery Guy left the group chat a few days ago and we've not texted since he told me he didn't wanna reschedule our coffee date."

Once he said that, I wasn't about to try to change his mind, but it still hurt. I don't know if it's normal to be sad about it or miss him after only spending a month chatting, but a part of me does.

"Screw him for not realizin' how amazing you are. Another reason to get on this app and find someone else who will. Use that photo you sent me of you dressed up that day, too. That was super cute."

Lifting my shoulder, I wrinkle my nose. "Maybe. I'll think about it."

But she's right. I did look cute.

"Please do. It's kinda fun. You can add message prompts and then decide if you wanna reply based on their answer. There's voice and video chat options too, so you don't even haveta give 'em your number."

Only With Me

"What kinda prompts?"

"Anything you want. Mine is: The way to win me over is and then my response is: Be witty, charming, and rich. Or tall enough that none of those matter."

My eyes crease as I burst out laughing at how unexpected that was. Knowing Natalie, I shouldn't be that surprised.

"That's genius," I mock. "Now I see how you landed a giant cowboy."

"Yep, and it gives 'em a little hint of your humor but also what you're lookin' for. Then you'll know a little about them based on what they say. For mine, most just replied with their heights and asked if that was tall enough, but the one guy I'm going out with said—*tall enough to have the best view in the room when you're bent over in front of me.*"

My jaw drops at his bold answer and the fact that it worked.

"Goddamn, that's a line alright…"

"Worked on me like a moth to a flame. Immediately, yes."

I snort. "Glad I have *your* location now. He basically waved chocolate in your face, and you hopped in his creepy white van."

"I'm just here to have fun. You don't haveta take it too seriously. But also, you can change up your prompt and see what works best for ya."

"I don't even know what I'd write."

"Could be about your dreams, goals, your type, what you look for in a man…"

"I'd need to have experience with dating to even know what those are," I deadpan, leaning back against my headboard.

"Okay, let's look for some simple but fun ones for you." She grabs her phone, begins scrolling, and then reads them aloud.

"Best way to ask me out—by naming a time and place."

"We're the same type of weird if—you put the milk in before the cereal."

"The one thing you should know about me is—I'm in my Reputation Era to some, Lover to others."

"Two truths and a lie—I'm hot, funny, and mentally sane."

"I'm looking for—nothing too serious, just the love of my life."

Brooke Montgomery

I burst out laughing after each one and soon Natalie is too.

"Okay, these are funny," I confess. "Though that cereal one is diabolical. Immediate block if you put in milk first."

"Even ones like that could help you find your soulmate in no time." She beams, and I can't deny her puppy dog eyes pleading with me to try it.

"I'll download it but…no promises."

She squeals and does a little happy dance. "Yay! I can't wait to hear about who you meet."

Hopefully not a serial killer.

"Daddy, do you need anythin' before I go?"

"No, sweetie. I'm fine, go ahead." He waves me off like an annoying stray cat.

I chuckle. "Okay, love you."

It's been a week since his fall. He came home from the hospital on Christmas Eve and then we celebrated together as a family. I've been home every day since to keep a close eye on him. With his concussion, I didn't want to leave him home alone when Mom had to work.

But today she's off, so I'm finally going to the ranch.

Since talking to Natalie last night, I've been thinking more about her suggestion about getting on that dating app. I'm not a hundred percent sold, but I'm considering it. It'd be nice to meet a nice guy.

Since it's only forty-five degrees, I'm bundled up in my fleece jacket, riding boots, a hat, and gloves. Piper loves the cold, so after I lunge her, we'll go on a short trail ride, and then I'll have my lesson with Noah.

Only With Me

"Hey, sweet girl."

Piper neighs when I approach. I rub her nose and then wrap my arms around her.

"I missed you."

After I brush her and secure her lunging tack, I lead her out of the barn. It's quiet on the ranch, which isn't too surprising for this time of year. Most riders aren't getting lessons during the holidays because they're away or spending time with family. I've been cooped up in the house long enough and was ready to come back.

As we walk to the corral, I hear voices coming from the training center that isn't Noah. That's where she normally is, but this is a man's voice.

"There ya go! You got it," he shouts.

"Yeehaw! Now I'm a cowboy." That excited voice sounds younger.

The older voice laughs.

It must be one of Noah's brothers, so I walk Piper across the gravel and that's when I see Waylon with a teenage boy roping with a steer dummy.

"Hey!" I grab their attention.

Waylon's smile drops when he sees me, which makes me second-guess coming in here.

"Hi." He nods.

"Who's this?" I grin at the boy.

"I'm Bentley."

"My little brother from the BBBS program," Waylon explains.

"Oh, I didn't know you did that. How sweet."

Then I shift my gaze back to Bentley. "I'm Harlow. Nice to meet you."

"You too. Is that your horse?" He nods behind me.

Grinning, I bring her next to me. "Yep. Her name is Piper. She's my show horse. Do you have one?"

"No." He frowns. "But Waylon's teachin' me how to ride and rope, so maybe someday."

"Wow, that's awesome. Sounds like you're doing well."

"He is." Waylon pats his shoulder and looks at him with pride. "He'll be learnin' to bull ride in no time."

My brows rise, impressed. "You wanna be a bull rider?"

"Undecided," Bentley confirms. "My mom would probably kill me first."

I chuckle. "It's a dangerous sport."

"Yeah, but he's tough. Ain't ya?" Waylon taunts, giving him a little push.

I can't help smiling at them. I would've never guessed Waylon volunteered for the Big Brothers Big Sisters program, but I'm not surprised either. He seems good with him, too.

"It was nice meetin' ya. I'm gonna lunge Piper before our ride and then do some jumpin' exercises."

"You do horse jumpin'?" Bentley asks curiously.

"Yep, we start competin' again in the spring."

"That's so cool. Could I stay and watch you?"

"Of course," I say at the same time Waylon says, "We shouldn't bother her."

"It's no trouble. I'd love an audience. It helps me practice for the real thing."

Bentley's face splits in half. "Cool."

"I'll be back in an hour."

Glancing at Waylon, he looks as comfortable as an ice cube on a hot day.

When he catches me staring at him, he sucks in his lips.

"See ya then," he finally says.

Piper and I head back the way we came and once I get her into the corral, she starts lunging. While I stand in the center as she circles around me, my mind flicks back to Waylon and how tense he seemed around me. We spoke briefly in the ER waiting room but only for a few minutes. We were both dealing with family emergencies.

I should've asked how his brother was doing. I didn't ask Noah for details, but she mentioned he had a reaction to taking ketamine and was able to go home the following day.

Only With Me

Remembering what Delilah's told me in the past, this isn't Wilder's first medical scare.

After we're done in the corral, Piper and I take a short ride around the retreat. Luckily, it's not crowded, but there's something peaceful about it—the chill in the air, the beautiful mountain views, and the lingering silence.

There aren't many moments like this anymore.

When we return, Noah's in the training center, waiting for me. She beams and greets Piper.

"Are y'all ready?" She pets Piper's nose and gives her some love.

"I think so. It feels like forever since we've practiced."

"Don't worry, I set up an easy obstacle of smaller jumps to get you back into it." She glances at Waylon and Bentley. "I see you have some fans today."

I giggle. "I guess so, which means the pressure is on."

"You're gonna do great," Noah says confidently, handing me a helmet.

I remove my fleece, hat, and gloves, then secure it over my head.

Once I'm settled on Piper, I guide her over to the start and wait for Noah to blow her whistle. She has a timer wrapped around her neck and a clipboard in her hand to record my times.

But Waylon and Bentley standing next to her makes me more anxious than it should. Bentley appears so excited to watch me, but Waylon's looking at me with an expression I've never seen on him before.

I get into a two-point position and then give Piper a little kick as soon as Noah gives me the go-ahead. Piper takes off and makes the first jump effortlessly. It helps that they're low and we've done this dozens of times, but after this past month, I've not been able to practice as much or focus as hard.

By the fifth jump, my face is in a permanent smile at how great she did. It's hard not to have a blast when I'm on her, but I'm glad Bentley didn't have to witness me screwing up.

"Whew, that was great!" Noah shouts.

Bentley claps and Waylon grins at him.

"Thanks, but now we need a real challenge."

"You want me to raise 'em already?" She arches a brow.

Glancing at Bentley quickly, I nod and meet Noah's gaze. "Yeah, let's give him a good show."

"Alright. Just remember to bend your waist more and fold in those elbows."

"You got it, boss." I smirk.

"Waylon, do you mind helpin' me adjust the rails?"

"Sure."

He follows her out into the arena while Piper and I wait.

"Do you wanna pet her?" I ask Bentley.

His eyes light up and he nods.

I move closer and show him where he can touch on her neck and nose.

She nudges his hand and neighs at him.

"She likes you."

"How can you tell?"

"She hasn't bitten you," I tease.

"Alright, it's ready," Noah announces. "I only did four to give y'all room in between. Don't forget to keep your head up and look through the jump."

"Got it!"

I ride Piper back to the beginning and wait for the whistle.

As soon as it goes off, Piper canters to the first one and successfully jumps over without knocking the rails down. When we do bigger jumps, I switch my positions from post to two-point to keep us balanced in between. When my legs squeeze slightly to signal for her to jump over the second and third, she does flawlessly.

Moments before the final one, a small animal runs inside and spooks Piper. She plants into the ground before my body has the chance to stop, and I fly off her back.

And that's why I wear the helmet.

Only With Me

"Oh my God, Harlow!" Noah shouts, rushing toward me.

"I'm fine..." I grunt, attempting to roll onto my side.

"Are you okay?" Waylon kneels beside me.

I groan at how hard my tailbone hit the ground. "Never been better."

Noah snorts, grabbing Piper's reins so she doesn't run off.

"Take it easy and get up slowly."

Waylon offers me his hand, and I take it. He helps me into a sitting position, but the pain already shoots down my back.

"Was that a *goat*?" I ask for clarification.

"Yep...looks like one got loose." Waylon shakes his head. "Pretty sure Wilder was movin' 'em into a different pasture."

"That explains it." Noah sighs.

"He's so cute!" Bentley gushes, and when the three of us look over, we find him playing with the little devil.

"Don't let him get away," Waylon tells him. "We'll need to bring him back."

"Can I keep him?"

Waylon shakes his head. "Not a chance your mom would be okay with that."

"Ugh." Bentley pouts.

"Think you can stand?" Waylon brings his attention back to me.

No. "Yeah, sure."

Waylon gets to his feet and gently pulls me to mine. We're nearly chest to chest when I get to my full height. Inhaling, I smell whatever he's wearing. Or maybe it's just *him*. Manly and musky with a hint of leather.

His gaze finds mine, but then it lowers to my mouth.

I brush a hand over my cheek, feeling self-conscious. "Do I have dirt on my face?"

He blinks and then shakes his head. "Oh no, you look good."

My brows furrow at his choice of words, and I almost get lost in his ocean blue eyes while staring into them.

"You're gonna probably be sore now," Noah interrupts, causing us to break apart. "Take somethin' when you get home."

"I will. My ass is gonna have a nice bruise on it again, so I'll be sittin' on ice for the rest of the day." I chuckle, but Waylon tenses next to me, and I worry that was the wrong thing to say. "I bruise easily, but I'll be fine."

He gives me that forced smile again, which confuses the hell out of me.

"Bentley and I will take the goat back, and then I can help you take down the rails," he tells Noah.

"Sounds good, thank you."

Noah hops on Piper. "I'll groom her and then put her back into the stall so you can get home."

"Are you sure?" I rub my palm over Piper's neck so she knows I'm not upset with her.

"Yeah, I don't want you ridin' anymore today. You need to go rest so you don't wake up stiff tomorrow. Trust me, been there, done that. It ain't fun."

I nod and then give Piper a quick kiss on her nose. "See ya soon, girl."

With New Year's Eve in two days, Noah's taking off from training, so I won't be back until after the first of the year.

I'm going to be bored, though, because I'll be at home while Mom's at work. The hospital is swamped this time of year, so she ends up working overtime.

Maybe I'll make that profile on CowboyMatch after all.

At the very least, it could entertain me for a while.

Chapter Fourteen
Harlow

After taking the hottest shower possible, I change into comfy clothes and lie in bed with an ice pack underneath me. I texted Natalie that I'll be on bedrest for a few days and that I'm making a profile to kill time.

Of course she was excited as hell and told me to *get laid* before the end of the year.

Considering that's in two days, she's delusional.

I can hardly move, nevertheless have sex for the first time.

But I'm still willing to put myself out there and try—even if it bites me in my bruised ass later.

So after getting a profile up with some photos and a simple prompt—*What's something interesting about you*? My obvious response: *I'm a horse show jumper.*

At the very least, it'll be a fun icebreaker.

And if not, then I'll change it.

I even added a picture of Piper and me in my show clothes.

Considering the type of app CowboyMatch is, I'm hopeful I'll find someone with shared hobbies and interests that involve horses.

Within five minutes, my notifications pop up with responses.

Damn. That was fast.

Brooke Montgomery

I'd let you jump on me.
How original. *Block.*
I used to ride bulls…maybe we can take turns riding each other?
C for cringe. *Block.*
Stud horses and I have a lot in common…if ya know what I mean.
I'm a virgin, and *I* know what you mean… *Block.*
I don't ride horses, but I can jump pretty high. Maybe you could teach me?
Okay, that's kinda wholesome.

I click on Brandon's profile and see that he plays college basketball in Johnson City, which is over an hour north of here. Then I look through his photos and notice how tall he is, but he's cute too.

Though I'm curious why he's on this app.

Now I just need to figure out how to respond to start a conversation.

HARLOW
> I could teach you but with your sports background, I doubt you'd need more than one lesson.

Oh God, that was lame. Wasn't it?

BRANDON
> That's okay. I guess we'd have to find something else to do for our second date then.

HARLOW
> You'll teach me to play basketball?

BRANDON
> For sure. Might be easier if I just lift you up to make the basket instead.

HARLOW
> Because I'm short or too dumb to learn?

Only With Me

BRANDON

Nah, I'm saying it'd be more fun touching you instead.

Okay...I can't tell if that's a cute one-liner or a gross one.

HARLOW

You'll have to tell me more about yourself. What are you studying there?

BRANDON

Engineering Technology.

HARLOW

Oh! So your athletic AND a brainiac. Why exactly are you here?

BRANDON

I'm kinda shy around girls so most of them put me in the friend zone before I get the courage to make a move.

Aww.

BRANDON

I figured girls on CowboyMatch would be looking for something a bit more serious versus a hookup.

HARLOW

Makes sense.

BRANDON

Why are you on here?

HARLOW

My bestie told me to try it. She says I need to "get out more." I'm from a small town of only two thousand people, so the options are limited.

Brooke Montgomery

BRANDON

> You should come up here some weekend. Tons of stuff to do, on and off campus. Well, it's kinda boring right now with the colder weather but come spring, I love to go hiking. In the summer, my friends and I go whitewater rafting and fishing.

HARLOW

> I'd love that!

We continue chatting for two hours before he tells me he has to get ready to visit some family. Things leave on a good note, so I'm optimistic. For now.

When I go back to check my other messages, there's ten more.

Only two aren't sexual, so I respond to them—Michael and Jayden.

"Okay, this is kinda fun…" I muse to myself.

Keeps me from getting bored, but the meds I took earlier are making me drowsy, so I lock my phone and take a nap.

When I wake up, it's dinnertime. Mom didn't have much energy after work, so she brought home a pizza, which is fine by me. I'm not super hungry anyway.

Instead of sitting at the table, we crash in the living room and watch one of Dad's favorite shows.

"How's your tailbone?" Mom asks.

"I think I'll survive," I tell her. "Feels fine when I'm sitting on ice, but it hurts when I walk."

"I brought some ointment home. It's in the kitchen. Just rub it on your skin and it should help in about twenty minutes."

Only With Me

"What's in it?" I ask reluctantly.

"It has CBD and some other stuff." The hesitation in her voice makes me suspicious.

"Mother! Is it illegal?"

Her jaw drops. "Of course not! I might've bought it from a friend at work who has a patient that makes all-natural type stuff."

Dad snorts, making me laugh because he calls bullshit too.

"Uh-huh, okay…" I muse.

"It's for sore muscles. Just try it."

Once we're done eating and Dad goes to bed, I decide to take a salt bath and check if I have any new responses.

This time I accept a few who gave sexual responses just to see how they react to my replies.

Not that I'm good at flirting because I know I'm not, but I promised Natalie I'd try, so here I am.

> DEVON
>
> So you're a cowgirl…that's my favorite reverse position.

What even is that?

A quick Google search makes me immediately regret looking at the images tab.

> HARLOW
>
> Is that because my ass would be right in your face?

Seriously, though, what an awkward way to sit on someone. How does one even move like that?

> DEVON
>
> Spreading those ass cheeks while you ride me gives me the perfect view of your pretty little hole.

My eyes widen, and I blink hard because there's no freaking way he said that.

Brooke Montgomery

> **HARLOW**
> You look there?

DEVON
Why wouldn't I?

> **HARLOW**
> Gross.

DEVON
I assure you, it's not. My tongue all up in there would have you coming in seconds.

His tongue?
Oh hell no.

> **HARLOW**
> So back to being a cowgirl...do you ride horses?

DEVON
I work on a cattle ranch, so yeah, we use them for roping and herding.

> **HARLOW**
> Oh cool. Tell me more about that.

Or literally anything else that doesn't involve my butt in his face.

While I wait for him to reply, I check back on my other messages.

JAYDEN
Besides riding, what else do you like to do?

> **HARLOW**
> I take care of my dad, mostly. He's disabled. I watch Grey's Anatomy with my best friend every Thursday. She's in Nashville, so we don't get to see each other in person very often. I work at a Western clothing boutique. That's pretty much it...

Only With Me

And I sound boring as fuck.

JAYDEN

That's cool. Do you watch anything else besides that with your friend?

I furrow my brows.

HARLOW

No, we're trying to catch up on all the seasons. We're only halfway through.

JAYDEN

Not even some girl on girl?

HARLOW

No?

JAYDEN

You should. It's pretty hot. I hear girls watch it together and then recreate the scene.

HARLOW

Um...well, she's an hour away from me, so we watch together over video chat.

JAYDEN

If you ever need someone to watch it with, let me know.

Instead of replying, I call Natalie.

"Hey! How ya feelin'?" She grins.

"Um, fine. But I'm talkin' to some of these guys on the app and this one asked if you and I watch girl on girl together and then recreate it on each other."

She barks out a laugh.

"Is this normal? Am I supposed to be fulfillin' some weird fantasy for 'em and going along with it?"

"Kinda, yeah. It gets their attention. Keeps the convo flowin' and leads to some dirty talk."

"Before even meetin' 'em?"

"Yeah! That's kinda the point."

I curl my lip in horror. "The point of what? Being a perv?"

"Harlow...don't take it so seriously. It's just fun."

"*Fun*? One guy said he wants to see my booty hole in reverse cowgirl position."

"Oh my God!" she hollers. "Was his name Devon?"

"Uh, yeah."

"He's harmless...he just has a little fetish."

I look at her like a deer in headlights. "I'm not experienced enough for that kinda talk. I feel so out of my element."

"Then ignore 'em if you want. No one says you haveta engage in those conversations."

"There was one guy, Brandon, who seemed somewhat normal. He plays college basketball in Johnson City."

"He's a player."

"You know him?"

"No, but he's an athlete on a datin' app."

"He said he's shy around girls, so that's why—"

"Yep, that's a line. He's full of shit."

"How do you know all this?"

"Because there's hundreds of guys just like him at my school. Trust me. They pretend to be one way but in reality are a bunch of manwhores."

"Well, that's disappointin'. We talked for two hours."

"If he's truly interested, he'll reach back out. If not, he'll block you."

"Seriously? Why does this feel like *The Hunger Games*."

"Because dating *is The Hunger Games*."

"I don't have any game whatsoever, so I ain't gonna survive..." I throw my head back with a groan.

"If you're uncomfortable, just exit the chat. Don't waste your time. You'll find someone on there worth talkin' to."

"Maybe...I dunno."

We chat for a few more minutes, mostly her giving me pep talks, and then once we hang up, I go back to the app.

Only With Me

Then I notice I'm unable to message Brandon.
He blocked me? What the fuck did I do?
He was the most normal guy out of the handful I spoke to.
I must've been more lame than I thought.
Or Natalie's right and it was all bullshit.
Ignoring the other messages, I close out of the app and turn on the TV.
I've done more socializing in one day than I do in a month and now I need to decompress.

I must fall asleep because my phone ringing wakes me up and it's almost midnight.
Even weirder is it's my sister.
"Hey," I answer, still groggy.
"Hi, sorry to wake you. I need you to pick me up at Sheriff Wagner's office."
I sit up and clear my throat. "You're in *jail?*"
"No…not me. But he brought me in as a witness and won't lemme drive because I was drinkin'."
"A witness to what? And whaddya mean not you? Who's in jail?"
She pauses briefly before exhaling sharply. "Waylon."

Chapter Fifteen
Waylon

"Are we goin' out tonight?" Wilder asks, walking into my room without knocking.

"I coulda been butt naked in here," I chastise him, grabbing a shirt from my closet since I'm only half-dressed. "And *I* am. You're not."

"Dude, what the fuck?" He leans against my doorway, folding his arms in a childish pout.

"You nearly overdosed a week ago. Keep your ass home for once."

"Goddamn. Who pissed in your Biscuits and Gravy?"

"You and Jake."

"Ah, shit. What're you gonna do?"

What I couldn't do earlier because of the holidays, but now that those are over and it's Friday night, I'm going to find him.

"Send a message." I walk around my room, getting everything I need for the night—watch, keys, phone, wallet. I shouldn't be gone too long since I don't plan on partying or drinking tonight. As soon as I find the motherfucker and take care of him, then I'm out of there.

"I don't need you fightin' my battles for me. Jake knows what

Only With Me

happened and won't give me any more stuff," he says, genuinely concerned.

"It's a little too late for that."

Jake fucking knew better. Each time Wilder was hospitalized, Jake saw how it wrecked me. He was aware of Wilder's history. All this time, I thought he was my friend and he went behind my back.

"Why're you pissed? Is something else goin' on?" He holds out his hand, stopping me from walking past him.

Besides liking a girl who I later found out is Delilah's little sister and a million percent off-limits…

"I'm fine."

"You're amped up."

"Damn right." I nudge his shoulder with mine as I walk around him and go to the front door.

"Lemme come with you at least. I won't drink, promise," he nearly begs.

Spinning around, I face him nearly chest to chest. "Unfortunately for you, I don't trust you. I can't deal with Jake and babysit you at the same time, so just this one goddamn time, listen to me and stay here."

He clamps his mouth shut and I take that as an agreement.

"I'll be back in less than an hour," I say before walking out the door.

I've been on edge for the past week, there's no denying that, and it's finally come to a head. Between Harlow wearing that fucking pink bow in her hair and crushing my heart that we had to stop talking and then Wilder's incident right after, I've barely had time to process my feelings.

But then Jake texted me this morning to ask why I left the group chat. I made up some bullshit lie about it blowing up my phone and being too distracting, but he's the reason.

Then he said he was going out to The Twisted Bull and invited Wilder and me to go out with him.

I told him to leave my brother alone.

He *laughed*.

That was enough to set me off.

Driving into town, the street is packed with cars, so I have to park three blocks away. The walk gives me time to get even more heated at the thought of him giving him Wilder street drugs that could've ended his life.

I tune out the blasting country music and loud talking, hyperfocused on finding him. It's nearly shoulder to shoulder in here, which I already hate, but eventually, I find his loud, obnoxious ass at the bar.

Next to my ex.

Bastard.

He already fucked with my brother, so why not go after her next?

His eyes light up when he spots me and he stands to his full height. "Bro, ya made it! Lemme get you a beer."

Hard pass.

"I ain't here for a drink, and I ain't stayin' long."

"Why not?"

"I only came to tell you to leave me and my brother the hell alone. Don't talk to either of us ever again." I flick my gaze to Delilah, who's sitting on my right side. "And don't talk to her either."

I'm not in love with her anymore, but I still care about her. Jake's bad news and she doesn't need to get wrapped up in his illegal shit.

"Whoa, calm down. What're you even talkin' about?"

I step closer, looking down my nose at him. "You know what I'm fuckin' talkin' about. The drugs. Whatever illegal shit you're in, don't involve us."

"I already apologized for that and said it wouldn't happen again." His palm cups my shoulder, trying to pull me closer. "C'mon, lemme get ya—"

I shake his hand off me, stepping back. "Don't touch me."

He pushes my chest. "Chill, bro."

Only With Me

"Don't. Fucking. Touch. Me." I shove him back into a barstool.

"Waylon, stop…" Delilah steps between us. "This ain't you. Walk away."

"It is now since he almost *killed* my brother," I hiss, looking at him above her head.

"And fightin' with him isn't gonna change what happened," she says calmly.

"So if the man who hurt Harlow was here, you're tellin' me you wouldn't knock him out because it wouldn't change the past?"

She visibly tenses, and I know I hit a nerve, but she should know from firsthand experience how painful it is to watch your sibling nearly die.

"That ain't the same and you know it. Jake didn't purposely hurt him."

"Shoulda thought about that before he gave him street drugs."

Only God knows what the hell was mixed in with the ketamine. Finding him even minutes later would've cost him his life.

"You wanna hit me, go ahead," Jake taunts, then wraps his arm around Delilah's shoulders, pulling her into him.

Narrowing my eyes, I stare at him intently, deciding if it's worth it for the few seconds of satisfaction.

"Delilah, move."

She blows out an aggravated breath and mutters, "Y'all are idiots."

Once she shrugs his arm off her and is out of the way, I step toward him. "If you come near my brother or me ever again, you'll be the one in the hospital next time."

The corners of his lips curve up into a taunting smirk. "Is that so?"

Without giving him time to react, I shove my fist into his gut and deliver a crushing blow through his body. Grunting in pain, he falls back against a crowd of people before landing on his ass, where he belongs.

"Waylon!" Delilah squeals, shoving my arm.

A second later, Jake's on his feet and charges at me, shoving me into the people behind me. Delilah falls to the ground, and I see red.

It's one thing to shove me, but it's never okay to hurt a woman.

I jump to my feet and punch him in the face, knocking him down again. "You pushed Delilah, asshole."

"Waylon, stop it!"

"Alright, get out!" one of the bartenders shouts. "Or I'm calling the sheriff."

Jake either doesn't hear him or doesn't care because he stands and barrels right into me, knocking us both into a table that snaps under our weight.

We wrestle each other on the ground, swinging at each other until we're pulled apart. When I get to my feet, blood drips down my face.

"Get 'em outta here!" one of the managers shouts, pointing toward the exit.

The bouncer shoves me toward the door and as soon as we're outside, I find Sheriff Wagner and one of his deputies.

"Hollis. Murphy. Get in." Sheriff Wagner opens the back door of his squad car.

"For what?" Jake stupidly asks.

"Vandalism. Disorderly conduct. Being fuckin' idiots." He waves his hand toward the back seat.

Delilah comes out and stands next to me.

"You in the front. I heard you witnessed it, so you need to come down, too."

She groans. "Thanks a lot, guys."

The three of us get in and the ride stays silent as we drive to the station. I stretch out my fingers, already feeling the pain that will be worse tomorrow.

But I don't care. It was worth it.

"Boys, you sit there with Diane." He points to his receptionist's desk. "Delilah, you're with me in my office."

Only With Me

"How long is this gonna take?" Jake asks, wiping under his nose. "I'm bleedin' here."

Sheriff Wagner nods to his deputy. "Take him to the First Aid room." His gaze meets mine. "You need to go, too?"

"No, I can wait," I deadpan.

"Great, then sit."

Delilah follows the sheriff but glances over her shoulder at me before walking into his office.

Diane hands me a form and tells me to fill it out.

"This is dumb," I mutter.

The last thing I want to do is write when my hand hurts, but I tough it out and fill in the stupid form anyway. Only Sheriff Wagner would make us do his own paperwork.

When Jake returns, he sits in the other chair, but neither of us speaks to each other.

Twenty minutes later, Delilah and the sheriff exit his office.

"You've been drinkin'. You need to call for a ride," he tells her.

"I only had a few."

He pierces her with a look.

"Fine, I'll call my sister."

Oh, fuck my life.

"Hollis, my office," he snaps.

When I stand, I meet Delilah's gaze and give her an appreciative grin for having my back at the bar. I know she warned me to stay out of trouble, but it was more important for me to send a message.

Once I'm in the chair, I explain what happened. He doesn't bother taking notes nor interrupt me, so I keep going until I tell him why I took the first hit.

"I thought someone told me the wrong name at first. Fully expected Wilder to walk out of the bar," he muses. "But I understand why ya did it and him eggin' ya on. Still, the bar's gonna press charges, so I have to write up a citation."

"Understood, sir."

After I sign all the paperwork, he escorts me out of his office, and I'm met with Delilah and her sister.

Harlow's in her PJ pants and was obviously sleeping. Her hair's pulled up into a messy bun and she's makeup free. But she's stunning as always.

Words I should not be thinking about her.

"Murphy, you're next," Sheriff Wagner orders, and once they're both gone, I step closer to the girls.

"Hey, how're you feelin'?" I ask Harlow.

Her green eyes meet mine. "Sore, but I'll live."

"Sore? What happened?" Delilah asks.

"She fell off Piper durin' her lesson," I explain before Harlow can. "She should be restin'."

"Oh my God, you didn't tell me that," Delilah scolds her.

"It's no biggie. Landed on my ass, mostly. But I wasn't about to miss seein' you in jail." Harlow snickers.

"I was a *witness* to this dumbass, who I told not to start a fight," Delilah clarifies, waving her hand at me. "Never listens to me."

Harlow crosses her arms, amused. "Yeah, let's talk about that."

I blow out a tense breath. "Let's not."

Delilah shoots her gaze at me. "And I got pushed down too. Thanks so much for askin' how I am."

"Sorry." I suppress a grin. "I knew you could hold your own."

"Damn right. Coulda fought better than you too."

I scoff, quickly glancing at Harlow, who's staring at me, and I avert my gaze before it gets awkward.

"Well, for what it's worth, sorry for gettin' you involved," I say earnestly, then turn to Harlow. "And for you havin' to come get her. I coulda driven her."

Harlow shrugs. "It's fine. I clearly had nothin' better to do on a Friday night except doom scroll through horrible datin' profiles."

My heart plummets into my stomach, and I almost blurt out the same question Delilah asks.

"Since when are you on a datin' app?"

Only With Me

"I only made one today. Natalie encouraged me. But it's already terrifying."

Who's Natalie?

"You're tellin' me." Delilah snorts. "Men in their mid-thirties seeking *friends with benefits*. Like, sir…being a fuck boy at your age ain't cute anymore. Grow up."

I purse my lips, wanting to ask which app she's on, but I know that's a bad fucking idea.

Still, I can't help being a little gutted that she signed up for one. After chatting to her for weeks and not at all this past one, I miss it.

I can't blame her, though, for moving on to find someone else to talk to.

"Well, I better get home. You guys drive safely." I walk around Harlow toward the exit.

"You too," Delilah calls out. "Oh, wait. Waylon?"

"Yeah?" I spin around.

"Tell Wilder we're prayin' for him."

I swallow hard. She knows better than anyone how challenging it's been and why I had to take action with Jake.

Nodding gratefully, I say, "Thanks, will do."

When I arrive home fifteen minutes later, Wilder's passed out on my couch. He's been waiting for me this whole time, not that I should be too surprised. He doesn't like being alone with his thoughts.

I turn off the TV, cover him up with a blanket, then pick up the beer bottles on my coffee table. Once I toss those out, I grab his phone and make sure his alarm is set for work tomorrow.

And because I know he could use the sleep, I give him an extra hour.

Chapter Sixteen
Waylon

"Howdy, Jail Bird."

"Funny," I deadpan, walking through my parents' kitchen.

Noah and Magnolia giggle at my sister's taunting words. They're leaning against the counter, helping Gramma Grace bake something for dessert.

"Sheriff Wagner didn't even cuff me or put me in a cell, so it hardly counts."

"That's a nice black eye, son." Dad smacks me hard on the shoulder, and I wince as he passes around me to get to the fridge. "Knuckles look rough, too."

I swallow hard, taking my seat at the table next to Wilder. "Barely hurts."

Jake managed to get one face punch, but I got at least two on him.

"Isn't this where you say *you should see the other guy?*" Noah mimics in a deep voice.

Narrowing my eyes at her, I scowl. "Don't ya have your own child to worry about? Leave me be."

"Who knew Waylon would kick anyone's ass, no less his best

Only With Me

friend's?" Wilder taunts, draping his arm around me. "I guess that means he loves me."

"Or that you're a huge pain in my ass and since I can't kick yours, I had to kick his."

"No cussin' at the dinner table." Mom strolls in with an apron around her waist and Mallory behind her, already gloating at my slipup.

"Pay up, cowboys. I'm savin' up for a big truck," Mallory muses, holding out her ridiculous swear jar.

"A big *what*?" Wilder hollers. "Whaddya need that for?"

"Noneya business, that's what."

"Here's a concept: get a job and pay for it yourself." Wilder pokes her arm when she sits next to him.

"Puttin' up with you *is* my job."

They continue bickering, but I'm just happy I'm no longer the topic of conversation.

The rest of the family filter into the dining area and soon we're all bowing our heads and saying grace. Mom makes an extra point to peek up at me when she mentions my name.

It's like I'm ten being scolded all over again, but this time without words. Instead, I get disappointed glares.

Meanwhile, the twin who's caused trouble since he came out of the womb gets a friendly pat on the back and a smile.

I hate it here.

But I don't regret it because Jake deserved it.

I'm grateful Sheriff Wagner didn't make me sit in a cell all night, so I'll take the small win.

After dessert, I bow out and skip scrapbooking so I can busy myself at the barn. It's New Year's Eve, so we didn't have any tours today and none tomorrow. Normally, I'd enjoy the break, but instead, it gives me more time to sulk.

I've spent the past two days signing up for every dating app I could find.

Pathetic, I know.

But I need to find Harlow. I can't stop thinking about what those men must be saying to her.

Nothing like the conversations we used to have.

I miss her telling me secrets about her romance wish list.

About her day and how she slept.

How my face would light up every time I checked my phone and a message was waiting for me.

God, I sound like a simp.

Maybe it just didn't mean as much to her, so it's easier for her to move on to talking to someone else.

Maybe that's what I'm telling myself so I don't feel like such a horrible person for what I did.

Would it have been so bad to sit across from her at that table and tell her I was the guy she was speaking to? Would she have freaked out the way I did?

It would've had to end either way.

She's so young and has gone through so much in her short life that it would've been wrong to tangle her into my shit when she's getting hers back on track.

But then why can't I get it out of my damn head?

So since I'm already at war with myself, why not add to it and see if she'll notice my profile and DM me on whichever app she's on. I could message her first…assuming I can figure out what to say and if I can find her.

Wilder's going out tonight, but I asked Delilah to keep an eye on him since she's going out too. I'm not going to bed until his drunk ass is home.

The Twisted Bull is having a whole New Year's bash and is staying open until four in the morning, so thank God we only have barn chores tomorrow. Wilder won't even be up until noon.

Once I bring in the final horse from the pasture and get them in their stall for the night, I close the barn door and turn off the lights. Then I head home.

When I pull into my driveway, Delilah's here, picking up Wilder.

Only With Me

"Hey." I smile weakly when they walk down the duplex stairs toward me.

"You sure you don't wanna come?" Wilder shouts, already acting tipsy.

They probably pregamed while I was at the barn.

"Oh, I'm positive. They wouldn't let me in anyway."

I already paid my citation and apologized to the owner in person when I gave him a check for the damages, but I'm not going to push my luck. Plus, being around hundreds of drunks with loud music blasting and sweaty bodies swarming me sounds like my personal hell.

Wilder jumps into the passenger seat like an excited kid on his way to see Santa Claus. When Delilah walks to the driver's side, I stop her.

"Thank you again for doing this. You don't know how much I appreciate it."

"You owe me big time." She grins mischievously. "And I'm gonna make it a *good* favor."

Snickering, I shake my head. "I have no doubts."

She gives my chest a little pat before I move out of her way and she hops inside her truck.

"Wilder, please, for the love of God, don't overdo it," I warn, holding open the door and peeking inside. "We have work tomorrow."

"Aye aye, boss." He gives me a cocky salute, and I roll my eyes.

"Drive safe," I tell Delilah. "If you need a ride, call me. *Please*."

"I will, but I plan to stop drinking at one, so that should be enough time to sober up and drive home."

I nod and thank her again before closing the door.

After I watch them drive away, I head inside my place and grab a beer to drink alone while I scroll through more dating apps to sign up for and look for the only profile I'm interested in.

Brooke Montgomery

My phone blows up with DMs from dozens of women. I ignore all of them and start wondering if this is a lost cause. Even if Harlow saw my profile, there's no way she'd—

A notification from the CowboyMatch app pops up with a message under her name.

That's the app she chose? I almost laugh because I shouldn't be that surprised.

This one allows you to directly message people or respond to their prompt to help break the ice.

And I cringe a little seeing she answered mine.

I didn't put a lot of effort into mine since I wasn't looking to chat with strangers.

One way to impress me is—know how to ride a horse.

It's lame, but I couldn't think of anything else. However, from the looks of the responses, no one's taking it seriously because they're all asking to ride me instead.

Great.

But when I see Harlow's message, I smile.

HARLOW
There's no way you thought that prompt was a good idea. If the girls are anything like the guys on here, 99% of them made it sexual.

WAYLON
You would be correct. I haven't even bothered to respond to them.

HARLOW
Can't be much worse than the reverse cowgirl comments I've gotten.

Only With Me

My jaw clenches.

WAYLON
So you've not been having much luck on here then?

HARLOW
Nope. A couple guys seemed nice but then turned it suggestive and I'm just not experienced enough to know how to play along. They end up ignoring or blocking me.

WAYLON
What do you mean not experienced enough? What the hell are they asking?

HARLOW
I've never had a boyfriend.

WAYLON
Okay?

HARLOW
Or kissed a guy.

What? I figured she didn't have an extensive dating history, but I would've never guessed she had...*none.*

It makes sense, though, because most of our texting conversations were genuine and innocent.

Minus the inside joke of her showing me her ass.

But that's what I liked about her.

Most girls who are interested in me never try to get to know me or engage in normal discussions. They just want me for sex. And because I was looking to block out my chaotic thoughts, I went along with it at the time.

WAYLON
Oh. Well then don't talk to those guys. I'm sure there are ones who aren't that way.

Except, probably not on dating apps.

Brooke Montgomery

> **HARLOW**
> Ha...yeah right. Even when they come across as nice, they eventually ask for a nude.

> **WAYLON**
> A nude pic?!

Oh fuck no.

> **HARLOW**
> Yep...I'm naive sometimes but not enough to send a naked pic of myself.

> **WAYLON**
> Good. Otherwise I'd have to give you the internet safety talk I just gave Bentley.

She sends me an eye roll emoji.

> **HARLOW**
> Oh like you've never sent a dick pic?

Why does her saying that make mine twitch? *Fuck, talking to her like this is a bad idea.*

> **WAYLON**
> We're not talking about me...we're talking about you.

> **HARLOW**
> Classic line of defense.

> **WAYLON**
> I just want you to be careful. There are a lot of creeps on these apps only looking for sex and some will do whatever it takes to get you into their beds.

> **HARLOW**
> Speaking of creeps, I'm honestly surprised to see you on here.

Only With Me

Chuckling at her effortless dig, I lean back against the couch, relieved that we've seemed to fall back into our easy conversation rhythm. Too bad she'll never know it was originally me.

> **WAYLON**
> Wow...you're funny.

HARLOW
I know. It's why I'm so unlikable.

> **WAYLON**
> You are not.
>
> Why are you surprised I'm on here?

HARLOW
Because I wouldn't have pegged you as the type who has trouble finding dates in the real world.

She's not wrong, but I'm not about to confess my sins on why I'm here.

> **WAYLON**
> I don't use these apps much. Kinda forgot I had them.

Mostly true.

HARLOW
Also surprised you're not out on New Year's Eve with your brother. Delilah told me she's "watching" him for the night.

> **WAYLON**
> I wasn't feeling it. Plus, I figured it wasn't a good idea to show my face in a place I just got kicked out of.

HARLOW
Speaking of that, how's your black eye and knuckles?

Brooke Montgomery

I stretch out my fingers, looking at the small cut.

> **WAYLON**
> Better than Jake's.

HARLOW

> Well, I'm glad neither of you ended up in the hospital. Not a fun place to be over the holidays.

No, it ain't.

> **WAYLON**
> How's your dad doing since his fall?

I should've asked earlier.

HARLOW
> He's hanging in there. Mostly miserable from his phantom pain but I've been trying to keep him occupied and his mind busy. Playing cards and board games, doing puzzles, reading him books, watching TV.

> **WAYLON**
> That's sweet of you.

HARLOW
> Yeah, but I think he's getting sick of me.

Now I'm the one laughing.

> **WAYLON**
> I don't think anyone could get sick of you.

HARLOW
> Really?

> **WAYLON**
> Yeah. How could they?

Only With Me

HARLOW

You don't ever seem excited when I'm around.

Shit. That stings.

WAYLON

Don't take it personally. I'm exhausted most days and keeping Wilder alive is a full-time job.

Both figuratively and literally.

HARLOW

I can understand that. I feel the same about my dad.

WAYLON

How so?

It's been years since I've seen Mr. Fanning, so I haven't stayed updated on him since Delilah and I broke up.

HARLOW

His mental health isn't great. Between his depression and pain, I'm always fearing the worst. When I first saw him unconscious on the bathroom floor, I assumed he was dead. I thought…yep, this is it. He's overdosed on pills or took something.

My heart jumps into my throat because I've been there too many times to count.

WAYLON

Damn, that's traumatic. I'm sorry you went through that. Unfortunately, I understand those fears all too well. Never gets easier either.

HARLOW

Nope, not in all the years since his accident but it got worse after I recovered. It was like as soon as I was back to "normal" he had nothing to live for anymore.

WAYLON

You gave meaning to his life during a time he felt like he had none. Now he needs to find a new meaning.

HARLOW

Sadly, I don't know that there is one besides his family, but he thinks he's a burden and that our lives would be easier without him. I always tell him he's wrong, but his mind is set on it.

WAYLON

He said that?

Damn, I can't imagine that's easy to hear from your own father.

HARLOW

A few times, usually during his darker moments when the pain has been nonstop for days and his meds aren't strong enough to help. Those are when my mom takes him to the ER for a morphine drip. It's stronger than pills but even if it's short-term relief, it's something to keep him off the ledge.

WAYLON

Fuck, that's a tough one. No one deserves to live that way. It's understandable he struggles mentally when you're constantly at war with your own body.

HARLOW

I know. I'm torn between begging him to fight to live and giving him my blessing to surrender. I can't imagine losing him, but it feels selfish to want him here when I know he's suffering.

Only With Me

> **WAYLON**
> Life can be so unfair sometimes. I think the best you can do is be there for him and love him as much as you can and it sounds like that's exactly what you're doing. You're not responsible for how he chooses to deal with the pain, but you can make sure he's not alone with it.

> **HARLOW**
> You're right. It's why I've been trying to keep him distracted from the pain as much as I can with activities. I even busted out my old paint set and we painted portraits of each other. They were both horrible and we laughed. But then it was ruined a couple minutes later when his pain got so intense it brought him to tears.

My heart aches for her. It's such a tough position to be in, and I wouldn't wish it upon anyone. Watching someone you love suffer and being helpless to stop or fix it is the worst.

> **WAYLON**
> Not to sound pushy on the topic, but does he see a psychiatrist for his mental health issues or a pain therapist?

> **HARLOW**
> He saw both the first three years but then got sick of going with no results—his words, not mine. Mom tried to talk him into going back but she got sick of fighting with him and let it go.

> **WAYLON**
> I know how that goes. Been trying to get Wilder to go to therapy for years so he can get the right medication for his depression, but he refuses. I've even offered to go with him, but he's so stuck on the stigma that he's too blinded to see how the benefits could outweigh it.

> **HARLOW**
> So we both have insufferable stubborn men in our lives...

> **WAYLON**
> Seems that way.

Grabbing my beer, I down the rest of it but then nearly choke when I read her next message.

> **HARLOW**
> A guy just messaged me and asked if my kitty cat was purring…I feel so dumb because I don't even know what that means?? I know kitty means pussy but what does purring mean?

Nothing in the world could've prepared me for that question. Or her so easily texting the word *pussy*.

> **WAYLON**
> It means he's a creep and you should block him.

> **HARLOW**
> Oh come on…tell me. No way I can Google it or ask him myself without looking stupid.

> **WAYLON**
> You really wanna know?

> **HARLOW**
> I wouldn't have asked if I didn't.

I sigh, blowing out a frustrated breath. At this point, she probably thinks of me like an older brother more than anything. No way she'd talk to me about guys she's chatting with if she saw me another way.

So fuck it. Might as well tell her.

> **WAYLON**
> He's asking if you're turned on. Ya know…purring like a cat in heat.

Only With Me

HARLOW

Oh God.

Okay, so while that makes sense, now he's asking if the kitty is thirsty? Thirsty for what...

Jesus Christ.
    She's gonna fucking kill me.

WAYLON

For his CUM, Harlow. He's asking if you want to fuck him.

HARLOW

I told you I was bad at this!

WAYLON

And I told you he was a creep.

HARLOW

Because he wants to fuck me?

I growl.

WAYLON

He wants to fuck anyone who will fuck him. Not the type of guy you should be with.

HARLOW

And what is my type?

WAYLON

I don't know but you have higher standards than that.

HARLOW

Maybe I wanna lose my virginity and get it over with so I don't sound like a prepubescent girl around these men.

WAYLON

Your first time should be special, not just some rando on a dating app looking to get his dick wet.

Brooke Montgomery

HARLOW
I'm tired of waiting.

WAYLON
You're only 20. You can't even buy alcohol, so I'd hardly say you've been "waiting" a long time.

HARLOW
And how old were you when you lost yours?

WAYLON
Again, we're not talking about me.

HARLOW
Was your first time "special"?

WAYLON
You don't want me answering that.

HARLOW
Why not? Tell me. I can handle it. I'm not a CHILD.

WAYLON
Harlow, drop it.

HARLOW
Why can't you just tell me how old you were?

WAYLON
Because it'll make things awkward so let's change the subject.

HARLOW
Or we could play hot and cold. I'll guess your age and you tell me if I'm getting close or not.

WAYLON
No.

HARLOW
15?

WAYLON
I'm not playing.

Only With Me

HARLOW
16?

WAYLON
Stop guessing.

HARLOW
17?

WAYLON
I'm not answering.

HARLOW
14?

WAYLON
No.

HARLOW
18??

Closing my eyes, I pinch the bridge of my nose and surrender.

WAYLON
20.

HARLOW
20?! No way. It's almost like…that's MY age. Which means I have to lose it before I'm 21 or I'm officially a loser.

WAYLON
Who'd think that?

HARLOW
Every man looking to hook up. I can't be 21 and tell them I've never had sex before. They'll know I'm inexperienced and won't be able to please them.

Brooke Montgomery

> **WAYLON**
> Not that I want to talk you into giving up your V-card to just anyone but most guys don't care about that. If they're into you, they'll respect your body and your boundaries enough to wait until you're ready.

> **HARLOW**
> Ugh, you sound like Delilah. Even though I know she was having sex before my age.

> **WAYLON**
> Then you know she's giving you advice based on experience and her wishing she hadn't rushed it.

> **HARLOW**
> Maybe…but let's backtrack to you being 20. That means you didn't have sex in high school. How's that possible? Didn't you and Wilder have the biggest manwhore reputations?

Of course that comes back to bite me in the ass over a decade later.

> **WAYLON**
> There's other stuff people can do that don't include penetration. Hooking up doesn't always mean sex.

> **HARLOW**
> Really? What does it mean then?

My head falls back against the couch in disbelief that I'm having this conversation with someone I *like* and having to pretend I don't in that way.

That'd be my damn luck.

But at this point, if this is the only way I get to talk to her, then I'll take it.

Consequences be damned.

Only With Me

> **WAYLON**
> It means getting each other off from touching or kissing down below. Could also be dry humping until you both come.

> **HARLOW**
> Ohh. Dry humping sounds fun. Does it feel better with the girl on top or the bottom?

I adjust myself because the more she talks about this, the more it's confusing my dick.

My jaw is also about to snap at how hard I'm grinding my teeth.

> **WAYLON**
> Both feel good but everyone has their own preferences.

> **HARLOW**
> What's yours?

Fuck me. How do I get out of this conversation without coming in my pants?

> **WAYLON**
> Uh...I guess I prefer the girl on top, straddling my lap and taking control. That way she can go as fast or slow as she needs to help her orgasm. And I can play with her nipples and kiss her neck easily to help her come harder.

And with that, I should burn my phone.

> **HARLOW**
> Jesus. See, now that's hot. Why can't these guys talk to me like that?

> **WAYLON**
> Because they're dipshits.

HARLOW

Clearly. One guy asked me how long it took to get myself off. I didn't know how to answer, so I lied and said five minutes.

I furrow my brow, confused.

WAYLON

Why would you have to lie about that?

HARLOW

Because I've never been able to.

WAYLON

Not even with a vibrator?

HARLOW

You think I have a toy? Please. I wouldn't even know where to buy one.

Holy fuck, she really is pure and innocent to the core.

WAYLON

There's only like a dozen sex shops within a fifty-mile radius and hundreds of online ones.

HARLOW

I'm not gonna order one to my house! I would die of embarrassment if my parents saw that. Perks of living at home.

I laugh at her upside-down smiley emoji.

WAYLON

I guess you'll have to use your hand like the rest of us mortals.

HARLOW

Ha! I've tried...I just don't know what I'm doing. Maybe you can teach me?

I blink twice to make sure I read that correctly.

Only With Me

> **WAYLON**
>
> Teach you? How?

HARLOW

Tell me what to do so I can get myself off. That way I don't have to risk my mother opening a package with a sex toy inside.

> **WAYLON**
>
> I don't know if that's a good idea.

HARLOW

Why not? Save me from the humiliation of my father somehow finding a rubber penis in the house.

Christ. I can't believe I'm about to agree to this…

> **WAYLON**
>
> Fine. But only because I don't want to give your old man a heart attack.

HARLOW

On behalf of my family, we thank you for your service.

I snort at her salute emoji.

> **WAYLON**
>
> Put two fingers together and then rub circles over your clit. Play around with the pressure and speed to see what you like or what helps get you there. You can also thrust them inside yourself and when you're nice and wet, rub the pad of your thumb over your clit to help you finish.

When she doesn't respond immediately like she has all night, I panic.

Oh God.

That was fucking creepy, wasn't it?

She's gonna think I'm a sicko.

Brooke Montgomery

I bang my head against the back of the sofa until she finally replies three minutes later.

> **HARLOW**
> Wow, that almost worked. I got close but like... lost the sensation? But that was helpful, so thank you. I'll keep trying.

How is she talking about masturbating so freely like we're discussing the weather? This is a new one, even for me.

> **WAYLON**
> Sure, no problem.

Because what else am I gonna say?

> **HARLOW**
> My friend Natalie says that it sometimes helps when a guy dirty talks you through it. Is that true?

> **WAYLON**
> Yeah, that can help elevate the fantasy of someone else touching you.

> **HARLOW**
> Okay, so I just need to find a guy who will voice or video chat while I try to give myself an orgasm.

> **WAYLON**
> I'll do it.

Fuck, why did I just volunteer?
Because I don't want anyone else to do it with her.

> **HARLOW**
> Really? Do you want to now?

NOW?
I'm seconds away from coming in my pants as it is.

180

Only With Me

WAYLON
Okay, sure.

HARLOW
Great, I'll video call you in a few...

How the hell am I going to compose myself and not completely lose it when she moans to the sound of my voice?

The simple answer is, I'm *not*.

Chapter Seventeen
Harlow

I've never been more turned on in my life and it should freak me out that Waylon's the guy on the other line, but it doesn't.

I feel safe with him.

Secure. *Somewhat* confident.

Maybe a *little* wrong because of who he is.

But he doesn't make me feel stupid for not knowing about sex and orgasms.

Even though I was a little surprised to see him on CowboyMatch, I was also relieved that I'd have someone to talk to about dating.

Maybe it's because we're not face-to-face, but he's easy to talk to. We've never chatted this much in all the years I've known him, but it's like we've been friends for ages.

And his voice…deep and rough…but somehow soothing at the same time.

A girl could get used to this.

"This'll be easier for you without bottoms and panties," he says sheepishly, but he's right.

His room is bathed in darkness, minus a dim light coming from the opposite side, so I can't see all of his face, but I can tell he's staring at me intently.

Only With Me

I shuffle under the covers, removing my PJ shorts and underwear, then get my blankets back in place.

"Okay, done."

"Put the phone close to your ear so it feels like I'm next to you," he orders.

"Okay," I say breathlessly, moving it up to my pillow and no longer able to see him.

"How's my voice? Too quiet?"

"No, it's perfect," I whisper.

And although it feels more intimate this way, it's a game changer compared to when I'm alone.

"Good. I'm gonna start talkin' you through it now. Are you ready?"

God, yes. "Yep."

We've barely started and my body's already buzzing. The anticipation has me both nervous and excited.

"I want you to spread your legs and put your hand between them. Rub two fingers in a steady circle over your clit."

Quickly doing as he said, I put my middle and ring finger between my folds.

I've tried going solo plenty of times, but it's much more thrilling now that I have someone telling me what to do.

"How's it feel?" he asks after I release an intense breath.

"Good…really…nice," I pant between each word.

"Once your clit is aching, slide your hand down and thrust a finger inside your pussy. And then when you're ready, add a second one."

It's so hot hearing him give me instructions. I wish I could record him because his demanding voice would be on repeat.

"Okay," I whisper, doing exactly as he says.

"Are you wet down there?"

"Yes." *Much more than usual.*

I swear he hisses after I hear him shuffling around.

"Tell me how it feels."

"A little weird, but I like it."

"Bend your legs at the knees so you can fill that tight cunt deeper."

Jesus Christ. His filthy mouth is my new obsession.

Once I have, I insert two fingers back in and gasp at how far I can go. My walls squeeze them when I move in and out.

"That's..." Unable to finish my sentence, a groan vibrates against my chest.

Undoubtedly, he can hear how wet I am now.

"Your body responds so well, Harlow." He swallows hard, and I wonder if he's as affected as I am right now. "Keep fucking yourself until your fingers are drownin' in your arousal."

"They're so wet right now," I tell him.

"Perfect. Now increase your speed."

"Oh my God..." My chest rises and falls rapidly at the intense warmth brewing low in my abdomen.

"Think you can add a third?"

"I don't think so. It's so tight and full."

Waylon's breathing picks up as if he's restraining himself.

"That's okay. Try curling 'em up inside, like a hook."

I prop up on one elbow as I try to reach farther but can't quite do it. "I think I need longer arms."

His breathy chuckle has my core tightening. "That's okay. Drag the wetness from your pussy up your slit and then rub it over your clit until more pressure builds."

His voice strains as he tells me what to do and it makes me more eager to come. I want to do this for him, too.

"Okay."

"And this time I wanna hear you moan, Harlow. The more responsive and louder you are, the more your body releases oxytocin to help you finish. Guys also like hearing it, so unless you haveta stay quiet, don't hold back."

All of my senses are on fire knowing he's listening to my reactions.

"Got it."

Only With Me

Once my fingers find my clit again, I move them in a circular motion and find the perfect pressure. My mouth spills open and a moan echoes around me.

"Good girl," he praises. "Keep your eyes closed and focus on my voice."

"I am."

"The trick to finishin' with self-pleasure is fantasizing about someone else being there, touchin' you, kissin' your neck, makin' you feel good. Play into your senses to build an intense orgasm."

"How?" I ask, my back arching as the pleasure increases.

"Listen to my voice and imagine I'm there. My hands on you. My lips on your skin. My breath mixin' with yours."

"God, yes. I think I'm close…" My legs stiffen and my breathing intensifies as I climb closer to the ledge.

"Continue your steady rhythm and keep going. Don't stop."

My free hand cups my breast over my shirt, imagining it's him so I don't lose the sensation.

My breath catches as the pleasure starts to take over. Slowly and gradually, a feeling I've never had before shoots down my spine and lingers in my core.

"Yes, yes…*fuck*…" I groan out the words, gasping for air as the orgasm takes over my body.

"That's it. Keep going, baby," he encourages. "I'm right here with you."

Baby? That does it for me.

I muffle my screams with my other hand and my back flies off the bed as the explosion rips through me. My screams turn to moans and then I give in to the pleasure, no longer caring how loud I am.

And I swear, I hear Waylon groaning through the phone.

"Fuck, you did it," he says once I go quiet.

"I've never been able to do that before," I say in between catching my breath. "You feel that every time you orgasm?"

"Yeah. It's even better when it's with someone else."

I shift to my side and prop up the phone so he can see me again. "I can't imagine that. No wonder people get addicted. I wanna experience that over and over again."

He chuckles softly, moving slightly so I can see the shadows over his face. "How do you feel now that you have?"

"Boneless and euphoric. Like I could sleep for ten hours straight."

He scratches his cheek. "Sounds about right."

"But I'm afraid it's gonna hurt the first time I have sex," I admit.

"It might, a little. But if your partner knows what they're doing, you should only feel some tightness and discomfort in the beginning. If you're wet and relaxed, it'll reduce the pain."

"So lots of foreplay?"

"Yes, lots."

"Does that include for him, too?"

He lifts a shoulder. "It can, yes. But it's most important for you, especially when it's your first or even second time."

I sigh, holding up my head with my palm. "I wanna do it again."

He bellows out a laugh. "Well, you can do it as much as you want now that you know what to do."

"I dunno if I'll be able to do it on my own, but I'll haveta try later."

"You'll get better at it...the more you do it."

"And I'm willing to bet the same goes for sex, right? I'm probably gonna be bad and awkward my first time."

"I doubt it. Just tell your partner what you need and don't be afraid to tell him to slow down or give you more time. Communication is key."

"Have you ever taken someone's virginity?"

It's hard to be sure in this light, but I swear his cheeks turn red.

"Uh, yeah. After I lost mine, I dated around and took a few others."

Only With Me

"A few?" I shriek. "No wonder you're good at this."

"At what?"

"Knowin' what a woman's needs are and being able to talk me through it. I assume most guys couldn't or wouldn't be able to successfully."

"Most are too lazy," he retorts. "Or they don't care."

"So now I just need to figure out which guys are worthy of my V-card." I snort because that's going to be easier said than done. "Sounds truly awful now that I'm thinkin' about it."

"Welcome to the dating world." His jaw clenches and I wonder if he's over talking about this.

"Is that why you're still single after all these years? You didn't wanna put in the effort anymore?"

"I didn't wanna get my heart broken again," he clarifies, sadness coating his voice. "Not only that, but my mental health wasn't great after Wilder's hospitalization. It's a miracle Delilah put up with me for those two years because I was always worryin' and would drag her out with me so I could keep an eye on him. It doesn't seem fair to put someone else through that, especially since I knew she had you and your dad to think about, too."

"I understand being a package deal. Whoever I end up dating or having a serious relationship with has to be okay with me being accessible to my dad and regularly checkin' in on him. I can't imagine every guy would be supportive of that."

"Sadly, you're right. People can be selfish and manipulative. They don't always show their true colors right away either. They'll do whatever it takes to get you, but they'll slowly reveal who they are by gaslightin' you or makin' you pick between them and your family."

"Wow, you're givin' me so much hope right now," I deadpan.

He lifts a shoulder, a sincere grin on his face. "Now you understand why datin' is hard. It ain't all flowers and candlelight dinners."

"Okay, but that sounds so sweet," I coo. "I'm addin' that to my romance wish list."

He noticeably stiffens before his shoulders fall again. "What's that?"

"A list of things I wanna experience in a relationship. Most are cute little gestures like that. Some are date night ideas."

"Whaddya have on there so far?"

I suck in my lips. "I can't tell you that."

He tilts his head. "I just taught you how to orgasm but sharing *that* is off-limits?"

Giggling, I shrug. "Some of it is personal—things I doubt would ever happen. But I'll tell you a few of the others."

"Okay, I'll take what I can get."

"Good." I smirk, then pull up my notes app where I keep a list. "A couple's massage. Not only does it sound super relaxing, but it feels like it'd be a fun bonding experience."

"Hell, I could use a massage. Let's go."

"Ha! Okay, another one is fruit pickin' and then baking a pie together with the fruit. My mama loves to bake, and it'd be cool to learn that with someone special, too."

"Strawberry or apple pie sounds delicious," he mocks.

"I agree."

"What else?"

"Hmm...let's see." I read over my list, wondering if I should share the ones I told Mystery Guy but then decide not to. "Horseback riding in the snowy mountains, a picnic in the sky while in a hot-air balloon, a cross country road trip, singing karaoke in a country bar, reading at the beach together except we read the letters we wrote to each other on our one-year dating anniversary, reenacting my favorite scene from *The Notebook*..." I list off and then wait for his reactions.

"Which scene?" he asks.

"You've seen the movie?"

"Of course."

"Then guess."

"Alright..." he drawls. "The one where Ryan Gosling says if she's a bird, then he's a bird, too."

Only With Me

"Good guess, but nope."

"The Ferris wheel scene where he's beggin' her to go on a date with him?"

"That's dangerous! I'd never risk that."

He snickers. "Had to check."

"It's the rain scene," I tell him. "Where they're fightin' about the letters and they kiss, then it leads to hot make-up sex. But mostly the kissin' in the rain part."

"Interestin' choice."

"See, you think I'm weird."

"Nope, not at all. Datin' you would never get boring, that's for sure."

"I'm gonna take that as a compliment."

He licks his bottom lip. "As you should."

"Do you have date ideas you wanna do before you get married?"

"I'm not sure I'll be gettin' married anytime soon. But I have non-negotiables that would make or break a relationship I'm in."

"Ooh, let's hear 'em. Maybe I'll haveta steal some for myself." I make a new note and type out the title at the top. "Okay, I'm ready."

He shakes his head, chuckling. "Alright, uhh...the top one is family comes first. If any of my siblings text an SOS, I drop everything and go. So if my girlfriend can't understand that, then we'd break up."

"That's a good one. Mine would be the same because I immediately go if anyone in my family needs me, especially if it's for my dad."

"Another is them having to be okay with me leavin' in the middle of the night to pick up Wilder. His number is programmed so it rings even when my phone's on silent. My partner would also haveta understand we have a special twin bond, and if he's hurting, I'll most likely feel it."

"Damn. So when he's depressed or in pain, you always know?"

"Yeah. Been that way for as long as I can remember."

"I think that's reasonable, honestly. Any more on your list?"

"Just one."

I meet his gaze through the screen. "What's that?"

"They have to scrapbook with my family on Sunday nights."

My lips spread into a wide smile. "That sounds like a fun tradition."

"It can be...I don't stay every week, but I try to at least once a month."

"How do I get invited?" I tease.

"You gotta marry a Hollis."

My brow arches. "Any Hollis?"

"Any of 'em that are available."

"Well, I don't see Wilder as the marryin' type—unless he's literally dragged down the aisle—so I guess I'll haveta somehow beg you so I can join."

"It wouldn't take that much to convince me," he mumbles almost too quietly for me to hear him.

"Oh? What're you doin' next weekend?" I quip.

He snorts. "What I always do...work and keep an eye on Wilder."

"He can be your best man, and we'll handcuff him to Delilah so he can't get into any trouble."

He barks out a deep laugh. "Trust me, he'd find a way to drag your sister into his madness."

"That's probably true. Have you heard from either of 'em tonight?"

His finger swipes over the screen, so I assume he's checking his texts. "Nope. Probably won't for another couple hours."

"And you're stayin' up until he's home?"

"Yep," he says, not looking at all amused about it.

We've already talked through the midnight celebration like it was nothing. But when I yawn, he notices.

"You should get some sleep. No point in you stayin' up too."

Only With Me

"I don't mind. I'm off work tomorrow anyway."

"I'm not."

"Whaddya have to do?"

"Muck stalls, disperse straw and feed, fill water buckets, check the water troughs, make sure the barn is picked up. It'll be an easy day since there are no tours, but something always comes up. Someone else will need help or a disaster will happen. A fence post needs replacing, a tractor or four-wheeler needs repairs…you name it."

"No wonder y'all stay busy."

"Pretty much every day."

"Not complainin' about your long hours should be one of your non-negotiables or they might start givin' ya a hard time about it."

"Valid point. I'll add it." He taps his temple. "Girls always wanna date a cowboy until they realize how much they're not home."

"When my dad worked on a farm, I remember there'd be specific times of the year where he'd be gone before I left for school and wouldn't be home until after I was in bed. Mama would keep his plate in the oven and stay up to warm it for him."

"Sounds right. Especially durin' the summer."

"He'd try to make it up to us on the one weekend a month he had off. Mama would cram as much family stuff as she could into those two days," I say with a laugh, remembering how chaotic things would be. "By Sunday nights, I'd be exhausted."

"At least y'all understood. It ain't for the faint of heart."

"Is it fun workin' on your family's ranch with your parents and siblings? You probably get to see 'em all the time, right?"

"Yeah, it's fun most days. But it's easy to get sick of each other, too."

We continue talking for a few more hours, moving effortlessly from topic to topic, and before I realize, it's after three in the morning.

"Your sister just texted. She's on her way to drop off Wilder."

"Did she say how drunk he is?"

"Uh…I assume somewhere between him thinking he can ride the mechanical bull for eight seconds and being passed out on the sidewalk. Which means he's at least half asleep."

"I can't believe how late we stayed up. I'm ready to pass out, too."

"Same. But you helped the time fly by, so I'm ain't complainin'."

"Me neither. It was fun. And I learned a lot." I giggle, my cheeks heating. I'm still in disbelief he volunteered. "Thanks again for helpin' me."

"Sure…"

"I'll talk to you soon," I hesitate, almost like a question.

"Yeah, for sure."

"Okay, good night."

"Night, Harlow."

As soon as I end the call, I'm mentally kicking and screaming.

I know I shouldn't crush on him, but it's impossible when he's this sweet and nice.

But it'd never be possible. For so many reasons…

1. He's twelve years older and is probably looking for a wife

2. He's way more experienced than me, so he'd have to literally teach me how to please him in the bedroom (no guy wants to do that, right?)

3. He sees me like a little sister or at the very least only a friend

4. He's Delilah's ex, which means she's already slept with him

5. See number four

Delilah would freak out if she ever found out what Waylon and I did tonight. Texting is one thing, but he helped me orgasm over the phone and talked to me in a way I've never experienced before. She might've forgiven him for "cheating" years ago, but hooking up with her little sister would be unforgivable.

Even on the off chance he was into me, we'd have to keep it a secret, and then what's the point?

Only With Me

I wouldn't want to risk our relationship either.

It's better not to even think anything more could happen between us, but I can still enjoy him teaching me things, if he's even up for it after tonight. It'd be nice to get tips before I go on a first date with someone.

Assuming I can even get one.

Chapter Eighteen
Waylon

"Way-Way…" Wilder drawls, walking sideways out of Delilah's truck. "You missed a goooood party."

"I'm sure," I deadpan, though I had a much better night staying home.

Delilah's arm wraps around his waist, heading toward the stairs, but at this rate, he's going to trip and bring them both down.

"I'll grab him." I push off my doorframe and take her place. "Thank you again for keepin' an eye on him. Appreciate it."

She licks her lips and brushes a sweaty strand of hair off her face. "No problem. He was on his *best* behavior."

I snort. "That'd be a first."

She walks behind us as I help Wilder upstairs, and eventually, I get him through the door. He stumbles into the living room, then drops to the sofa and kicks up his feet.

"You gonna sleep here with your clothes and boots on?"

"Wouldn't be the first time," he mumbles, already drifting off to sleep.

Sighing, I grab his hand and pull him up to his full height. "C'mon, go to your bed so you don't wake up with a stiff back. We're not spring chickens anymore."

Only With Me

"I saw your buddy Teddy," he mumbles.

I roll my eyes. "You mean Jake?"

He laughs at himself. "Yeah, him. You gave him a nice shiner."

"And I'll give him another if he goes near you."

"Don't worry, she told him off and to get lost before he could even speak to me." He sighs. "Not that I planned to anyway."

Delilah giggles, following as I direct Wilder where to go. Glancing back at her, I mouth, "Thank you."

"I'm gonna marry her..." he drunkenly announces before plopping down on his bed with his shoes on the floor.

"Who?" I ask.

"*Delly*..." he singsongs, then points to her standing next to me.

That's a new nickname I've never heard before.

Shaking my head, I kneel to untie his boots. "I don't think so."

"Why not?" he asks, his tone tripping with offense.

"Because she's my ex-girlfriend."

I almost feel bad saying that, considering what I did with her little sister tonight. If I'm not allowed to date Harlow, he's not allowed to date my ex.

Except Delilah would never be interested in him anyway, so there's no use in hurting his feelings.

He scoffs. "So what?"

"So you're too much of a handful as it is and she has enough on her plate," I say, removing one boot and then going to the other.

"You're the one who said it was my fault you have no datin' life because I'm *too much work*, so if I get married, I'm no longer your problem."

"I didn't say you were too much work."

Not in those exact words anyway.

"And you should focus on yourself before gettin' a wife," I tell him, taking off the second boot.

"We're not gettin' any younger..." he drones. "You said it — we're not fall chickens."

Standing, I pull him into a sitting position and lift his shirt, then yank it over his head.

"*Spring* chickens," I clarify.

"Yeah, that." He drops back on the mattress.

"Women don't like comin' home to husbands who drink themselves stupid. So until then, you can't get married."

"That's not fair!" He pouts like a prepubescent child. "Plus, I'm not even drunk…" He attempts to wiggle out of his jeans without undoing the button. "And fine, I'll quit if it means you'll lemme get married."

I stifle a laugh at how ridiculous this conversation is. "Please do."

"And then she'll marry me." He throws his pants, leaving him in his boxer briefs. "Right, Delly baby?"

"*Baby?*" I look between them.

"Sorry, I don't marry men who wear red briefs," she quips.

When I glance back at her, I can tell she's toying with him.

To be fair, he makes it too easy. Especially when he's wasted.

"Nadda problem. I'll take 'em off." His hands go to his waist, and I quickly stop him.

"Dude, no. Wait until I'm outta here."

"Me too," Delilah adds.

"Don't ya wanna see my new tattoo and piercing?" He waggles his brows with half-open eyelids. "They're under the briefs…"

I pinch the bridge of my nose at his taunting voice. "Jesus Christ. Just get under the covers and go to sleep," I beg.

I find his phone in the pocket of his jeans and set his alarm. "You get six hours and then your ass better meet me in the barn."

Pulling back the covers, I motion for him to get under, and he finally does.

"I'll be there at noon," he confirms, collapsing against his pillows.

"*Ten*," I counter. "I wanna be done by noon."

"Then you won't even need me by the time I get there."

Only With Me

I blow out a frustrated breath because it's not even worth arguing with him. "Shut up and go to sleep."

"There's room in my bed if you wanna snuggle, Delly."

"As temptin' as that is, I prefer wakin' up without vomit all over me."

Her snarky response causes me to laugh. "Damn, you're brutal."

"I gotta be to handle him." She waves toward him and by the time I look back at him, he's already snoring.

"Well, I'll walk ya out."

I flick off the lights and close the door behind us.

Once we're at the driver's side of her truck, I open the door for her. "Did you at least get to enjoy your night?"

She nods, smiling. "Wilder knows how to have a good time and he made sure I did, too. He rode the bull and made it six seconds."

I stuff my hands in my pockets and grin. "Wow, he's gettin' better."

She snickers. "I know he's a party animal and has a lot of growin' up to do, but he was mostly a gentleman all night."

"Well, that's somewhat reassurin'."

The air grows tense between us.

Delilah and I rarely talk, and it's never just the two of us.

"You must be tired. Are you okay to drive home? I have a couch you could crash on…"

"Nah, I'm fine." She jumps into the seat and starts the engine. "I switched to water at one and then I had a Red Bull before we left."

"Thank you again, *Delly*. I owe ya one."

"You sure do, *Way-Way*."

Brooke Montgomery

My alarm goes off way too fucking soon. I roll over and hit the snooze, grumbling at the sun beaming through my blinds.

Even though I went to bed at four, I slept better than I have in a long time.

And woke up with Harlow on my mind.

I knew I missed talking to her but getting to chat the way we did last night makes me realize just how much I depended on seeing her messages every day. They always made me smile and excited for the next one.

This morning's no different. My chest squeezes at the memory of hearing her moan and orgasming to my voice. I've never done anything like that before, but I can't wait to do it again.

Hopefully with her moaning *my* name.

She was so open and honest about wanting to learn, and honestly, it was refreshing to talk to someone so vulnerable. It made me feel like I could be, too.

It was impossible not to be turned on as she obeyed my commands. The more she followed instructions, the harder I got. It was the hottest thing I've ever experienced on the phone.

She was so eager to learn and do as I say, my cock was nearly busting through my zipper by the time she was finger-fucking her pussy and telling me how wet she was.

I couldn't get enough of it.

Between talking her through it and hearing her breathy moans, I couldn't hold back anymore. I lowered my jeans and stroked my shaft until I came all over myself at the same time she finished.

I doubt she realized it, though, since she's never been with a

Only With Me

guy to know how badly I was struggling to speak. I had to put her on mute for a few seconds so she didn't hear me.

However, I'm surprised she didn't call me out for calling her *baby*. That slipped out by accident, but she didn't seem to notice.

Even though I have no claim to her, I hate the thought of her talking to other guys. She sees me as a friend, a *teacher* even, but I know if she knew I was the guy from the group chat, she'd think differently.

The more I think about last night and how easy it was talking to her, even before we got on video chat, the more I want to do it again and want her to do that only with me.

Instead of getting ready for work like I normally would after my alarm goes off, I decide to shower and deal with this erection that won't go away. Thinking of her first thing in the morning has my cock hard and needy. The last thing I should be imagining is her in my bed or how I'd worship her body and take her virginity, but here we are, jerking off in the shower to those very thoughts.

As I fuck my fist to the memories of her soft whimpers and her telling me exactly how it feels, the tighter I squeeze. The tip is red and desperate, badly needing a release, and my thighs burn with tense muscles. I flatten my palm against the wall, aggressively abusing my cock, and come harder than I have in years.

Except this time when I moan through my release, it's with her name on the tip of my tongue.

Brooke Montgomery

> **HARLOW**
> I have a sex question.

The corners of my lips curve up when I get the notification she's messaged me through the app.

I've been off work for a few hours and sitting on my couch with a beer, trying to come up with any reason to message her first.

Thank God she doesn't overthink like me.

> **WAYLON**
> Okay, shoot.

> **HARLOW**
> Do men think scars are gross? I'm concerned mine could turn someone off during sex because they're on my upper thighs, the sides of my chest, and abdomen. Granted, most are faded, but if their faces are all up in there, it's likely they'll see or at the very least, feel them.

The fuck? Who made her worry about that?

> **HARLOW**
> Also, Happy New Year's Day! Hope you got a little sleep after waiting up for Wilder. Delilah told me she didn't get home until almost four-thirty.

The drastic change from one message to another gives me whiplash, but I send her separate replies anyway.

> **WAYLON**
> First, any guy who comments about body scarring is a piece of shit and shouldn't be anywhere near your naked body anyway. Second, if they can't understand the trauma you went through and how you survived against many odds, again, they shouldn't be anywhere near you.

Only With Me

> **WAYLON**
> Also, I got about five and a half hours, so about normal. How about you?

HARLOW

After the first and unarguably best orgasm of my life, I slept for nine hours.

Fuck me.

HARLOW

That's a relief to hear. It was just something I was thinking about and wondered if I should warn a guy first. Like a piercing…I'd wanna know if they have a Prince Albert ring beforehand.

> **WAYLON**
> Did you Google that?

HARLOW

Yep, after Natalie mentioned the various piercings men can have down there, I got curious.

Of course she did.

> **WAYLON**
> And did you look at the images?

HARLOW

Unfortunately, yes I did.

> **WAYLON**
> You're comparing a piercing someone got on purpose to scars on your body during an assault…so not the same thing. A piercing affects a woman during sex, so it would make sense you'd wanna know. But your scars have no effect on a man. They don't need to know unless you want them to but it shouldn't deter a guy wanting to be with you if he's a decent person.

Brooke Montgomery

I hate that in reassuring her, I'm also giving her pointers on finding a worthy man to lose her virginity to because in my eyes no one is deserving.

> **HARLOW**
> But it could be considered unattractive, right?

I bite my cheek because she's right—some superficial men would have issues with it—but I don't want her to feel insecure about any inch of herself. Harlow's perfect and beautiful, and I love how she's not jaded about relationships—yet.

> **WAYLON**
> Yes, just like anything else about a person. Everyone has preferences. What I find attractive, someone else might not, and vice versa.

> **HARLOW**
> What's your opinion about them?

Jesus Christ, she's making it harder to act unaffected.

> **WAYLON**
> It doesn't bother me. I'd probably make an effort to kiss them and reassure her how much they don't bother me.

> **HARLOW**
> That would make me melt like butter.

I chuckle.

> **WAYLON**
> That's the point. We all have imperfections, no use trying to hide what makes you special and unique.

Only With Me

HARLOW

I don't think I'm ready to tell just anyone what happened to me. I was talking to this one guy, as a friend, before I signed up for this app, and even after a month of texting, I never told him. Kinda glad I didn't because the day we were supposed to finally meet in person, the day you and I ran into each other at The Grindhouse, he stood me up. He texted later apologizing because he had a work thing come up, but then said he didn't think rescheduling was a good idea. I haven't talked to him since. I keep wondering what I did to make him ghost me.

And there it is.

Fuck.

I unintentionally made her insecure and now I need to do whatever I can to fix it.

WAYLON

It's perfectly normal to want to protect yourself. Sharing that part of your life, the worst moment you've ever experienced, isn't exactly a first date conversation. And even if you have sex before you share what happened to you, a guy should always respect your body and your boundaries.

God, I sound like an old youth minister.

No wonder she has no interest in me when I give her "the talk" like a father would.

HARLOW

I don't know that I'd be able to tell anyone exactly what happened without it giving me an anxiety attack. I had nightmares for years.

WAYLON

Do you still?

HARLOW

I hadn't for a long time until a month ago.

> **WAYLON**
>
> Just out of the blue?

> **HARLOW**
>
> Yes, well…kinda. He's up for probation soon and I'm anxious he'll get it.

Holy fuck, already?
He deserved way more time than he got.

> **WAYLON**
>
> When do you find out if he'll be released?

> **HARLOW**
>
> I check his case every week, but I think our lawyer would inform us on the exact date if he does.

> **WAYLON**
>
> I hope you plan to get a protective order from him right away.

> **HARLOW**
>
> That's always been the plan. But the scary thing is, I don't know who the other two accomplices were. They all wore masks. Three teenage boys broke in and when I came out with a bat, two of them ran off and were never caught. The other, well, he's the one behind bars.

I'm furious just thinking about what this punk did to her and even more now that I know he could be back on the streets soon.

> **WAYLON**
>
> I wish I had some comforting words to say but I don't blame you for having those fears. I'd put all three in the hospital if I knew who the other two were.

> **HARLOW**
>
> You know, violence is never the answer

Only With Me

WAYLON

> It is when they tried to kill a teenage girl.

HARLOW

> To keep from a complete meltdown, I've convinced myself that the other two were bad kids and are probably in prison for other crimes. There's no way my house was their first and only attempt.

WAYLON

> I would be surprised if it was, too, but it's possible they don't even live around here. They'd be in their mid-twenties now. They could be anywhere.

HARLOW

> Hopefully nowhere near me.

God save their souls if they ever come near her again.

Chapter Nineteen
Harlow

> **HARLOW**
> What feels better for a guy? Jerking off or having someone else do it? And then do men prefer a woman's mouth or hand more?

> **WAYLON**
> Harlow…it's seven in the morning.

> **HARLOW**
> Oh, shit. Were you sleeping? Sorry!

> **WAYLON**
> Physically, no. Mentally, yes.

> **HARLOW**
> I thought you were up at like 5.

> **WAYLON**
> 5:30-6ish.

> **HARLOW**
> Okay, so you've been up for over an hour. What's the problem?

Only With Me

WAYLON

I don't usually talk about blow jobs before noon. Especially on a Monday.

I roll my eyes because I know he's messing with me.

We've been talking every day, all day, for the past week and it's been a lot of fun. Way better than having to Google or read through Reddit forums. But we've also talked about other stuff, some more personal, and some simple like our favorite movies and artists.

It's made the anxiety about the incident go away and my attacker's potential probation.

Even more so now that I found out he was denied probation. There were added pending charges to his case that weren't there before. When I looked up the codes, they were for assault with a deadly weapon and attempted murder. I can only assume without asking my lawyer to look into it that he must've been in a prison fight, perhaps with a shank, and it must've been bad enough that they're adding time to his existing time.

Thank God.

I won't know for sure until he gets sentenced, but it was enough of a relief not to stress about it in the meantime.

Safe to say, I've been in a great mood for several reasons.

HARLOW

I might have more questions by then.

WAYLON

I have no doubt.

Guys like being touched anywhere, in any variety. We're not picky.

HARLOW

Will you show me?

WAYLON

Show you what?

HARLOW

How you jerk off…like the movements and what feels good. I imagine there's some kind of rhythm to it…I want to see how guys touch themselves so I know what they like.

WAYLON

You want to watch me come?

HARLOW

Yeah…you watched me.

WAYLON

Technically, I didn't. I only heard you.

HARLOW

Well you weren't the one learning, so you didn't need to. If it makes you uncomfortable, you can use a banana to demonstrate.

WAYLON

Jesus Christ.

I laugh because I can hear his annoyed voice in my head.

HARLOW

Or I'll get a banana and you tell me what to do.

WAYLON

No banana.

HARLOW

What about a cucumber?

WAYLON

No.

HARLOW

An eggplant? 🍆

WAYLON

The fuck? No.

Only With Me

HARLOW
Then WHAT??

WAYLON
I'll show you on myself.

I do a little happy dance in my bed because I knew he'd cave.

HARLOW
Great. When?

WAYLON
When do you need to learn by?

HARLOW
Well, I have a date on Friday afternoon at the cafe.

I've been talking to this guy from the app, Emery. Since I need the experience and figured there was no harm in it, I agreed. He's a few years older and prefers getting to know someone in person, so we've only been texting a little here and there.

But I'm only teasing about needing to learn by then. No way I'm touching anyone's dick on the first date.

But I enjoy Waylon's reactions too much not to mess with him.

Except, when he doesn't respond after an hour, I message him again in case he got busy at work and forgot.

HARLOW
Are you free tonight?

It takes him twenty more minutes, but he finally responds.

WAYLON
Sure. How's 8?

HARLOW
Works for me.

Last Thursday during Natalie's and my weekly virtual hangout, we spent most of the time catching up and her squealing at everything I told her about Waylon.

She claims he must like me because no other guy would "teach" a girl how to masturbate and answer all my questions. But I told her she was crazy because Waylon doesn't see me that way. If he did, there's no way he'd be okay with me talking about dating other guys and wanting to learn so I can hook up with them.

But when I told her I wasn't having much luck on the app, she told me about the "emoji test."

"Send them one emoji—completely random, it doesn't have to be anything specific—and see how they respond. If they play along and send one back, they're worth talkin' to. If they reply with something snarky or rude, block. No more wastin' your time."

I figured I had nothing to lose at this point. Almost every guy I've started a conversation with ended in ghosting me or I blocked them for being a creep.

So when Emery responded to my prompt, I replied with a duck emoji.

He responded with a goose.

Then I sent a turtle.

He replied with a fish.

But then I sent an eagle with a fish.

Finally, he broke the emoji battle and said I'd won because my eagle ate his fish.

I found it humorous enough to give him thirty minutes of my time to chat. The following day, another thirty minutes. And then yesterday, he asked to meet in person.

Since I'll only go to public places, I suggested The Grindhouse. It's the one place in Sugarland Creek that won't put on a lot of pressure to sit through a whole meal. If things go well, maybe he'll ask me out for a second date. Until then, meeting over coffee will do.

Only With Me

Admittedly, I'm not overly excited about it. Mostly because I don't know that much about him. However, he seems cool enough and looks cute in his photos to at least give him a chance. Even if we're not compatible, it'll be nice to get experience to find out what is or isn't my type.

HARLOW
> I have my session with Noah at three. You wanna come watch?

I only had one last week, with the holiday, but went out on my days off to ride Piper. The weather has been in the forties and fifties, and even dropping to the thirties at night, but if I don't get out of my house when I'm not working, I'll go stir crazy. My seasonal depression comes out in full force and although it's been better than when I was diagnosed with it years ago, I know I need to keep myself busy during the winter so I don't become a hermit in my bed.

However, Moose very much enjoys it when I do.

WAYLON
We start getting the trail horses ready for the afternoon tour around 3:30, but if I can, I'll swing by for a few.

HARLOW
> Okay, cool. When are you bringing Bentley to the ranch again?

WAYLON
Saturday afternoon. Why?

HARLOW
> Thought it might be cool to hang out with him again. Maybe the three of us can go riding.

WAYLON
He's a little young for you, don't you think?

Brooke Montgomery

HARLOW
Very funny, you sicko. I thought he'd enjoy riding up the mountains, especially with the snowcaps. It'd be a beautiful view.

WAYLON
I'm sure he would. I'll ask him.

HARLOW
Just don't let me fall on my ass again. I bruise easily as it is.

WAYLON
I won't.

HARLOW
Okay, I'm off to work for a few hours. Then I gotta find a cute outfit for Friday. If he's on the shorter side, should I wear flats instead of heels?

WAYLON
Uhh...how short are we talking?

HARLOW
His profile says he's 5'9, but Natalie says guys always lie about their height on dating apps, so he could be shorter.

Considering I'm five-foot-seven, I don't want to make him uncomfortable if he doesn't like girls being taller than him. Waylon's a good six or seven inches taller than me, so he probably doesn't care either way if girls wear flats or heels.

WAYLON
No, I'd definitely wear heels. The taller the better. Short guys like that.

I contemplate asking if he's lying, but he's been nothing but honest with me, especially when it comes to sex stuff and dating. So I take his word for it.

Only With Me

HARLOW

Okay, perfect because the boutique got in the cutest ankle boots but they have a five-inch heel.

WAYLON

That should work. He'll feel more confident knowing his height isn't an issue for you.

HARLOW

Great, thanks!

I get ready for work and am relieved I'm not working with Ashley today. She's nice enough, but she talks nonstop and as someone who was homeschooled for five years and didn't have a normal high school experience, I find it uncomfortable when someone gossips about their "friends." It's one thing if she was saying nice things about them, but she's not.

I've concluded she was probably a mean girl in high school, and ten years later, she's still mentally there. Maybe it's because I didn't have a lot of friends growing up, but I've never been interested in talking shit about my so-called friends. After everything I've experienced, I've learned that you never know what someone else is going through behind closed doors, so it costs nothing to be nice.

Even now, I don't have many friends. Although I have a lot of acquaintances—the other girls at work, Noah, Magnolia, Ellie from the ranch, the people in the horse club group chat, and some others I've met at show horse jumping events—I don't consistently talk to them or share personal details of my life.

Delilah and Natalie were the only two, and now Waylon, who I consider being close to.

And I can't imagine ever saying anything mean or hurtful about them.

"Hello, welcome!" I greet as another customer walks through the door. "Lemme know if I can help y'all find anything."

"Thanks." Two women smile at me before browsing the other side of the store.

"So this date on Friday…" Marissa comes and stands next to me, grabbing sweaters to fold so we look busy. "What're you wearin'?"

I showed her Emery's profile earlier when the store was empty and told her we were meeting up Friday for coffee. She's a couple years older and way more experienced in the world of dating than me.

"Those new ankle boots we got in, with jeans and a blue sweater."

"The ones with the five-inch heels?"

"Yeah. Thought they'd be cute, but hopefully I won't slip or fall on my ass. That wouldn't make a good first impression," I say with a nervous chuckle.

"You're gonna wear *heels*? On a date with a man who's less than six feet tall?"

My shoulders drop, and I turn to look at her. "Is that bad?"

"It is if you don't wanna be taller than him."

"I thought that meant I was showin' him I was okay with his height and that he didn't haveta be insecure if I was taller than him with heels?"

"Who told you that?" she asks around a fit of giggles.

My heart pounds in frustration because why would Waylon lie to me?

"A guy friend."

This time her head falls back on her shoulders she's cackling so hard. "A guy friend…who's clearly in love with you."

"No, he's not!" I almost laugh at the idea of Waylon liking me that way.

"Why else would he try to jeopardize your date?"

"To be fair, he's like six-two, so maybe he doesn't know because he's always taller than most girls."

Marissa's face twists in an expression that tells me she's not buying it.

"What?" I ask.

"That man doesn't want your date to go well."

Only With Me

I'm not about to admit I'm a virgin and that he's been teaching me about sex, so I shrug and drop it.

And fuck worrying about a man's height. I'm getting the cute ankle boots for *me*.

When I finish my shift at work, I go home and change into riding clothes. I kiss my parents goodbye, give Moose some love and attention, and then drive to the ranch.

"Hey, sweet girl…" I rub my palm up Piper's nose and give her some praise. "You ready to get outta here and stretch your legs?"

After I put on her tack, I lead us out to the training center. Noah's helping me sign up for local events that'll start up in a few months, and although I'm still new to the sport, I'm looking forward to this next season. It'll be a nice change of pace and keep me busy.

"Hi," I say when I see Waylon and Wilder bundled up in hats and jackets standing next to Noah, surprised they're both here.

"Hey," they reply in unison.

"Looks like you have an audience today, so we'll start with a course run before we do her exercises," Noah says, looking suspiciously at her brothers.

"He dragged me here to help with the rails." Wilder points to Waylon. "But I don't think I've seen you jump before, so you better show me your best." He winks.

"I'll try, just for you." I smirk, securing on my helmet. "But I need to warm her up quickly."

I hop on and run a few laps around the arena. Every time I pass by Waylon, he's watching me intently while Wilder plays on his phone. Noah's watching me too, but she's looking at my posture and Piper's trotting.

"You ready?" Noah asks.

"As long as no more loose goats come in and scare my horse…" I arch a brow at Wilder and his mouth drops open.

"Oh, come on. That was one time!"

Waylon shakes his head. "And you're the reason she fell on her ass."

"Blame that on Landen for not helpin' me when I asked him for an extra hand. Those little fuckers are quick and feisty. Be happy only one got out."

Noah snorts. "I made sure the back doors are closed. That way we won't freeze our asses off either."

"Good call," Waylon says, glancing up at me, but then shifts his gaze back to Noah.

We haven't exactly told anyone in his family that we've been talking or that he's been *coaching* me on dating. I'm not sure how they'd react to that news, so I don't blame him entirely for not wanting to make it obvious with his siblings around.

"Anyway…let's show 'em whatcha got." Noah grins, grabbing her clipboard and timer.

The rails are about three feet from the ground, but I'm hoping to start practicing closer to four feet and eventually two rails so I can enter more challenging competitions. Even if I don't compete in national shows, I like pushing myself and making goals to prove I can do it.

Piper and I get into position and when Noah gives the signal, she takes off for the first jump. I stay focused on the obstacle and guide her with each jump. After the fifth, she's flawlessly completed all of them and then I hear cheering on the sidelines, almost forgetting they were watching.

"Wow, y'all killed that one!" Noah claps. "You didn't come to play 'round today."

Wilder looks impressed, but Waylon looks proud and in awe.

Honestly, though, I was zoned in and wanted to show all of them that we still had it after a few rough weeks.

"Damn, girl. You got the moves." Wilder holds out his hand for a high-five and I bring Piper closer to reach him.

"You did tell me to do my best." I shrug bashfully. "Maybe you're my lucky charm."

Only With Me

Although I'm only teasing, Waylon's shoulders tense the more Wilder beams at me.

"Guess I'll haveta come to all of your practices and shows from now on."

"Please, Lord, no." Noah groans, and I laugh at her reaction.

"I take offense to that!" Wilder nudges her.

"Good, it was meant to be offensive."

Waylon chuckles at Noah and Wilder's antics as he walks away from them and comes to my other side. He clasps his hand around my upper thigh and squeezes. "Thanks for lettin' us watch. We gotta get the horses ready for the next tour, but I'll talk to you tonight?" He lowers his voice so only I can hear him, even though I'm certain Wilder is trying to eavesdrop.

"Yeah, sounds good." I smile, overly aware of his fingers digging into my riding pants and how close they are to the inside of my leg.

He nods once, then releases me, but my heart continues to pound.

"Wilder, let's go," he hollers, walking toward the exit, and then waits for his brother to catch up before they leave together.

"Well, now that I know you can put on a show, let's do some flatwork and get her prepared to go to the next level," Noah says.

"Sounds good!"

Flatwork improves her responsiveness to various gait transitions and then we'll work on patterns and side movement. Between that, jumping exercises, and conditioning, my lesson goes by quickly. When we're closer to the season starting, I'll have extra sessions so we can work on show prep and go through everything the judges look for in a performance.

I'm still thinking about how Waylon touched me hours later after practice and wondering if Marissa is right. Would he give me bad dating advice on purpose because he thinks of me as more than a friend?

There's just no way.

Brooke Montgomery

Waylon's a fantasy, like crushing on a celebrity. There's no point in even considering it could happen or getting your hopes up because it's so farfetched.

But the more I try to talk to guys on the dating app, the less invested I get in wanting to date any of them. The only reason I agreed to one with Emery is because he didn't say anything creepy, rude, or offensive.

God.

The bar is truly in hell if those are the only requirements.

Chapter Twenty
Waylon

"So you wanna tell me what's goin' on with you and Little Miss Heart Eyes?" Wilder taunts after we finish our afternoon tour.

"What're you talkin' about?" I scoop out a bucket of feed and then hear him follow as I walk down the barn aisle.

"I saw the way you and Harlow were lookin' at each other."

"Nothing's going on. We're friends," I say, sprinkling the feed over hay in one of the stalls.

"Does Delilah know?"

"Know what? There's nothin' to tell her."

"That you're *friendly* with her little sister…"

"I dunno what she knows or what you think you know, but you're wrong."

"So I could ask Harlow out, then?"

By the tone in his voice, he's fucking with me and waiting to see how I'll react.

"Sure, go ahead," I deadpan, grabbing more feed.

"You like her…" He blocks my path. "Does she like you?"

"No and *no*."

"Have you asked her?"

I blow out a frustrated breath. "No."

"So I could be right?" he gloats.

"It doesn't matter. She's my ex's little sister and it could never happen."

"Is that what you think or just what you're tellin' yourself to avoid being happy for once?"

"Mm-hmm." I ignore his interrogation and step around him to go to the next stall.

"Is this you not wantin' to date because of me?" he asks my back.

My spine straightens, but I don't turn to face him. "It's a little of everything."

He pats my shoulder before coming in front of me. "I told ya, you don't haveta put your life on hold for me. Get a life outside of worryin' about me."

Easier said than done.

"I wish I could."

"So what, I've had a few episodes over the past decade or so. That doesn't mean you can't allow yourself to be in a relationship."

I arch a brow. "A *few*?"

"Stop using me as an excuse."

"I'm not gonna go after a twenty-year-old who's related to the last girl I dated," I say matter-of-factly.

*Or at least I shouldn't...*is what I tell myself.

"This is because she's too young for you?"

"And innocent," I add. "She and I started talkin' when she asked me questions about datin'. So that's how I know she's not interested, and I just need to get over it."

"So you *do* like her. Who's she datin'?"

I shrug. "Some guy she met from CowboyMatch. Today, she asked if she should wear five-inch heels because he's only a couple inches taller than her, and instead of tellin' her the truth, I lied. Made up some bullshit about how it'll show she doesn't care about his height."

Only With Me

Which I feel guilty as hell about. I shouldn't have done that.

But I hate the thought of some punk taking advantage of her. She's young and inexperienced enough that she wouldn't even realize it.

"Dude, you gave her bad advice on purpose?" He's full-on laughing. "That's some shit I would pull."

"Trust me, I know. It was a low moment, and I plan to confess later."

Along with telling her the truth about the horse club group chat. I thought not telling her would be best, but the closer we get and the more we open up to each other, it feels wrong to hide it from her. I'm not sure how she'll take it, but as soon as the right time approaches, I'll do my best to explain why I had to pretend I wasn't there to meet her that day at the café. And why I had to stop communication.

When she approached me in the dating app to ask about getting experience and learning, I was so shocked at how much she opened up and trusted me, I didn't want her to shut down if I told her. But then I started liking her more and more, so if I don't tell her soon, she could get pissed enough to walk away from our entire friendship. And I'd be devastated if that happened.

"No way. Unless you want her to fall for someone else, let her show up in heels. Hell, tell her to wear eight-inch boots with a knife strapped to her thigh. Scare away the dude for good."

I scoff because of course that'd be his advice. "I can't do that to her. She's tryin' so hard to put herself out there and live her life after everything she went through. She trusts me, and I shouldn't sabotage her."

"Fuck…" He shakes his head. "You're *really* into her, aren't ya?"

Stepping around him, I smack into his shoulder as I walk away.

And now tonight, I'm supposed to let her watch me jerk off.

Yeah, I'm fucked.

Brooke Montgomery

Once I eat dinner and take a shower, I put on gray sweatpants and a T-shirt. It took everything in me not to jerk off in the shower since chatting with Harlow always makes me tense and tonight's going to be so much worse.

Why did I even agree to this?

I should've gone with the banana option.

HARLOW
Are you ready for me to call?

I reread her message that she sent ten minutes ago.

Maybe I should back out of this and tell her I'm too tired. It's not like she needs to learn for her date on Friday unless she plans to get a public indecency charge.

But who knows.

She's eager as hell to lose her virginity, and I shouldn't stand in the way of that just because I can't have her.

WAYLON
Yep.

She video calls through the app a moment later.

"Hi!" Her bright smile captures my attention as soon as I pick it up.

"Hey. How's it goin'?"

"Great. How was the rest of your workday?"

I casually lift a shoulder. "Fine. Nothin' special. Well, unless you consider Wilder *not* flirtin' with the tour guests for once a special occasion."

She giggles. "Sounds unlike him."

"I know, I almost checked his temperature."

Only With Me

She laughs again and it makes my heart race.

"So, uh…before I *show* you…I need to tell ya something."

"Okay?"

"Earlier when you asked me if you should wear five-inch heels on your date, I gave you bad advice."

"I was wonderin' about that. My coworker, Marissa, said that most guys who are on the shorter side probably wouldn't prefer the heels—at least not on the first date. I told her you probably didn't know any better because of how tall you are. There's no way for you to know from a short guy's perspective."

She trusts me so much, she assumes it was by accident.

God, I suck.

But if I elaborate and tell her I did it on purpose, I'll have to tell her why, and I can't do that.

Dating her is out of the question, but there's no point in ruining our friendship we're both enjoying.

"Right, sorry," I say.

"Nah, it's okay. I decided I'm wearin' them anyway…for me. If he has an issue with it, then I'll know we won't be a good match."

Oh. "Okay."

"And I'm not confident he'll show up anyway, so…" She shrugs. "But I guess that's part of the datin' process."

"Pretty much," I agree.

"Do you watch porn?" she asks abruptly.

"*What?*"

"When you touch yourself. I was wonderin' if you needed to watch it to get hard so you could show me how you do it."

"Uh, no…I can use my imagination."

"Okay, cool. That's what I did the last time and it worked."

"The last time?"

"Yeah, I wanted to see if I could make myself orgasm without you talkin' me through it. You said practice makes perfect, so I just repeated the words you said to me in my head, and I finished."

Fucking hell.

Brooke Montgomery

It's one thing to know she's capable of doing it herself now, but it's another knowing she thought of me while doing it.

"That's...great," I drawl. "Glad it worked."

"Me too. It's quite the stress reliever."

I chuckle at her bluntness. "Yeah, I'd say so."

"Which is even better for you tonight. You'll probably sleep great."

Oh, I wouldn't count on it...

"Yeah, let's hope so."

"I'm ready whenever you are."

Sitting back against my headboard, I prop up my phone against my lamp on the nightstand.

"How's this angle?"

"This should work. Maybe zoom in a bit."

I pinch the screen until she's satisfied and then make sure the phone's steady.

"Okay...I'm gonna lower my boxer briefs now."

"What's the difference between briefs and boxers?"

"Harlow..." I swallow hard. "You can't ask a million questions while I'm doing this. I need to focus."

"Shit, sorry..." She mimics zipping her lips and throwing out the key.

I inhale a deep breath before releasing it and then slide down my underwear. My cock's already half hard and smacks against my stomach.

Palming my shaft with my right hand so she can see everything from my left side, I make slow, steady strokes up and down, then gently swirl my thumb around the tip.

"The crown is very sensitive, so it feels good when you touch or suck up here," I tell her, repeating the motion a few more times. "But the shaft needs attention too, especially when your mouth is on it. Going as deep as you can feels incredible."

Glancing at the screen, I make sure she hasn't bailed on me, but she's still there, watching intently as if she does this every day.

Only With Me

I continue stroking myself and then grab the bottle of lube I set aside.

"When you're giving a hand job or having sex, lube can be a nice way to enhance pleasure and decrease friction. It can also prevent condoms from breaking, so I'd suggest using it, especially for your first time or if you're not on any birth control," I explain, adding some of the lube to my palm before touching myself again.

Her face is angled differently on the screen and then I hear her writing on some paper.

"Are you takin' notes?" I ask.

"I don't wanna forget anything."

I breathe out a laugh of disbelief. "There's not a test after this."

"Yes, I know...but it doesn't hurt to remind myself for later."

"Okay..." I increase my pace, my cock fully hard now, and I can't contain the deep groans that echo in my throat.

When I glance at her again, her cheeks are redder than before, and I can't help wondering if this turns her on.

"Harlow..." I grab her attention and she quickly finds my eyes on hers. "You can touch yourself, too, if you want."

She bites her lower lip as if she's contemplating it before she nods and shuffles around on her bed.

"Can you still talk about what you're doing and what feels good?"

"Sure." I tighten my grip. "You wanna squeeze around the shaft and twist your wrist while you stroke up and down, but don't do it too hard. We're sensitive down here, especially the balls."

She grins. "Is there a trick to findin' the right amount of pressure?"

"You'll know from how the guy's responding to your touch. Some like it very hard and rough while others prefer a gentler approach. Most guys will be vocal about it if they want you to do something else."

"Mmm..." She's lying on her bed and although I can't see past her shoulders, I can tell by her facial expression that she's touching herself.

"Does that feel good?" I ask her, gripping my tip and watching her.

"Mm-hmm." She smiles with her eyes closed. "Can you keep talkin'? Tell me how good it feels for you."

I lean back and continue my steady movements. "Fuckin' amazing. All the blood's rushin' to my cock and my balls are full and tight. The buildup and anticipation make it hard to breathe sometimes."

"What about when a girl's mouth is on you? How does that work?"

"Usually, they switch between their hand and mouth or they do both—their fingers wrap around the bottom of the shaft while they suck the tip. That's the best way for a girl to do it so they can control how far deep into their mouths it goes."

"But I'm betting guys like it when they put the whole thing down their throats, right?"

Fuck, she's gonna make me come too damn soon.

"Mm-hmm. It feels incredible any way—hand, mouth, throat. All very...satisfying."

"Do you like going down on girls?"

"Uh, yeah. Very much actually."

"I wonder how that feels..." She breathes out like she's already close. "It seems it'd feel weird having a face between my legs—all up in there."

"For some girls it is, but for others it can amplify the intimacy between their partners. It's all personal preference."

"I'd like to experience it just once to see if I like it."

"Well, you gotta make sure you have the right partner who knows what they're doing. Some guys don't...and might deter you from wantin' to experience it ever again."

"How will I know if they're bad at it if I've never done it before?"

"If they don't make you come, they suck."

Only With Me

"Really? You can come from just their tongue down there?"

"Yes." I chuckle lightly. "It's foreplay, so you should always finish from oral."

"And I assume a guy always finishes from that too?"

"Typically, yes. Or they'll finish off themselves with their hand. And then some like to come on their partner."

"*On* them? Ain't it...sticky?"

"Very."

"Does cum taste good?"

"That's subjective, I guess."

"What about girls when they come? How do they taste?"

"Uh...sweet? It depends. Every woman's different."

"So you've done oral a lot?"

"Depends what you consider a lot."

The corner of her lips tilts up. "Way to evade."

"I've been sexually active for twelve years, so..."

The deep moan Harlow releases cuts off my words.

"Fuck, you're close..." My grip loosens. "I need you to finish before me."

"Are you almost there?" she asks.

"Yeah, but I'm waitin' for you. You wanted to watch and I don't want you to miss it."

"Okay, I-I...can you talk me through it like you're here so I get there faster?"

Christ. It's going to take a miracle for me to hold myself back if I do that.

But I agree anyway.

"Okay..." I exhale through my nose, trying to slow down my pounding heart. "Pretend my fingers are seeded deep inside you while my tongue flicks your needy little clit. Your fingers are in my hair and your legs are wrapped around my shoulders."

"Oh God...yes. Just like that." Her little moans make my skin burn hotter and I have to tell myself to slow down and hold off, but fuck, it's getting harder.

"I reach up and pinch your pebbled nipple before massaging your breast. I bury my face in your pussy and taste—"

"Yes, yes…fuck, I'm—"

And then she releases the most beautifully aroused moan I've ever heard.

"Holy shit, that was more intense than my last one." She fully pants, then adjusts the phone so her whole face is back in view. "If ranchin' doesn't work out, you should start your own phone sex business, because *goddamn*. Ten out of ten stars."

"As much as I appreciate the compliment, I'm gonna explode, so I need you to focus on me."

"Okay." She nods, her face still flushed, and shit, that turns me on even more.

I bring my phone closer, holding it in my left hand so she can get a better view.

"When a guy gets close, you'll feel him tense and then—" I fuck my fist a few more seconds before I groan through my release, shooting cum over my fingers.

"Whoa. That's hot…" She licks her lips. "Girls normally swallow that, right?"

"Uh, well…if they want. Or they can spit it out."

"Whaddya like?"

Jesus Christ.

"It doesn't matter to me. I'd rather my partner do whatever makes 'em comfortable."

"I'll haveta try it and judge for myself. It kinda looks nasty, though. Like why is it so slimy? Girls' cum don't look like that, right?"

"I dunno why it's slimy and no, yours is more liquidy." I set the phone back on my nightstand. "I need to clean up. Hold on."

She giggles. "Me too. I'll be right back."

Well, I can't say I've ever done that before, but somehow with Harlow, she makes awkward things not feel awkward at all. She's so damn wholesome, she doesn't even realize how we technically got each other off during phone sex.

Only With Me

To her, it was a learning experience.
But for me, I've fallen deeper.
And now, there's no point in even trying to ignore my feelings.
They're front and center, but if I don't control them, she's going to see right through me.

Chapter Twenty-One
Harlow

Waylon showing me how he likes to be touched while I got off to watching him is all I've been able to think about for the past four days.

I've never seen a cock in person and even though he was through a screen, it was still jarring to see how thick and big he is.

I was tempted to ask how *that* is supposed to fit inside someone, because even though I have no references to compare it to, I assume he's above average. When he wrapped his hand around his shaft, I couldn't help wondering if my fingers would even touch around his girth.

And then I tried to picture how it'd fit in my mouth…
I would choke to death.

But then I read somewhere about gag reflexes and how some people practice with a dildo to go deeper down their throats. Since I'm not about to buy one of those, I'll have to learn another way.

The more he teaches me about sex and what guys like the more the lines blur between us. I've tried pushing my feelings aside so things don't get awkward when he's answering my questions, but it's getting harder now that we're growing closer as friends.

Today's my coffee date with Emery so I need to shove all my

Only With Me

unrequited feelings to the back burner and at least try to give him a chance. He messaged this morning to confirm we're still meeting at noon and then said he'd be waiting for me with a black baseball cap on and leather jacket.

Should be easy enough to find him, especially since I've seen his photos on the app. But I'm still not super eager about it. I'm more excited to wear my new boots out of the house.

I'll never get proper dating experience if I don't try, so I get myself ready and try to give myself a pep talk. Who knows, he could be very sweet in person, we could have a lot in common, and I would've never known if I hadn't given him a chance.

Yeah, that's what I'm telling myself.

Before I head out, Natalie video calls, and I prop up my phone while I finish my makeup and hair.

"I still have your location in case this Emery dude turns out to be a psycho," she tells me.

"I'm not going anywhere with him so you don't need to worry."

"After the last book I read, I will always worry. Girl went on a date with an *actual* serial killer…"

"Oh God."

"And he ate his victims!"

"I'm gonna throw up if you keep talkin'."

"She was an undercover detective and managed to escape but he beat her up badly beforehand…"

"Then what happened?" I ask, annoyed that I'm invested.

"Oh, she got revenge in the best way. Returned with a huge ass knife—like a machete—and tortured him the same way he did his victims."

"Please don't tell me she ate him…"

"No, she chopped him up and fed him to alligators."

I mimic a gag reaction because what the fuck is she reading?

"That's disgusting."

"That's what he gets."

"I guess?" I chuckle. "You're gonna scare me away from wantin' to date at all."

"Speakin' of that, how're things with Waylon?" she taunts in that bubbly voice of hers.

"Well…" I lower my voice before continuing. "I saw his dick."

"*What?*" she chokes out, nearly spewing her drink everywhere. "When did this happen? How're you now just tellin' me?"

"Calm down…it was through video chat. I asked him to show me how he jerks off and teach me how guys like to be touched."

"Fucking hell, and he just agreed to that?"

I shrug. "Yeah. Then he told me to touch myself because he could tell it was turning me on, so I did, and we came together."

"Holy shit, that's so hot."

"It was, but it was just a learning experience. Once we finished and cleaned up, we talked for a little bit and then said goodnight."

We've talked every day since then too but nothing out of our ordinary conversation.

"That man is either not into women or he's incredibly obsessed with you. There's no in between."

"That would be neither."

"I will die on this hill. He wants you." She gives me a serious look. "And I'll say this again because what man would *teach* you about sex and orgasms, show you how he masturbates, and then talk you through how to touch yourself if he wasn't interested in you?"

"A man who's my friend and doesn't want me to get hurt by datin' the wrong men."

She snorts. "You mean, dating *other* men."

"Well…" I shrug. "If he was interested, then he should ask me out himself. And since he hasn't, I just haveta assume it's because he doesn't wanna."

"He's probably scared just like you are. He's older and dated your sister. He's more experienced than you. Might also be jaded from other bad datin' experiences."

Only With Me

"Yes, I'm well aware of the list of reasons," I deadpan. "Which is why I'm going on a date with Emery. It'd be much easier to date someone who I'm allowed to like and likes me back."

I check the time. "Speakin' of which, I better go so I'm not late."

"Okay, good luck. Don't get murdered."

I chuckle, hovering my finger over the end call button. "Bye!"

Before heading out, I give Moose a little goodbye kiss and then check on my dad who's still napping, so I don't bother him. I shouldn't be gone more than an hour, but I still have PTSD from the day of my dad's accident. I never saw him that morning to tell him I loved him. He was in a medically induced coma for two weeks, and during that time, I feared I'd never get to tell him again. But fortunately, he woke up and I was finally able to.

I never leave the house without telling either of my parents for fear it'll be the last time I see them.

Then I message Emery to let him know I'm on my way.

HARLOW

I'll be there in five minutes.

EMERY

Take your time. I'm here, sitting at a table in front of the big window.

HARLOW

Sounds good!

The nerves kick in as I drive down Main Street and find a parking spot. Once I get out and walk to the cafe, I see him right away and he stands to greet me.

He's decent looking in person, charming smile and kind eyes. With my boots, I'm at least a few inches taller than him but if it bothers him, it's not obvious.

"I'm so glad you could come," he says, leaning in to give me a side hug. "You look beautiful."

I return it the best I can before I take my seat.

"Did you wanna order something?"

"Yeah, sure." I'm about to stand when he stops me.

"I'll grab it for you. What would you like?"

"I'll do an iced caramel soy latte."

"You got it." He winks.

Nervously, I smile and then wait for him to return.

I can't help wondering how things would've gone if Mystery Guy had shown up. Would he have offered to order for me? Would we have sat and talked for hours? I can't imagine things would've felt this tense after how much we texted.

While Emery stands at the coffee bar waiting for our order, I quickly pull out my phone and decide to text him.

HARLOW

> Hey, it's been a while. I'm just checking in and seeing how you're doing. The group chat hasn't been the same without you. I miss talking to you and have just been thinking about the conversations we had. Hope all is well.

Oh God, that sounds so fucking lame.

I haven't been active in the group chat in a couple weeks but it's not the same anymore.

When Emery grabs our order, I put my phone away, but make sure it's on silent so we don't get interrupted. If I'm going to give him a chance, I need to give him my full attention.

"Here you go." He sets mine down in front of me.

"Thank you. I appreciate it."

"Of course."

He sits across from me, keeping his eyes on me. "I'm excited to get to know you. So you're twenty, right?"

"Yep, I'll be twenty-one in a few months."

"Nice. Gonna celebrate big?"

"Probably not, but I'm not sure. We'll see."

"Cool, cool. You do show horse jumping. How's that going?"

Only With Me

"Great. Just a lot of trainin' right now before the season starts in the spring. Mostly doing practice runs and conditioning."

"I love that. I only ride for fun on my friend's ranch. But I'd love to watch you sometime."

"Yeah, maybe!"

"Whaddya do outside of that?"

"I work at Rodeo Belle, the Western clothing boutique, a few times a week."

"Oh that's close to here, ain't it?"

"Yeah, just a block or two away."

He continues asking me questions, and I barely get a chance to ask him anything. I guess that means he's interested? But it would've been nice to get some details about him.

After thirty minutes of feeling like I'm being interviewed, I tell him I have to go and check on my dad. He asks if he can walk me to my truck, and it seems harmless, so I agree.

He opens my door and I thank him again for the date.

"I hope we can do it again soon," he says.

"Yeah, maybe. I'll let you know."

He grabs my hand and then kisses my knuckles—something I've only seen in movies.

"Bye, Harlow. Have a lovely rest of your day."

I force a smile, slowly prying my hand out of his grip.

"Thanks, you too."

Finally, he walks away, toward his car that's a few ahead of me.

When I hop into my truck, I toss my purse onto the passenger seat and put my phone in one of my cup holders. As soon as I go to close my door, a body approaches, scaring the living shit out of me.

"Oh my God, Waylon!" My hand smacks against my racing heart, and I breathe out in relief when I realize it's him.

He stands with a taunting grin. "How was your date?"

"Are you stalkin' me? What're you doing here?"

"No, I was across the street buyin' a new phone and saw you

gettin' in your truck, so I thought I'd come over." He thumbs over his shoulder, and I see the cell phone store sign.

"Next time, say something before you creep up on me! I thought you were a murderer."

He smirks. "Yeah, lots of serial killers in Sugarland Creek."

I playfully smack him. "You know what I mean."

He chuckles. "How'd things go? Did he say anything about your heels?"

"It was fine," I say dryly. "And no. He said I looked beautiful."

His gaze roams down my body and he's not even trying to hide that he's checking me out. "I agree. Very nice."

"Thanks," I say hesitantly, then nod toward the bag in his hand. "So wait, what happened to your phone?"

"Uh...I dropped it twenty feet when I was up in the loft and then Wilder ran it over with a tractor."

"Jesus. What a brutal death."

"Yeah, I had to get a new phone number, too. My dad said being on his cell plan at my age was pathetic."

I stifle a laugh, but it comes out as a snort anyway. "I mean, he's not wrong."

He shrugs. "Well, now I need to get your number since I don't plan to redownload the CowboyMatch app."

"No?"

"Nah, I ignored every message that came through, but I kept it so I could talk to you since we never exchanged phone numbers."

That has my whole stomach fluttering and heart pounding because it's undeniable how sweet that is considering he knows I was on there talking to guys.

"Well, gimme your phone, and I'll program my number." I hold out my palm and he hands it over without a second thought.

"Whaddya want my name in here to be?" I ask, clicking on the add new contact button.

"Um..." He purses his lips for a moment and squints one eye. "How about *Favorite Student*?"

"Seriously?" Chuckling, I roll my eyes but type it in anyway

Only With Me

and then text myself so I have his number. "Guess that means you'll be *Favorite Teacher* in mine." I hand him back his phone and then grab mine from inside my truck.

"Favorite *Hot* Teacher," he counters. "At least gimme that."

"More like Mr. *Grumpy* Teacher," I tease, clicking on the text message and programming his number.

"Don't do me dirty like that."

Smirking, I give in. "Fine, *Favorite Hot Teacher* it is. But if anyone ever breaks into my phone and sees that, they're gonna think you're a creep for textin' your student."

"That'll be the least of their worries once they find all the weird sexual questions you ask me."

"They're not weird!" I defend, pocketing my phone once I'm done. "They're for educational purposes."

"That's one way to put it," he muses.

"Well, now that we officially have each other's numbers, what time should I meet you and Bentley at the ranch tomorrow?"

"I was gonna pick him up at one, but I can swing through town and grab you first?"

"Are you sure? Then you'll haveta drop me off."

"I don't mind."

"That works for me."

"Great, we'll see ya then."

Right as I go to turn around, he captures my hand, lifts it to his lips, and grins around my knuckles before pressing a gentle kiss there.

"Is this how he did it?" His mocking tone has my whole face burning red.

"Saw that, did ya?" I yank my hand out of his grip. "You're so mean."

He holds up his hand in feign innocence. "What? I thought that's how you liked sayin' goodbye?"

"Wow, you're so funny." I playfully punch his arm, but before I can step back, he quickly grabs my wrist and pulls me to his chest. Our bodies smash together along with all the air getting sucked out of my lungs.

His gaze pierces mine, and I swallow hard at the intensity of his stare. He's made me speechless, which is hard to do.

When he grabs my chin and tilts it up so my mouth is closer to his, I brace for contact—hoping this is finally it.

But then he shifts slightly and kisses my cheek.

"Have a good rest of your day. I'll see ya tomorrow."

Before stepping away, he winks and then walks across the street to his truck—leaving me in a puddle of disbelief.

Chapter Twenty-Two
Waylon

Knowing I'll get to spend time with Harlow and Bentley today had me waking up in the best mood. We texted briefly last night to confirm what time I'd be at her house, but otherwise we haven't spoken much since I saw her in town.

I might've stretched the truth a *smidge* when I told Harlow I broke my phone.

After she texted me as Poison Ivy Girl, I knew I had to get a new number. I feel awful that she's going to lose access to "him" from the group chat, but it'd only be a matter of time before she asked to exchange numbers and then realized she already had it.

Then I'd have to explain everything.

At this point, maybe I should rip off the Band-Aid and tell her.

But she's opened up to me so much and she's the first person in years I've felt comfortable being vulnerable around, so maybe I'm being selfish now because I don't want to ruin that.

Plus, I don't want to keep messaging her through that stupid dating app, but I couldn't randomly change my number without my siblings questioning it.

When I told Wilder I was getting my own plan and that it included a free phone, he asked if we could test my current phone's durability. *For fun*.

That's where the tractor came in.

And if I'm being completely honest, I knew she was meeting her date at the café at noon, so I purposely went into town and parked close by during my lunch break.

But...she doesn't need to know that.

I'm no expert in dating, but even I could see how uncomfortable she was from across the street. Her body was tense, she hardly smiled or laughed, and she looked like she'd rather be anywhere else. The guy was leaning on the table toward her. Meanwhile, she had her back pressed against the chair so she was farther away.

If you didn't know they were on a date, you'd assume she was on a job interview.

But I couldn't help kissing her knuckles the way he had because the look on her face while he did it was priceless—like she was taken so aback, she didn't know how to react. I didn't want her to leave with a bad taste in her mouth, so I mimicked what he'd done and then moved to her cheek. Even though I wanted to kiss her lips, I knew I couldn't without consequences.

I could feel the tension between us, and I think she did too, so it's probably a good thing Bentley will be with us for a few hours this afternoon.

WAYLON

I'm leaving now, be there in 15.

HARLOW

Okay...my father would like to talk to you first.

Oh fuck.

WAYLON

Should I come armed?

HARLOW

Only if you think you can't outrun a man in a wheelchair.

Only With Me

> **WAYLON**
> Nah, I think I'm good then.

> **HARLOW**
> He just wants to give you the "If you hurt my daughter, I'll hurt you" talk.

> **WAYLON**
> Oh...how fun.

It's been years since I've seen or talked to Mr. Fanning. His work accident had happened shortly after Delilah and I started dating, so we never got to know each other. But I don't blame him for wanting to speak to the guy who's picking up his daughter. Considering what she went through, I'm glad he's overprotective.

> **HARLOW**
> You'll be fine. Just don't stare at my chest in front of him.

> **WAYLON**
> I don't do that when he's not around.

Do I?

By the time I park in front of her house, I'm more nervous than I thought I'd be. We're friends, so this shouldn't be a big deal, but maybe he doesn't like that his oldest daughter's ex is *friendly* with his youngest daughter.

I wouldn't blame him either.

From the outside, it looks bad.

Walking up the wheelchair ramp, I clear my throat, then knock on the door.

I hear barking and moments later, Harlow appears.

"Hey, c'mon in. Don't mind the dogs. They sound scarier than they look."

I nervously chuckle as I try to make my way through the entryway and into the kitchen.

"Dad's in the livin' room." She walks away before I can say anything, so I follow until I see him.

"Waylon, hello. Long time no see."

"Mr. Fanning, nice to see you. How're you?" I ask, standing next to Harlow.

"I'm alive. How about you?"

"Same, good. Thanks."

"Harlow tells me you're a Big Brother?"

"Yes, sir. To a fifteen-year-old boy named Bentley. He lives in the town over, so I pick him up and bring him to the ranch to hang out a couple times a month."

"Fifteen, huh? He's closer in age to Harlow than you are."

And there it is.

"Yeah, I guess so. He enjoys watchin' her jump with Piper."

"That's what she says. What're you plannin' for today?"

"I told you, Daddy. We're gonna horseback ride up the mountains," Harlow chimes in.

"That sounds dangerous," Mr. Fanning says.

"It's not. I give ridin' tours twice a day. I know those mountains in my sleep."

"You know she's not legal to drink, so I expect you won't either."

"Of course not."

"Daddy, he's responsible," Harlow tells him. "As am I."

"I know you are, sweetheart, but I just wanna make sure you're safe."

She hugs him in his recliner and he wraps an arm around her gently. "I'll be fine, I promise. I'll be home later, okay?"

"Drive safe." He shifts his gaze to me.

"Yes, sir. I'll bring her back in the same condition I took her."

"Love you, Daddy."

"Love you, too."

I say a quick goodbye and then she leads me out to the kitchen where the dogs are waiting.

Only With Me

"This is Moose. He's my little snuggle buddy at night." She holds him up and I give him some pets.

"He's a cutie."

"My little protector." She chuckles, then kisses him before setting him down. "Okay, we can go now."

I hold open the door while she locks up and then we walk to my truck, except I go to the passenger side to help her in.

"Thanks," she says with a little blush across her cheeks.

I smirk. "You're welcome."

Once we're buckled up and driving on the road, I point to my radio and tell her she can pick the music.

"So, did my dad scare you away?" she asks, shuffling through the stations.

"Nah. I can tell he worries about you."

"I worry about him, too. His mental health is not in a good place right now. It's bad enough he's stuck inside most of the day, but the gloomy weather doesn't help either."

"Doesn't he use his power wheelchair when he's out?"

"Yeah, but it can be a hassle for Mom to get it lifted onto the lift at the back of the truck. He suffers with so much social anxiety, he doesn't like being around a lot of people out of the house." She turns and looks at me. "There's times he won't leave the house for three months straight."

"Damn, that's tough. Do you think he'd feel more comfortable if someone stronger was there to bring his chair with him?"

"Stronger, like you?" she muses.

"Yeah. Give your mom a break from doing it. Even if it were to go to the store, he could do short trips to get used to being out, and then gradually do longer ones."

"You'd do that?"

"Well, sure. I get one day off a week where I could come and help out with anything or anywhere he wanted to go. Maybe he feels like a burden because he knows how much work it is on your mom, but if it's someone like me, who could lift his chair with one arm, he wouldn't feel so guilty about acceptin' help."

"With one arm, huh?" She laugh-snorts, and it's fucking adorable. "You're pretty sure of yourself."

"I work on a ranch, Harlow...since I was like in middle school. I've had to carry bales of hay and straw up and down stairs for two hours straight. I've had to push thousand-pound horses to get into trailers while they try kickin' me. Lifting a power chair onto a lift wouldn't even register as heavy."

"Okay, Mr. Big Shot. Return me back in one piece and he might trust ya."

Amused, I chuckle. "As long as you don't fall in poison ivy, I think you'll be fine."

"What?" she asks.

I realize my slipup when she looks at me with furrowed brows. Fuck, this is where I should come clean, but it feels wrong to do it now when we have a full afternoon planned with Bentley.

"I was jokin'. It's dormant this time of year."

"Yeah, I know. I got poison ivy in November."

"Oh." I stay focused on the road but glance quickly at her. "I bet that wasn't fun."

She frowns, looking down at her lap, and I wonder if she's thinking about "him."

"No, it wasn't. But a guy I met in a group chat helped me with ideas on how to deal with the itch. I stayed in bed for like two or three weeks because it was all over my arms and chest."

"Wilder and I got it once. It sucked big time."

"Really? It must be quite normal out here."

I wonder if she's thinking about the conversations we had and if they're feeling similar. I can't remember how much I told her about when Wilder and I had it in high school, but now that I brought it up, I have to find a way to change topics.

"That was the same summer I got a tick in my neck."

"Oh shit, that sounds painful."

"Well, I've gotten lots of ticks over the years, but it was extra brutal being in my neck. I had to go to the ER to have 'em take it out."

Only With Me

She visibly shivers. "I would cry if that happened to me. I hate 'em so much."

"When we went back to school that fall, there was a lice outbreak."

"Oh my gosh! What in the world happened to y'all that year?"

"It was madness. My mom was inspectin' everyone's heads and pickin' out lice."

"Gross." She laughs. "Your poor mother."

"She's been through it with havin' five kids."

"And with four boys? I don't envy that."

"Do you think you want kids when you settle down?"

"Yeah, I think a couple. When I'm old, like thirty."

"*Old*, really?" I glower at her, and she laughs again.

"You're just too easy to tease. But in all seriousness, I'd love to have a family, but it's hard thinkin' that far ahead with my dad's health issues. I don't wanna leave my mom responsible for him all by herself and she'll never put him in an assisted living home unless it's her last resort."

"I told Wilder somethin' similar..." I admit.

"What's that?"

"That I couldn't settle down because of how much his mental health affected me and with his reluctance to get help, I had to be the one to stick around and watch him."

"What did he say to that?"

"Recently, he told me to stop using him as an excuse not to be happy." I lick my lips, glancing over at her staring at me. "And I'm startin' to think he's right."

Before she can respond, I'm pulling up to Bentley's apartment complex.

Brooke Montgomery

The afternoon riding with Bentley and Harlow turned out to be a huge success. Bentley had a blast and even tried to race us down one of the trails. Considering we have years of experience on him, Harlow and I crushed him. But he had fun trying.

Once we make it back to the barn, we head to The Lodge for an early dinner. I told my siblings we'd be there if any of them wanted to come and eat with us. None of them besides my twin have questioned why Harlow and I are hanging out, which I appreciate. I'm not ready to fully explain how all of this happened.

Wilder, Landen, and Ellie showed up, which was a nice treat for Bentley. He lost his mind when he found out Ellie just won at the NFR last month and got so excited to ask her all kinds of questions about being a pro barrel racer.

I almost felt bad because now Harlow didn't look as cool in his eyes. But to be fair, Ellie has years of competition experience.

Either way, Harlow is great with him and even if she is close in age to him, she's a great role model. We had a good time and shared a lot of laughs.

It was the most fun I've had in a long time.

It's so effortless making conversation and finding things to talk about with Harlow. One of the things that intrigues me so much is that she doesn't try to impress me. She's just herself, all the time, and is never afraid to ask me anything.

Some of her questions can be a little jarring, but I've come to love the randomness that spills out of her mouth. Hell, I look forward to it now.

"Did you wanna hang out at my house after I take Bentley home?" I ask Harlow when we walk out of The Lodge.

Her brows pinch together and she narrows her eyes in confusion.

"I wasn't sure if you wanted to go home right away since it's still kinda early," I clarify.

And I'm not done spending time with her.

"Oh, sure. I just assumed you probably had to get up early tomorrow."

Only With Me

"I'm off."

Actually, I told Wilder he owed me one so I didn't have to wake up early.

"Okay, cool. Could we try something?"

"Name it."

She glances behind us at Bentley and then leans in closer.

"Dry humping...you mentioned it once, and I've been wantin' to know what it feels like ever since," she whispers.

"Harlow..." I lower my voice. "That's...pretty intimate."

"Oh." She shrugs casually like she didn't just ask to grind against my cock. "Okay."

Except it's not okay because it's all I can think about on the drive to Bentley's house. The two of them talk while I'm having a mental crisis between right and wrong.

One minute, I'm trying my damnedest to be a gentleman and keep my hands off her.

And then the next, she's snapping my last ounce of restraint.

"I'll be right back. I'm gonna walk him to his door," I tell Harlow once I'm parked.

"Bye, Bentley! Hope to see you again soon!" She waves at him out the window.

"Bye, Harlow!" He waves in return, and I smile at how cute they are.

"Did ya have fun today?" I ask, wrapping my arm around his shoulders as we approach his apartment.

"One of the best days ever."

My heart swells with happiness. "Good, I'm glad."

"Is she gonna be around for a while?"

I tilt my head. "Whaddya mean?"

He shrugs dismissively. "I don't wanna get attached if y'all break up or something."

I don't bother correcting him because it doesn't matter for what he's asking. He's had so many people come and go in his life, so it's no wonder he'd worry about that.

"If I have it my way, she'll be around for a very, very long time."

"Good, because I've never seen you this happy."

Chuckling, I playfully nudge him. "Yeah, it feels nice."

He punches me in the arm. "Don't screw it up."

I bark out a laugh, but that's exactly what I'm worried about.

Chapter Twenty-Three
Harlow

I'm so glad Waylon let me hang out with him and Bentley today. I didn't grow up with younger siblings, so it was kind of nice talking to him and hearing about his school and home life. It's no secret he doesn't have a stable home, but you'd never be able to tell with how kind and well-mannered he is.

I also love seeing how he looks up to Waylon. It's easy to tell they have a special bond.

When we're halfway back to the ranch, on some country road, Waylon turns down a dirt country road and then parks to the side. Music's the only sound in the truck, but when I look at him, his eyes are hooded with hunger.

"What're we doin'? This feels straight outta one of Natalie's thriller novels."

My heart hammers in my chest at the way he's looking at me.

Waylon unbuckles and then leans down and pushes the lever that makes the bench seat move all the way back. Then he pushes up the steering wheel as high as it'll go.

"Come here."

"Whaddya mean?" I ask, unbuckling my belt—either to jump out of his truck and run because Natalie's made me fear the worst about taking country drives with potential serial killers—or to climb in his lap. I'm not sure yet.

"You wanna experience dry humping, so come straddle my thighs."

Oh!

"I thought you said—"

"I changed my mind."

Well then.

I maneuver myself across the seat and then grab onto his shoulders, lifting myself over his legs. His palms grip my hips as I situate myself on top of him.

"But are you sure you still wanna try this?" he asks, his face only inches from mine.

"Yes." I nod confidently so he doesn't second-guess his decision. "I've only made myself come with my hand, so I'd like to know what it feels like with another person."

"There's a couple different positions for dry humping, but this one will allow you to take control of the pressure and speed."

"Okay…" I dig my fingers into his shoulders, feeling nervous with how close we are, and still, we haven't kissed. "So what do I do now?"

His hands squeeze my hips and he pushes me down on his erection. I swallow hard at how good it feels against my core.

"Rock against me. Use my cock like a vibrator and rub your pussy over it until you orgasm."

Holy hell.

I should've thought this through before suggesting it, but I'm here now, and it's too late to back out. Plus, I want to feel him close to me and for us to experience this together.

I just need to get over my fear of being too inexperienced for him.

He lifts his hips slightly, encouraging me to move.

"Are you gonna stare at me the whole time?" I ask nervously.

"Not if you don't want me to. I can kiss your neck, if you prefer?"

Only With Me

Um...yes! I didn't know that was an option.

"Yeah, I think that'd be nice..." I stammer.

His body moves underneath mine as he pulls me in closer and breathes softly under my ear. Then he presses his lips there and gives it a little suck. My head tilts to the side, giving him more access to put his mouth all over me.

"I'm painfully hard, Harlow. I need you to move now, okay?"

I nod, trying to get myself to stay focused on what I'm supposed to do, but it's so damn hard with him so close and kissing the sensitive areas across my skin.

"This feels so much better than my fingers," I confess in a whisper when we find a rhythm. My palms wrap around his neck, securing myself in place.

"It feels fuckin' phenomenal..." He groans, his face buried in my neck. "You're doing so good, Harlow."

"Really?"

He releases another throaty moan, and I wonder if he's close.

"Yes, fuckin' perfect," he says. "Keep goin' until you find your release. Grind as hard or fast on me as you need to."

My eyes float to the back of my head at how good the pressure feels on my clit. His tight grip on my hips as we rock back and forth against each other, our shared moans echoing between us, and the way my breasts press into him have every inch of my body on fire. I'm burning up with desire and it's only a matter of time before I come on top of him.

He moves from one side of my neck to the other, but for whatever reason, skips over my mouth. I don't know if it's because he knows I've never kissed a guy before, but I'm seconds away from begging him to finally do it.

Put me out of my damn misery already.

It's not like I want to share that with anyone else.

"Waylon..." I mutter his name desperately. "Touch me... please."

"Where?"

I chicken out at the last minute. "My boobs. Under my shirt."

He pulls back slightly until there's enough room between us to grab the hem of my T-shirt and pull it up over my head, exposing me in only my bra.

"Fuck…" He whispers the word like a prayer. "You're truly breathtaking."

"Kiss me there," I beg.

He cups my breasts, pushing them up, then slides his tongue across them. He feathers kisses down between them and then sucks in one nipple through the fabric.

"Oh my God, that's…" My head falls back and he does it again to the other breast.

Who knew getting your nipples sucked and touched would feel so good?

"Mm, baby…keep ridin' me. Don't stop."

Fuck me, he threw that word out again, knowing it'd push me over the edge.

I manage to spread my legs wider until I drop deeper onto his erection and rub my clit as fast as I can over his length.

"Good girl, just like that." His words come out muffled between kissing and sucking, but it's those two words—*good girl*—that have me shooting up like a rocket.

My fingers dig into his shoulder muscles as my legs tense and waves of pleasure rush through me. Shivers run down my spine, my thighs quiver, and my lungs gasp for air. Inhaling sharply, I moan through the sensations that erupt like fireworks, and moments later, I feel liquid pooling between my thighs.

"Waylon…" I breathe out his name, sated and exhausted. "That was the most intense thing I've ever felt."

He pulls back, and I laugh at how swollen his lips are.

"Is my chest red now?" I ask, breaking the silence.

"Uh-huh, your neck too. I wouldn't be shocked if you get a few hickeys."

My hand shoots up, covering where he was. "You sucked that hard?"

Only With Me

"To be fair, it doesn't take much for someone who bruises easily."

"Hey, I've been takin' vitamin K supplements for almost two months."

He chuckles. "I know, but it takes longer than that to have an effect."

My brows furrow, trying to remember when I told him I was taking those. I'm pretty sure I didn't, but I must've if he knew about it.

Waylon hands me my shirt, so I shift my body back onto the seat next to him.

"Wait…" I say after pulling it over my head, looking down at his groin. "You didn't finish?"

"Uh, no. That would be a very sticky mess and we still have ten minutes to the ranch."

"Waylon! Ain't that painful when you're that hard?" I can't stop looking at how big the bulge is in his jeans and how he's going to suffer through it.

"Yeah, it's not the best feelin' in the world, but I'll survive. I'll take care of it when I get home."

"Why don't ya let me instead?"

I bring my hand to his zipper, but he quickly stops me.

"You can teach me."

"Harlow, you don't haveta do that…"

"But I wanna learn… ain't that why you're my *teacher*?" I playfully remind him. "Unless you want me to do it on a banana. I think the real thing would benefit both of us."

He digs one of his hands into his hair and scratches his nails through as if he's fighting with himself. "Fuck, it's hard to say no to you when you flutter those big green doe eyes at me."

I giggle at his confession, his voice strained and desperate.

"Is that so? I'm gonna start usin' that to my advantage," I quip.

"I never say no to you anyway."

My cheeks heat at how true that is. Waylon's been on board for every crazy thing I've asked of him.

"Okay, so start tellin' me what to do." I nod toward his legs.

"Alright." He gets comfortable in the seat, spreading his legs wider. "Carefully...lower my zipper and unbutton my jeans. There's an openin' in the briefs and you can pull out my cock through there."

I shift my body toward him and do exactly as he says, but the moment I feel how soft his shaft is against my palm, my mouth waters to taste him.

"Wow...it's so smooth." I stroke my hand up and down just like how he taught me during our video call.

"Slide your tongue underneath from the base to the tip and then swirl it around the top. Then, when you're comfortable, slide your mouth up and down my length."

It's easier than I thought because once I get the hang of it, I don't need his instructions.

I spit on it before I take him into my mouth again.

"Jesus Christ, baby. You are incredible at that." His words are strained between his breathy moans. His fingers wrap into my hair and around his palm, holding it back, out of my face. He uses the tight grip at the base of my head to bob my mouth up and down the way he likes.

"Do you wanna try going deeper?" he asks hoarsely. "Only if you're ready."

"Mm-hmm," I say around his cock, nodding.

"Okay, tap my thigh if it's too much. Got it?"

I nod again.

"First, I need you to relax your jaw for me. The looser your mouth is, the more you'll be able to take without hurtin' yourself."

I release the tension in my face and let it go slack until he's satisfied I'm able to slide down deeper.

"Good fuckin' girl...just like that, sweetheart." He slowly moves me down a bit more. "The back of your throat feels so goddamn good."

Only With Me

He doesn't keep me there for long before he pulls me back.

"I'm so close. Keep suckin' me and then I'll let you know when you can back up."

I groan out a no and shake my head.

"You don't haveta swallow, Harlow."

I tighten my mouth around him, hollowing my cheeks so he knows I'm doing it my way. I want the full experience.

"Shit, okay…I'm right there. Don't stop."

When his hand squeezes harder in my hair, I know he's about to come in my mouth.

"Oh fuck…I—" His whole body stops moving and then I feel it—warm, sticky bursts on my tongue.

As soon as he exhales with a sated groan, I slide my mouth off his cock but make sure to take all his cum with me.

"I can't believe you did that."

Sitting up, I make sure he watches me swallow.

"And I can't believe you did *that*." His brows shoot up like he's impressed.

That makes two of us, but I *especially* can't believe that happened before we've kissed on the mouth.

"It was a lot of fun," I finally tell him. "I'm honestly surprised how turned on it made me knowing how aroused you were."

All this time I thought there was no way it'd fit in my mouth, and I'd choke to death. But now I'm addicted to his reactions and crave hearing him praise me for doing a good job.

He adjusts his jeans, tucking himself back inside his briefs. "That's what should happen, especially with someone you trust."

"In case you wondered, cum has a weird texture and is a little bitter and salty."

Waylon bursts out laughing. "Yeah, so I've heard."

"Girls don't taste like that, right?"

"No, not at all."

"I felt it when I came earlier…almost like I peed myself a little."

"That's common. Some women can squirt and it makes a huge mess."

"Whaddya mean by *squirt*? Like how?"

"Like...a waterfall, almost?"

"A waterfall? You're messin' with me."

"I swear, I'm not!" He holds up his palms in mock surrender. "There's like a bunch of studies and articles on how to do it."

"Wow...more stuff I need to research and learn."

"It's easiest with fingers and clit stimulation."

"Really?" I arch a brow. "So you've made someone squirt before?"

"Uh, you want me to answer that?"

"I might be a virgin, but I'm well aware you're not. I know you've been intimate with other women."

"That doesn't bother you?"

"Why would it?"

He shrugs, glancing away, and I wonder if that was the wrong thing to say. I suppose most people wouldn't want to hear about the previous partners of the person they like, but I have no right to be upset about something that happened before we even started talking or hanging out.

"It doesn't bother me because it's in the past. It'd be different if you were teachin' me and three other girls at the same time."

"*Three?*" He huffs a laugh.

"I'm just sayin'! And I only asked because I wanted you to try it on me."

"You want me to go down on you?"

"Only if you wanna. It'd be cool to experience it with someone who knows what they're doing. Like you said, it's important to have the right partner who can make it good for me."

"Right, I did say that." He scratches his cheek.

"You don't haveta if it's uncomfortable for you," I tell him. "You're allowed to say no to me, by the way." I chuckle, hoping to slice away the tension between us.

Only With Me

"It's not that I don't want to, Harlow…trust me, I've thought of nothin' else than makin' you cum on my tongue."

"Oh…" My face flushes at his blunt confession.

"But before we go further, I think we need to talk about the elephant in the room."

Licking my bottom lip, I suck it in between my teeth and hold my breath as I anticipate his next words.

"Okay…"

"I want you." His blue eyes meet mine. "As more than a friend. I want you all to myself. And I know you being Delilah's sister and much younger than me might cause issues, but I couldn't go another second without tellin' you how I feel."

I swallow hard, trying to suck in as much air as possible, but all the blood drains from my face and then I get dizzy.

"Harlow?"

I beg my head to catch up so I can say the right thing, but the longer I say nothing at all, the more awkward it gets.

"Are you okay?" he asks.

Finally, I blink away the fog and shake my head.

"S-sorry. You…I…" I swallow again because my throat's gone dry. "I wasn't expectin' that and am tryin' to find the right words to say."

He lowers his gaze as if he anticipates something bad. "Say whatever you feel."

"I feel…like you could do so much better than me."

He tilts his head, narrowing his eyes as they meet mine. "Why would you think that?"

"I've crushed on you for a while, but in the way someone crushes on a famous singer—not someone who's within arm's reach and could like you back. You have so much more to offer than I could give you in return."

"I don't agree with that. But you didn't know I liked you?"

"I mean, Natalie suggested that you did, but I told her she was wrong. I thought you were just being helpful and friendly."

The corner of his lips tilts up in amusement. "Natalie was not wrong. Although I was being helpful, I'm not usually this *friendly* with girls I don't like."

"Dammit, she's gonna love rubbin' that in my face." I laugh, then ask him the million-dollar question. "Why haven't you kissed me?"

"I was tryin' not to cross the line between teachin' you the things you asked and makin' things intimate between us in a way that a couple would be," he explains. "I also didn't wanna steal your first kiss if you didn't have the same feelings toward me."

"I *only* have feelings for you…like…a lot of 'em," I admit shyly.

He blows out a breath of relief, grinning. "Good…then get back in my lap so I can kiss you the way you deserve."

Chapter Twenty-Four
Waylon

The weight of uncertainty finally lifts off my shoulders, so when Harlow is seated in my lap, I pull her into me without hesitation.

"You're so beautiful and perfect," I whisper, stroking my thumb over her cheek.

"I'd argue about the perfect part," she sasses.

"Perfect for *me*," I clarify, brushing the strands of loose hair behind her ear. "Do you need me to talk you through this?"

I'm only half-teasing, but I want this to be a good experience for her and to make sure she's comfortable even though we've done far more than kissing at this point.

"I think I'll be okay. Take the lead, and I'll follow," she says confidently.

Slowly, I lean in closer but not quite touching. My hand slides around her neck and up into her hair. Pressing my forehead to hers, I inhale her scent and breathe her in.

Her chest presses into mine with every deep exhale, and I know she's anxiously waiting.

"Harlow…" I say her name gently, hoping it calms her nerves. "Wrap your arms around me."

Only With Me

She slides her hands up my shoulders and around my head, then grips her fingers into my hair.

I love the feel of her hands on me, touching me, craving me as much as I crave her.

Our breaths mingle together before I tilt her head back and then glide my lips over her soft ones. I move against her, slowly at first, and then she kisses me back with fervor.

Sliding my tongue in her mouth, she massages it with hers and we quickly form a rhythm. I tighten my grip around her, then lift my hips so she feels how hard she's made me *again*.

"Yes…" She moans when she rocks against me. "Dry humping is even better with kissing."

I chuckle softly, teasing her bottom lip between my teeth before deepening it.

"Do you want me to rub your clit for you?" I ask.

The more she grinds on top of me, the harder it is to hold back from coming in my jeans.

"You can do that in this position?"

"Are you doubtin' me?" I quip, lowering my hand to the button of her jeans.

"Never…" She pants, almost nervously.

"If you want me to stop, just tell me, okay?"

She nods.

"Sit up slightly so I can grab your zipper," I demand.

She holds on to my arms as she lifts on her knees, giving me better access to lower her jeans. I teasingly slide my finger along the top of her panties and watch for her reaction.

"Are you okay?"

"I feel like every nerve in my body is on fire," she admits, blushing. "Keep going. I want you to touch me."

I twist my wrist as I lower my hand and then press the pad of my thumb over her clit. As I rub circles over it, her breathing picks up and her eyes flutter closed.

With my free hand, I grip her chin and bring her mouth back to mine so I can overwhelm her senses until she comes on my lap.

"Waylon..." She struggles through the buildup, needing more.

"I've got you, sweetheart...you can let go."

"I'm tryin'. I'm so close."

Bringing my lips to her neck, I kiss and suck under her ear.

"That's my good girl, baby. Ride me while I touch your pussy."

I quickly learned how much she likes it when I say filthy things to her and that it helps get her off so easily.

"It feels so different when you do it," she says in between deep breaths.

"Different bad?"

"No, definitely not...the pressure is so good."

"Your clit is so needy, fuck. I can't wait to taste it."

Her nails dig into my skin as she moves her hips with mine.

"Put 'em inside me. Your fingers. *Please*," she begs, and I almost don't recognize her desperate plea.

With another twist of my wrist, I slowly move two digits to her opening.

"Brace yourself, Harlow. It's gonna be tight and there might be some pressure."

"I don't care...I just wanna feel you there."

Fuck.

I'm trying so damn hard to go slow and be gentle with her, but she's so eager to experience everything all at once.

"I don't wanna hurt you."

"I'm so wet, they'll slide right in."

I almost chuckle at how confident she sounds because even though she's aroused, she's never had someone else put anything inside her.

"Tell me if it hurts," I remind her, sliding two fingers between her folds before slowly entering inside.

Her body tenses, and I do my best to ease in and out.

"Are you okay?"

"Yes...*perfect*," she hums.

I bring my lips to hers again so she'll relax, and when she finally does, I thrust in deeper.

Only With Me

"How's that?"

"You can go faster."

I do as she says and increase my pace, finger-fucking her fast and deep.

"Oh my God, that's so good...don't stop."

"Fuck, you're so wet for me, baby. You wanna come on my fingers?"

"Yes, so close...I'm—"

Her head falls back between her shoulders, body shaking, and frantic moaning echoes around us and I know she's there— riding the high of her first orgasm given by someone who's not herself.

"Holy shit," she exhales the words with a sated smile.

I bring up my hand and hold up the two fingers before sliding them in my mouth.

"What do I taste like?" she asks, watching me intently.

"Sweet...like fruit."

"No way."

Once I've cleaned off my fingers, I bring my lips to hers and slide my tongue between them so she can see for herself.

"You taste like my *favorite* strawberry."

"I like tastin' myself on you. Maybe next time I should spit your cum back into your mouth so you can see for yourself."

I arch a brow, wondering where the hell that came from.

"Do you have a spitting kink I'm just now learnin' about?"

She giggles against me, tightening her hold around my neck and kissing me again.

"You're not the only one who can teach."

"We'll circle back to that one later." I grin against her.

"Mm. But I'm also learning how much I really like kissin' you."

"Glad to hear it because I don't think I coulda gone another day without it."

"Am I good at it?" She pulls back. "You can be honest."

"Harlow..." I laugh between my words. "You have nothin' to

worry about. Everything we've done has been better than anything I've ever experienced."

"Can I ask you a question?"

"You should know the answer to that by now," I quip. "But yes, go ahead."

"If you've liked me for a while now, why did you agree to teach me about sex and orgasms when you knew it was so I could find someone on that datin' app?"

"Because I didn't want anyone else teachin' you. I wanted you to have those experiences only with me."

"Okay, fair enough." She licks her lips. "I kinda stopped tryin' to meet anyone because I much rather spend my time with you."

"Is it safe to say you won't be goin' on a second date with Ethan?"

She snorts. "Emery, and definitely not. He was kinda weird and way too invasive."

"Invasive, how?"

"He asked about me the entire time, never said much about himself, and wanted to know a lot of personal details."

My brows rise in concern. "I hope you didn't tell him where you live."

"No, but he did ask where I worked."

"Harlow..." I sigh. "What's the point in meetin' in a public spot if you're just gonna tell him how to find you later?"

"I thought it was harmless...he looked like a normal guy."

"They all do until they hunt you down like prey."

"Now you sound like Natalie. She makes me share my location with her because she reads all these horror novels about serial killers. Oh shit, speakin' of—" She reaches for her bag and takes out her phone. "If she's watchin' me now, she's gonna freak out that I've been sittin' in the middle of nowhere for a half an hour."

"I think I like this Natalie..."

"I'm sure you would," she mocks, scrolling through her messages. "Yep, seventeen texts askin' if I'm alive."

"I'm glad she cares about you, though."

Only With Me

"Oh no…" Her eyes grow wider.

"What?"

"She called the sheriff and gave him our location."

"Oh shit…we better go."

When I look in my rearview mirror, I realize it's too late. He's parked behind me.

"Fuck, you better get over." I help her move next to me but then realize her pants are still undone. "Button your jeans."

Then I scramble to adjust myself and hide my erection.

There's a knuckle tap on the window and an angry sheriff with a phone to his ear.

"Hey, Sheriff Wagner," I say once the window's down. "Nice day out, ain't it?"

"Yes, Miss Rhodes, I see 'em." He speaks into the phone, his tone laced with annoyance as he glares at me. "Alive, not murdered." His gaze moves to Harlow. "She looks fine to me. By the looks on their faces, I interrupted somethin'."

And then a loud squeal through the phone's speaker, "I knew it!"

"Oh my God," Harlow mutters, her palm colliding with her forehead. "I'm so sorry."

Her apology to the sheriff gets ignored as he pulls his phone away from his ear and dramatically hangs up on her.

"Mr. Hollis…" His pointed stare makes me uneasy. "Ms. Fanning."

"We were just—"

"Save it." He holds up a hand. "I *highly* encourage y'all to get a move on because if y'all make me do more paperwork on my *day off*, imma be pissed."

"Yes, sir." I lower my steering wheel and then pull the lever to move up the seat. "We're leavin' now."

I watch in my side mirror as he walks back to his car, shaking his head. Once I'm buckled, I signal to turn onto the road and drive back toward the ranch.

"Holy crap, he scares me."

I chuckle. "He's all growl and no bite."

"I can't believe Natalie called him and made him find me. She's gonna kill me for makin' her worry."

"Better text her that you were *too busy* to answer." I smirk.

"Yeah, see...that'll require a whole Thursday night topic of conversation where she'll demand a play-by-play of what happened."

"Not...*everything* that's happened, right?"

She shrugs innocently.

"What have you told her so far?"

She purses her lips, then pretends to seal them.

"Well, that's not fair...who am I supposed to tell?" I'm only messing with her because I'd never reveal intimate details to someone else.

"Your twin brother."

I scoff. "He has the biggest mouth of anyone I know and unless you want your sister findin' out through him, I can't tell him shit."

Even though he already suspects something's going on between us, I don't have to confirm anything yet.

"That's true, but I'll need to tell her eventually."

I reach over, interconnecting my fingers with hers. "I know. We can do it together, if you want."

"Yeah, maybe. But I think she'll be happy for us. At least that's my hope."

"For you, maybe. I have a feelin' she'll wanna kick my ass."

"Well, that might be the price you pay if you wanna be with me," she taunts.

I bring her hand up and kiss her knuckles. "In that case, I'll let her get in a few good punches before I tell Wilder to hold her back."

"How sweet of you." She giggles. "But I think you're gonna haveta tell my dad first."

Chapter Twenty-Five
Harlow

After Natalie thoroughly cusses me out for ignoring her messages and reminding me about country drives being serial killer territory, she makes me tell her every little detail during our next Thursday night hangout session—although I skipped the details, but she doesn't need to know that. She enjoyed gloating about how she *knew it*. After the sheriff busted us, I texted and thanked her for *so kindly* sending the sheriff to come interrupt us, but I appreciated the sentiment that she was worried about me.

But then my dad found out and he was less than happy. The sheriff's wife works at the same hospital as my mom, who mentioned it to her, and then she told my father.

Even though I'm an adult, he'll always see me as a little girl. He's not used to me being interested in dating or staying out late. Although he goes to bed early, he often wakes up with pain a couple times throughout the night, so when I quietly walked into the house after midnight, it was unusual for him to see me coming in from a night out with Waylon.

It's not so much that Waylon dated Delilah, but my parents are concerned he's too old for me and will push me into marriage and having babies before I'm ready. Waylon isn't pushy like that, considering how respectful he's been of my boundaries and always asks if I'm comfortable doing certain things, he's not the type.

But I'm hoping they'll warm up to him the more they get to know him again and see how happy I am and that they have nothing to worry about.

Now I just have to find a way to tell my sister before she finds out on her own.

But that day won't be now because Waylon planned a whole Saturday to take me and my dad out to an elite equine center for premier riders an hour and a half away. Waylon bought a carrier attachment for the back of his truck so he can drive us and make sure Dad has everything he needs.

It took a little convincing for my dad to agree to come along, but once Mom talked to him, he changed his mind. I know it's not easy for him with his anxiety and chronic pain, but I hope getting him out of the house will be good for his mental state.

He's been struggling more lately, which I think is somewhat due to being in the middle of the winter season, but this place has heated lounges for comfortable viewing of the arena. Better yet, everything's handicapped accessible, so he should have no issues being in his power chair.

I'm also excited to watch the show horse jumpers. They're professionals who've been riding for two decades or more and they do some intense courses and high jumps.

By ten, I'm ready to go and waiting in the living room for Dad to finish. As I play on my phone, I'm reminded that I need to remove the CowboyMatch app. But first I need to delete my profile.

Except when I go to my most recent messages, I see an unread one from Emery. I know how it feels to be stood up and ghosted, so I'd like to give him the courtesy of telling him I'm no longer interested.

Only With Me

EMERY

Hey gorgeous, I was hoping we could set up a second date. Are you busy Saturday?

He sent that three days ago.

HARLOW

Hi Emery. I'm so sorry for not replying sooner. Honestly, I forgot to check my messages on here. I'm actually seeing someone now and will be deleting my profile, but I wanted to tell you so you weren't left wondering.

I think that sounds okay, right? I'm being direct and honest, and if he gets mad about that, then that's his problem.

EMERY

Oh too bad. But I appreciate you telling me. Maybe I'll see ya around your store sometime. Have a good one!

Before I can reply, his profile disappears.
Did he just block me?
How strange.
I delete my profile and then delete the app for good.

WAYLON

I'm on my way, baby. Be there in 15.

I'll never get over him calling me that.

In person when his hands are all over me, when we're video chatting casually about our day, or in a text. It sends butterflies to my stomach within seconds.

"Hey, Daddy? Are you almost ready?" I call out through his bedroom door.

When no one answers, I knock a few times, then twist the knob.

"Daddy?"

He's sitting on the edge of the bed with his one foot on the floor, still dressed in his comfy clothes. His head's bowed down and he's shaking his stump.

I walk in and rest a hand on his shoulder. "Are you okay?"

He startles at my voice as if he didn't hear me calling his name or knocking on the door.

"Oh, hi, sweetheart." He looks up at me with sad eyes, and I notice that expression. "I'm sorry. I don't think I can go today."

"You don't wanna get outta the house and see some horses?" I ask gently.

"The pain is bad today. The weather changes are messin' with me and makin' it worse."

The temperatures have been jumping all over the place for the past couple weeks. It'll be in the low thirties one day and high fifties the next. Not great for those who suffer with chronic pain.

"Can I do anythin'?" I ask, knowing there isn't, but I offer anyway.

I'm disappointed he can't go, but I understand.

"No, no. You and Waylon go and have fun. I'm gonna take a sleepin' pill and lie down."

"Please be careful with that," I remind him.

It sucks he has to be dependent on medication to help him sleep through the pain, but I mostly worry when it's this intense and he takes so much of it.

"Don't worry about me. Mom will be home in an hour."

Since she's off work today, she went grocery shopping and to pick up his monthly meds at the pharmacy.

"Waylon and I can wait until she's home," I tell him.

"Okay, sweetheart."

I kiss his cheek. "Love you."

"Love you, too."

Before I shut the bedroom door, I call in my mom's two dogs to go inside. They love snuggling on the bed with him and it gives me some comfort that he's not alone.

Only With Me

Moose follows me into my room and sits on the bed with me while I text Waylon.

> HARLOW
>
> Hey, change of plans. My dad's unable to go today. He's in a lot of pain, so he's going to bed. My mom's out running errands so I told him we'd wait to leave until she returns.

It can be hard for some people who don't live with chronic pain or aren't disabled—or live with someone who is—to truly understand that it's not as easy as jumping in the car and going whenever we want. You don't recognize what a privilege it is to have mobile freedom until it's taken away or realize how many public places aren't handicapped accessible. Between Dad losing his leg and me having two broken legs a year later, I can hardly remember a time in my childhood when we didn't have to think twice about leaving the house and making sure there was a wheelchair ramp, an accessible bathroom, and wide enough doors for him to get through.

There's been several times over the years where we'd go somewhere and then quickly find out how inaccessible it was, even when they claimed they were. Doorways too small, aisles between tables and chairs too tight, and only one or two handicapped parking spaces. I think his bad experiences worsened his feelings about being a burden and added to his anxiety to the point where he stopped wanting to go anywhere.

> WAYLON
>
> No worries. We can even hang out until he wakes up and then see if he wants to play a board game or do a puzzle. Or even watch TV.

> HARLOW
>
> You'd spend your only day off sitting in my house and playing games?

WAYLON

> Of course. I can't think of anything else I'd rather do.

Gah, he's sweet.

When he arrives five minutes later, I throw myself into his arms and kiss the hell out of him.

"What was that for?" he asks when I finally let him breathe. "Not that I'm complainin', but I was gonna limit the PDA around your folks."

Laughing, I grab his hand and lead him into the hallway where we keep the games. "It's just us for now."

When I open the closet, his eyes widen in surprise. "Wow, you have a lot of options."

"Yep, and I can probably whip your ass in most of 'em."

"Oh, I didn't realize you were one of those."

"One of what?"

"A competitive game freak."

"Excuse you?" I push him with my hip. "It was all I could do being in a half-body cast."

"Alright, fair enough. So what do ya wanna play?"

"You're the guest, so you choose."

He steps closer, looking through all the games. "I've not played this in years, but I remember Noah always tried to cheat."

I grin when he grabs the Clue box. "That's one of my favorites. I'm gonna *crush* you."

"You sound awfully confident." His taunting voice makes me giggle.

"Well, let's play and see."

Only With Me

"You're cheating!" I exclaim when Waylon reveals the final card from the envelope.

This is the fourth game in a row he's won. Or rather, *cheated*.

His eyes crinkle as he bellows out a laugh. "How can I cheat when you're right there?"

"Forgive her, we let her win so much as a child, she thinks we cheat if she loses," my dad says, sitting next to me and suddenly on Waylon's side.

"You did not *let* me win!" I argue. "I had good intuition!"

"Sweetie, you always guessed the same person," Mom interjects. "So we made sure that card was always in the envelope so you had a better chance at guessin' right."

My jaw falls to the floor. "You're tellin' me y'all let me think I was winnin' on my own for seven years?"

"You were the baby of the family, and we felt bad. You could barely walk," Mom explains.

"Oh my gosh! A pity win? Unbelievable."

"If it makes ya feel better, I'll never let you win on purpose." Waylon beams.

"You know what"—I point my finger at him—"you're banned from game night."

"Don't be a sore loser," Dad says. "You just need more practice."

I glare at him for being part of the reason I apparently suck at this game.

"Fine." I force a smile. "How about Uno? Did y'all let me win at Uno?"

The room goes silent.

"Oh my God!" I throw my arms up in disbelief and then smack my forehead against the table. "I'm a fraud."

"We can play Monopoly. You rarely wanted to play that because of how long it lasted, so most times, we never even finished a game," Mom says.

I lift my head and burst out laughing at this whole situation with my parents letting me win and the fact that Waylon is here on a Saturday night, playing games with me and my parents. And he looks like he's genuinely having a good time.

"Are you good at that one?" I ask him, playfully narrowing my eyes at him.

"I've only played a handful of times back in high school, so we'll be on equal playin' ground."

"Alright, it's on."

Mom puts a pizza in the oven while Dad and I set up the game board. We put him in charge of the money and then I organize the cards. Waylon reading over the instructions has me giggling.

"What? I wanna make sure when I beat you, it's fair and square."

"Very funny," I mock. "Hope you're ready to embarrass yourself in front of my parents when I win."

My dad turns and looks at Waylon. "Now you know why we *let* her win."

Three hours and landing on Waylon's multiple houses and hotels later, I finally surrender when I go bankrupt.

"What was that about me being embarrassed?" He cups his ear as if he's waiting for me to admit I was wrong.

"Ya know, it's not very gentlemanly to *gloat*."

He smirks, helping my mom clean up the table.

"If you want, I can *teach* you how to better strategize so you don't lose all your money before you're able to make investments." The way he emphasizes that word as a subtle hint has me squeezing my legs.

Well played, cowboy.

Only With Me

At seven, Dad's ready for bed and Mom has an early shift in the morning, so she calls it a night too.

"It was nice of you to stay," Dad tells Waylon, and my heart beats with happiness. Even though Dad's day started out rough, I think having company and staying distracted helped him manage his pain.

"It was my pleasure, sir. Thank you for havin' me."

Dad's chair maneuvers around the table until he's next to me. "I like him."

I can't help grinning as I look at Waylon out of the corner of my eyes. "Yeah, I like him too."

"Now don't scare him off with your overcompetitiveness."

I roll my eyes. "Whose fault is that now?"

Dad shrugs, chuckling. "He's good for you. Doesn't let you win out of pity."

He's not even trying to speak quietly, so I know Waylon hears him, but it fills me with pride to get his approval.

"Love you, Daddy." I lean in and kiss his cheek, then he heads toward his room.

Mom says good night next and thanks Waylon for spending time with them.

"Thank you for dinner," Waylon says.

Mom blushes, waving him off. "Oh, it was nothin'."

She comes around and hugs me, then leans in to my ear. "Have fun. Don't stay up too late."

"I won't. Love you."

Once she's out of view, I walk over to Waylon and sit on his lap, then press my lips to his.

"It meant a lot that you stayed and hung out with us."

"I had fun...especially kickin' your ass."

I elbow him in the chest. "Okay, you can stop sayin' that now."

He chuckles, gripping my chin and pulling me in for another kiss. "I will always let you win first when we *play* in private."

"Is that so? I think you might haveta prove that to me..."

He reveals a cocky smirk. "Take me to your room and I will."

"With my parents here?" I whisper.

I've never had a boy in my room before, and I'm not so sure what they'd think if they found him in there.

He leans in and seductively presses his mouth to my ear. "You're gonna haveta be quiet. Think you can do that?"

When he kisses my neck, I inhale sharply at how good it feels when he touches me. "That's so not fair."

"Not complainin' about my skills now, are ya?"

Definitely not.

Chapter Twenty-Six
Waylon

It's been three days since I've seen Harlow and I'm already having withdrawals. I never thought I'd be that guy who wants to see a girl all the time, but when we're apart, I miss her like crazy.

I'm obsessed.

Between our work schedules and her staying home with her dad, we haven't been able to hang out. But we text throughout the day as much as we can.

Then at night, we video chat and I talk her through giving herself an orgasm—but now I don't have to hold back like I did before. I can tell her all the filthy ways I'd touch and pleasure her if I were there with her.

> **HARLOW**
> What time should I come over tonight?

Since she only works until four and her mom will be home, we can finally make plans.

> **WAYLON**
> I'll be done and showered by 6. Do you want to grab something to eat then?

Brooke Montgomery

> **HARLOW**
> Sure, and then we can go back to your place and you can eat me for dessert.

Jesus Christ.

> **WAYLON**
> Baby! You can't just say that when I'm working.

> **HARLOW**
> Why not?

> **WAYLON**
> Safety hazard. I could've driven into something.

> **HARLOW**
> Are you driving right now?

> **WAYLON**
> No, I'm about to walk to The Lodge to eat breakfast with Wilder.

> **HARLOW**
> So I shouldn't tell you that tonight I'd like your tongue between my thighs? 😈 For educational purposes…

> **WAYLON**
> I'm about to ditch work and speed over to your house right now if you don't stop torturing me.

And because she loves to tease the hell out of me, she sends a photo of herself only wearing panties in bed.

> **HARLOW**
> Strawberries for dessert sound good, doesn't it?

> **WAYLON**
> Fuck yes, it does. But now I'm gonna be walking around all day with a hard-on, so thank you for that.

Only With Me

HARLOW
If you feel the need to take care of that before I get there, send me a video.

WAYLON
You're killing me, woman.

HARLOW
I'll send you one of me and how wet I am just thinking about you.

Fuck me.

WAYLON
That's cheating when I can't stop what I'm doing to make one for you.

HARLOW
Cheating…or knowing how to win fair and square? 😈

I can't help smirking at her competitive nature, but I adore her for it.

WAYLON
It's like that, huh? Okay, you just wait…I'm gonna edge you over and over until you're begging me to let you come. And even then, I won't let you until you admit you lost.

HARLOW
Never gonna happen.

WAYLON
We'll see about that, baby.

"Stop sexting your girlfriend before you run into a door."

Wilder's voice startles me, and I realize we're in front of The Lodge.

"Quit readin' over my shoulder." I lock my phone and slide it into my pocket.

"When're you tellin' Delilah?" he asks as we walk inside.

"Whenever Harlow's ready."

Confessing to her sister isn't the only thing hanging over my head right now. The truth about the group chat still sits in my stomach like a piece of meat I can't digest. The more I think about how to tell her, the more scared I get that I'll lose her when I do. This is the first relationship I've had in years and the last thing I want to do is complicate things, especially because of how much I like her and how much she trusts me.

I just need to find the right time.

"Look, I want you to be happy. Hell, I'm glad you're finally gettin' some and outta my hair. But you gotta tell her before she finds out."

"We will. But it's nice not havin' everyone in our business and feedin' us their opinions while we get to know each other," I tell him as we approach the buffet.

"You gonna tell Mom and Dad?"

"Eventually." I grab a plate and add as much food as I can to last me for the next twelve hours. Once I get Harlow to myself, I'm not eating anything besides her.

At exactly six, there's a knock on the door. I grin, knowing she's going to be pissed when she sees I'm in only a towel.

But when I open the door, I'm the one surprised.

Biting my cheek to keep from smiling, I lean against the doorframe with my arms crossed. "What're you wearin'?"

She looks down at her short skirt, thigh-high boots, and black lace corset top. "Just a new outfit I got at work yesterday."

"Since when does Rodeo Belle sell lingerie?"

Only With Me

"Oh, right..." She playfully smacks her head. "I stopped at Lacey's after. Don't ya like it?"

Unable to hold back, I smirk at her feigned innocence.

"At least I'm wearin' clothes..." Her gaze drops down my chest, stomach, and to the towel that's barely hanging on. "You've been holdin' out on me with all of that."

"Well, why don't ya come in and see more of it for yourself." I step back, giving her room to enter.

She stops mid-step to meet my stare. "And you say *I'm* the cheater."

I hold up my hands. "I literally had ten minutes to shower."

"Mm-hmm..." She walks in and drops her bag next to the shoe rack.

Closing the door behind her, I grab her wrist and pull her in front of me until she's caged against the wood and my body.

Tilting up her chin, I say, "You're the one who sent me a naughty video and then I had to wait hours until I could take care of myself. So if anyone's playin' dirty here, it's you, baby."

"It's not my fault you're playing Checkers when I'm playin' Chess." She bites her bottom lip like the little seductress she is.

In that case...

Dinner can wait.

Lowering my hand to the towel, I release the knot and it falls to the floor. Her eyes follow and widen when they land on my half-erect cock. Wrapping my hand around the shaft, I pump it a few times, pushing into her stomach with each stroke.

"Be a good little student and get on your knees."

The fire behind her eyes tells me she's fighting between being defiant and giving in to what we both want.

"C'mon, now. I know how much you love followin' my instructions."

Her gaze stays locked on mine when she finally obliges and kneels between my feet.

There's a pink ribbon at the back of her head, pulling half of her hair back and reminding me of the day we were supposed to meet in person. I wish I could say it causes me to stop and tell her right now, but truthfully, there's no natural disaster that could prevent me from experiencing this with her right now.

Tomorrow. I'll tell her tomorrow.

I cup her chin with my other hand. "Such a good girl. Now show me your tongue."

When she does, I slap my cock against it a couple times, giving her a moment to get used to it. Although she's done it once before in my truck, it's different at this angle when I'm standing above her.

"Tap my thigh twice if you need me to stop, okay?"

She nods, sticking it out further. I slide deeper into her hot mouth and then she takes over with her hand around the bottom of my shaft, sucking and licking. When she wraps her lips around my length and then hollows her cheeks to take in more, I lose myself to the pleasure.

"Fuck, Harlow." My palm rests on the door behind her, and I watch in amazement at how well she's swallowing me whole. "Just like that, so good."

The sensations shoot right up my spine with every teasing swirl around the tip. She smiles around my cock, looking up devilishly as if she knows she's going to win this round.

"Can you take more?" I ask and she nods eagerly.

I cup a hand around the back of her head. "Relax your jaw, sweetheart. I'm gonna fuck this perfect mouth until I come down your throat."

When I feel it loosen, I thrust in and out, keeping eye contact as tears slip down her cheeks, but I watch her hands closely in case she needs me to stop.

"So close, baby. Squeeze me harder."

And when she does, it only takes a few more seconds before I'm losing my breath and feeding her my release.

"Fuck, how'd you get so good at that?" I pant out the words, trying to fill my lungs.

She grins up at me, licking her lips. "I had a good teacher."

Only With Me

Holding out my hand, she puts hers in mine, and then I pull her up against me. Cupping her face, I kiss her hard and taste myself on her.

"You're gonna haveta be in a lot less clothing if you want me to eat your pussy, baby."

"What about dinner?"

"You had the appetizer and now I'm skipping right to dessert."

Before she can respond, I lift her by the back of her thighs and she quickly wraps them around me. Her hands clasp to my shoulders as I walk us to the kitchen.

"I'd like to try somethin' new…for educational purposes," I tease, throwing her words back at her. "I've never done this on the kitchen counter before…you wanna try it?"

"Try what exactly?"

I set her down on the kitchen island, stand between her legs, and then bury my face in her hair.

"Feastin' on your sweet cunt right here on full display. Devourin' every inch of your body between these thighs and not stoppin' until you come shakin' and screamin' on my tongue."

"Okay, you win…" She pants out the words, spreading her legs wider around me.

I chuckle with amusement, gliding my nose down her neck and then sucking on her collarbone.

"Remove your clothes for me…one by one."

I'm already hard again at watching her strip for me. First, her corset drops to the floor. Then I help her out of her boots and skirt. Next, the panties slide down her bare legs, and I finish tearing them off her ankles with my teeth.

"Fuck. You're so beautiful, baby. So goddamn perfect." I cup her breast, then bring my mouth to her nipple. "Lean back on your hands so I can taste you."

Once she's in a comfortable position, I make my way down her stomach, licking and kissing before I kneel between her legs.

"If you don't like the sensation or anything I'm doing, tap my shoulder or tell me to stop. Okay?"

She nods, biting her lower lip.

Although I've had my fingers inside her, swiping my tongue through her wet folds is pure bliss and enough to make me crave more.

"Mm…so fuckin' sweet, Harlow."

I tease her clit and circle my fingers through the slickness at her entrance. When her breathing turns deep with needy sighs, I know she's ready for more.

Sliding two digits inside her, I bury my face in her pussy, flicking and sucking, waking up all her nerve cells. Harlow's groans fill the kitchen, her fingers tangle in my hair, and soon she's edging closer toward her release.

But then I slow my strokes, pull my fingers back slightly, and peek up at her wide eyes.

"Why'd you stop?"

Licking my lips, I smirk. "That's called edgin', sweetheart."

"That's torture! Punishable in fifty states with a lifetime sentence in federal prison."

I cackle at her quick wit, thrusting my fingers back inside.

"Is that so? You gonna put me in handcuffs and turn me in?" I quip, giving her clit another flick.

"I should, and then sit on your face as punishment."

"Oh, don't worry, baby. I'll teach you to do that before I let you leave tonight."

Harlow's sweet, needy moans keep me fed while I devour her. Fingers soaked in her juices, my face covered with her scent, and her thighs shaking around me as I edge her over and over—getting her close, almost to the finish line—and then pulling back.

"Please, I'll do anything," she hisses, begging for mercy.

"I can't get enough of my favorite strawberry…" I taunt, my groans vibrating against her pussy. "I'm addicted."

Obsessed.

Before she can continue pleading, I scoop her up and walk us to my bedroom. My cock's so hard, it's almost throbbing in pain.

But I'm not having sex with her tonight. I want to take my

Only With Me

time with her, make sure she's ready mentally and physically, and make it as special as I can. She deserves that and so much more.

"I want you to finish by ridin' my face."

"How do I do that exactly?" she asks when I sit on the edge of the mattress and motion for her to stand.

"I'm gonna lie back, like this..." I get into position with my head in the middle of the bed. "And you're gonna straddle my face with your thighs so I can eat your pussy."

She climbs on top of me until she's kneeling above me.

"Perfect, now lower your body so I can taste you."

"All the way down?" she asks.

I nod. "All. The. Way. Down."

"Seems like a breathin' hazard, but okay..." she drawls and then sits right where I need her.

When I look at her, she meets my eyes and a beautiful blush covers her chest and face. Reaching up, I cup her breast and pinch her little pebbled nipple.

I pull her throbbing clit between my lips before rubbing circles over her sweet spot with my tongue.

"Holy shit, that feels so good..." Her head falls back slightly as she braces her palms on the wall in front of her.

Cupping her ass with my other hand, I move her back and forth so she gets the hint to rock against my face.

"Fuck, Waylon. Right there...don't ya dare stop this time."

Groaning against her flesh, I continue rotating between sucking and licking until she's screaming through her release and I taste her sweet cum.

"Yes, yes...oh my God." Her body twitches, and I moan into her inner thigh, then tap it twice.

Once she lifts off me, I roll my body until I'm towering over her.

"Jesus Christ, you did so good." Then I bring my mouth down to hers so she can see how delicious she is.

"My whole body is numb," she whimpers.

Brooke Montgomery

Chuckling against her neck, I feather kisses along her jawline and ear. "I think we'll call this round a draw. Whaddya think?"

"Okay…" She snickers. "Guess that means we'll haveta find a way to break the tie to determine a winner."

"Maybe if you're a good girl, I'll let you win next time and then you can claim your prize."

"Hmm." She grins with a mischievous look in her eyes. "What kinda prize are we talkin' about?"

I trace my finger over her cheek, down her chin, and then slide it between her lips until she's sucking on it. "The kind that makes you lose your voice and need three to five business days to recover."

Chapter Twenty-Seven
Harlow

The day after the best oral of my life, I have training with Noah but can still feel Waylon between my thighs.

After I came down from my orgasmic high, I noticed Waylon was hard again. But this time, I told him to get himself off so I could watch in person. It was even sexier than through a screen, especially since this time, he shot his cum on my chest and then licked it off me.

Safe to say, last night was one of the hottest nights I've ever experienced. Feeling his facial hair scratch against my pussy and thighs was a new kind of sensation I hope to relive over and over.

Once we cleaned up and got dressed, he made dinner and we watched *The Notebook* so I could refresh his memory on the fighting in the rain scene. That led to him asking if I had more things on my romance wish list.

Go-karting and whoever wins gets to make the loser do whatever they want—sexual or not

Wine tasting but with coffee drinks

Eat something off each other—preferably non-sticky but make it fun and erotic

Buddy read a book together

Each time I think of another thing I want to experience or do

Only With Me

with him, I add it to my notes app. I'm up to a hundred and seventeen.

The rails aren't set up in the training center today, which means Noah's going to have me do exercises and conditioning with Piper. It's as important as practice jumps, but considering I'm more tired today than usual, we drag ass and Noah notices.

"You okay?"

"Yeah, why?" I ask, grabbing Piper's lead rope and walking toward her.

She shrugs one shoulder. "You're lower energy than normal."

I swallow hard because as far as I know, Waylon hasn't told his family, except Wilder.

"Didn't get much sleep last night, but I promise to be on my A-game next time."

She hides a knowing grin with her clipboard. "Okay, no biggie. We all have our off days."

"I'll take Piper to the groomin' stall and put her back in," I tell her.

"Your sister should be here any minute for her session if you wanna stick around."

Delilah's a professional trick-rider, so she doesn't need a lot of extra training but likes to practice more during the off-season so she doesn't get rusty.

"Sounds good. I'll come back out when I'm done."

After guiding Piper into the barn, I tie her up in the grooming stall and take off her tack. When I carry her saddle into the tack room, Waylon's in there, waiting for me.

"What're ya doing?" I whisper even though no one else's here.

"I was missin' ya and saw you were almost done, so I wanted to surprise you." He scoops me in his arms, tilts my chin, and presses his lips to mine. "And I was hopin' we could talk."

"Well, ain't you sweet." I giggle in his arms, kissing him back. "Noah noticed I was draggin' ass today."

"You're not the only one. Wilder's been on my case all mornin' about it, which is hilarious comin' from *him*." He scoffs. "But oh well, totally worth it."

"Definitely worth it."

He sinks his tongue into my mouth, and I get so lost in him, I don't hear the door open, but it's followed up with a loud gasp.

Waylon's eyes widen and I glance over my shoulder to see my sister in the doorway, looking like she's ready to murder him.

"Oh shit." I turn around and wipe my chin.

"My little *sister*?" Delilah snaps at him, folding her arms across her chest. "How long has this been goin' on?"

"A month," I say at the same time Waylon says, "A couple weeks."

I narrow my eyes and look back at him. We weren't *together* at the start of my lessons, but we started talking before he confessed he wanted me.

Delilah's brows furrow in confusion. "Which one is it?"

Waylon scrubs a hand over his scruffy jawline. "We started talkin' New Year's Eve."

"So…over three weeks?" She gives him a pointed look.

Before either of us can answer, Noah opens the door, not realizing what she's walking into.

"Oh, hey." Noah notices Delilah's pissed off expression and then glances at Waylon and me. "Uh-oh…did y'all not tell her yet?"

Delilah shoots daggers at Waylon and me. "Am I the last one to know?"

"To be fair, I didn't know that Noah did," Waylon says.

"Oh, please." Noah snorts. "I know a secret relationship when I see it. Y'all weren't very discreet. He never came to watch you practice in the four years since you started and suddenly he's showin' up. Waylon's on his phone way more than I've ever seen him. Harlow coming to trainin' exhausted like she stayed out the night before. I was young and sneakin' around with Fisher once, too."

Oh my God.

Only With Me

My cheeks flush with embarrassment.

"*Great...*" Delilah feigns excitement. "So glad my ex is corruptin' my baby sister."

Like a dagger to my heart, I hate that she still sees me as a little kid.

"If anythin', I've corrupted him," I blurt. "I'm not a child anymore, Delilah."

I turn twenty-one in less than two months. But in her eyes, I'm a fragile kid who's on bedrest and needs her help for everything.

"Yeah, I don't need details." Delilah moves her gaze to me. "Do Mom and Dad know?"

I swallow hard and nod. "Yeah, he spent Saturday at the house playing games."

"And they're okay with you datin' my ex?" she asks in shock. "Who's over a decade older than you?"

Nervously, I suck in my lip. "Yeah, they love him."

And I'm falling hard for him, too.

After an awkward amount of silence, Delilah says, "Okay, well, I need to grab Jasmine's saddle. Excuse me."

Realizing we're in her way, Waylon and I move to the side, and she silently grabs it from the rack.

Noah grabs what she came in for, then Waylon and I are left alone.

"Well...that went as expected," I say. "She'll come around."

Waylon sighs. "Hopefully. I thought she was gonna kick me in the balls before Noah came in."

I chuckle lightly. "Saved by your sister."

He scratches his cheek. "Yeah, I can't believe she knew..."

"Do you think that means the rest of your family does?"

"There's only one way to find out." He takes my hand and leads me to the door. "Wanna go to lunch at The Lodge and then we can talk at my house after?"

"Really?" I ask about showing up around his siblings together.

"Yeah." He winks, bringing my hand to his lips and kissing my knuckles. "No point in hidin' it now that your sister knows."

Brooke Montgomery

When we walk into The Lodge hand in hand, the rest of his siblings who are there to eat all hoot and holler, embarrassing us in front of the guests.

Waylon leans into me as we get closer to the tables. "Oh yeah, they knew."

I giggle and blush at the attention. "*Great.*"

Magnolia and Ellie are here too, so when I sit across from them and they smile sweetly at me, I return the gesture.

"So..." Magnolia waves her fork between Waylon and me. "How'd this happen?"

Tripp snickers next to her. "So nosy."

"As if you're not wonderin' the same thing," she drawls.

"The shortened version..." I begin. "I messaged him through a dating app and we started talking."

Speaking of the app, I need to tell Waylon about Emery showing up at my work yesterday. But I forgot the moment I arrived at his house and he opened the door in only a towel, his hair still dripping wet from his shower.

"She asked me to teach her how to orgasm," Waylon abruptly adds in the most casual way and then takes a bite of his food.

I elbow him and he winks at me. The little blabbermouth. "They didn't need to know *that*."

"Oh my God, yes, we do!" Magnolia squeals, leaning over the table to get closer.

Ellie checks her pretend watch on her wrist. "I've got the whole afternoon free."

"Did you tell Delilah finally?" Wilder asks.

"She kinda walked in on us makin' out." I wince, scooping mashed potatoes and taking a bite.

"Yeah, she ain't happy with me," Waylon adds.

"To be fair, she wasn't happy with you when y'all were datin', so who cares what she thinks now?" Landen quips, and Ellie shoots him a glare that can only be translated to *Shut up, you idiot.*

"I think she's madder we didn't tell her because she still sees me as her little sister who needs her," I explain. "My parents are

Only With Me

okay with it, so I think she will be too once the shock wears off."

"If y'all get married and Delilah's your maid of honor, Waylon's gonna haveta see his ex-girlfriend walk down the aisle before his new wife does." Magnolia giggles.

"That's not awkward *at all*, Sunny." Tripp gives her a pointed look.

"Oh, c'mon. It's kinda funny. She's his ex's *sister*! That'd be like you and me breakin' up and then I go on to date Wilder."

Wilder leans over the table and winks at her.

"Don't even think about it," Tripp warns him.

It's hard not to laugh at their antics.

"Or I can hook up with Delilah and level the playin' field." Wilder waggles his brows.

"That's even crazier!" Magnolia blurts. "Your twin's ex-girlfriend? That's some straight to jail shit."

"Wouldn't be the first time he's slept with someone I was interested in…" I give him a pointed look.

"That was one time!" Wilder defends. "And how was I supposed to know you were actually gonna tell her? You dragged your feet for so long, she got married and knocked up six months later."

Waylon leans down closer. "Don't listen to him."

Wilder rolls his eyes, then looks at me. "Wait, I thought y'all started talkin' in that group chat first?"

Waylon visibly stiffens next to me and my heart races at his reaction.

"What're ya talkin' about?" I ask Wilder, leaning toward him.

"Jake told me y'all were in the horse club group chat together. I assumed y'all started talkin' through there."

"Wilder, shut up," Waylon demands through clenched teeth.

I've never seen him act this way toward his brother.

I nudge Waylon to grab his attention. "What's he talkin' about? You were in Jake's group chat?"

There's no way. Jake never introduced him.

Waylon's gaze lowers as stress lines cover his forehead. "I was gonna tell you after this," he mutters softly.

"Tell me what?" I ask, but I already have a sneaking suspicion that it's going to piss me off. "You're the one who told me I had poison ivy, aren't you? The one who told me about havin' a vitamin K deficiency?"

He nods.

I push my chair back. "We texted for a month and then you stood me up at the café!"

"Harlow, lemme explain..." He reaches for my hand, but I retreat out of his reach.

"You *fooled* me!"

He stands, covering me from his siblings' views. "I was gonna tell you this afternoon, I promise. I've been tryin' to, but there was never a good time."

"It doesn't matter now because our relationship is based on lies." I push against his chest when he tries coming closer, and then I walk away, storming through the doors until I'm outside.

Joke's on me now because my truck's all the way on the other side of the ranch.

A moment later, Ellie calls out my name behind me.

"Harlow, wait!" She catches up to me. "I'll drive you."

Tears fill my eyes, and I quickly wipe my cheek. "Thank you."

She leads me to her truck and once we're buckled in, she starts it. For a minute, it's silent between us, but then she glances over at me.

"I know my situation ain't exactly the same, but Landen's and my relationship didn't start out with the truth either."

"How so?" I ask, keeping my gaze low as I fight the urge to burst out crying.

"I hated him for four years before I lost my memory in a barrel racing accident."

I vaguely remember that from two years ago, but I was never in their circle to know the details.

Only With Me

"But when I forgot him, I realized I liked him. He was so kind and attractive, I couldn't fathom why I hated him."

"Did you figure it out?"

"Oh yeah...after I was deeply in love with him, too. So that sucked."

"How'd you react?"

"Well, I knew since the beginning that he was someone I was supposed to hate. Everyone kept tellin' me, 'you can't stand him, Ellie'...and Landen tried hard not to let me get too close. He knew as soon as my memory returned, I'd hate him even more. He was constantly waiting for the moment it came back and it felt like an evil trick. No one knew why I didn't like him, so no one could tell me why."

"Yikes, that'd be so frustrating."

"It was! But even after I remembered, there were moments it felt like our relationship wasn't real because of the four years prior, but me losing my memory gave us a real chance to explore our feelings. If I hadn't, there's no way we woulda ended up together."

I nod, understanding her position.

"So what I'm sayin' is, if it hadn't happened exactly how it was meant to, everything would be different, and that makes me sad because I can't imagine a life without him. So even if your relationship started out with deceptions, it brought you two together now. If you wanna make it work, you're gonna need to hear him out. Listen to why he did what he did and then decide if you can forgive him and move forward."

She parks next to my truck, then turns toward me.

"For what it's worth, none of us have seen him this happy before. Wilder spilled his big fat mouth about y'all and then I started noticin' the signs when I'd see him at The Lodge or during family dinner nights. His eyes are brighter. He laughs and smiles more than I've ever seen. And although I dunno him super well, I know he'd never hurt anyone on purpose."

"I know…he's been very patient and open with me." I wave out a hand. "Minus this one thing."

"And you have every right to be upset about it. In fact, make that man grovel like he's never groveled before." She smirks. "But don't punish yourself by not being with him outta fear if he's who you wanna be with in the end."

"I do want him, but I can't help questionin' everythin' I told him when I didn't know it was *him*. It'd be one thing if we never had contact again, but then I found him on CowboyMatch and sent him a message to tease him about his prompt. We started casually chattin' about how awful the guys on there were and that I had no datin' experience. He had so many opportunities to tell me before he confessed his feelings to me."

"If I know anything about the Hollis boys, they fall hard and get scared easily that they'll lose it."

"Yeah." I release my belt. "Appreciate you drivin' me."

"No problem. Good luck, Harlow."

I jump out. "Thanks, Ellie."

When I get into my truck, I pull out my phone and find a message waiting for me.

> **WAYLON**
> Harlow, I am so sorry you found out this way. I'll explain everything whenever you're ready to see me again. But please know I never wanted to hurt you or make you second-guess my feelings for you.

Because I don't want to have this conversation over text, I type out a quick reply.

> **HARLOW**
> Give me a few days. I'll text you when I'm ready to talk.

> **WAYLON**
> I can do that.

Only With Me

Dropping my phone, I let the tears welling in the corner of my eyes fall down my face.

When we started texting in a separate thread, I opened up and shared so much with him that didn't involve my past and it made me feel seen for the first time in my life. I wasn't the girl with the trauma. I was just *me*.

Realization hits when I think back to the day we were supposed to meet. He saw the pink ribbon in my hair before he saw my face and that's when he acted like he was only there to grab coffee. While I sat and waited for *him* to show up, he let me think I'd been stood up.

But why?

Why would he pretend he wasn't the person I was there to meet?

I guess that's the answer I need from him.

Chapter Twenty-Eight
Waylon

It's only been seventy-two hours since my last message to Harlow and I'm going crazy not hearing from her.

I know this is my fault, and I need to deal with the consequences of not telling her sooner, but fuck, I'm more miserable than I've ever been before.

And I don't know how to handle it.

Wilder came over last night to apologize for slipping up and even though I'm pissed he brought it up, it's not his fault. Of course he'd assume Harlow and I knew we were talking to each other being in the same group chat.

But fuck Jake for telling him when he was giving him pills behind my back.

I should've knocked him out cold when I had the chance.

But then I think about his little brother and how murdering Jake would affect Kenny's life, so then I pull back my rage.

Jake and Kenny work on their parents' ranch about fifteen minutes from mine, so we grew up close, and it sucks now how much has changed.

"Hey, bro!" Wilder walks into my bedroom and starts digging through my closet.

"The fuck are you doin'?"

Only With Me

He ignores me.

"I gotta start lockin' my door," I mutter, pulling the blankets over my head and rolling over. I worked a full day, mostly feeling numb, and then came home. I haven't left my bed since then.

"Gettin' your ass up and movin'," Wilder says, pulling out a clean T-shirt and jeans.

"No, I'm stayin' right here."

He yanks off the covers and then throws my clothes at me. "You're not gonna win her back sulkin' in bed. So get the fuck up and meet me in the living room in five minutes."

When the hell did he get so bossy?

Reluctantly, I pull myself out of bed and put on the shirt and jeans he picked out. I'm not sure what he has planned, but it's gotta be better than my current plan of doing nothing.

"Alright, so what're we doing?" I ask once I find him sitting in the kitchen.

"We're gonna brainstorm on how to fix this."

"*Brainstorm*? When have you ever brainstormed in your life?"

"You gonna insult me when I'm tryin' to help?"

"Considerin' it was your loudmouth that blurted it out...I should do a lot more than that."

"I didn't know it was a secret!"

"I know," I say, defeated. "I wanted to tell her so many times but didn't wanna ruin what we had."

"Well, there's gotta be a way to fix it, and I'm not leavin' until we figure it out."

Considering it's been three days with no contact, I'm not sure there's anything at this point.

"Wait, it's Saturday night. You're not goin' out?" I ask, grabbing a drink from the fridge.

"No, not when you're home alone being sad and pathetic."

"Wow, thanks," I deadpan. "But you go out almost every weekend. Don't let my heartbreak stop you."

"Nah, not until you get your girl back."

"Okay, love expert. What's your advice?"

"What's somethin' she's passionate about? Or somethin' specific y'all talked about that would be special to her?"

"Hmm…" I sit across from him at the table and scroll through Harlow's and my text messages.

"She loves romance…she has a whole romance wish list of things she wants to experience."

"Okay?" Wilder arches a brow. "Like what?"

"Dancin' outside at sunset, kissin' in the rain, a couples massage, go-kartin'…" I list off a few of my favorites I wanted to experience with her too.

"Like date night ideas?"

"Yeah, kinda."

"Okay, I can work with that." He grabs my keys from the counter. "Grab your shit. Let's go."

Standing, I follow him toward the door, then put on my boots.

"Where're we goin'?" I ask once we're outside.

"To the craft store."

The fucking what?

"Whaddya know about crafts?"

"Excuse you, we've been doing scrapbookin' on family nights for years."

"Yeah, and you rarely stick 'round for it."

"I do sometimes, but if you don't trust me, then fine—we'll pick up Noah and make her help us, too."

I groan. "Great."

Three hours, a glass jar with hand-painted hearts on it, and two hundred and twenty-five paper hearts cut out later—I'm tapped out.

Only With Me

Bringing Noah was a big mistake.

The moment Wilder told her his craft idea, she took it to the next level.

Noah painted different colored hearts around the jar, Wilder cut heart shapes out of construction paper, and then I wrote one of her romance wish list items on each piece. Since Harlow didn't tell me every single one of hers, I added in some of my own that I want us to do.

Noah and Wilder might've chimed in with some ideas, too.

Waylon's Jar of Hearts for Harlow is written on a tag and tied with pink ribbon around the top of the jar. I'm hoping she'll accept it as my promise to her that not only will we do these together but that I'll never keep anything from her again.

"Look at us being all crafty and shit." Wilder smirks at the mess we've made on my kitchen table. He grabs another two beers from my fridge and then sets one down in front of me.

"So now what? You gotta wait for her to reach out and then give it to her?"

I lift one shoulder, staring into space. "I guess."

"Wait, no way. This needs to be a grand romantic gesture. You get the biggest floral arrangement you can find, write her a sincere apology and letter about what this Jar of Hearts means, and that you hope she'll accept you back into her life. Then you leave it for her to find and hopefully she'll reach out to you sooner rather than later. That way you aren't being pushy, but you're lettin' her know she's on your mind."

"And if she doesn't accept it or reach out?"

"Then we go to a strip club!" Wilder hollers.

"No!" Noah and I shout in unison.

"Y'all are no fun." He pouts.

"If I know Harlow, she'll give you a second chance. But you gotta wait for it to be on her terms, not yours."

I sigh, knowing she's right.

Noah helps me clean up the kitchen, and when my phone rings

and I see Delilah's name on the screen, I hold it up and show them.

"Oh, shit. Put it on speaker! I wanna hear her chew your ass out." Wilder grins.

I roll my eyes, connecting the call. "Hey, Delilah."

"Waylon, have you seen Harlow?" Her frantic voice has me sitting upright.

"No, I haven't in three days and she hasn't reached out yet. Why?"

"Dad's in the hospital. I called her at work to come right away and she hasn't shown up. She's not answerin' my calls or texts now either. When I called her job, they said she left over an hour ago."

"Oh my God. Is your dad gonna be okay? Any idea where Harlow would go?"

"He's not in good shape. Mom found him unconscious after he went to lie down, and he hasn't woken up. She found several empty pill bottles and called 911. But Harlow shoulda been here over a half an hour ago."

"Oh, shit." I scrub a hand down my face, sweating with nerves. "I'll drive into town and see if I can find her."

"Thanks, lemme know if you hear from her, please."

"I will. And keep me updated if she shows up."

Delilah agrees and then we hang up.

"I gotta go." I rush to grab my keys, but then Wilder pulls out his.

"You're a mess. I'll drive."

"Drive safe! Text me if you need me to do anything," Noah calls as we rush out the door.

"I have a bad feelin' about this," I tell Wilder as he guns it down the gravel driveway. "She'd go right to the hospital or at least keep her sister updated on where she is."

"We're gonna find her," Wilder tries to reassure me, but my stomach's in knots.

Only With Me

Wilder gets us into town in twelve minutes and then goes downtown.

"Drive behind the building," I tell him. "That's where most of the employees park."

"There's her truck!" I point toward it so he knows where to go.

As soon as we get close enough, I jump out and look inside. The door's locked and her bag isn't inside.

"I'm gonna go into the store and double-check if she's still here," I tell Wilder.

"I'll come with you," he says, turning off the engine.

When we walk inside, I find her manager, Ashley.

"Waylon! Wilder! Oh my gosh. Hey!" Her eyes light up in a way that creeps me out.

"Is Harlow here?"

"No. She had a family emergency."

"Her truck's still in the parking lot, so she didn't leave."

"It is? She rushed outta here as soon as she heard her dad was in the hospital."

"Where the hell is she?" I spin around, ripping at my hair.

"Maybe she got a ride from her friend."

I turn back around and meet her eyes. "What friend? Who?"

"I dunno his name, just that he's been visitin' her all week."

My heart drops into my gut.

"What's he look like?" Wilder asks.

"Uh…brown hair, clean-shaved jawline…short."

"How short?" I quickly ask.

"Five-nine, five-ten?"

"Motherfucker," I hiss. "Was his name Emery?"

She shrugs. "She never told me. Just that they had a date a few weeks ago."

Why the hell wouldn't she tell me that he was coming to her job?

"Thanks, Ashley. Wilder, let's go."

I storm out and call Delilah back.

"Hey, did ya find her?"

"Not yet. Do you know her friend Natalie?" I ask urgently.

"Yeah, of course."

"Any chance you have her number?"

"Yeah, what's this about?"

"Natalie tracks her location. I need you to ask if she can see Harlow's location. Assuming she still has her phone with her, Natalie might be able to see where he took her."

"Where who took her?"

"A guy named Emery. They met on a dating app, but according to Harlow's manager, he's been showing up here," I explain, pacing back and forth in the parking lot. "Her truck is still here."

"Oh my God. She never said anything to you?"

"No." I clench my jaw. "But if he's been stalkin' her, who knows what else he's capable of."

"I'm texting Natalie right now, hold on."

After what feels like an eternity, Delilah finally gets a response. "Natalie sent me her location. It's pinging at…" She pauses. "That can't be right. It says she's at Murphy's ranch."

"Jake's parents' house?" I ask in disbelief.

"Yeah…why the hell would she be there?"

Good fucking question.

"I dunno, but we're gonna find out. I'll call you back."

"Waylon!" she quickly blurts. "Call the sheriff and have him meet you out there."

"I will, bye."

Wilder and I hop in the truck, then we head out of town toward Jake's parents'.

"You're not callin' the sheriff, are you?"

I look over at him, my pulse beating erratically. "You still have your shotgun in the back?"

"Yeah?"

I look straight ahead at the road. "Then no. I'm not callin' him."

Chapter Twenty-Nine
Harlow

"Daddy's going to the hospital. You need to come right away."

Delilah's frantic voice has my heart racing.

She never calls me at work, so when Ashley told me my sister was on the phone, I had a gut feeling something bad happened.

"Oh my God." I suck in my breath. "Is he okay?"

"I dunno. The ambulance took him ten minutes ago. Mama found him unconscious."

My worst nightmare has come to life.

"I'll be there as soon as possible," I tell her, then inform Ashley I have to go.

"Drive safe. Lemme know how it goes!" she calls out as I rush toward the back door.

With my bag over my shoulder, I sprint toward my truck.

I hate that I haven't talked to Waylon in three days, but my plan was to call him after my shift and ask to come over. I'd rather talk in person, but my dad takes priority above all else, so that's gonna have to wait.

Before I can open the door, someone calls out my name.

"Harlow!"

Spinning around, my mouth opens. *"Emery*? What're you doin'?"

He's been lurking around the store every day this week I've been here. I don't know how he knows my schedule or if he's stalking it every day until I show up, but it's starting to get creepy.

His face splits into a mischievous smirk. "I came to get you."

"Wha—" Something hard hits me from behind before I fall to my knees.

"Dude, I think I hit her too hard."

"Nah, she deserved it."

My eyes struggle to open, but I can tell I'm no longer in the parking lot at work. I'm on something hard. And cold.

My limbs are fighting to move as if I'm paralyzed.

Throbbing pain in my head makes me feel like I need to throw up.

But all I can think about is my dad. I should be at his bedside, not here. I didn't even get all the details on what happened and have no idea how he's doing.

"Do you think she's gonna wake up?"

"Just give her a little kick and she will."

I recognize Emery's voice and then he bellows out the evilest laugh I've ever heard.

The other sounds familiar, but I can't place him. Both sound terrifying.

Boots step closer and then a kick to my ribs has me groaning out loud.

"See, told ya. She's fine," Emery says.

"Now what?"

Only With Me

"Now...we do what we came here to do." Emery chuckles darkly.

The other one cackles. "Karma's a bitch."

My eyes flutter open to a recognizable face leaning down in front of me.

"Kenny?" I snarl.

"Hello, Harlow." He grins, then slides his tongue across his top lip.

"Don't touch me," I hiss.

"Aw, c'mon. Don't be like that."

Jake's younger brother is five years older than me, but everyone knows everyone in our small town. Even if I never went to school with him, I've seen him at rodeo events with Jake.

But I have no idea what he and Emery want with me.

"Lemme go," I demand. "I haveta get to the hospital to see my dad."

"That's not gonna happen..." Emery grabs a metal baseball bat and spins it around in his hand. "Not until you pay."

"For not wantin' to go on a second date with you?" I hardly get out the words because the blood rushing through my skull makes me dizzy with stars.

"Oh, you wish, sweetheart."

Emery smacks the bat into my thigh, and I release a blood-curdling scream that makes the throbbing in my head even worse.

"Every second lookin' at you was torture."

He presses the bottom of his boot against the spot on my leg he just bruised. And then another hit lands on my hip.

"Aaahhh..." I groan, reaching down where the pain settles. "Please, stop."

"Should we tell her why she's here?" Kenny taunts, crouching down to make eye contact with me. "Are you feelin' a little déjà vu?"

Emery lifts the bat again, but this time, he slams it into my ribcage.

All the air gets sucked out of my lungs, and I gasp, struggling to breathe.

"It's a shame Henry couldn't be here for our little reunion. He was my brother, you little *rat*," Emery says.

I swallow hard at the name of my previous attacker—*Henry Gibbons*.

Brothers?

"What'd ya think, Kenny? We can still have fun with just the two of us, right?"

"Mm-hmm. I think he'll appreciate the dedication. We've waited years for this moment," he responds.

That's when it hits me.

Emery must've recognized my face and name on the CowboyMatch app and then tried to lure me in by acting interested and wanting to get to know me in person. No wonder he was so persistent and asked a million questions about me.

Fucking psychopath.

It's no coincidence he messaged me after Henry's parole was denied.

Emery probably didn't anticipate me rejecting a second date and that's when he resorted to stalking me. Who knows what he would've done to me if I'd willingly dated him and he'd gotten me alone?

The thought sends a shiver of nerves down my spine.

And Kenny? All these years, he was right under my nose, and I had no idea he was one of the three. There's no way Jake knew... he couldn't have.

A truck engine roars outside, grabbing their attention. Kenny picks up some kind of large weapon and holds it up when noises come from the other side of the door.

God, please let it be the sheriff or someone with a loaded gun.

I try to shift my body so I can look over my shoulder, but the pain is too much.

"Go check out who's here," Emery tells Kenny.

When he walks around me, I try pulling myself up.

Only With Me

"And where do you think you're going?" Emery stomps on my ankle, and I hiss at the pain.

"Let me go," I sneer.

Commotion outside grabs Emery's attention and then I hear popping sounds.

"Stay here," he demands.

When he goes to step over me, I lift my leg as high as I can and make him trip. His knees bend before they collide with the ground and when he tries to catch himself, he loses his grip on the bat.

It bounces and rolls, landing a foot away from me. With as much strength as I can produce, I roll over and reach for it. Before I can grab it, Kenny stands over me and stomps on my wrist.

"And whaddya think you're gonna do with that, you little bitch?"

I think about the countless book plots Natalie's told me over the years. The girls who get murdered in those stories always do something stupid before their throats get ripped out. If I become one of them, Natalie will summon me from the dead just to kill me again for being so stupid.

When more popping noises echo outside, Emery's attention goes to the door. Without hesitation, I reach over with my other hand and grab the bat. Before he can stop me, I swing the bat between his legs.

I hear his high-pitched shriek before his knees buckle and then he collapses on his side with his back to me. Part of him lands on my arm, but I fight through the pain to slide out from under him.

When I attempt to stand, the dizziness and throbbing almost knock me down again, but I refuse to give up when I'm this close.

Crawling toward the bat that dropped between his legs, I hiss through the pain that's radiating through my body until I wrap my hand around it. Even as I struggle to breathe, a surge of adrenaline fuels just enough strength to lift the bat over my head.

"You can tell Henry I'm not thirteen anymore!" Then I slam it down against his rib cage—once, twice, three times—until I hear them crack.

Drained of energy, the weight of my injuries is too much to hold myself up, and I fall to the ground next to him.

The last sounds I hear are the metal bat rolling away and someone screaming my name.

Chapter Thirty
Waylon

The moment we pull into the Murphys' gravel driveway, I know something's off. Jake's not here, but his brother is. Kenny's truck is parked by the shed behind their house instead of in front of the garage like normal.

"Go back there," I direct Wilder to park behind Kenny's truck.

"Why would Kenny take her?" he asks.

"We're about to fuckin' find out. Grab your shotgun," I tell him when he parks.

As soon as Wilder and I open the tailgate, I get hit in the shoulder.

"The fuck?" I hiss at the stinging sensation.

I fall to my knees and put my hand over where it hurts, but there's no blood.

"I think he hit me with a fuckin' paintball gun," I tell Wilder, who's kneeling beside me. "What the hell? Did you see where that came from?"

"Pretty sure it was Kenny behind those doors."

"Motherfucker. He's about to be sorry he brought a knife to a gunfight." I pull myself up to my feet but stay crouched down.

"Waylon…lemme go first." He pulls out his shotgun, loads it, and then removes the safety. "Stay behind me."

I roll my shoulder, pissed that punk got me when I wasn't looking. That's gonna leave a nasty bruise.

A couple more pops sound off, but he misses.

We move to the driver's side of the truck and stay out of his view.

"Do you have a visual on him?" I ask when he props the gun up on the side of the bed. "Don't shoot if you're not sure. Harlow's in there somewhere."

Without a warning, he squeezes the trigger and a loud bang echoes through the air. Wilder stands to his full height and ejects the spent shell, the metallic casing clattering to the ground.

"He's down."

His calmness is eerie.

"Call the sheriff," I tell him before I round the truck and rush over to the shed door. Kenny doesn't move as I push through it, but it looks like Wilder got him in the upper thigh, so he should be fine as long as an ambulance gets here before he bleeds out.

I follow the sound of wailing and then find Harlow crashing to the ground, a metal bat falling from her grip.

"Harlow!" I shout, but she's knocked out before I can catch her.

I rush to her side and lift her in my arms.

Looking over, I see Emery rolled on his side, knocked out. Presumably from the beating she gave him with the bat.

"You did good, baby. Now I need you to wake up for me." Standing with her against my chest, I rush out of the shed. Wilder quickly notices and opens the passenger door.

"We gotta get her to the ER." I climb inside, holding Harlow in my arms. "I think he clubbed her with a bat a few times."

And if I ever get my hands on him, it won't be pretty. That bat would live so far up his ass, he'd beg me to put him out of his misery.

"Jesus Christ," Wilder hisses. "The sheriff and ambulance are on their way."

Wilder shuts my door and then hops into the driver's seat, tires squealing as he guns us out of there.

Only With Me

I keep my finger to the pulse point on her neck, making sure she stays with me. I'm furious with myself that I didn't protect her from him.

"Harlow, if you can hear me, I need you to try to look at me," I tell her softly.

Her eyelids flutter open and closed.

"Hang on, my love." I pull her closer and she winces. "Shit, sorry."

The bastard hit her in the ribs and only God knows where else.

I haven't felt this type of fear since the night I found Wilder in the bathroom.

"She's gonna be okay," Wilder says as if he knows I need to hear it.

"She has to be," I murmur, then brush my finger softly against her cheek. "She's survived once before. She can do it again."

Twenty miserable minutes later, Wilder pulls up to the side of the hospital, and I carry her in. He called ahead of time so they could expect us. Then he called Delilah and broke the news to her.

Based on Harlow going in and out of consciousness, I'd guess she has a concussion and possible internal bleeding if he hit her hard enough.

The thought makes me want to go find him and finish the job.

The ambulance that brought Kenny and Emery in arrived five minutes ago.

The sheriff is also here, asking for statements.

It's a fucking mess.

"How the hell did this happen?" Delilah cries next to me.

I wrap my arm around her shoulders, pulling her into me. "I dunno. He must've struck her in the parking lot and then the two of 'em took her to the Murphys'."

"Why would Jake's brother be involved?"

"I dunno that either."

Mrs. Fanning's a mess, and I feel awful because she's still

waiting for news about her husband. Last they heard, he was intubated after they pumped his stomach. Now it's a waiting game to see if he'll breathe on his own.

I'm so overwhelmed by my emotions—a level of anger I've never felt before consumes me, the fear that Harlow won't survive this suffocates me, and the sadness that she's having to go through it again makes me want to trade places with her.

I don't know how to deal with this level of pain, but I have to be strong for her.

Within the hour, the waiting room is full of my family members, Jake and his parents, and a few friends from the horse club group chat.

I refuse to look at Jake's family and getting into a fistfight with the sheriff here would be a dumb move.

But I will get to the bottom of this.

The next sixty hours go by in a blur of exhaustion and mental autopilot. I don't leave her side after she had surgery to remove her spleen that ruptured from the impact of the bat and to stop the internal bleeding caused by her re-fractured ribs. She's also covered in bruises and was diagnosed with a mild concussion.

Her recovery is going to take months, and that's if she doesn't have any complications post-surgery with infections, but I know my girl is tough. If anyone can get through this, it's her. I hate that she'll be out of the horse jumping season for the next year, but at this point, I'm just relieved she made it through surgery.

She's on heavy pain meds while her body heals, so she hasn't been able to keep her eyes open for more than a few seconds at a

Only With Me

time. Unfortunately, that means she still doesn't know about her dad.

Mr. Fanning still can't breathe on his own and hasn't regained consciousness.

When they asked about his living will and end-of-life wishes, Mrs. Fanning broke down in tears because Mr. Fanning doesn't want to be kept on life-saving interventions. That means if he continues not to breathe on his own, they have to remove the ventilator.

Delilah's spiraling, which, given the circumstances, I understand. Both her father and sister are fighting for their lives, and it's even worse than last time when their incidents happened a year apart.

I can't fathom how this is happening to them again.

The community of our small town has come together to bring food for the Fannings and everyone affected, which has helped, but no one has an appetite. My siblings take turns checking on me and making sure I eat. Wilder brought me a bag of clean clothes and toiletries so I can shower here.

He's stepped up in a way I've never seen before.

While I appreciate it more than I can express, all I want is to talk to Harlow and tell her how sorry I am for deceiving her. For not being there to protect her.

To tell her how much I love her.

Tell her how much I want to hold her and keep her forever.

I wanna give her my jar of hearts and do all the items inside with her. She deserves that and so much more.

I wish I could go back to a week ago before Wilder blurted the secret I should've told her myself. Her finding out and still unable to talk it out is killing me.

I wanna take away her pain of going through this again and losing her dad at the same time.

And I want those two assholes to pay.

Kenny had surgery for his bullet wound and is now on house

arrest while he recovers. Sheriff Wagner has reassured us he'll be charged with kidnapping and conspiracy.

Emery's injuries weren't major enough for surgery, so he's suffering with pain in a cold jail cell, pending his arraignment for aggravated assault and kidnapping.

The sheriff could've given him house arrest too while he recovers from his broken ribs, but I have a feeling he purposely didn't go easy on him after finding out how badly he'd beaten Harlow.

He's hopeful they'll both take plea deals so she doesn't have to be re-traumatized with another trial.

"Waylon?" Delilah grabs my attention, and I blink a few times to clear my vision.

"Yeah?" I stand from my chair as she walks into the room.

Her eyes are bloodshot. "They're removing his ventilator tonight."

"I'm so sorry, Delilah." I shake my head with grief, walking closer so I can wrap my arms around her.

"I can't believe this is happening."

I rub her back, wishing I could steal away her pain, too. Just because we didn't work out as a couple doesn't mean I can't be her friend and support her through one of the worst weeks of her life.

"Mom wants to tell Harlow before they do it, so they're gonna start weanin' her off the pain meds."

"Harlow would wanna say goodbye," I reassure her that it's the right thing to do. "Hopefully, they can keep her comfortable with less drowsy meds."

"I wouldn't be surprised if she's out of it and doesn't remember anything we tell her. That's what happened last time. Her memory was foggy for days."

The nurse comes in, followed by Mrs. Fanning, and she adjusts her morphine drip schedule.

"She should start waking up within a couple hours, maybe sooner, but she might not be very aware," the nurse explains.

Only With Me

The three of us wait by her bed and within forty-five minutes, she begins opening her eyes and moving her hand against mine.

"Mom?"

"Right here, sweetheart. Delilah and Waylon are here, too."

Harlow looks around until her gaze finds mine. Tears well in my eyes for the hundredth time in three days, but this time I let them fall. I've never been so happy to see those beautiful green eyes staring back at me.

"Hi, baby," I say softly, choking down my emotions.

"What happened?" she asks hoarsely.

After a few seconds of looking back at her mom and sister, I respond, "Emery and Kenny, do you remember 'em attackin' you?"

She blinks a few times and then moves her hand to the side of her stomach. "They took me in the parkin' lot at work."

"Yeah. Do you remember where you were going?" Delilah asks.

Harlow's eyes widen and then she looks between her sister and mom.

"Daddy. Is he okay?"

The room stays silent long enough for Harlow to figure it out. Tears fill her eyes within seconds and they fall down her cheeks. She closes them for so long, I worry she's fallen back asleep.

"What happened?" she finally asks.

I'm glad she seems more aware than we expected, but I hate that it's the first thing she has to hear after she wakes up.

Mrs. Fanning explains everything from the moment she went to check on him and realizing he wasn't breathing to calling 911 and then finding his empty medicine bottles.

From what Harlow's shared with me, this was always a fear of theirs.

"You can still say goodbye if you want to," Mrs. Fanning says. "We have a little time before they remove it."

"Will they let me sit in a wheelchair so I can sit with him?" she asks, and when she makes a slight movement to adjust, she winces in pain.

"Take it easy. Lemme help." I stand, fluffing her pillows that are secured by her side to keep the ice packs in place.

Once she's comfortable, Mrs. Fanning tells her that they'll do whatever they can to accommodate her as long as she doesn't overdo it.

Then we go through the events of Wilder and me finding her, what injuries she's sustained, and what her recovery for the next several months looks like. I tell her everything Sheriff Wagner said about Emery's and Kenny's charges and that they're going to pay for what they did.

"I can't believe this happened again."

"But you fought back this time, Harlow," I remind her. "You got some good hits in and didn't make it easy for him. Even after you were in pain, you put up a fight. I'm so proud of you."

"Is it weird that I'm glad Daddy doesn't know about this? He'd be so distraught knowin' he couldn't protect me from 'em again."

Her mom and sister cry with her, holding her hand and giving each other a safe space to let out their emotions.

"Daddy knew you were in good hands." Delilah looks at me with sincerity. "He told me the day after I found out about y'all that he knew Waylon would take good care of you."

That makes me choke up, knowing I not only let Harlow down, but her father, too.

After another hour of talking about the incident and her dad, Mrs. Fanning says she wants to go home and freshen up before returning this evening to say goodbye. She also wants to make some phone calls, get their pastor to come, and notify a few friends.

I hate this for her. No one should have to go through this.

Delilah offers to go with her, so I stay with Harlow for some alone time.

"Are you doing okay without the morphine?"

Only With Me

"Unless it numbs the heartache I'm feelin', morphine won't be enough anyway."

"I can't tell you how sorry I am. For what you're goin' through. For what happened to you. For keepin' a secret from you."

"Well, you're only responsible for one out of the three."

"You're the strongest person I know, baby. You're gonna get through this. I know it'll be hard, but if you'll let me, I'll be by your side every step of the way."

She swallows, fighting back her emotions as if she's saving them for what's coming later.

"I'd like that." She squeezes my hand. "But if Ellie asks, tell her I made you grovel."

I laugh for the first time in days because of course she'd be the one to do it. "I dunno what that means, but I'll say whatever you want."

Later that evening, after Mrs. Fanning and Delilah return, we get Harlow situated in a wheelchair. I can tell she's trying hard not to complain about the discomfort, but I see it written all over her face.

Before they go to Mr. Fanning's room, Delilah brushes Harlow's hair and braids it for her. Then she covers her in a blanket from home so she has something comforting to hold while she sits next to his bedside.

I can't even pretend this isn't affecting me. Getting to be around him, even for that short period while we played board games, was an honor. It was obvious how much he loves and adores his family.

But I hate that he had to suffer in pain every day.

It's not fair. None of this is for any of them.

But I'll be here to support her and help her fight through the pain for the rest of our lives if she lets me.

"Okay, I'm ready," Harlow says softly.

Her nurse pushes her wheelchair out of her room and then brings her to Mr. Fanning's on a different floor.

Brooke Montgomery

I stand behind Delilah and her mom, keeping my distance so they have enough space around his bed.

"His doctor will be here in thirty minutes, but please feel free to take all the time you need," the nurse says before shutting the door.

It's silent for the first several minutes. Harlow holds his hand and stares at him while she quietly cries.

"Mom?" Harlow grabs her attention. "We should tell Daddy it's okay to go. He needs us to say the words so he knows we'll love him no matter what."

Delilah breaks down and it's impossible not to at this point.

Harlow goes first, choking through her words, but she eventually gets them out. Delilah goes next. Then Mrs. Fanning.

And if it's possible, I lose it even more after hearing his wife say goodbye to the man she's been married to for thirty-three years.

"Waylon…" Harlow calls for me, and I quickly wipe my cheeks and kneel next to her. "You haveta tell him, too."

Fuck me.

I nod, trying my best to get it together.

When I can finally speak, I step closer to his bedside.

"Thank you for sharing your family with me, sir. I promise to take care of 'em for as long as I live." I close my eyes, trying to breathe through the tears so I can say my final words. "You're free to go, Mr. Fanning. I'll take it from here."

"That was beautiful, Waylon," Mrs. Fanning says, pulling me in for a hug.

"It was," Delilah says, patting my arm. "You're a good man, Way-Way."

I choke out a laugh at her trying to ease the tension.

"Dad woulda loved hearin' you say that." Harlow grabs my hand. "Thank you."

"You're welcome," I mouth the words.

When their pastor arrives, he reads Bible verses and prays over Mr. Fanning. It's a bittersweet experience because while it's

Only With Me

sad as hell, there's also something beautiful about being surrounded by your loved ones while you leave this earth.

And less than an hour later, he does.

Peacefully in his sleep, he passes with his wife and two daughters telling him they love him and that they'll see him again someday soon.

Chapter Thirty-One
Harlow

Dad's funeral was beautiful. Sad and tragic, but still beautiful to witness the hundreds of people from our community come pay their respects.

Although he was cremated, we had a lovely memorial to honor him. Delilah and I spoke about what a fighter he was and how despite his challenges, he always put his family first.

Mom tried to read a poem about true love but choked up to the point she couldn't finish, so Waylon stood up and finished reading it for her.

I wouldn't have been able to get through these past couple weeks without him.

Although my body is still recovering, I'm doing my best to take it slow and rest. Mom barely lets me lift a finger and Waylon comes over every night so I'm not alone.

Not that I'm complaining about spending time with him, but I know he's trying to keep my mind occupied so I don't cry or sulk about my injuries.

Truthfully, I've not allowed myself to think too much about what happened that day. It was the worst week of my life, but I'm leaning on Waylon and my family as much as I can. Now that I'm older, I feel stronger and braver than the last time, but it still

Only With Me

bothers me that I was tricked and assaulted again. I've already told them I'll go to counseling when I feel mentally ready to handle it.

The silver lining—if you want to consider there is one—no broken legs this time. Bruised my thighs badly enough, but at the very least, I can still walk, so I'm grateful for that.

I'm also grateful Emery and Kenny took a plea deal, so we don't have to spend months waiting for a trial. They're both going to prison for a long time. And as much as I feel sorry for Jake, especially since he had no idea what his brother was into, I've ended all communication with him.

I'm also pissed I won't be able to do any horse shows this season. There's no way with my ribs and recovering from spleen surgery, so for now, Waylon checks in on Piper for me. He'll video chat with me so I can talk to her. At the very least, I'm hoping I can lunge her in a few weeks after my doctor gives me the clear.

Once I was home from the hospital, Natalie came and stayed with me through the funeral. It was interesting introducing her to Waylon and seeing her blush over him.

I swear, Waylon could charm a nun.

Now she understood why I went on that country drive with him after she warned me only serial killers do that.

Then I had to remind her a few times he was off the market but that he had a single twin brother.

That seemed to distract her long enough to stop flirting with my boyfriend.

Boyfriend.

It still feels surreal to call him that after having such bad luck on that dating app.

Turns out, I never needed it anyway.

But it's part of how Waylon and I started, so I'm not upset about it.

Speaking of...

We finally sat down and had the conversation about the group chat. I told him how I felt betrayed and that our relationship started on a lie.

He admitted that he screwed up and should've told me before things progressed between us. He vowed to never deceive me again and that he'd spend the rest of his life proving how sorry he is.

Waylon has a good heart, and I believe he had good intentions to tell me that day. So even though I didn't make him grovel for days, I accepted his sincere apology and gave him a second chance.

We agreed to make a fresh start and let the past stay in the past. No more secrets.

Then he surprised me with a jar of hearts filled with ideas from my wish list and some of his, and it brought me to tears. No one had ever done anything like that for me and to know Wilder and Noah helped too makes it extra sweet.

I imagine the three of them at a table, forming an assembly line of painting, cutting, and writing. Some cute sibling bonding.

I keep the jar on my nightstand, and when he tells me to pick one, we go do that thing as long as it isn't a physical activity.

So far, we've done a painting night at a local art studio and then a night where we made homemade muffins and drank apple cider in front of the fireplace.

Admittedly, it's earned him a *lot* of brownie points.

For the past couple weeks, Mom's been trying to keep herself busy while she grieves, as we all are, but it's almost unhealthy how much she doesn't sit still. She comes home from work, makes dinner, cleans the house, does laundry, tidies up again before bed, and then when she finally gets tired, she sleeps on the couch.

She's not ready to be in their bed.

Not that I blame her.

It's hard seeing Dad's power chair, his recliner, and his things around the house.

I asked Mom if we could spread some of his ashes around and

Only With Me

she hesitantly agreed, so Waylon's taking us somewhere to do that.

"Are y'all ready?" he asks uncomfortably after waiting twenty minutes with the urn on the coffee table in front of him.

"Mom?" I call. "It's time to go before it gets dark out."

I walk down the hallway, and when I find her, she's sitting on their bed with a photo album in her lap.

"Mama? Are you okay?" I step inside and stand next to her.

"Yeah, sweetie. Just missin' him, is all."

I rub her back, knowing there's nothing I can say or do to make this easier and all I can do is comfort her the best way I can.

"If you're not up for this, we don't—"

"No. It's fine, sweetie. I think Dad would love one more tractor ride around the farm."

I beam with tears in my eyes. Although that's what caused his injury in the first place, he loved working on that farm and being a part of something that mattered. So when I asked the family he used to work for if we could spread his ashes on their land, they were more than happy to let us.

Mom stands and we meet Waylon in the living room. He greets her with a warm smile and a side hug. I appreciate how much he's there for her, too.

We walk out to Waylon's truck and then he drives us to the Fosters'. It's a ten-minute drive and when we arrive, Mr. Foster already pulled out the tractor for us.

Waylon hands me the urn, then climbs inside before taking it again so Mom and I can climb up next.

"We good to go?" he asks once the doors are closed.

"Yep."

He drives us out into one of the fields and then lowers the loader. Once he parks, he climbs back down and then I hand him the urn one final time.

Waylon pours Dad's ashes inside the bucket of the front-end loader and returns to the tractor.

"Okay, Mr. Fanning. One more ride around the field we go!"

I can't help but laugh and cry at how silly this probably looks from the outside, but I don't care. Dad would've loved this.

Waylon raises and tilts the bucket so the ashes can blow in the wind as he drives.

After losing his leg, Dad never got to drive a tractor again or spend another day on this farm, and now he'll forever rest in the place that brought him so much pride.

"Thank you for today," I tell Waylon as we sit in his truck, just the two of us.

Mom went inside to get ready for bed and I wanted to say good night in private.

"You're welcome, baby. I was happy to do it and get to experience it with y'all."

"Can I sit on you quickly?" I nod toward his lap.

"You think you're up for it?"

"For sittin'? Yeah, pretty sure I can manage that," I quip.

He teasingly rolls his eyes. "You know what I mean."

Once he lifts the steering wheel, he pulls the lever underneath the bench seat. "Hop on." He pats his lap like I'm getting on a saddle.

I crawl over, straddle his thighs, and then wrap my arms around his neck.

"I've been wantin' to tell you something, and I think now's the perfect moment for it."

His hands grasp my hips, then he pulls me in closer. "Okay."

I nervously rub my hand over his cheek, playing with his scruffy jawline.

"We've been through so much together in a short amount of

Only With Me

time, but I can't imagine a better man for me. Someone who's been nothin' but kind and patient, as well as sweet and caring to my family. I've experienced all my firsts with you, and I'm so glad I did because I'm head over heels in love with you, Waylon."

His face splits in two as he grabs my chin and tenderly brings my mouth to his. Then he rests his forehead on mine. "I'm madly in love with you, Harlow. I have been for a long time, and honestly that's a first for me, too. My feelings for you are the strongest I've ever had for someone."

"Really?" I bite down on my lower lip, leaning back so I can look at him. "How come you haven't told me this before?"

He gently brushes the hair out of my face. "Because I woulda run you off if I'd said it the first time you were sittin' on my lap like this."

I snort at his implication that he's been in love with me that long.

Maybe he has.

"Does this mean I get invited to scrapbookin' night now?"

He snickers, shaking his head. "Nope, sorry."

"That's so unfair. I'm gonna haveta talk to upper management about this."

He leans into my neck and slides his tongue under my ear before capturing it between his teeth.

"Patience, my love."

"I have none." I rock against his groin, attempting to tease him enough to make him hard.

He gently squeezes my hips. "Harlow..."

His deep warning voice makes me want him more.

"As much as I wanna fuck you to the moon and back, we haveta wait for your checkup."

I playfully pout, frowning.

"You had a serious attack on you two weeks ago."

"Okay, and? You can't be gentle?"

"Of course I can, especially when it'll be your first time, which is why it's even more important we don't rush it with your injuries."

I know he's right, but that doesn't make it easier to wait when I've wanted him for so long.

"But I'd be happy to help you get off if you need some assistance..." He lifts his hips, poking me with his cock.

And the devilish grin spread across his face tells me exactly what type of *assistance* he's referring to.

"Add in lettin' me suck your cock and you've gotta deal."

He barks out an amused laugh, shaking his head at my counteroffer. "I guess I can handle that."

"Oh, but I want us to do it in the middle of the woods."

"Uhh...is that some kinda weird serial killer fantasy from your romance wish list?"

I giggle at his shocked expression. "I wanna see how long it takes Natalie to freak out and call the sheriff on us again."

"That's an arrest waitin' to happen."

"Not if we outrun him."

"Harlow Fanning...I think you're the one corruptin' me after all."

But he doesn't say no. Instead, he drives us twenty minutes away, deep into the woods, where it's pitch black.

If I didn't trust him with my whole heart, I'd be terrified out here. But it adds to the thrill.

"Use me, baby. Use me to get off," Waylon softly demands in my ear.

I rock on top of him, feeling his cock harden underneath me, and moan at how good it feels against my clit.

"Just like that, you're doing so good."

Wrapping my hands around his shoulders, I grind faster, desperate to find my release before we get caught.

He slides his hand to my breast, teasing my nipple through the fabric of my shirt and groaning as he kisses along my jaw.

"Don't hold back. I wanna hear you scream while you come on me."

Only With Me

"Can you help me? Talk me through it..." I plead. There's nothing hotter than Waylon telling me all the ways he wants to touch me.

"Imagine my tongue on this needy little clit while you ride my fingers deep and fast until your sweet cunt juices make a mess on my face. Then I slide down and tease your tight hole until you beg me to let you come again."

"Oh my God..." My eyes roll back as he tightens his grip on me.

"You look so fuckin' perfect when you get close..." He brings his lips to mine, slides his tongue between them, and kisses me deeply and urgently. "So beautiful and *mine*."

This is the first time he's ever called me *his* and it's such a turn-on.

"I'm so close. Say it again," I beg between catching my breath.

"You're all mine, baby. I'm so in love with you." He tilts up my chin with the pads of his thumbs, locking his eyes on mine. "All *mine, mine, mine.*"

The deep hoarseness of his voice echoes in my ears and shoots straight down to my core like a lightning bolt.

And as requested, I don't hold back. I scream out his name like a desperate prayer. Every inch of my body vibrates with pleasure. When I catch my breath, Waylon collides his mouth with mine and claims me in a way he never has before.

"I'm gonna come in my pants if you don't climb off me, baby."

"Is that so?" I rotate my hips once more over him.

He grabs my thighs and holds them in place. "Don't torture me like that."

"Then lemme help you with that problem."

He looks outside, making sure we're still alone. I crawl off his lap and release his cock, then bring my mouth down on him.

"Fuck, I'm not gonna last long."

After I lick up his shaft and suck on him a few times, I hollow my cheeks and squeeze my fingers around his shaft.

His hand tightens in my hair and he comes down my throat

with a roar. I do my best to lick him clean before he pulls me up and quickly kisses me.

"We've gotta go." He pulls himself into his jeans and shifts into drive.

I look behind us and see the sheriff's SUV, his bright light shining directly into Waylon's truck.

He slams on the gas, and I burst out laughing as I pull on my seat belt. Luckily, the sheriff doesn't even bother following us.

"Natalie's getting rusty," I say once we're back on the road. "Took her fifteen minutes longer than last time to have someone find us."

"I have a feelin' the sheriff didn't come lookin' for us right away."

"He's gonna chew our asses when we see him next, ain't he?" I wince.

Waylon smirks at me. "Yep."

Chapter Thirty-Two
Waylon

SIX WEEKS LATER

Harlow's turning twenty-one, and since she's not interested in spending it at a bar, I've decided to give her the best birthday celebration I can. But first, I need Wilder's help with part of it.

"Wilder? You here?" I call into his apartment.

Unlike him, I know how to knock and not walk into someone's home unannounced.

When he doesn't answer, I step inside. "Hello? You better not be naked."

After no response and not seeing him in his room or the kitchen, I check his location and see he's two minutes away, so I go outside and wait for him next to my truck.

He pulls in and I'm ready to give him a hard time about being late, but I notice the look on his face—a mixture of emotions I'm not used to seeing from him.

"Hey, you okay?" I push off my door and walk toward him.

"Yeah, just had an appointment and it ran a little longer than usual."

"What kinda appointment?"

He goes to walk past me, but I quickly grab his arm.

"What's going on? Are you sick?"

"No…well, depends how you look at it." He shrugs.

I stare at him, waiting for him to explain what he means by that.

"What kinda appointment was it?" I ask again.

He blows out a defeated breath like he knows he's not gonna get away from this conversation. "I started seein' a therapist a few weeks ago."

My eyes widen in shock and relief. "Really? That's…great. Why wouldn't you tell me that?"

He lifts his shoulders again, avoiding eye contact with me. He's embarrassed, and I get it, but he has no reason to be.

"Because I knew you'd be all… *Wilder, I'm so proud of you. You're doing the right thing. Good job workin' through your issues…*" His mocking tone has me snorting.

"Oh God, how dare I care about my twin brother? What an asshole, am I?"

"Yeah, you are. Glad you finally admitted it."

I roll my eyes. "Well, I *am* proud of you. What made you finally decide to go?"

I've only been begging him for fifteen years.

He leans against the truck, folding his arms and staring at the dirt. "It was after Mr. Fanning died and I realized how many people his death impacted. Worst of all, I saw how much pain his family was in, even you. He lived with chronic pain for years before he decided he couldn't live with it anymore. I guess it made me realize that could be me someday if I continued ignorin' my mental health. Granted, it's not physical pain, but there's some shit I need to work through so I don't get to the point where I can't do it anymore. Seein' how sad and upset y'all were got to me. I'd never wanna be the reason y'all feel that way, and if I can do somethin' about it now before I lose the ability to reason with myself, then I owe it to my family to try. Just because I'm not

Only With Me

there now doesn't mean someday I couldn't be and that thought scared the shit outta me."

"Wow...I'm so impressed. And damn proud you came to that realization." I pull him into a hug even though he resists at first.

"I hate that it took something like that for it to happen."

"Either way, this is a huge step. You deserve to be happy, too. Workin' through your issues in a healthy way will help you see there's so much more to life than drinkin' and random hookups."

"Yeah, being sober and abstinent is fuckin' hard," he grumbles, and I crack up, but I'm glad he's trying. "And I was so close to makin' it eight seconds on the mechanical bull."

I snort. *Sure he was.*

"If you ever want me to join you for a session, just lemme know."

"Yeah, my therapist and I have talked about it, but I'd like to spend a bit more time with him on my own first. He's gonna refer me to a psychiatrist so we can discuss medication options, too."

I nod, patting his back. Although he looks less than thrilled about it, I'm glad he's doing it. "Take all the time you need. I'll be here."

"Thanks. Appreciate it."

"Well, are you ready to help me now with Harlow's birthday surprise?"

"You mean, so you can reap the rewards and get laid?"

I smirk, shrugging unapologetically.

We've messed around some once she started feeling better, and I even surprised her with a toy so she could start getting used to the size and feeling of having it inside her. But we've been waiting for her ribs and body to heal post-surgery. She just got the okay from her doctor to ride Piper again, so now she can start getting back into her practice routine.

"Alright, whaddya need me to do?" he asks, and then I give him a list of instructions.

Brooke Montgomery

One of the items on Harlow's romance wish list is something I've been waiting to do until the weather warms up, but with it being her birthday, I wanted to do it tonight.

I also want to do something extra to cheer her up. As much as she's been acting fine about what happened to her and Mr. Fanning passing, I can tell she's struggling. Fortunately, she started therapy last week and is still going to grief counseling with her family.

But the other one I've planned includes my family.

Even though it's not a Sunday, I have Wilder helping me get things ready for a special occasion at our parents' house that Harlow's been begging to be included in.

Once I'm ready, I text her that I'm on my way.

When I was in town earlier, I bought two rose arrangements so I could give one to Mrs. Fanning. I've been trying to make sure Harlow and I spend equal time between our places so her mom isn't left alone too often. Delilah goes over on the nights she doesn't work and we've even had a game night in Mr. Fanning's honor.

The three of them started going to a grief support group, and I think it's been helpful being around others going through the same thing.

I know nothing will take away their pain completely, but it's still good to see Mrs. Fanning smile from time to time.

When I knock, she answers the door. "Waylon, sweetheart. C'mon in. She's almost ready."

"These are for you." I walk through the threshold and hand her one of the bouquets.

Only With Me

"Oh my goodness, after everythin' you've already done today." She holds the pink roses up to her nose. "They're breathtaking."

"Just like you." I wink.

"Stop it," she says, getting all flustered.

"Are you hittin' on my mama right in front of me?" Harlow waltzes into the living room, taking *my* breath away.

She's in a gorgeous white dress with lace trim that hits her knees, a blue jacket, and cowboy boots.

"You look incredible…" I lower my gaze down her body and press my lips to hers. Then I reveal the other bouquet from behind my back. "And these are for you."

"Red roses…my favorites." She grins sweetly, smelling them. "You've already spoiled me all day."

I brush a piece of golden-brown hair behind her ear. "I wanted today to be extra special for you."

"Thank you. I appreciate everything. The cupcakes were delicious!"

"They really were!" Mrs. Fanning adds, then grabs the red roses from Harlow. "I'll put these in a vase for you."

When we're alone, I cup Harlow's face and kiss her again. "Happy birthday, love."

"Thank you. I'm finally allowed to buy alcohol. Look out, world. Me and a strawberry margarita are gonna tear it up."

Chuckling, I take her hand and intertwine it with mine. "Are you ready to go? I have a lot for us to do tonight."

"Yep, just gotta grab my stuff and give Mama a hug first."

Since we made plans for her to sleep over, she packed an overnight bag. She's stayed over a few times already, but since I always have to get up early for work, she ends up waking up too.

However, tomorrow I'm going in late.

"I've remembered somethin' I wanted to ask you," she says during the drive.

"Okay?"

"When we were textin' under the group chat, what'd you have my number saved as?"

335

"Um...why do you wanna know?"

"Because I was scrollin' through my old texts and saw the contact name I had you listed under."

I hadn't even considered she put a name in for me.

"What was it?" I look over.

"You first!"

I sigh. "You can't get mad."

She arches a brow. "No promises."

"It was Poison Ivy Girl."

Her mouth falls open and her eyes widen. "That's horrible! Out of all the options you had, you picked that?"

"Shoulda seen what I labeled the others." I chuckle, remembering Scrawny Perverted Asshole. "So what did you label me?"

"Mystery Guy, but now I'm thinkin' I shoulda done somethin' like Liar Liar Pants On Fire."

I glance at her, trying to fight back a smile and act angry.

"It's not as catchy as Mystery Guy, though." I wink and she finally laughs.

Once we arrive at the ranch, I take her to my parents' house instead of mine.

"What're we doin' here?" she asks when I open her door.

"This is your first surprise." I smile, taking her hand and helping her out of the truck.

I guide her into the house and as soon as we walk into the kitchen, her jaw drops at seeing everyone inside waiting for her.

"Happy birthday!" they scream, and I beam at Harlow's shocked reaction.

"Oh my gosh, what is this?" She turns and looks at me.

"It's your scrapbookin' birthday party."

"Shut up!" She jumps into my arms, laughing in disbelief. "You said you had to be married to a Hollis to be invited."

"Well..." I shrug. "I spoke to *upper management* about it and made an executive decision to get you an early access pass."

"We have all the craft supplies you could possibly need and

Only With Me

new books for you to make your own scrapbook," my mom says, coming over to give her a hug.

"Y'all are too freakin' sweet. I can't believe this. You dunno how much this means to me." Tears well in her eyes, and I feel guilty for making her cry. "I promise these are happy tears."

"Gramma Grace baked you a cake, so we can eat and scrapbook for a couple hours. That sound okay?" I ask, pulling out a chair for her to sit.

"That sounds perfect." She gives me a quick kiss before taking a seat.

There's snacks and appetizer finger foods spread out on the kitchen island, so I put some of her favorites on a plate and then sit next to her.

"How'd you get these?" She opens a box of her family pictures and starts flipping through them. Lots of her and Delilah, their parents, and some of her at show horse jumping events.

"I asked your mom for some a few days ago and snuck over when you were at work." I grin. "I figured if we were gonna scrapbook, you'd wanna make one with your own photos."

She sticks out her bottom lip and fights back more tears. "This is the sweetest thing anyone's ever done for me. Thank you."

I press a soft kiss to her lips, wiping her cheeks with my thumbs.

She continues looking through them, stopping at the ones with her dad and silently crying. I figured it might be hard for her to see them, but I also knew she wouldn't want to miss an opportunity to make a scrapbook she can cherish forever.

With thirty minutes before sunset, I tell her we have to go so we don't miss her next surprise. She got half the book pages done, but I promised she'd be invited again to keep working on it.

"Where're we goin'?"

"You'll see...it's close."

I drive us farther into the ranch property, near a wooded area.

"Okay, we're here..." I say, parking on a pathway between the trees so we can see the sunset.

"Is this some serial killer fantasy where I'm supposed to run and you chase me with a knife and then catch me and—"

She pauses when she sees the horror on my face.

"I'm startin' to get a little concerned about Natalie's tastes in books."

She cackles. "Remind me to tell you about the one with the priest plot."

"Anyway...we're doing something from your romance wish list. So pick a song."

I hand her my phone with my music and she scrolls through until she lands on "Creek Will Rise" by Conner Smith.

"Perfect choice." I grin, then blast it through my truck speakers and lower all the windows. "Let's go, love."

I leave the lights on and meet her in front of the truck.

"I'm sorry I couldn't get it to rain, but I'd still love to dance with you." I hold out my hand and she takes it with a huge smile on her face.

"I can't believe you remembered this after all these months."

Pulling her closer, I spin her around before tilting up her face for a kiss.

"I remember everythin' you tell or ask me." I wink. "Especially the weird stuff."

"What weird stuff?" she asks, offended.

Spinning her around again, I laugh at her faux scowl.

"I can think about a dozen or more questions revolving around orgasms, penises, and cum, if it hurts the balls to be squeezed—"

"Those are genuine questions!"

Beaming, I pull her into my chest and wrap an arm around. "And I love every single one you ask me."

I kiss her forehead and spin her around a few more times. We continue dancing until the sun sets and then we drive to my house so I can finally give her my gift.

Chapter Thirty-Three
Harlow

Waylon has already made my birthday so magical—one I'll remember forever—I can't imagine what other surprises he has planned after everything he did.

This morning, I woke up to the sweetest message from him about how much he loves me and couldn't wait to see me tonight.

An hour later, someone from The Grindhouse delivered Mom's and my favorite lattes and muffins.

At noon, Maria's Kitchen showed up to bring us our favorite Mexican dishes for lunch.

After that, the bakery owner from Tillie's brought us specialty chocolate fudge cupcakes topped with strawberries.

Safe to say, by the time he picked me up, I was more than ready to kiss him.

Scrapbooking with his family and dancing at sunset in front of headlights topped everything off perfectly.

When we enter Waylon's house, there's gotta be a hundred balloons covering his living room and a big Happy Birthday banner.

"You've gone crazy!" I laugh, removing my jacket and setting it on top of my bag. "How did you even blow all these up?"

"I recruited a couple helpers." He smirks. "Bentley came over and then I bribed Wilder to donate some of that hot air in his head."

"So mean." I playfully swat his chest and he captures my wrist.

"Just wanted today to be extra special for you."

"You've made it unforgettable."

"Good." He winks, then takes me by surprise when he lifts me up and carries me through the balloons and into the kitchen.

When he sets me down on the kitchen island, he stands between my legs.

"I have a gift for you."

"Waylon, you've already done so much today."

"Just one more."

He reaches for something from the drawer and my eyes widen when I see it's a jewelry box.

"When I first realized I was thinking about you as more than a friend, I knew I was in trouble. I was either gonna get my heart broken or have to break yours because people wouldn't accept us being together. But then I started fallin' in love with you and those fears no longer mattered because I only wanted you. And to prove that you will always have my heart, no matter what, I wanted to give you this locket."

He opens the box, revealing a very unique type of necklace I've never seen before.

"When you press the button, it plays my heartbeat. Which means, you're the only one who will ever have it. I'm giving it to you to keep forever."

My mouth drops at the sentimental way he's promising me that I'll always be his and he'll always be mine.

"This is the sweetest thing I've ever received," I gush. "Can I try it on?"

"Yes, but only"—he pulls it out of the box, then holds it up for me to see—"if that's the only thing you're wearin'."

"Hm…" I bite down on my lower lip. "You might change your mind about that when you see what I have underneath this dress."

He lifts his brows. "You play dirty, don't ya?"

Only With Me

"Haven't you learned by now? I'm always playin' to win."

Waylon smirks, then puts the necklace around my neck. When I press the button and hear his steady heartbeat, I almost start crying again. Considering I just lost my dad, this gift means so much. It'll make me feel like I'm not alone, even when I am, and that I'll always have him close to my heart, too.

"That looks beautiful on you." He cups my face and tenderly kisses me.

I touch it against my neck. "Thank you. I love it so much."

"And I love you."

"Now take me to your bedroom. I'm done waitin'."

"Harlow Fanning, are you sayin' you only want me for sex?"

"Right now, yes," I deadpan, but he knows I'm messing with him.

We've talked about how my doctor approved me for light physical activity, so I'm taking that as a go-ahead on the whole losing my virginity thing.

"You"—he lifts me back up into his arms—"are about to be sorry you said that."

Waylon places me on his bed, then puts his knee between my thighs and leans in until I rest back on my elbows.

He lifts my dress over my hips and finds the red lace thong and corset with little white bows on them. "Fuck, are you wearin' lingerie?"

"Mm-hmm. I thought you'd like red for *strawberries*," I taunt.

"Mmm...my favorite." He licks his lips, then strokes a finger down my panties and back up again until he rubs over my clit.

"Grind against my knee," he orders, rocking it back and forth against me. "Lie back and put your arms up."

I do as he says and then he slides off my dress the rest of the way.

"Jesus Christ, you look gorgeous. So fuckin' perfect." He cups my breast that's spilling out of the cup. My sister helped pick out this set for me once she got over the ick factor that she was picking it out for her ex-boyfriend, who was going to sleep with her little sister.

She made me swear to never utter a single detail.

Waylon towers over me, brings his lips to mine, and rubs his knee between my thighs. It feels good, but I'm ready for the real thing. No more dry humping or grinding on the outside of his clothes. I want to feel all of him.

My hands go to his belt buckle, attempting to undo it so I can unbutton and lower the zipper.

"Patience, baby. I wanna take my time with you and make sure you can take all of me."

"I don't care if you haveta shove it in there with a bottle of lube. I want you inside me."

"Harlow…" He chuckles against me as if he knows better than to be surprised by what comes out of my mouth.

"It's not my fault you showed up in sexy tight jeans and a cowboy hat. You've been edgin' me ever since then."

He left it in his truck when we got to his place, but now I'm tempted to ask him to put it back on.

"Oh, is that what does it for ya?"

"Um, yeah…pretty much guaranteed to get some if you show up lookin' like a hot cowboy."

"In that case, I'll make sure I always have one on."

"As long as you're prepared to pay the consequences," I quip, wiggling underneath him. "Because after tonight, you'll be lucky if I ever let you get dressed again."

"That sounds like a threat."

"Now you're catchin' on, cowboy."

As if he can't help smiling, the corners of his lips reach his eyes. Then he leans back and takes off his shirt with one hand behind his neck.

Fuck, that's a sexy move.

Then he slides his jeans and boxer briefs down his legs—I finally learned the difference between boxers and briefs and definitely prefer the latter. And once he's completely naked, he

Only With Me

grabs a condom and bottle of lube from his nightstand and sets them on top.

"I'm gonna get you ready first so you're nice and wet," he says, dropping to his knees, then spreads my legs wider.

He kisses my thighs, the right first, and then the left. Slow, taunting licks around my pussy until he finally moves the thin strap of fabric and puts his tongue where I need him the most.

Waylon's oral game is always so damn good, but it feels extra sensitive with how turned on I am. He ravishes every inch of me, my clit and down to my opening. Then he slides two fingers in and eats like he's been starved for me.

"That's so good," I moan out the words, threading my fingers through his hair.

"I'm gonna add in a third finger. Lemme know if it's too much," he says.

"You could put all ten in as long as it means you'll fit inside me."

"Harlow..." He shakes his head, grinning. "I'll stretch you out nice and slow."

All my confidence vanishes when that third finger is enough to set me off because of how tight and full it makes me.

"Relax your muscles, baby. Lemme in all the way."

He wasn't even in all the way?

I release a breath and he slides in deeper.

"Good girl...just like that."

He thrusts slow and steady, flicking my clit as my wetness coats his fingers.

"Lemme taste my *favorite* strawberry..." he murmurs, twisting his wrist and pushing against something inside me that has me moaning louder than before. "There we go, just like that. Do it again."

He repeats the movement, but this time, pleasure bolts through my body like an explosion erupting inside me.

At this point, I beg God for mercy because my body can't stop shaking. I come harder than I have before when we've fooled around, even with that vibrator he bought me. This feels so much more intense.

"Holy shit," I finally spit out when I can inhale again. "How did you do that?"

He lifts until I can see him, licking his lips like he just had his favorite dessert.

"You're not the only one who can ask for sex tips."

Who would he ask for—

"Did you seriously ask your brother?"

He gives a one-shoulder shrug. "It's been a while for me, too. You're not the only one who's nervous. And I wanted to make sure you were properly prepped."

"Remind me to thank him later."

He barks out a laugh. "I'll have you screamin' loud enough to thank him for both of us."

My eyes fly to the ceiling, realizing Wilder's right above us.

"Is his room right there?" I point up.

Waylon presses his mouth down to my chest, licking a straight line from between my breasts up to my neck. "Yep. And payback's a bitch for all the times I overheard him, so you better *scream*, baby."

In a weird way, that turns me on even more.

"Then you better gimme something to scream about, cowboy."

Without warning, he stands and pulls my legs nearly off the bed. I yelp as I hang onto the edge so I don't fall.

"You're gonna be sorry you said that."

His taunting warning tone should scare me, but I want everything he has to offer.

Waylon pulls me up to my feet. "Everything off...I wanna see all of you."

He helps me out of the corset and then my panties. His gaze lowers down my naked body, appreciating every curve and scar. He's kissed them dozens of times when we've fooled around, but it never gets old to watch him openly accept that my skin isn't perfect. But to him, I am, and that's all that matters.

Only With Me

Waylon moves us to the bed, with me on top, and him flat underneath me. He rolls the condom over his impressive, hard length, and he coats himself with lube.

"Being on top will give you more control of the pace and rhythm. Slide down on my shaft and then rock against me like you normally would if we were dry humpin' in the truck."

I love that he voluntarily talks me through it without me having to ask because he knows I'd want instructions beforehand.

Straddling his legs, I lift on my knees and position him between my thighs. I grab his shaft and slowly push it inside me.

Waylon holds my hips in place, watching my face for any discomfort, but I'm focusing on him because I want to see the moment he's fully seated inside me for the first time.

"Fuck, you're so tight." His eyes nearly roll to the back of his head.

I don't think he's even all the way in.

"Am I okay to keep going?" I ask.

"Yeah, as long as it's not hurtin' you."

I'm ready to get the pain over with because I know it'll be there initially anyway.

With one quick exhale, I push all the way down.

I gasp at the tightness and wait for my body to adjust before I inhale.

"Are you okay?" He squeezes my side to grab my attention.

"Uh-huh…" There's a sharp pain, but it's not unbearable.

I lift slightly before sliding back down, the pain now a dull sensation. "I think the worst is over."

"Put your hands on my chest and then you can move however you want."

When Waylon put the vibrator inside me, he was slow and gentle, but I want more. The lube seems to have helped because I can slide up and down him much easier than with the toy.

With my palms flat on his abs, I grind on top of him, slowly at first, but then we find a rhythm. I relax my muscles and he bends his knees slightly so we can rock back and forth.

"Fuck, baby. You feel incredible."

He sits up, wrapping a hand around my neck and pulling us together in a heated kiss.

"Are you doing okay?"

I nod in between panting. "Can we do another position?"

He lifts his brow, smirking. Without a word, he flips us over so he's on top and my legs are wrapped around his waist.

"Go deeper," I tell him. "I can handle it."

He sinks lower on top of me, grabs one of my legs, and then pulls it up to rest on his shoulder.

"Holy shit!" I gasp as he moves, his cock penetrating me so freaking deep. "Don't stop."

Waylon kisses and sucks my neck, plays with my nipples, and thrusts hard and deep until I'm seeing stars.

"Scream my name, baby. Nice and loud."

And I do, over and over, until I can't take it anymore and beg him to let me come.

"Waylon, please. I'm so close." My legs wrap around him, and I dig my heels into his ass to push him deeper.

He's a master at edging me even if it was meant to make me so wet that it no longer hurts. Now it's pure bliss. Pleasure overload. And I want him to feel that too.

"Say the magic words, baby girl, and I'll give you anything you want."

Baby girl? Oh fuck, that's a new one.

Turns out it works on me because it makes my core tighten even more.

"Please lemme come on your cock…I need to so badly," I beg, squeezing my pussy so he can feel how needy I am.

"Such a good girl for me, Harlow…" He lifts both of my arms above my head and locks them with one hand. The other pulls him up slightly before he slams back down on top, tickling a spot inside me that has me screaming again.

He wraps his hand around to cup my ass and then lifts me up to meet his thrusts again and again. The hard penetration

Only With Me

movements send me over the edge and then I'm falling, moaning through the waves of pleasure, and squeezing his dick.

Waylon buries his face in my neck, groaning through his own release.

This feeling we just shared is almost indescribable. *Euphoric. Blissful. Heaven on earth.*

What I imagine being high is like.

No wonder people get addicted.

I've only experienced it once, and I'm ready to give up my life savings and everything I own just to have it again.

"Harlow, talk to me. Are you okay?"

Blinking through the lavender haze, I look up at him with a sated smile.

"When can we do that again?"

"Christ, woman." He falls back on the bed, sweat coating his forehead and into his hair. "You're seriously gonna kill me, aren't you?"

I lean up on my elbow so I can look at him. "Oh, right. You're older, so you probably need like five minutes to rest, right?"

"*Five minutes?* Yeah, sure..." He pants out between the words, and I laugh.

He wraps his arms around me and pulls me into his chest, kissing my shoulder. "Baby, you're gonna be very sore tomorrow. I'll get you some pain reliever and a cold towel so I can clean you."

Arching a brow, I try to look down between us. "Did we make a mess?"

"You bled a little, most likely from how deep I went, and it mixed in with the lube."

I scrunch my nose. "That's probably not attractive, huh?"

"You think your blood is a turn-off for me?"

"I dunno...I thought it would be gross to you. Or maybe a part of the trauma from what happened to Wilder."

Although Waylon told me a while ago some more details about

Wilder's past, we don't bring it up, so I can only assume he'd associate blood with what happened.

"There's no part of you that would ever be a turn-off or unattractive to me. You could squirt piss all over me, and I'd still be hard inside you."

"Okay, ew. Wait a minute."

He chuckles like he knew that would get my attention.

"Women squirt piss?"

"That's what some of the researchers say…that it comes from the bladder. There's mixed opinions about it, though."

"Why am I just learnin' about this now? You were supposed to teach me all things sex before we got here."

He kisses the tip of my nose. "Haveta save some stuff for extra credit lessons."

"There's more?"

He brings his fingers to my nipple, pinching it until it gets hard. "We haven't even touched on anal play yet."

He flashes a playful smirk, thinking I don't know about butt stuff, but thanks to Natalie and her tendencies to overshare, I've already been educated in that department.

Doesn't mean he has to know that.

"Hmm…" I feign innocence. "For you or me, cowboy?"

When I waggle my brows, his face lights up. "Very funny." Then he rolls over me to get off the bed. He takes out a bottle from his nightstand drawer and then shakes two pills out.

"Sit up, and I'll grab you some water."

He puts the meds in my palm and then slides on his briefs. But before he leaves the room, he glances over his shoulder.

"And to answer your question, *both*." Then he winks and walks out.

Epilogue
Harlow

"Spit on it, baby. We don't have much time."

Lifting up slightly, I spit on his cock and then stroke his shaft until it's lubricated. I line us up and then slide down his hard length.

"Fuck…" His head falls back on the bed as he grips my thighs that are straddling his.

"You better get me there faster if I'm on limited time," I teasingly warn because he knows exactly what I need.

His thumb perfectly rubs over my clit like he's done hundreds of times before. Waylon knows my body better than I do, and I love him more than anything for accepting me exactly the way I am. Imperfect skin and all.

"Ride my cock just like that…" he says when I lean back and rest my hands on his thighs. He gets a full view of my pussy and it helps him go deeper as he plays with my clit.

One of my favorite positions besides doggy style.

And yes, we've tried several over the past eight and a half months.

I wanted to experience as many as possible that didn't exceed my gymnastics ability and since he's a great teacher, he was all for trying anything once—including anal play.

Only With Me

Turns out I'm basic when it comes to sex because I love when he slams into me from behind, slaps my ass, or wraps his hand around my waist and pinches my clit.

I love when he buries his face between my thighs and eats me until I come all over his face.

But I mostly love the way he cherishes my body and makes me scream.

Wilder would probably disagree.

I bought him some top-of-the-line noise-canceling headphones for his birthday.

He didn't find it as hilarious as Waylon and I did.

From the moment Waylon and I started officially dating, we've been inseparable.

So when we had thirty minutes to spare before we had to go back to the arena to watch Ellie compete on the ninth day of the NFR, we took full advantage of a quiet hotel room.

Everyone in the Hollis family came to Vegas for the championship, and I brought my mom and sister, too. It's almost the middle of December, so it was a nice way to celebrate before the holidays.

It's been a blast watching Ellie kick ass. She won last year and is expected to win again this year, but she has some big competitors, so the scores have been close.

Waylon and I decided to road trip it here, one of my romance wish list items, but we're going to fly back so he can get back to work.

"Alright, I'm close..." He groans. "Come sit on my face."

I crawl up his stomach and straddle his head so I can finish on his tongue. He fucks his fist while eating me so we can get off together.

Normally, he'd wear a condom, but *someone* forgot to buy more and we didn't realize we were out until we were already naked.

Since I'm not looking to get pregnant anytime soon, we're not taking any risks.

"Right there..." I tell him, bouncing on his face, and then I cover my mouth to muffle my screams.

We've already been warned by hotel security twice to keep it down.

The first time, they thought there was a domestic dispute, and I had to prove it wasn't by showing them the hickeys on my neck and my torn panties on the floor.

The second time, they said they'd kick us out if we couldn't control ourselves.

You'd think we were on our honeymoon, but with Waylon's work schedule keeping him tired and busy, we don't get to spend many nights together unless he has off the next day or is willing to go in late.

But I'm not complaining because I knew what I was getting into and we still make it work the best we can.

Waylon groans through his release, spilling out onto his stomach. I roll off him but then crawl over to lick up his mess.

"Jesus, baby. That's hot."

I smile up at him as I clean his cock next. "No time to shower."

He laughs. "Yeah, we better go before Landen starts askin' questions again."

We were ten minutes late for the barrel racing event yesterday and he glared at us as we snuck in.

Rushing to get dressed and fix my hair, we make it to the lobby with two minutes to spare.

"Where's Wilder?" I ask him.

"Who knows...I'll text him."

Wilder's been consistent in going to therapy and not drinking as much, but while we've been here, he's been a lot more free with it. Not that it's a huge deal, considering we're in Vegas, after all, and the guys don't get a lot of downtime with their schedules.

"We'll just meet him there," Waylon says, grabbing my hand.

We spend the next couple hours at the NFR arena and cheer loudly when it's Ellie's turn. She comes in second, which is

Only With Me

honestly amazing. Her last event is tomorrow and then depending on how she scores will decide if she's the overall champion.

We spend the rest of the evening with his family, eating and hanging out at the casinos. I don't gamble, but I watch some of them play slots and other card games. Waylon sticks to water, so I let myself get drunk on margaritas since I know he'll make sure nothing happens to me.

It's shortly after sunrise when Waylon's phone rings. We'd just fallen asleep a few hours ago, but he always keeps his on for emergencies, so it wakes us both.

"Delilah?" Waylon mutters, putting it on speakerphone.

"Hey, sorry to bother you. But have you seen Wilder?"

"Uh…no. He texted me hours ago saying that he was *out*. Why? Everything okay?"

"Remember that big favor you owe me?" she asks.

"Huh? Whaddya talkin' about?" Waylon's half-asleep, but he sits up and turns on the bedside lamp.

"New Year's Eve, I babysat your brother for you, and you said ya owed me. That time has come."

"Okay…it's like seven in the mornin'."

"Yeah, well…I just woke up and noticed Wilder was missin'. So I need you to go find him for me."

"Missin' from where?"

"We got drunk last night."

"Oh my God, Delilah…did you fuck my brother?" Waylon rubs his temples.

"I'm afraid it's worse than that."

"What could be—"

"We ended up at the Little White Wedding Chapel," she admits.

"Oh my God!" I screech.

Delilah sighs through the phone. "Yeah."

"Wait, wait, wait…" Waylon shakes his head. "Y'all got *hitched*?"

Brooke Montgomery

"Yep...say hello to your new sister-in-law."

I burst out laughing at Waylon's shell-shocked face.

"How the fuck did this happen, Delilah? You were supposed to make sure he doesn't go out and do stupid shit like this!"

"Because he got me drunk too! Who knew Long Island drinks were that strong? Not to mention the tequila shots at the strip club."

I snort. *Of course they went there.*

"Motherfucker." He pinches the bridge of his nose, clearly not amused with either of them. "Didn't realize I needed a babysitter for his babysitter."

"It could be worse, babe..." I tell him. "He coulda married a complete stranger."

He glares. "That doesn't make things better."

"I should be the one mad here. My sister got married before me and they weren't even datin'!"

"My twin brother married my ex," Waylon counters.

"Okay, so we're mad equally." I cackle. "But not really because this is funny. Mom's gonna pop a blood vessel when she finds out."

"Yeah, please don't tell her. At least not until I can find my *husband* so I can get this annulled."

"Lemme see if I can find his location..." Waylon goes to his app and clicks on Wilder's name. "It says he's in the hotel."

I look at the screen to see if we can find which floor.

"It looks like he's on the roof," I say. "That can't be right."

Waylon's face turns ghost white as he checks for himself. "We gotta go. Call hotel security now," he tells Delilah.

Waylon grabs his jeans, yanks them on, then pulls on a shirt. I quickly follow suit and then slide on my boots.

"What the hell is goin' on?" Delilah panics. "The roof access is all blocked off."

"I dunno, but it's possible he's passed out somewhere. Or worse, he relapsed and hurt himself."

Only With Me

My heart pounds with the fear that he could be right. It's not uncommon for people who struggle with depression and substance abuse.

Waylon grabs the room key, and I quickly pick up the phone so he doesn't forget it. "Delilah, we'll call you back," I tell her, then hang up.

Waylon grabs my hand and we rush toward the door.

As soon as he opens it, we find Wilder lying on the floor.

"What the fuck? Wilder!" Waylon shakes him.

Wilder opens his eyes and smiles when he notices his brother. "Hey...*finally.*"

"What the hell are you doin' out here?"

"I forgot my key."

"This ain't your room," Waylon reminds him, helping him to his feet. "Where's your phone? It says your location is like on the roof or something."

"I dunno, I lost it," he slurs, still clearly tipsy. "And I lost my key, so that's why I came here."

"You wanna tell me about this?" Waylon grabs his left hand with a brand-new wedding band on his ring finger.

"Oh shit..." He stares at it like it's the first time he's seeing it. "Who'd I marry?"

"Jesus Christ," Waylon mutters, scrubbing a hand down his face. "My ex-girlfriend, you fucker."

I suck in my lips to stop myself from laughing.

"*Delilah?*" Wilder says it like even he's shocked she agreed to marry him.

"Yep," I say.

"Fuck...she's gonna kill me, ain't she?" He scratches his head like he knows this is bad even for him.

"Oh yeah..." Waylon shakes his head, crossing his arms. "I might as well start writin' your eulogy now."

Brooke Montgomery

Read Waylon & Harlow's bonus scene on my website
brookewritesromance.com/bonus-scenes

```
Curious about Wilder and Delilah?
Find their story next in Sin With Me
```

Sin With Me

A hidden identities stand-alone from small-town romance author Brooke Montgomery about a girl who wakes up married in Vegas to her ex-boyfriend's twin brother...

From the moment he calls the crisis hotline, I'm drawn to his voice.

As I help him through his darkest moments, we slowly get to know each other. The more he needs me, the more I need him, too.

A family emergency forces me away from my volunteer job, and I fear I'll never talk to him again.

Until I'm introduced to my new boyfriend's twin brother.

For years, we ignore the undeniable tension between us. Even after my break up with his brother, neither of us says a word about our history. He's a player, and I'm too afraid of getting hurt again.

Sin With Me

But then my restraint snaps, and I lose myself in a searing hot kiss.

When he doesn't hold back, I realize he wants this as desperately as I do. Before things can go further, he stops us, and my insecurities rush in.

Dealing with the pain of losing my dad, I'm more confused about my feelings than before.

My lapse in judgment leads to getting pulled over, and when chaos erupts, he knocks out the deputy—rewarding himself with a backseat ride in the sheriff's SUV.

An article releases that tarnishes his reputation and threatens his family's business. But when I bail out another man for a crime he didn't commit, I get a target on my back, too.

My world flips upside down when we go to Vegas and wake up married. He begs me to give him a chance—thirty days to prove we should stay together.

But the honeymoon can't last forever in a Southern small town.

About the Author

Brooke has been writing romance since 2013 under the *USA Today* Bestselling author pen names: Brooke Cumberland and Kennedy Fox, and now, **Brooke Montgomery** and **Brooke Fox**. She loves writing small town romance with big families and happily ever afters! She lives in the frozen tundra of Packer Nation with her husband, wild teenager, and four dogs. Brooke's addicted to iced coffee, leggings, and naps. She found her passion for telling stories during winter break one year in grad school—and she hasn't stopped since.

Find her on her website at
www.brookewritesromance.com
and follow her on social media:

facebook.com/brookemontgomeryauthor
instagram.com/brookewritesromance
amazon.com/author/brookemontgomery
tiktok.com/@brookewritesromance
goodreads.com/brookemontgomery
bookbub.com/authors/brooke-montgomery
threads.net/@brookewritesromance
bsky.app/profile/brookemontgomery.bsky.social

Made in United States
North Haven, CT
23 August 2025